Little Beauty

Alison Jameson

Doubleday Ireland

LONDON · TORONTO · SYDNEY · AUCKLAND · JOHANNESBURG

DOUBLEDAY IRELAND
an imprint of The Random House Group Limited
20 Vauxhall Bridge Road, London SW1V 2SA
www.transworldbooks.co.uk

First published in 2013 by Doubleday Ireland,
a division of Transworld Ireland

A CIP catalogue record for this book
is available from the British Library.

ISBN 9781781620007 (cased)
9781781620014 (tpb)

Addresses for Random House Group Ltd companies outside the UK
can be found at: www.randomhouse.co.uk
The Random House Group Ltd Reg. No. 954009

The Random House Group Limited supports the Forest Stewardship Council (FSC®),
the leading international forest-certification organization. Our books carrying the
FSC label are printed on FSC®-certified paper. FSC is the only forest-certification
scheme endorsed by the leading environmental organizations, including Greenpeace.
Our paper procurement policy can be found at www.randomhouse.co.uk/environment.

Typeset in 11/15pt Electra by Falcon Oast Graphic Art Ltd
Printed and bound by CPI Group
(UK) Ltd, Croydon, CR0 4YY

2 4 6 8 10 9 7 5 3 1

For Steve

Whale Island –
18 September 1975

1

Thursday

Like the island itself, Laura Quinn was lonely. The house her mother left her offered her nothing. Not a home or warmth, just grey cedar wood that looked wet in all seasons and windows that were filling up with geraniums, growing wild inside. It was a wet morning in September when the letter came. She read it twice and pulled her wellingtons on. Whale Island, Inis Míol Mór, a small wet sponge off the west coast of Ireland. There were only forty-two square miles and a few hundred people and she couldn't stand any of them. It was the *Titanic* of islands. Floating to America. Stone walls crumbling. There was one village built around a little harbour and facing the mainland. It had a handful of whitewashed shops, the Catholic church and McKenna's Select Bar. A new shop had just opened and everyone was talking about it. They laid the groceries out on tables there, strange displays involving Kimberley biscuits, bars of soap, buckets and spades.

Laura let the front door close quietly behind her. There was a key somewhere but no one locked anything up around here. Her house was three miles from the village, built much higher up and looking out over a sandy beach called Fintra.

She put the letter into her pocket and stood for a moment on the road in her nightdress. There was nothing at all for her to do here. The silence and cold wind emptied her out. There was a wet hen standing on her gatepost. Two sheep were waiting with curled horns and angry yellow eyes. On the bend of the road she met five of them running, their small hooves making a gentle rock-falling sound. Something had frightened them. They were galloping. They passed her without a glance and without slowing down. Sleepy Joe had come early with the post and her first reaction was to walk the two miles to her lover, Martin Cronin, who lived higher up, in the lighthouse on the coast road.

She could not remember the last time she got a letter from anyone and she already knew the contents of this one by heart.

Tuesday, September 16th
Dear Miss Quinn,
I would appreciate if you would attend an interview for the
position of Housekeeper at Bishopstown House at 3pm on
Monday next, September 22nd. When you reach the mainland
take the Bridestown bus from the harbour – it goes through the
town of Drumquin first and will drop you at Bishopstown village
after that. You can call the house from Shaw's grocery shop and
someone will collect you. If the bus is running on time it should
take less than an hour to get here from the harbour.
Yours sincerely,
Mrs Audrey Campbell

Laura buttoned her coat down over her nightdress. The wind was blowing sticky rain into her face, misting her glasses and wrapping the flannel around her legs. From the top of the road she could see Lucas Boyle out playing. He was climbing the Black Rocks like a mountain goat. She watched him for a moment, smiling, and then his blond head turned and he gave her a big wave.

The wellingtons were too big but she wasn't going to splash through these potholes in her new platform shoes. Her gait was slanted, ungainly, shoulders moving from side to side. A sudden gust of wind lifted her blonde hair and she moved under the brief canopy of it. She let the wind blow her coat open again. She let it blow in her front and out through her spine. She allowed the wind to swim inside her and around the empty barnacle of herself. There was a heart in there somewhere. Only the other night she had heard it. It had felt like something alive and warm and under a heavy weight.

On her next birthday she would be thirty-eight, a spinster, nailed to the shelf. She needed to know if Martin Cronin would ever make an honest woman of her – or if it was finally time to get a proper job and leave the island. Everyone said Inis Míol Mór was lovely. The tourists followed the coast road from the harbour, through the village and up the long winding path to Laura's house and Fintra Beach – and on then to the lighthouse at the furthest point. They would cross the island to the other side and see Bee's Beach, a real beauty in any kind of light. They got out of their cars and stood high on the rocks, laughing into the wind that after so many days scratched and clawed at her face. 'How lovely', they said, 'how beautiful' and 'wow', the Americans gasped. But it wasn't 'lovely' or 'beautiful' or 'wow', not when it persisted in showing itself to you, over and over, like some old biddy who didn't know any better. And they loved the sheep and marvelled at how they never seemed to come tumbling down the cliffs on their heads. What did they expect – the panic-stricken BAAAAAAAAAAAAAAAAAAAAAAAAA of a rock-falling sheep?

The sheep never fell. Laura could give them that and admire them for it if she wasn't so sick of their dirty wet wool and small

11

black feet. The only decent part of Inis Míol Mór was the little lighthouse painted white and red, if she could ever get over the person who lived in it. Apart from Martin, she only liked Lucas Boyle and he was a seven-year-old child who couldn't talk.

Martin might not be up yet. She would ask him her question and he would say yes. He would talk about the future then, *their* future, and she would write back to Mrs Audrey Campbell and politely tell her, 'No, thanks.' Every morning he climbed the steps to the lighthouse and then swept each step on his way back down. The rocks at the foot of the lighthouse were like teeth gone rotten. Last week there had been another bad storm. He had stayed up all night, keeping the light burning and saving two trawlers from running aground. She was proud of him then instead of how she usually felt now, which was ashamed.

The letter could have stayed on the mantelpiece and she would never have to deal with it. But here was lonely. Here was miserable – especially at night – and that was because – and this was the voice in her head, the one that made sense some of the time and reminded her that she was not dead – Martin did not seem to want her at night now. When he stayed at her house he preferred to leave in the dark while she was still asleep. He seemed to love her more at his own house and in daylight – the divan sliding on the lino floor, the smell of moss there in the sheets with them, the afternoon sun making flowers on the ceiling overhead.

And yet everything on the island was familiar. So she was still sad about her mother but what was sadness when she could keep the outside world at arm's length? What was a feeling of emptiness? Wasn't everyone empty at times? What was an empty heart when she was safe?

Martin lived in a low grey bungalow that was attached to the lighthouse. He kept pedigree sheep in the fields around it and had a cat, named Francis after the saint. He went to mass every morning and did the church collections. When there was a storm he climbed into the lighthouse like he was boarding a spaceship. He was very proud of that. But they only met in the afternoons now. He wanted to see her face in daylight, he said. Most days she would walk to his house after lunch, through the creaking gate and around to the back door – the lighthouse in the background casting a long dark shadow instead of a light.

'Don't come to the front door,' he said. And she would find him waiting in the warm kitchen for her, in the smell of his turf fire, with the same lino his dead mother had picked out and nailed to the floor for him, a low cloud of cigarette smoke hanging over his head. She would come in through the scullery and see the dresser, weighed down with several layers of old paint, peeling here and there, drawers that were crooked and went in with a rattle of knives and forks. There was a big deep sink in the scullery and plates standing on the draining board, the faint smell of a rasher, an egg, porridge, burnt and stuck to the pot. The mantelpiece over the Rayburn stove was crowded, the kitchen too hot and the bedroom down the hall always cold.

She would stand in the doorway and he would look up and smile at her. Sometimes they would make tea and watch the television. Her favourite programme was *Fawlty Towers*. He loved *Morecambe and Wise*. Sooner or later they would head for the bedroom. That was how she got him in the first place, three years ago now. They had come back from McKenna's pub drunk and falling into each other and into the walls and on to the low red couch. They had met in the back bar earlier and she was wearing a new pair of denim flares that she was proud of. 'American Pie' was playing and they started dancing. Laura had noticed him before because he kept to himself and, like her, steered clear of the other people on the island. He seemed to float over everyone and she liked his dark eyes and his sallow skin and his hands, smooth for a fisherman. Later she would wonder if she fell for him because he was a bit of a loner, an outsider like her. They had found the bedroom together then, knocking the Sacred Heart picture sideways as they went. There was no talk between them at all, but what were words when two souls could die empty in a place like this.

Her glasses were left on the nightstand and she liked that he came to her in a blur. She had opened her legs for him then and he had responded. She could remember the sound of his belt buckle, a zip, and then he was kneeling on the bed, climbing over her. This is love, she had thought, the clumsy island version of it. Two awkward people together at a disco and now this. He had opened her legs wider, got in under her, lifted her up and opened her blouse at the front. Her breasts were big and flat when she lay down like that. Her nipples brown, round, there was nothing pretty here. He wore his own glasses into the bed. Later he would say that he wanted to see her and when he went into her she made a sound like a cat's meow, the wind forced out from under her ribcage, and then he kept at it, the rubbing and scratching and lovely discomfort of two strangers now joined but who had never actually met.

The word she said inside then was 'Why' and 'Why' and 'Why' and really she didn't know why she said it or what it meant. The glass lightshade in the middle of the ceiling was starting to spin and he, his stubble scratching her face, a red burn being left on her upper cheek, said 'Atch ... atch ... atch' over and over under his breath and it sounded like 'Bitch ... bitch ... bitch' and she felt very cold and still grateful for it.

So that was how they found each other. That was how Laura avoided being separate from everyone else in the world and avoided being killed by the grey stones and the heather and avoided putting any real value on herself.

2

The same postman looked in the window at Martin Cronin and nearly frightened the life out of him. He had just come in from early mass and could still smell the church on his clothes. He could hear the priest's voice and his own shy laugh as he closed up the doors to the church. His fingers were black from counting the coppers in the plate. Sleepy Joe was tapping on the glass and grinning in at him like a simpleton. And he had no post for him at all. He only wanted to give him the sheep show catalogue and then tell him that he had been over at Fintra earlier and that Laura Quinn had got a small white letter from the mainland.

'She's fond of the bed, that one,' he added with a little wink, 'I nearly had to drag her out of it.'

Martin turned a deaf ear to that. He didn't want this imbecile talking about her and the bed and her being fond of it. It wasn't respectful and besides he was only trying to goad him. The same man was known to put the postbag over his head and sleep in the ditch. He took the catalogue off him and banged the door shut. There was no peace in a place where everyone knew what you had for your breakfast.

When Martin rang the bell for mass, the collie dog at the new shop pointed his muzzle upwards and howled at it. Martin liked the silence of the empty church, the feeling that when he said his prayers early he started the day with a nice clean slate. He wondered if Laura would be around later. The mention of her name had him thinking about her again. Would he hear her foot on the step, the latch being lifted on the door, the sound of her wool coat brushing the walls? He wasn't sure if he really loved her but he loved the dark sin of it. The dog. The bell. The priest. His helping. Her. And her. And her. When he closed his eyes he could see her breasts. He wanted them now. He did. He would have to have them but he would not marry her. She was a nice-looking woman but people said she was a bit odd. His own mother, Lord rest her, said she was a fast one and the idea of Laura wearing her old engagement ring would be enough to bring her back from the grave. So he was not content to stand at the altar with her. No. At least not yet. He closed his eyes for a second. He put his head in his hands and tried to think about the sheep show instead.

At the beginning, he had admired her from a distance. He had looked into her blue eyes and smiled when he went around with the collection plate. Most women turned shy and went burrowing into their prayer books, rattling their rosary beads, but not her; she looked back at him, held his gaze, dropped her coins into the plate with some defiance. Her skin was the same as her mother's, Lord have mercy on her soul, fresh and fair like a child's, pink cheeks, freckles. The Quinns had a lot of bad luck, building their house facing the sea and so close to it. The islanders were always very superstitious about that and built their own houses facing the road.

He didn't like staying at Laura's house and preferred to leave before the sun was up. There was sand on the kitchen floor, geraniums in clumps around the windows. It was an awful mess of a place. She was no housekeeper anyway. But what would you expect without a mother to show her, to guide her – wasn't she just a girl when she was left to fend for herself? First the father and then the mother and they were decent, respectable types. Eliza, that was the mother's name, known for reading tea leaves and the mother and daughter would be seen walking on Fintra Beach in the evenings, always hand in hand, talking and laughing, close.

Joe Quinn was a fisherman. It was not too surprising that he drowned. But Laura's mother, that was a different story entirely.

Martin had woken at six as usual with the air around him feeling wet. The sea was lifting part of itself up, the mist creeping like a ghost into his house. It had driven a slug inside overnight. It sat now like a piece of fresh liquorice over the mantelpiece. He turned on the radio for the weather forecast and heard that another storm was coming to the west coast of Ireland. The worst storms came in September, winter pushing its way in and summer putting up a fight. It would hit Inis Míol Mór by midnight. These wild autumn winds were blowing the last days of sunshine off the beach. The Birmingham Six had been convicted, they were still talking about it – and Margaret Thatcher was on a visit to America, striking the fear of God into that poor Gerald Ford.

Martin needed to open up the lighthouse. He turned off the radio and put some more turf on to the fire to warm the kitchen up. He should close the house windows at night. Laura herself had said this – to keep out the sea mist. They were going out three years now. Not quite. At the start she had asked to stay the night and he could not agree to it. He was used to being on his own and he was afraid of her two feet planting themselves under his table. He didn't want a woman who turned into a vine around his neck. Her scent had stayed on his body though. He remembered being wet and sticky with it. After that first time with her

17

he had panicked. He had wanted to throw her out and wash himself. He remembered pulling back the bedclothes and gently helping her up. He had handed her her glasses. He had taken her elbow and then they had both seen her underthings in a ball near the bed. She had leaned down to retrieve them and he had gone to the window and looked out.

He had not asked Laura to go but he had driven her out with silence. He was afraid of being trapped and he was worried about a woman attaching herself to him, limpet-style, and him not being able to shake her off. On a small island like this it would be awkward to say the least. Deep down he was also afraid that Laura might bring him some of her own bad luck.

He had not liked himself for it and yet, at that time, he had needed to get her out. He had stood with his back to her and frozen her. He had looked through the window and imagined pushing her. He had closed his mouth tight and drowned her. Out. Out. Out. And yet as the back door closed, he felt like she had covered him in a glittering cobweb, that she had written her name on his skin and that it would never wash out.

Her mother had jumped from White's Cliff and it was Laura who found her. A smiling thirteen-year-old running along the beach with rosy cheeks. Even now Martin would find himself thinking about it. The whole island went quiet over it. The people couldn't even bring themselves to see Laura or to do anything to help. Just the idea of what she had found seemed to send them into shock. And they knew it wasn't an accident because she had left a note. They said she couldn't get over losing her husband and even the daughter couldn't mend her heart.

'A kind of madness,' most people said.

Madness because it left Laura on her own with no one to raise her and no one to show her wrong from right. She was a wild girl anyway, she needed guidance, but her mother did not seem to think about that part.

It's a wonder, Martin thought, that Laura is even half right in the head.

The drop from White's Cliff was close to four hundred feet, the rocks below jagged, merciless.

Laura never mentioned it, except the once.

'To do a thing like that,' she said, 'Mam must have hated her life and everything in it.'

Now Martin tried again. He did not want to think about her. One day without her and then two and then perhaps three and he might be rid of the curse. Without her glasses she was really lovely. He tried to think about the lighthouse again. How his feet sounded on the two hundred and five spiral steps.

The bolt on his gate creaked. The sound of her coming opened his heart up raw as if it had a mouth and it was taking a big breath. For a minute he thought about running down the hall and hiding in the lighthouse. He waited, not breathing at all. He imagined her footsteps on the wet path. He saw her wet boots, the white knees, bare with freckles and light golden hairs. In a second, he might be kneeling over her, the soft dull whiteness of her thighs making his mouth open up. He could see her through the net curtains, long hair wet from the mist. Big drops of rain were beginning to land on the rhubarb leaves and there was no sound of footsteps at all after the sound from the gate. Then he heard her lift the brass knocker.

Before the sound came he tried to remember the time of the next ferry to the mainland. He wondered if that ram lamb was ready for the sheep show. Any thought at all but he could only think, she's coming to the front.

3

Martin was a cowardly sort. She knew that now. It was in the way his eyes came at her through the crack in the door, wide and dark with fear, and why should he be so afraid? Even now she could see that he was very handsome but he still didn't want her to be seen coming to the front door of his house. He did not want her wellies on the black and amber tiles. He did not want her feet tracking through his dust. He wouldn't let her go into the lighthouse either. All she wanted was to see the view of the island and the sea. And why not? She wanted to know. Why would he not let her go up those steps? When she had let him climb inside herself.

He hadn't shaved and the silver in his stubble glistened at her. He had not taken himself into the new green bathroom that he was so proud of. His shirt was open under braces that held up a pair of brown trousers. She could see a vest that was growing yellow at the neck. And yet she wanted to be in this small grey bungalow that was perched on the cliff, reached by a lane that stretched in a soft pencil line from the last turning on the coast road. There was a window on either side of the green door, one for the kitchen and the other for the parlour. The bedroom and the new bathroom jutted out the back. And inside he kept the sea safe for them to look at, divided up and packaged in different windows. The bedroom looked out over the Atlantic and the coastguard's station, abandoned to broken windows and green pebbledash. The parlour was for looking out at the mountain, the brown and green and grey sweeping upwards, the sheep gathered in his field, a sliver of sea caught in between them.

His house was full of sea pictures and she knew each one by heart. Old ships dashed with waves. Seahorses and starfish. A mermaid here and there. But he never wanted to talk to her about anything like that. He only wanted her to see the new bathroom extension with the toilet and matching sink and the furry green mats. A few people on the island were still using an outhouse but Martin had always wanted a nice modern bathroom. He was a bit too proud to have a piss-pot under the bed.

She put her hands down into her coat pockets and waited, not that she was being defiant or brave but more that she was already weak with the wave of rejection that she felt. He opened the door wider and she saw how a cobweb stretched with it.

She waited. He waited.

The sea rushed and made waves on the rocks at the end of his field. For once she could not hear them. He stepped back in socks, his heels visible through a weave of maroon threads. She realized that she had seen every part of him but never the backs of his legs, never his heels. He opened the door an inch wider and she stepped forward, feeling, as she smelled the turf fire, that she was sinking into the bog.

The idea in her mind felt old and outdated now. With it came the same feeling she had when she couldn't remember a dream or put a name to a face. When she was younger she really did believe that there would be a wedding one day and that she would be in it. That there would eventually be someone carved from the same stone as she. Her mother had seen it in the tea leaves and told her. There was someone *even* for her – was that what she meant? Someone as odd as she.

And now she was standing in the hall with Martin Cronin, whose hands were always oily from handling the wool on his sheep, whose eyes were wide and suspicious and also dark and lovely and while there was no welcome whatever, if she had crossed the hall to the bedroom, he would have followed her as if he was on roller skates.

But Martin did not move at all and so she turned left into the kitchen, feeling like an intruder. There was the low red velvet couch with springs rising up in small hillocks, the mantelpiece with the clock and last year's Christmas cards still up, faded and warped from the heat. She moved towards his armchair under the window, the one that looked out over his rhubarb patch and his sheep.

She sat on the edge of the chair, feeling the tweed from the cushion scratch through her coat and nightdress. How would she begin now? Straight for the main artery and not hit any minor blood vessels on the way. Minor blood vessels, she supposed, would be an American-style question – something along the lines of 'Where are we going?' or 'Where do you see us in a year's time?' or 'Martin, would you ever marry me, for fuck sake?'

Once, after sex, he had held her hand loosely against his chest and she had felt how he tightened and relaxed his grip and then held her hand up to the light to see it – as if he didn't quite know how another human being looked and felt. He had made no move to push her out that day. His hand was warm and relaxed and hers was happy inside it. And after that he took her to see *One Flew Over the Cuckoo's Nest* at that new cinema in Bridestown on the mainland. She knew he was capable of kindness and he could be thoughtful enough in his own way. He had given her a bottle of Charlie perfume once but when she wore it

22

to the pub Maddy Hughes, the hairdresser, said it smelled like cat's piss.

'You're up early,' Martin said. He was putting the kettle on to the Rayburn's hotplate. He had walked into the scullery to fill it and she had listened to the tap rattle and watched the broad line of his shoulders.

'It's the best part of the day . . . or so I'm told.'

'I suppose it is . . . I did the early mass with Father Meehan.'

The teapot was being scalded and two spoons of tea leaves scooped out.

'Sleepy Joe woke me at seven . . . I didn't have much choice.'

'So I heard. The eejit was around here a while ago telling me you got a letter in the post.'

He filled the pot and they waited for the tea to draw.

Laura swallowed. When she moved her legs the letter seemed to rattle in her pocket.

'Oh, that's today's big news, I suppose,' she said.

'Not really,' he replied.

And now Martin was crossing his arms and grinning down at her.

'Patricia McKenna got one of those new curly perms,' he said. 'I saw her at early mass and her like one of the Jackson Five.'

'She was bad enough when her hair was straight,' she said.

Patricia and Irene McKenna were the two spinster sisters who owned the only pub on the island. In Laura's worst nightmare she would end up like one of them.

'Middle-aged women . . .' and Martin stopped for a moment as if to order his thoughts, 'can get some very funny ideas about themselves. I saw Maddy Hughes down the village last week, wearing these giant sunglasses. She looked like an alien.'

He made big rings around his eyes with his fingers and peered at Laura.

She wondered who else he was talking about when he said 'middle-aged'.

The teapot hissed and he got up and filled two cups. He added milk to hers and handed the cup to her and only then did their eyes really meet.

Laura took a breath and looked up at him.

'I'm thinking of leaving the island.'

Her voice came out too suddenly. Martin lifted a kitchen chair away from the wall and parked it close to her and when he sat down he was watching the side of her face.

He was a man of few words, always.

'Where would you go?' he asked.

'To a job.'

And here she stopped, the sudden foolishness of it all catching her breath.

And yet her voice struck up again, a voice that she had no real control of.

'I answered an ad for a housekeeper's job in the *Western People*. It's in a place called Bishopstown House.'

'Bishopstown? The Campbells' place?'

'Do you know them?'

'I've heard of them. They're only about forty miles from the harbour on the mainland.'

'Well, I would clean and cook,' she said. 'I'd be a housekeeper . . . for them.'

'A housekeeper for them.' He whispered it back to her and they were both silent again. He sounded astonished by the idea of it. He scratched his head then, one finger behind his ear as if all the answers to his questions might be in there.

'Aren't you the dark horse?' he said suddenly. 'Making plans and writing away to ads in the newspaper . . .'

He stopped scratching and looked at her squarely.

'I didn't think you were too fond of housekeeping,' he said.

'I might like it more if I was being paid for it.'

She took the letter out of her pocket and handed it to him. He read it and put it back on her lap.

'This is what you want to do?' he asked.

'It's better than picking seaweed.'

'There's nothing wrong with picking seaweed for a living . . . Didn't your mother do it before you?'

Yes, Laura thought, by the time she died I was an expert.

By some strange law of nature the best black seaweed got washed up on her part of Fintra Beach and Kennedy's Bath House bought all of it. She spent every morning there with the light changing around her, lifting great wigs of black seaweed into a cage with a pitchfork.

'Yes,' Laura said, 'but that was when my mother still wanted to stay here. Before my father died she loved Whale Island.'

'And you?' he asked then. 'Do *you* not love Whale Island?'

'I don't,' she said simply.

She could feel herself shrinking into the chair. They stared at each other without speaking.

'But why not?'

And in that moment his voice suddenly softened.

'Because . . .' and Laura stopped, frightened by what she was going to come out with.

'I'm not sure there is anything here for me.'

She looked at the floor sadly. It was only now that she had realized this herself.

She looked up slowly and into his eyes. She wanted him to challenge her, to give her reasons to stay, but so far between them it was the usual lukewarm stuff.

'Is there, Martin?'

He leaned back in his chair and studied her. He crossed his

25

arms and frowned as if he was looking at some rare species. She was still waiting for him to somehow save her.

'Would you like to see the parlour?' he asked.

He was supposed to reach for her, to comfort her – and instead he wanted to show her the three-piece suite in that odd pink buff colour, the china cabinet, the new television on its own stand in the corner, the Swiss cuckoo clock.

Laura saw the poker beside the range and she wanted to cut the arse off him with it.

He got up and after a moment, out of habit, she followed him. They crossed the hall and stood in this odd place. It was clean and untouched and smelled of mothballs. They stood together in this dark little room, like the two oddities that they were, survey-ing the scene, looking at the furniture, the framed photographs of his sister's wedding, the carpet, covered in brown and maroon swirls, soft under their feet.

There was a click behind her and a small wooden door in the clock opened and the tiny bird shot out.

'Cuckoo,' it said.

Martin smiled. He gave a little laugh then, delighted with it. Their eyes met. He could imagine her in his kitchen peeling potatoes, wearing a blue apron, her hands rough and sticky from the starch. He could see the nights with her, the ease of it. He liked how she smelled. When she stood next to him now he wanted to put his nose to her neck.

'Will you come into the room?' he asked.

'Yes,' she said because she needed him to hold her and then he might tell her that there was no need to go away and that she could stay with him instead. But all she could hear was the cuckoo over her head. She was still waiting for him to give her something. She had no friends at all and her parents were gone now. He was the only person she knew like this. Without him, she had the ticket to the mainland and not much else.

The bed was not made and they got into the small hollow without getting undressed. The curtains were still drawn, the fabric of brown and black stripes making shadows that were both light and dark. He pulled her face into his chest and placed a firm hand tight on her head. He held her there. Kept her. His chest lifting her up and down with every breath. She felt him grow colder and opened her coat out and covered him with it. She could feel her head beginning to swim with the idea that he loved her because he wanted to hold her like this. The strangest of people paired off and were happy enough. He held her tighter now, his breath going deep into her scalp and making it damp. Any moment now and he would speak to her. He would open up and say the words she wanted to hear, which were 'Laura, please stay with me.'

She waited on and could hear the alarm clock ticking on the bedside table.

But Martin said nothing. Instead he yawned so deeply that his jaws clicked.

She could hear the familiar sound of sheep, their feet tapping as they made their way up the garden path, and she could not wait any longer. She could not bear the further embarrassment to herself.

'The sheep are in again,' she told him and she sat up slowly, pulling her hair into a damp ponytail low at the back of her neck. She got up then and left him, walking across the room in the boots she had worn into his bed. She straightened her coat and would not look at him.

'They must have jumped the grid,' he said.

Laura opened the bedroom door and walked down the hall past the parlour and left in time to avoid the creak from the tiny door in the cuckoo clock. Martin went to the bedroom window and watched her leaving. He made a ball of the curtain in his fist and opened his mouth to call her. But the wind was rising and the waves around the island getting higher – the storm was coming and that was more important. He left the bedroom and, turning right, opened the heavy door to the lighthouse.

4

Monday

Laura carried her blue suitcase to the harbour and waited for the ferry. The old grey pier was at the far end of the village, built out into the water and pointing towards the mainland. She sat under the corrugated shelter surrounded by fishing nets and lobster pots. From there she could see the church spire and some of the village shops. Kennedy's Bath House was already open, the steam puffing out a window at the back. Beside it, Joe Levy's butchers with its smell of blood and sawdust. Maddy Hughes's hair 'saloon', as they called it, was next and then Ben and Eileen McGrath's restaurant, an ugly pink house with the word LUNCH painted on the gable. The soggy smell of cabbage and chops came wafting towards her and she wanted to get away from it. She had only just eaten breakfast.

An old man and a child in a red hat joined her on the bench. They were from the other side of the island and she nodded even though she didn't know them. When she sat next to other people now, she was worried she smelled of damp, that if anyone touched her she would feel cold.

'Do you want the ferry?' the woman in the ticket booth had asked. 'Bohemian Rhapsody' was blasting out on a small transistor beside her and she was trying to sing along to it.

'Yes,' Laura said and in her mind she saw the ferry being lifted up and placed in her back yard.

She had not always been like this. She had dreamt of finding a good man once, a great love. She had read romance novels and hoped to be moved by the fizz of it herself. She wished that she didn't know that real love could exist. A love that could change a heart, change its shape – change the shape of her own eyes and her face. All she knew now was disappointment. Loss. Too much crying flattened a face – she knew that now too. It washed the personality out. It put a plug into laughing. Her mouth still opened up expecting it but the special bubbling noise, the sound of pure joy, would not come out. She had been funny once. She had made her parents laugh. She could remember it. Their laughing had made their house bright and full of hope. But being funny was not enough to keep her mother away from White's Cliff.

And they would not give her a proper funeral. Taking her own life, Father Meehan explained, was a terrible sin. It meant she wasn't allowed into the Catholic cemetery but maybe she could rest with the unbaptized babies on the side of that hill, he said. The carpenter, Paddy Sweeney, made the white cross and two more islanders were paid to do the digging. Laura couldn't remember who they were. 'It's canon law,' the priest said. Apart from him and the two men with shovels there was no one else at the burial. Then Laura walked back to the house and sat in the dark and listened to her own lungs breathing. Outside, the sea seemed to breathe with her and apart from that there was no sound, no car on the road, no other person.

And then there was Martin Cronin. She might be better off without him now but she wasn't sure yet. There were not as many fish in the sea as people thought. At the beginning it had been different and she could still remember that. They were mad about each other and he didn't seem to care what people thought. Then about a year ago he began to cool off a bit. He was a confirmed bachelor, everyone knew that, but since meeting her he seemed to soften up. Then Joe Levy, the butcher, made trouble for her. He was full of drink one night in McKenna's and saying far too much. It was a long time ago when she went down the boreen lane with him and let him put his hand up her skirt. She had never expected him to sidle up to her boyfriend in the pub five years later and tell him about it. Martin was different after that. He was like a hen on a hot griddle then, jumpy and restless.

She could see her house from the harbour. It had the best view on the island but no one ever spoke about that. It sat high on a peak over Fintra, made of wood, like a boat, with a big open room for sitting in and two bedrooms underneath. 'An upside-down house,' people said. The islanders always turned their houses away from the sea. They said it brought them better luck. Her mother was the sort of woman who laughed at things like that. She wanted a wooden house with a porch and seven windows in a row so the sea would fill their lives up.

'Modern,' the islanders murmured as they queued with baskets at the new shop. 'Like the hovercraft,' someone said.

'No carpets or lino, living on the bare boards,' someone else remarked.

Before she left for the job interview Laura had a go at the cleaning. She had been neglecting the house and wanted to leave it clean before her new life could start. Her mother had always been very particular about it and if she saw it now Laura knew she would be disappointed. She dragged the furniture out on to the grass and got down on her knees and scrubbed the floor. Then she hung the rugs over the line and when she imagined

31

Martin's face in the silk and wool patterns she was able to beat them senseless. The plates and cups in the kitchen she scoured with baking soda. The red and white curtains were washed and ironed and put back up again. It was getting dark when she finished and all she had to do was to turn the lights on and sit on the floor and look around her. It was a long time ago now but she had a vague memory of her mother showing her how to clean a house.

The blue sofa and the two rockers were still parked at a wood stove. 'Carpet cutters', her mother called them but there was no carpet to cut. The high trussed ceiling was painted milk white and a yellow model aeroplane had landed on one of the cross-beams overhead. They had often talked about taking it down. The stepladder was mentioned or a long-handled brush – but the pilot looked so happy, her mother said, that she didn't have the heart and, besides, the broom would knock it down and it would break. Laura would remember her mother in that single frag-ment. How it summed her up. How she was. How empty the house was after she died. How the colour seemed to drain out of every part of it. How the blue couch was suddenly faded and the yellow plane almost white. She realized now that she had been thinking about leaving the island since the day they refused to bury her mother in a decent place.

The ferry was still making its way back from the mainland now. It forged ahead, bobbing and rocking, against the waves, a row of cheerful navy and white stripes covering up the rust. There were only eight seats on it, back to back, under a wooden shelter in the middle of the deck. Most of the time, the people stood around the rail and talked, watching the water. Now and then, a farmer would get on with a jumpy heifer on a rope or a few loose sheep.

When Laura turned around she saw that the islanders had

begun to gather on the pier beside her. Sleepy Joe had spread the story that she was leaving and they had come to give her a send-off. It had been a tradition since before the famine when the youngsters left to pick potatoes in Scotland. There was a quiet shame, a loss of pride attached to leaving. The island was not overly generous but a *real* islander could make a go of it and others, like the potato pickers, like Laura, needed to jump off.

'We'll give you a good send-off anyway,' Joe Levy said. He had a fresh cigarette behind his ear and he was still wearing his white wellies and his bloodstained apron.

'I might be back,' Laura said.

She lit a cigarette herself and blew the smoke towards him. His thick curly hair was going grey now. If he had brought a cleaver up from the shop she would have used it to cut his head off.

She watched as a red Ford Escort pulled into the car park and knew that it was Toilet O'Riordan with the dwarf sitting up beside him. His real name was Bernard O'Riordan ·but because he had campaigned for public toilets on the beach the rest of the islanders now called him 'Toilet'. He had gone too far with it. They did not want anything that spoiled Fintra. To them the shore was sacred, fixed for ever and no one could touch the perfect unending line of it.

The women appeared next in bedroom slippers, their husbands' coats thrown over their shoulders.

'Where are you off to, Laura?' someone asked.

'We noticed the suitcase when you passed the shop.'

'Who will gather the seaweed, Laura?'

'What will we do with it, Laura?'

And the questions came from Toilet O'Riordan and Maddy Hughes and Patricia and Irene McKenna and John Evers and Joe Levy and Ben McGrath and Eugene Murray and the dwarf.

'Did you say goodbye to Martin Cronin?' Patricia McKenna

asked in a sly voice. 'I thought I saw you up at the lighthouse last week . . . and you soaked,' and Laura watched as the men pushed their hands deep into their pockets and laughed down towards their feet.

Patricia McKenna had only spoken to Laura once. She stood now with her arms crossed and her two feet pointed out like a duck. Her dark hair was in a frizz around her weather-beaten face.

'Are you a less-bean?' she had asked then.

Laura wished she had had the courage to answer yes. Yes would have made Patricia's wiry hair stand on end and now she was winding her up about Martin Cronin.

Laura looked up at her from the bench and said, 'No, Patricia, but maybe you saw a ghost.'

'That's right . . . a ghost in a white nightdress.'

Two of the men burst out laughing over this.

Laura watched Patricia for a minute.

'And what are you gawking at, Laura?'

'You remind me of someone famous with that new hairdo,' she said.

'It's all the rage now,' Maddy Hughes piped up.

Patricia smiled and gave a quick little toss of her head.

'You're like one of the Wombles,' Laura said.

The sky was grey and getting darker and she knew that there was a storm hidden in it. She hoped the ferry would load up quickly and get to the mainland before it broke. Her tweed coat had opened when she sat down and she showed off her two knees underneath. They were round, smooth, grey, like field mushrooms, almost good enough to eat. If she was closer to the water she would hear the sound of shingles, rocks, shells, rolling back. There was no more talk on the pier, just the child in the red hat and his little questions, the gulls dropping and rising, the ferry coming closer, turning now, backing itself into the pier in a mist of white spray and diesel smoke.

Lucas Boyle and his mother came next. He was a strange, shy child, born with white hair, a mute. The only time he ever smiled was when he saw Laura Quinn. He was smiling now too, coming towards her and carrying a bunch of lavender.

'It must be the hair,' his mother had said once. It seemed that Lucas felt safe with Laura because of her light hair colour. He stood back for a minute and then handed her the lavender.

She took a good big sniff of it and pinned it into the lapel of her coat.

'I'm just going for a short visit,' she told him. 'Then I'll be back again to see you, sure maybe I'll bring you something nice from the mainland.'

Lucas stood and watched her face closely.

'Would you like one of those Curly Wurlies . . . or maybe a lucky bag?'

Here his face cracked into a wide smile and he nodded. He clasped his hands together and began skipping around the pier. His mother watched him, her face without expression.

'I want him to talk, to have a voice,' she said, 'and you won't be able to get him that on the mainland.' She was a tired-looking woman, her own blonde hair dried up and faded. Laura didn't like her much either. When she looked at Lucas, her own child, her eyes were always full of worry and disappointment and Laura couldn't understand that. When she looked at him he seemed to light up and glow a bit – and she only had to smile at him with her eyes.

On Saturday a whale had been washed up and they had tried to save it. It had come too close to the shore, smelling like the sea and death, leaving what it needed behind, not knowing any better and suffocating on the beach. Poor Lucas had tumbled down from the Black Rocks in his effort to claim it. It was Laura who lifted him off the sand when no one else seemed to notice. She had carried him up through the dunes and then sat him on the end of her kitchen table to bandage his knees up. Then she wrote 'T-A-B-L-E' on the wood with a crayon and tried to get him to make the sounds – and he had tried too and she couldn't understand why his own mother didn't do that.

The islanders began to move away and Laura felt happy about that. The ferry ramp was lowered and she walked towards a vacant seat, her body being rocked as she turned to look back at the island. More people climbed aboard and sat around her. She had taken her only suitcase, a navy cardboard one with a dent in the lid, an embarrassment in itself. With these storms there was always a chance you might get stuck on the mainland. There was nothing inside, except a magazine and some underwear and a sod of black turf. She had found that on the road on the way to the boat and couldn't leave it. The islanders always said it was lucky to find a sod of turf and she needed all the luck she could get.

The letter was well crumpled now and hidden behind a zip in her handbag. How many times had she read it now? How many times had she imagined the woman writing in the drawing room – that's what they would call it – not a parlour or a sitting room – with plush green velvet and long floral drapes. There would be a smell of expensive soap and fresh-cut flowers and then she would arrive – Laura – bringing the surf in with her, a waft of seaweed lifting from some part of her, a sound of shingle when she dragged those big feet.

The wind gave a sudden gust and lifted the child's hat and Laura's hands went grabbing for it. The ferry began to bob a little on the waves. Laura sat perfectly still then holding her case and watching as everyone moved together in the same rhythm in this old trawler called *Princess Grace*.

'They should have called the ferry *Peig Sayers*,' Martin had said once.

That had made her laugh a bit, not a big hearty laugh but a soft 'Ha ha' under her breath and now she missed him, the bad seed that he was. She knew she was better, worth more, but lately she had begun to wonder what was the point – if she was the only one who knew it. Her mouth went dry when she heard a thick chain dragging on wood at the back of the boat. She was going to the gallows. She felt sure of it. Where was her case? If the ferry sank or she changed her mind she would cling to it and make a raft. Suddenly she saw Martin's car swing into the car park. It was a navy Ford Cortina, with a sticker that said 'Honk if you love Jesus' on it. He jumped out, quicker than she had ever seen him move before, and ran to the edge. He stood, eyes searching, his mouth set, a new pair of flares swinging around his legs. To her he was a wooden man now, a metal man, a man without a heart.

Laura swallowed and got up, her legs drunk from the movement. Trying not to slip, she walked towards him and the ferry blew its hooter and the ferryman tipped his cap at Martin. He was frozen to the spot and then she watched as he lifted his foot and pushed the boat off. For a minute she had thought he was calling her back, and yet a kick was what she got. A kick in the backside or just as good. She refused to take her seat under the shelter again and stood holding on to the white railing at the end of the deck. She held on tightly and watched as he grew smaller, her hair blowing all around her. She wanted to see him shrink.

The waves sent a light spray up and Laura felt it like a dew on her face. She knew that when she licked her lips next she would taste salt. She didn't bother. There was no novelty in it. Turn around, she told herself. Turn around. At least be the one to turn around first. She watched and watched and then used her hands on the rail to push herself back and then forced her shoulder left and then finally gave him the back of her tweed coat. 'This is right. This is right. This is right,' she whispered. 'If I am to have any kind of life, this is right.' She felt sure that when she turned again she would find the navy car gone and a deserted car park, so she was surprised when she turned around and saw a tiny Martin Cronin, his hands deep in his pockets, rooted in the same place.

The radio from the driver's cabin began to play 'Rhinestone Cowboy' and the engine moved up a notch and another and another so that Laura had to stumble back to her seat and the ferry began to lurch up and down on the waves. In that moment she felt like she was riding a horse and she wanted to laugh a bit. Around her, reluctant smiles formed on other faces and off they went to the sound of Glen Campbell and she wondered where they would all end up.

5

Martin did feel the loss of her. The sight of her leaving with her shoulders rounded in that old coat made his heart drop down into the long hollow of his legs. She was gone. And who would buy her a new coat now? He had been thinking about getting her one of those big duffels since the day he met her. Everlasting and as warm as a blanket. What woman wouldn't want one of those? When she left his house he knew that the wind would draw tears from her eyes, that in no time at all she would be soaked. But new coats weren't cheap and now she had beaten him to it. She had her own surprise for him instead. She was leaving. Had left. Seeing her move away on the ferry was the final blow. He went home and the sudden loneliness he felt there was sharp and jagged. It seemed to run in cold rivers down the walls of his house.

He put the kettle on for tea even though it was too early for it. He poured a mug for himself and then forgot about it. He opened a tin of sardines for a cat that wasn't interested. He climbed the steps to the lighthouse, looked out and then came straight back down again. It was a serious affliction to love a woman who was beneath him. She was a grand woman really but he couldn't marry a girl who already had a 'reputation' – and whose mother had jumped off a cliff. On the island where people were scarce

Martin was considered the catch. He had a good house and he had forty acres. He had a job and he was good-looking with it. There were others waiting in the wings, other girls who smiled at him when he went around with the collection plate. And yet he felt strangely chilled now without Laura. The idea of her not being on the same island as him hit him in his heart.

He put on his coat and drove to the village to buy a bag of crisps.

There were other things he could think about. He could think about the Legion of Mary meeting on Friday where he had read the opening prayer and watched Father Meehan swallowing the ham sandwiches down like a duck. There was not much else to do there anyway – except say a few Hail Marys and eat the sandwiches if there were any left.

When Brid Molloy got to the altar for communion on Sunday, she gave her arse a little twist. He could also try thinking about that.

'I wouldn't mind but it was the worst arse on the island . . . the size of a television set.'

When he was younger he too had wanted to leave the island. Those grand ideas were not exclusive to Laura Quinn's head. As a boy he had watched the ferry come and go and he had wanted nothing more than to be on it. And he had wanted to go further than Bridestown or Drumquin or Bishopstown. He wanted to go to Italy and see the Punta Penna Lighthouse and every other lighthouse he could find after that. But then his sister went off to get married and there was only Martin and his widowed mother left. And then she got sick but still lived and lived and he got older but couldn't remember any of it, nights and days being the same and crashing into each other. And still she lived and was prone to having big nosebleeds on the sheets and rambling up the lane at night carrying a scythe and him after her, afraid she would cut her two legs off. She got older and took him there with her and he forgot about taking the ferry and seeing that very tall lighthouse in Italy. And finally she died and left him there, worn out like a dishcloth. He would never forget sitting in the parlour – with her in the coffin before the wake and before the islanders started calling. Just the two of them there together with stacks of ham sandwiches on plates and no one at all talking. Who would he talk to? And still he was glad, glad that she was gone and never so heartbroken.

He remembered seeing Laura Quinn at the church a few months later, her hair freshly washed and out around her shoulders. What could he do? He was only human. He had asked her to dance at McKenna's the following Friday, hooking his thumbs into the belt loops of her jeans and squeezing her to him. After all that sheet changing and mopping and fetching and carrying, she felt alive and very lovely to him. It was like being on a holiday for the first time in his life. They got on great for the first year and a half, not dwelling too much on the future but they seemed to be going somewhere together. He did love her, he supposed, and at the start he thought he would marry her. And then things got a bit rocky after that. Some eejit in McKenna's had made a joke about being in a car with her. 'She's a bit of a goer,' he said. She wasn't a saint, Martin already knew that. But he wasn't sure he could marry a girl who already had a bit of a name for herself. There seemed to be less said between them after that and yet neither of them could let go completely.

And now she was gone because he had let her.

Martin knew that behind a row of ice-cream-coloured houses just before you came to the Esso garage and after the square of wet concrete and the row of wooden benches under the corrugated shelter – there was the sea and the ferry that was taking Laura with it. And the worst part was that he could have

41

stopped her but he wasn't going to do that. He was bad enough without making a promise he wasn't sure he could keep. He ate the crisps in the car and took the bog road home so he would avoid the coast road and seeing her house with the blinds down and the curtains shut.

At home Martin climbed the steps to the lighthouse again and watched the ferry until a mist came down and the sky darkened. He could not see the boat at all then and didn't know where she was any more but there was a new raw feeling behind his ribcage, an empty space that poked him like a needle and he suspected that she was hiding in it.

6

The Bridestown bus was late leaving the harbour. It climbed up a wet hill and then moved slowly towards the town of Drumquin. The driver took them through narrow roads and farmland, waving at farmers who lifted their cattle sticks to salute him. He slowed down and crawled behind tractors and stopped when cows crossed the road to be milked. The air was different here and Laura could already sense it. It was the sound of people, more traffic, more noise, more life.

'Where are you off to yourself?' the man beside her asked. He was a lot older than her with snow-white hair and he had the same saintly way about him as a priest.

'Bishopstown.'

'Ah Bishopstown, I know it well . . . and where in Bishopstown are you going?'

'To the village first and then Bishopstown House.'

Here he smiled kindly at her, nodding. In that moment he had sized her up, she was one of the islanders, hoping to be a servant in a big house.

'It's a lovely place,' a voice behind her said and Laura turned to see a young woman in a long paisley dress standing up.

'That's out past the lake, isn't it?' the woman asked the man and before he could answer another voice shouted up from the back.

'That's the lake where people get the itch.'

'That's right,' the old man beside her nodded. 'The White Lake, one swim and they're covered in big red welts.'

Laura didn't know what to say to this.

'I don't think I'll be swimming in it today,' she said and the woman behind her laughed.

In a few minutes the old man's head was nodding and he was asleep and Laura watched the road signs so she would know how far she was from the village. She saw a sign for Bishopstown finally and the bus came down a long, smooth hill and arrived in a neat little place built around a crossroads. There were three pubs, Shaw's grocery shop and a village pump under a small thatched roof.

In Shaw's shop she asked for the phone and when the man behind the counter showed her into his own hallway, she stood and took a good long look at it. It was black Bakelite with a tiny handle on the side. It was dark back there and the phone sat on a pot stand covered in dust. They had had to walk together past the shelf of groceries and into the drapery part where there was a counter with a brass tape measure on it. The bolts of gingham were faded. There were lucky bags for sale on the window. She thought about Lucas Boyle and missed him. For 2p she could buy him a bag of luck.

'Calling the boyfriend?' Shaw asked and he gave a little twist of his head.

Laura stood for a moment and waited and then the shop bell rang and he gave a sigh and left. She caught her reflection in a speckled mirror and the girl she saw wanted to laugh. She didn't want to use this phone. She could imagine another phone ringing in a big house and how awkward she would feel speaking into it. She would walk. That would calm her down and she had a good idea where Bishopstown House was. Out past the lake, the woman on the bus had said. Laura used the front door of the shopkeeper's house to avoid going back through the shop. The sun was coming out and the village seemed yellow now and warm in it. It was almost autumn and the leaves on the beech trees were beginning to change. She watched as an old woman with a dog walked towards her.

What now? she wondered.

The woman moved slowly with a stick and when she stopped to rest, the dog stopped too, allowing her to catch her breath.

'Is Dooley collecting you?' the old woman asked. 'For the job at the big house,' she continued. 'Decent folk . . . cracked in the head, of course. But they'll see you right,' and she sat on the low windowsill in the sun and turned her face up to it.

The dog wagged his tail and seemed to smile up at Laura. He stood quietly and placed his head on her lap. Laura hesitated and then put her hand on his head, feeling his warm coat, his skull like a hard seashell underneath.

'A good Christian dog,' the old woman said and her voice was full of pride.

The shop door opened and Shaw stood and pretended to look out over the street. He watched her then with his hands on his hips. She could feel his eyes on the side of her face, making her cheeks hot and red.

'She won't fill you with chat, Bridie,' he announced and he let the door slam as he went back into the shop.

'Which way is it to Bishopstown House?' she asked.

'That road there, past the lake and follow the river after that. It's about two miles . . . you can't miss it,' she said and Laura started to walk.

The White Lake was pale blue and calm, not at all like the Atlantic. There was a high diving board which needed painting, a rusty ladder and a red boat forgotten in the grass. She wanted to lie down in it and drift away to sleep. She did not like to admit it now but her courage was fading. The lake had made her quiet. It had stopped her steady walk and it made her think. She was going for a job that she had no chance of getting and now she would be late. The ferry had made a slow crossing and the bus seemed to stop at every house. She should turn around now and go back. Her wooden house would be there waiting for her. She could go home in darkness and light each of her mother's standard lamps. In the morning she would go down to the beach as if nothing had happened and make her living as usual with the crate and pitchfork.

A car passed her on the road and then slowed down for a look. She stayed where she was and when it moved on, reluctantly she felt, she turned again and began to walk. She met an old tramp who was leaning heavily on a stick and they looked at each other. There was no house in sight yet. He looked like he lived inside the hedge. He was wearing an oversized suit jacket and smelled sour, like strong tea and burnt toast. She passed him without speaking and then, because she felt his eyes were on her, turned around again to look.

'Don't be lookin' back,' he shouted and he waved his big stick. His face was the colour of redcurrants. There were just the two of them on the road and she was embarrassed by it. It was beginning to rain. She could hear it on the leaves at first.

Another car slowed down behind her and this one was playing music. It sounded like the Osmonds. The car crawled behind her for a minute and then the music suddenly stopped. Laura felt herself grow tense and her hair felt coarse and heavy on the back of her neck. Who would save her now? The man with the fiery cheeks? With a sudden rev the car changed gear and then lurched past her and swung, bonnet first, into the grass verge.

The Ford Cortina. Had he actually followed her? 'Honk if you love Jesus'. There was no doubt. There was only one idiot who had a sticker like that. His face seemed unusual here, still handsome, she had to admit, but without the dunes and sea grass Martin was out of place.

He was twisted in the driver's seat so he could see her. He wound the window down and stuck his head out.

'Get in,' he shouted. There was rain hitting the windscreen now. Not enough. The left wiper was beginning to squeak.

She straightened her coat, pulled it down, adjusted the buttons and then noticed her feet. They were odd-looking in her mother's navy shoes. She realized now that there were bows on the toes of them. Where did she think she was going, she wondered, with toes like these?

'For God's sake . . .' and here he paused, 'Laura, get in.' Her name nearly choked him. When he said it out it was sticking between his teeth.

She opened the door and got in beside him. He turned off the engine and looked at her face.

'You're obviously confused,' he said. Laura glanced over at him.

Around them the windows were misting. She wanted to tip his ashtray on to the floor and get back out. She would have enjoyed vandalizing his car. She could use her finger on the mirror and write the word 'fuck' on to it. Then she would add an exclamation point. That was the important part. Someone had written 'Cunt!' on the side of Murray's shop once. The exclamation point made it nicer. It took the harm out of it. It didn't matter anyway, Murray was a cunt and everyone knew it.

'I'm taking you back to your house.' He started the engine, looked in the mirror and flicked the indicator switch.

'Why would you do that?' she asked, looking straight ahead.

47

She put her hands on the dashboard as if she could stop the car from taking off.

'It's where you belong.' He said the words quietly and he waited for a moment before speaking again.

'Do you know where you're going, Laura? That house, everyone knows about it . . . The Campbells are *important* people, *fancy* people, *rich*. You'd hate it, no ocean, no wind, locked inside cleaning up their mess . . . and for what?'

If he promised her something they would be all right.

For once, she told herself firmly, will you speak?

She placed her hands flat on her suitcase lid.

'Martin,' she began slowly. 'If you promise me something . . . I mean,' and here she almost stopped, 'offer me something . . . then I think we might be all right.'

Martin blew a long sigh out through his lips.

'I can't promise anything . . . *definite*.'

Laura felt her heart grow weak but she was getting used to that.

'But I do want you to come back,' he said. 'And we could continue, we could agree on that.'

She waited for more. Something like 'And then . . .' but she realized he was waiting for her to speak.

'And we could continue.' She repeated his words back to him slowly and then turned to face him in his seat.

'Continue what?' she asked quietly. 'Me calling around to your house in the afternoons, using the back door, sitting on your couch, lying down on your bed, drinking tea and then leaving to go back to my own empty house again. Sure, what woman wouldn't be delighted with that arrangement, Martin?'

'There's no need for the sarcasm,' he said.

She said nothing. It was the first time they had had a fight. The idea was almost exhilarating. She would throw him a punch next.

'I think you're confused,' he said again.

Laura took a deep breath. She needed a few clear words to pull herself out of this swamp.

'All you do,' she said very slowly, 'is make me feel bad about myself and I'm not confused about that.'

He looked up at the roof of the car.

'And you think leaving the island is going to change that?'

'I think it might be a start.'

'And what about the seaweed . . . are you going to leave it on the beach to rot?'

'John Joe Kennedy can come and collect it himself. You can tell him I said that.'

'You can tell him yourself,' Martin said. He was annoyed with her now because he could see he wasn't getting what he wanted.

Laura didn't care about the seaweed or Kennedy's.

'Did you hear one of the Americans got stuck in a bath there last week?' he asked suddenly. He was changing his approach now, trying to get her to laugh.

'They used a big crowbar to get her out, I think. John Joe said she was wedged in good and tight.'

Laura had never felt less like laughing in her life.

'I'm going to be late for the interview,' she said.

They sat there together in silence.

'You'll live to regret this, Laura,' Martin said eventually. He sounded cold now and there was no laughter at all in his voice.

'Could you drive me to Bishopstown House, do you think?' she asked.

She looked out her window as if the lake was of great interest to her. She was a hitchhiker now and she was going to get a free lift. Because he was angry he would drive fast and she might not be too late. The car pulled away from the verge quickly and it took off, only hitting the road in spots. He was breathing quickly through his nose and feeling for his cigarettes in his shirt pockets.

Twenty Major appeared and a small yellow box of matches fell and landed between her feet. She left it there. She knew he was dying for a smoke. She liked the idea of that. Then they were at tall wrought-iron gates. A stag on each pier. He slowed down briefly and then took off down a long stretch of gravel to another high red gate with a padlock.

'The servants' entrance,' and here he gave a little sniff, satisfied with himself.

She got out and he drove away with her door still open, flapping out wildly and then slamming itself shut.

Grow up, she thought.

It was almost four o'clock on her watch. She would find some excuse. Despite being stepped on again by him, she was glad she had had the wit to ask for a lift.

7

Bishopstown House, when it appeared, was not the barracks she had expected. It was low to the ground, long and rambling and painted canary yellow. 'Strawberry gothic,' the old man on the bus had said. There were croquet hoops on the lawn and two wooden mallets painted in fairground colours. Through the trees she had seen a tall yellow chimney. She would escape from the island by following the smoke. Lucas Boyle was the only person she liked but he couldn't talk to her. Patricia McKenna was convinced she was a less-bean. Martin would go home and admire his mother's wallpaper. The thought of that propelled her up the long gravel path as if someone had turned a key in her back. A man in green waders was fly-fishing on the river. She stood for a moment and watched his hands spool and cast. Feathers covered the grass around him as if someone had burst a pillow. Further back it was overgrown with ivy and moss and higher up there were oaks, sycamores, beeches, willows.

The storm was coming in fast now. She had seen the clouds thicken from the ferry. The seagulls cackled over her. They seemed to follow her wherever she went and arrived in a tribe then, flapping and screeching.

Fighting like tinkers, Laura thought.

The rain came down suddenly and she had to run across the

lawn to the house for shelter. She lifted the knocker but no one answered. She had expected to hear a dog barking somewhere but there was only silence at the front of the house. Thunder banged over her head and the heavens opened. Laura had no choice but to step into the hall and shut the door behind her.

Two people were talking in the kitchen.

'I couldn't give a damn,' a man's voice said.

'Well, you'll give a damn if she doesn't show up at all,' a woman replied.

'Sure, she's only an hour late.'

A kettle was dropped heavily on to a hotplate and cold water began to hiss.

'She has no real experience anyway . . . and no letters of recommendation,' the woman said.

'If she can cook a blasted egg, she can have the job,' he said. 'And it'll give you a rest.'

'Well, where is she . . . to cook the blasted egg?'

'The ferry was late getting in, Dooley said.'

'This weather is a disgrace, where's the Indian summer we were promised? Two storms in one week . . . I told Dooley to clear those gutters at the front.'

'I saw him heading off with his fishing rod a while ago.'

'It's a wonder he wasn't heading to the pub. That fellow is so lazy he'll grow corns on his arse.'

Here there was a pause and the man began to chuckle and the woman made a laughing sound down low in her throat.

Laura knocked softly and pushed the kitchen door open.

'Hello,' she said.

She was aware that she was appearing in their kitchen like a ghost.

'Jesus, Mary and Joseph,' the woman whispered and she

put one hand nervously to her throat as if to protect herself.

She was standing with her long denim skirt lifted at an Aga cooker, the top oven door open, warming her backside. The man, who had thick black hair and sideburns, was sitting near her in an armchair, his long legs stretched out. On the table there was the remains of breakfast at one end and, at the other, what looked like the remains of lunch. The man's cap was beside him and there were three flat field mushrooms inside it. Someone had left a basket of fresh-looking eggs on the dresser.

'I'm Laura,' she said. 'I knocked on the front door but no one answered.'

By now she was soaking. She could hear herself drip on to their floor. Her hair hung around her face like wet shoelaces. At times like this she frightened herself.

The man jumped up and spoke loudly.

'Come in, come in,' he said. 'We thought you were one of the Jehovah Witnesses.'

'I'm sorry I'm late.' The words came out in one quick breath but this was something they had already forgotten about.

She had the letter ready, twisted like a used Christmas cracker in her fist. If anyone needed to know, she had permission to be there.

'Mr Campbell?' she whispered.

'Finn,' he announced.

He looked younger than she had expected but he was at least forty-five. He was a big handsome fellow who wore his dark hair longer than other men and had it swept back off his face.

'This is my wife, Audrey. She's the boss in the house.'

'The Jehovahs have started calling,' Audrey said and she was speaking to Laura as if she had known her all her life. 'They came around here last week and did a reading for me, can you imagine that? On the front doorstep. They must think I'm soft in the head.

So I stood and listened and when she was finished I said, "Thanks very much" and banged the door shut.'

Laura looked around the kitchen.

'You have a lovely house,' she said.

'Give me your coat, you're soaking wet.'

And before Laura could speak Audrey was up beside her, tugging at the old buttons, unwrapping her, opening her up. She pulled the coat from her and began hoisting it up over the Aga. In that moment when they were close to each other Laura could only glance at the other woman and then look away, ashamed of herself. Audrey was a good deal younger than her husband. She was probably in her early thirties but would pass for twenty-five. She had skin that seemed to glisten, elegant hands, slender fingers, hair in soft black curls, perfume that smelled like apples. On the radio in the corner a newsreader was saying that the American president, Gerald Ford, was alive. They had tried to shoot him again but he wouldn't die, not yet.

Laura tried to remember what she had put on that morning. When she looked down she saw bare white legs splashed with dirt. Her mother's shoes were mangled-looking. There was a blue skirt, a blue cardigan and the blue cardboard suitcase at her feet. Audrey was wearing a long skirt and a pretty silk blouse covered in pink and red flowers.

'Come here,' she went on, 'you'll catch your death,' and she was pulling a chair from the table to the Aga and putting both hands lightly on her shoulders to make her sit. Laura looked at Finn. He glanced back at her, met her eyes and then turned to the window and looked out. Whatever he saw had embarrassed him. Without her coat Laura felt as if she was naked and she was glad he was looking away, looking out. She knew that he could see her plainly. That she was a woman with old-fashioned clothes who needed work. That his wife was relaxed and casual and not

54

afraid to touch her because she was well used to dealing with the help.

By now the room had grown dark and the rain was hopping off the garden path. Over the wall were fields waiting to be harvested.

'Any more of that rain and the barley will be flattened,' Finn said.

'Jesus, the hens,' Audrey gasped suddenly and without saying another word, she grabbed her husband's coat off a chair and ran out.

There was a small door in the middle of the cooker. Here Laura tried to concentrate on this hot red square of her life. Audrey had opened it up to let out more heat for her. She sat facing the red and orange embers, feeling it roast her face and her legs. She knew that Finn was still standing quietly at the window. She knew that he was still looking at the rain and that he had not turned towards her yet because she would have felt that. The kitchen was getting darker and somewhere far away Audrey could be heard calling, 'Chucky chucky chuck.'

'She puts up with a lot for a fresh egg,' he said and he sounded saddened by it.

He moved away from the window and walked to the blue-painted dresser and turned on a brass lamp. From where she was sitting Laura could see their underclothes drying over the cooker, his white trunks, her white lace bras and stockings, hanging there with her awful coat. What was she doing here? It was as if a wet sheep had strayed into their house.

The dresser where he was standing was filled with hand-painted pottery and delft. There were rows of dinner plates covered in silver flowers. She could count ten coloured cups, each with its own hook. There was a row of copper saucepans on the sideboard to her right. She looked at all of these things and then realized that he was watching her. She blushed and went back to looking at the Aga.

Lightning flashed suddenly and Laura jumped off her seat and knocked against the bowl of eggs. They both watched as one rolled off. There was a pause, and it fell to the floor and broke.

'Ha ha ha ha ha,' he went. 'Ha ha ha ha!'

Finn's laugh had a loud bell ring to it. He stood looking at the egg on the floor and laughed with his hands in his pockets and his feet apart.

'You better get that cleaned up before Audrey sees it,' and he was walking towards the big white sink. 'Eggs are very precious around here.'

He was pretending to be serious and before Laura could move he had scooped it up with his handkerchief.

'So tell me,' he said and his eyes were still laughing at her, 'are you able to cook one or do you just like to throw them around? We need them done every way in this house – fried, scrambled, poached, boiled.'

The scullery door opened and Audrey came inside.

'Here she is,' he announced and he was smiling again as his wife pulled off her boots and wet coat. He began taking the mushrooms out of his cap and then as if talking to himself, 'With a nice salty rasher and a soft fried egg, what could be better than that?' and he looked at Laura and his eyebrows gave a little jump.

'I don't think there'll be a ferry back tonight,' Audrey said. She was taking a cake out of a round tin and rattling side plates. 'That sky is very black.'

Laura thought about the old ferry bobbing in a storm and in that moment she would have preferred to be on it.

'How did you get from the village?' Audrey asked suddenly. She was beginning to slice what looked like a burnt fruitcake.

'The bus was a bit slow. Then I walked. I got directions.'

Laura was aware that she sounded like a woodpecker but at least she was finding her tongue at last.

The broken egg was not mentioned. As Finn walked around the table he lifted his hand and touched the back of Audrey's head. She slapped him away gently and he gave a sigh like a man who was tired.

Big loud man, Laura thought, not as tough as he looks.

Audrey smiled and began to arrange the fruitcake on a plate.

'I baked it this morning,' she said. 'When there's a storm coming the oven is like a furnace.'

Finn stood at the table and lifted a slice. He leaned against the sink and took a bite. Laura wondered where he had hidden the broken egg.

'Well?' Audrey asked.

'You burnt the arse out of it,' he said cheerfully.

Three burnt raisins rolled across the plate.

'These remind me of sheep-shit,' Laura said. Sometimes when she was thinking the words came out through her mouth.

A few seconds passed but to her it was a lifetime. She had forgotten where she was and had let the words slip out. They might have offered her the job and now they would take it back. Audrey's mouth twisted a little and she frowned into her cup and Laura realized that she was trying not to laugh.

'Finish your tea,' she said 'I'll show you around the house.'

Laura poured milk into her cup and it splashed the tea out. She was not surprised that her hand was beginning to shake.

Audrey said, 'A proper fruitcake is very nice.'

'Or a Victoria sandwich,' Finn offered. 'I love a good Victoria sandwich.'

'Roast beef with Yorkshire pudding. Roast chicken with sage and parsley stuffing . . .' Audrey went on.

'Can you do a pudding?' Finn asked and Laura wrinkled her forehead.

'We love steamed puddings,' Audrey said. 'Apple Charlotte, queen of puddings, spotted dick.'

Laura could feel the heat from the oven on her ankles. Her skin was turning red because they were frying her now like meat. A shotgun hung over the dresser. Her wet coat was making the windows fog up. She followed Audrey out of the kitchen and felt his blue eyes on her again. She did not want to think too much about them.

'Important people, fancy people, rich people,' that was what Martin had said.

Now she saw old paintings and polished furniture. She saw long narrow landings with floorboards that creaked. There were fireplaces where the ashes had piled up and had begun to fall out of the grate. She saw a library where the walls were lined with books. Their bedroom was in its own wing when you turned left at the top of the stairs. In the mirror of an open wardrobe door Laura saw their tumbled sheets.

Outside they could hear Finn shouting at his dogs, 'Come up, come up, come up.'

'He has a tendency to shout but he has a heart of corn,' Audrey said.

Laura stood beside her at a window and did not know how to respond to this. When she glanced at Audrey her eyes were shining as she looked out at her husband. They climbed the stairs to the attic and stood in the main room looking around.

'This would be yours,' Audrey said. 'And you could bring your own furniture if you like, make a home here for yourself.'

A half-made dress was pinned on a mannequin and, around it, spools of thread and scraps of red velvet.

'This is beautiful,' Laura said and she reached towards it and then seeing her own fingernails stopped herself.

Audrey pretended not to notice.

'Do you like it?' she asked kindly. 'It's an evening dress. Red is my favourite colour and Finn has always liked me in it.'

Laura watched as Audrey picked a tiny white feather off the velvet and blew it quickly from her fingertip. She had never seen a woman as pretty in her life or one who was so confident and sure of herself.

It was getting dark when they got back to the kitchen. Audrey made more tea and talked to Laura about the work.

'There's a lot of cleaning to be done given the size of the house,' she said, 'but if you have a system and do the silver one day and the brass the next . . . then it won't get ahead of you.'

And Laura nodded. She had never cleaned silver or brass in her life.

And what will you be doing? she wanted to ask but this time she had the sense to stop herself.

'I love being outside in the garden,' Audrey said then as if she'd guessed. 'And I've been told to slow down a bit, take a rest,' and here she rolled her eyes as if it was a joke.

Finn came out of the scullery, carrying a flashlight and dressed in a long oilskin coat and waders.

'It's like asking a racing car to put on its brakes,' he said.

And now Audrey put her head back and laughed.

'Have you ever worked anywhere else?' Finn asked then.

'Only at home,' Laura answered. 'My mother showed me how to clean a house. She was very particular about it. Otherwise I gather my own seaweed and sell it to the bath house.'

'You're a strong girl so,' he said, 'and not afraid of hard work,' and his voice seemed to be full of admiration.

The wind whistled in the chimney again and the thunder banged and was followed by another flash of lightning.

'I want to check the cattle in the river field,' Finn said. 'That lightning will drive them stone mad.'

When the thunder rolled again it seemed to be right over the house.

The light over the table gave a gentle flicker and they all looked at each other.

There was another flicker and they heard a loud click from the fridge in the corner and then the room was dark and silent.

'Well, that's that,' Audrey said, her voice coming out through the dark.

The red glow from the Aga was making a gentle pink light on the floor around them.

Finn turned on his flashlight and nodded at Laura. He pointed the light at the blue suitcase down near her feet.

'Have you a sleeping bag in that?' he asked. Even in the dim light she could see that his eyes were laughing at her.

Audrey gave a little chuckle and said, 'Thank God for a solid fuel cooker . . . at least I can heat up some stew for us.'

She had lifted a hurricane lamp from under the sink and it was glowing yellow now from the middle of the kitchen table.

Finn left, banging the scullery door behind him, and in the distance Laura could hear him calling up the dogs.

'He's worried about the barley,' Audrey said. 'Fifty acres of it, cracking ripe and now . . .' She gave a sigh and shook her head. 'Can you cook?' she asked suddenly.

She had lifted a big red saucepan on to the cooker and was turning to face her.

Laura considered telling a lie. It would have been easy in this half-light.

'Only a bit,' she said, 'but I'm able to clean. I'm very good at that.'

'Right so,' Audrey said and she smiled at her. 'Well, I don't mind showing you how to cook, if you're prepared to listen and concentrate.'

'I can do that,' Laura said.

'Four weeks' trial at the start. That should be enough time . . .' Audrey turned away again and began to stir whatever it was she had in the pot.

Enough time, Laura decided, to make a fool of myself.

The kitchen door opened again and Finn reappeared. His cap was soaked and small rivers were running off his coat down to his feet.

He stood for a moment and peered through the dark at the two women.

'I met Dooley in the yard. The phone lines are down in the village. He was talking to someone on the road and the ferries are all cancelled.'

'You'll stay the night,' Audrey said. She was beginning to ladle a beef stew into three deep green bowls. She glanced up at Laura and nodded as if it was all decided.

'But . . .'

'You can start work next week if you like. Would that be all right? Dooley will take you to the ferry tomorrow and he can bring everything you need back here in the horsebox.'

'He'll bring everything I need in a shoebox,' Laura said and Finn looked at her and laughed.

'We'll let you have the horsebox,' he said and she imagined herself standing up in a bridle, her head sticking out the back.

Laura felt like a child sitting there in this big, warm kitchen. But Finn and Audrey opened a bottle of wine and they ate their supper quietly and didn't seem to mind her being there. She said no to the wine. She had only ever drunk Guinness on the island and the wine she saw was usually on the altar and Martin said it tasted desperate. She finished her stew and listened as the wind dropped and she could hear the sound of the rain falling in the yard.

Finn found a big square battery for the radio and they told Laura how they liked to dance in the evenings.

'We love to have dinner parties,' Audrey said. 'Last week we had everyone doing the conga . . . out through the kitchen and all the way down to the garden and back. Doctor Reilly's wife fell into the flowerbed,' and here Finn and Audrey looked at each other and started to laugh.

'Head first into the rose bushes, two heels sticking out,' Finn added, 'if you can imagine that.'

'She can't hold her drink,' Audrey said.

Soft music came from the radio and she turned the volume up.

'Finn does a lovely foxtrot and he can waltz better than any man I ever met,' Audrey told her proudly.

Her arms and face were tanned from working in the garden and as Audrey sat there in candlelight sipping her wine, Laura felt amazed by how lovely some women could get. Finn saw it too and when the music changed he took his wife in his arms without a word and twirled and waltzed her up to the Aga and back and then around the kitchen table twice. They seemed to follow a pattern of steps already mapped out in their house over many nights – and Laura watched and wondered if they were right in the head.

There was a knock on the back door and Audrey went out through the scullery to answer it.

'That'll be Dooley,' she said.

And without a word Finn took Laura's hand instead and pulled her to her feet and began to move her around the kitchen in time to the music.

She had only ever been to the Friday night disco at McKenna's where everyone got out on the floor and shook themselves – but here Finn seemed to make a quiet space with just the two of them in it. He held her close to him and with the music in her ears she wanted to follow him and it felt strangely warm and safe. She forgot about Audrey going to the back door and the storm and Martin and the island and she could get the clean smell of soap from him and see how the sun had left the backs of his hands brown with the tiny hairs turning gold on them.

Audrey came back and her face broke into a wide smile when she saw them.

'See,' she said proudly. 'He's a good dancer, isn't he?'

'Well,' Finn said, 'I won't have a girl sitting down if there's music playing.'

And Laura stopped and stood there, awkward again and feeling too big for the kitchen. She couldn't tell them that until now she didn't know what a real dance was, that for her a dance was something the men on the island asked for when they were planning something else. That kind of dance made her feel like a lawnmower being pushed around the floor in straight lines and circles. Martin could dance well but not the way Finn could. He could always keep time to the music, but it wasn't anything like this.

A man in a raincoat and wellingtons stepped out of the shadows and took his wet cap off.

'Well, Dooley,' Finn asked. 'What's the latest from the village?'

He was leaning back against the cooker now with his arms

63

folded. His feet were crossed at the ankle and he seemed to have forgotten all about the dance.

'This is Laura,' he added, tilting his head towards her. 'She's afraid we're holding her hostage.'

Dooley was tall and thin, a reed of a man with a raindrop hanging on the tip of his nose. When he took his cap off, his bald head was shiny and wet.

He nodded to Laura and she could get the smell of drink from him before he opened his mouth.

'The ferry should be back by tomorrow evening – there are a few people stranded in the village and can't get back.'

Martin, Laura thought and she felt bad for him now. She imagined him huddled in a corner somewhere like a drowned rat and blaming her for all of it.

The house became very quiet then without the noise of the storm to fill it. Dooley left with a flask of hot tea under his arm and they climbed the wide stairs together in candlelight. It was too early to go to bed but what else could they do, three people left in the dark but who had only just met. The stairs were made from solid oak with a worn green carpet running down the middle. Laura looked down over the wide tiled hall to the kitchen door, a big grandfather clock, a yellow wall covered in photographs and a telephone that was silent. Audrey walked her to a bedroom at the far end of the landing and said goodnight to her and she felt embarrassed by this. She could not remember the last time any-one had wished her a goodnight and she knew that it could only have been her mother and her father before that. The thought made her sad and settled down on her a bit. She sat on the side of the bed and thought about Martin and missed him then too, the smell of his skin, the times when he smiled at her, his voice. She found a flannel nightdress on the bed and a hot-water bottle under the covers. She was their servant and they were treating her like a guest and she found it hard to understand this. She got undressed and felt peculiar doing it. She was afraid one of them would come through the door just as she was taking off her knickers. She didn't know yet that they were the kind of people who would always knock, even in their own house.

The gutter at her window was overflowing and Laura liked the sound it made. She lay down in the bed and clung to it. There was no sound of the sea here and the river was too far away and quiet. The sheets were white and fresh and Laura could feel that they had been starched and ironed. From now on, she would have to do everything Audrey wanted. She would try to please a woman who was kind enough to fill a hot-water bottle for her feet.

She had tired herself out walking from the village and sleep came quickly and surprised her. She felt herself falling down and then woke with a jump and then down again, deeper this time, until she was really asleep.

The old house settled and creaked around her and she dreamt she was out in a boat with Martin and then they were at mass together and he was passing around an apple tart instead of the collection plate. In the same dream she was dancing and twirling with Finn and she was laughing so hard that she was smiling and chuckling in her sleep.

8

Finn lay awake beside Audrey. When he closed his eyes he saw acres of ripe barley flattened to the ground, knocked by the wind and rain into big wheels and circles. John Nolan, the man with the combine, had promised to come the day before but he had stopped to do someone else's field first, the blackguard. That was the way it was at harvest time – the farmers shouting down the phone at John Nolan and then walking the ripe cornfields, cursing him. They watched the sky and prayed for sun but not too much of it in case the crop got too dry and light. Then they prayed for clouds to block that sun, clouds that didn't have any rain in them. And all this in a little country, thought Finn, where you could have four seasons together any day or night. They were all waiting for the same rumble of tractors and trailers and then the big combine behind them, with Nolan at the wheel, like the Queen of bloody Sheba. For one month of the year he was the most important man on the planet. He wouldn't mind but last year Finn had caught him helping himself to diesel from his own tank in the yard, the robber. Now none of it mattered. The barley was probably lost and there was nothing he or John Nolan could do about it.

And the girl came in the middle of everything. A raw-looking sort. A grand girl but like one who had never been let out. She was a fair bit older than Audrey but he would think of her as a girl because she had no wedding band and she seemed a bit at sea in herself. He smiled when he remembered the egg falling on the kitchen floor – splat! – and how she had taken such fright, how she had looked up at him in a blind panic. It could make him laugh now even though he was so worried about the crop.

Audrey was sleeping quietly beside him. With all his heart he wanted to turn over and take her into his arms for comfort. After she lost the last baby there was none of that sort of thing going on at all. Doctor Reilly said they should wait a bit, forget about it, get a housekeeper in and give Audrey a good rest. It wasn't the first baby that was lost and when he lay down beside her now he felt them standing between him and his wife, the headstones, like white dominoes, keeping them further apart.

He got up as soon as the first bird gave a chirp. It would be bright in half an hour. He went downstairs, made a pot of strong tea and headed out into the yard. The air outside was still damp and smelled of blossoms. It was getting warm again and everything in the garden, on the lawn, in the hedges, had grown some more overnight. This was his favourite time of the day, striding out early on a summer morning in shirtsleeves with the birds singing and the sound of his boots on the gravel and then whipping through the long wet grass in the lower paddock.

The cattle got up and stretched when they saw him. He loved to see them like this, through the low fog of a warm September morning, chewing their cud and stretching, bursting with good health. Next year he would plough up the cornfields and plant grass, he knew where he stood with livestock and he wouldn't have to suffer Nolan after that.

He crossed the gate into the barley, jumping down and causing a flock of crows to take flight. They had already settled in like vultures and it was worse than he'd thought. The sun was coming up over the tall pine trees at the end of the field and he took a deep breath and began to walk over the barley towards it. The whole field had been flattened, as if a giant in big boots had come in and had a barn dance on it. He leaned down to pick up an ear of barley, the seeds fat and ripe, asking to be harvested. The combine wouldn't be able to lift much of it. Most of it would stay where it was and rot. The birds and mice would have a feast. He took a deep breath and took his cap off and threw it on the ground at his feet. He looked up into the pale blue of the morning sky and tried not to shout out a curse. There were only a few things that could make him cry – that good Friesian cow that went down and couldn't get up, his own mare put to sleep after she broke her leg on the hunt and now this. He wanted to blame Nolan but he couldn't. As usual everything in this country came down to the bloody weather and all the blaming and cursing of Nolan in the world wouldn't change that. He sank down on to his haunches and crushed the barley seeds between his fingers and took a deep breath. The two collie dogs bounced over the field towards him, licking his hand and expecting nothing in response.

Finn stood up again. He would save his crying for other things – Audrey and what she had been through over the last few years. At night after supper he could hear her crying quietly in her bath. He cried over it himself in the outside toilet – the one with the damp toilet paper and the wooden seat and the old bathroom scales given over to rust. He had sat in there a few times and let his crying out; he could have washed the walls down with it.

And then he turned towards the back lane, the one that ran around behind the copse of pine trees and went in a straight line to the back gate, and he saw the girl, Laura, with her head down into the light wind and carrying the blue suitcase. He watched her for a minute, seeing her feet moving quickly in those dowdy old shoes, the suitcase swinging – he had carried it up the stairs the night before and it had seemed too light, as if there was nothing in it. He considered letting her go and yet now, in spite of the flattened field, the sight of her heading off amused him. He guessed she was bolting and he wasn't surprised by it. She had a wild look in her eyes like someone who would see a door and want to run through it. He could let her go and pretend he saw nothing. He watched her for a moment longer and then, putting his fingers up to his lips, whistled, a long sharp whistle, the kind he used to call the dogs up from the furthest field and it stopped her in her tracks.

When Finn looked down at his boots it was because he didn't want her to see the smile on his face. She had tried to do a runner before anyone was up – or so she thought. He watched as she stopped short and then looked around. The poor girl had a look of such fear on her face that he couldn't help but feel sorry for her. He raised a hand and then walked towards the fence and she stood there, her shoulders drooping, all the determination gone from her. She was beginning to turn red as he got closer, the kind of blush that was big and travelling up from somewhere under her cardigan and he felt sorry he had caused that.

'You're up early,' he said.

'I thought I'd try to get the ferry back, get an early start.'

'Well, we can give you a lift into the village – or to the port – it's a long walk.'

She let out a little sigh and looked towards the gate at the end of the lane. Finn wondered if she would start running again and then jump over it.

'Is Audrey up?' he asked.

'I didn't see her.'

'You're not one for goodbyes then . . . not one to stand on ceremony.'

69

She was staring back at him as if she didn't know what ceremony he was talking about.

'The first ferry won't leave until this evening – come back and have a bit of breakfast,' Finn said and then without waiting for an answer he climbed over the fence and began to walk down the lane towards the house. He walked quickly with one ear listening for her footsteps behind him but all he heard were the crows as they dropped down into the barley, the scarecrows standing by, useless now and looking humiliated.

When he turned the corner into the yard he caught sight of her and she was beginning to follow him. He got to the first gate and climbed over it with the two sheepdogs sliding in under the lower bars out of habit. He waited and watched as Laura pushed her case under the gate and then climbed up and over it herself. She stopped for a moment on the top bar, her hands keeping her steady on either side as if it was a seat. She glanced up at the sky and then at the darker clouds that were new and low on the horizon. She gave him a shy smile and he smiled back at her. She moved to come down and Finn raised his hands instinctively to guide her and then, worried she would fall, put them on her waist and lifted her down to the ground without a thought. Some part of him was surprised at how light she was and that her waist felt neat under that baggy skirt. To him she was just a girl sitting on a gate but still important enough not to drop.

Finn felt tired suddenly. It would take some time to forget about a whole harvest lost but he would drink tea now and cook an egg or two and wait for Audrey to get up. And this raw-looking girl, with the blonde hair that kept falling into her eyes and that he wanted to push back so he could see them, would sit with him and be company and he was glad about that.

9

Laura fried bacon and eggs for his breakfast. She knew how to cook the bacon first and then fry the eggs so they were crisp around the edges and had a nice salty taste. She knew how to slice bread for a man too, good and thick with an inch of butter on it. She did this with her coat still on and the suitcase parked at her feet. And Finn sat quietly at the table, tapping his toe and listening to the weather forecast. She warmed his plate in the lower oven and then put it in front of him. He had given her some field mushrooms and she wiped them clean and cooked them on one side until they were full of their own black juice – and then Audrey was up. She came into the kitchen smiling at them with her dark hair in a high ponytail and her arms slender in a sleeveless, blue linen dress. She glanced at Laura and nodded at Finn's breakfast plate.

'Now, that looks like a very nice breakfast,' she said.

She reached for an orange from the bowl herself and began to peel it. It was still early but everything Audrey did was calm and smooth and all her colours seemed perfect – the dark gloss of her ponytail and the scrap of red ribbon tying it. The orange held between her hands, up close to the pale blue of her dress. And she was smiling and relaxed and well rested and only Laura knew that her husband had been out in a field of flattened barley, practically crying over it. There was a secret between them already and she hadn't planned for that.

'I hear Dooley in the yard,' Finn said. 'I'll go out and see if he knows what's happening with the ferry.'

'Tell him he's to take Laura back to the island later,' Audrey said. She seemed to forget for a moment that Laura was sitting between them and she was talking to Finn over her head.

'Maybe we should ask Laura if that's all right,' Finn said and he looked straight at Laura and gave her the smallest wink.

'That would be grand,' Laura said.

And Finn left the kitchen, wearing a straw hat and singing a song under his breath.

Audrey showed her how to make brown bread after breakfast, mixing the wholemeal flour into the buttermilk so that it wasn't too wet but just moist enough and then making a cross on the dough to stop the hot crust from cracking and falling off.

'Or to let the fairies out,' she joked, 'as we like to say in Kerry.'

She slid the loaf tin into the oven and closed the hot door with the corner of her apron.

'So you're not from around here at all?' Laura asked.

'No, I'm from Kerry. My brother still lives there in the home-place . . . but Finn was born here, in Bishopstown House.'

'And have you been here for long?'

'Nearly twelve years. We moved in after we got married – and Finn's mother moved out. She was finding it hard to manage the big house anyway and she got a smaller place in Drumquin. You would have passed it on the bus.'

Laura washed the mixing bowl and the wooden spoon and laid them out on the draining board beside the sink.

'So now you know how to make brown bread and I know you can fry eggs to perfection . . . so we'll have a good breakfast anyway,' Audrey said and she gave a little laugh.

Then she went upstairs and came back with a long white summer dress covered in small pink flowers.

'I bought this a while ago but it doesn't suit me. Would you like it? It's one of those new maxis and it's going to be hot today . . . you'll need a lighter dress.'

Laura had seen a dress like it in a magazine but there was no shop that sold them on the island. Audrey handed it to her and the cotton was smooth and soft.

'Here,' she said, 'I want you to have it.'

In her room at the end of the landing, Laura took off her old blouse and skirt and put on the dress. It had no sleeves, just two wide straps over her shoulders and a long line of white buttons down the back. Then she took her glasses off because she thought she might look a bit better without them. When she went downstairs again Audrey smiled at her as if she was really delighted.

'Well now, don't you look lovely in that,' she said and she leaned her little backside on the table and folded her arms to take a proper look. Laura knew she was older than Audrey but she felt very young in this light dress and even pretty in it.

'Sit down here,' Audrey said and she reached for a hairbrush and took Laura's hair back from her face and began making a bun at the back of her neck. In the distance Laura could hear the sound of a tractor coming into the yard and the men shouting. Here and there, one of the collie dogs gave a few short barks and the other one answered.

Audrey held a mirror up to Laura and they both started to laugh.

'Now, there you are,' Audrey said. 'You have a nice tan on your shoulders and you should let people see those lovely blue eyes that you have.'

Finn came through the kitchen door suddenly then. He looked hot and was heading towards the sink for some water.

He was wearing the same wide-brimmed straw hat and his cream cotton trousers were covered in dust. He stopped short when he saw Laura in this new outfit as if he was confused by it. And she felt small and like a girl in the first pretty thing she had ever worn in her life.

'Where's Dooley?' Audrey asked.

'Picking apples in the orchard,' Finn said.

He was filling a tall glass of cold water from the tap and seemed to avoid looking at Audrey and Laura.

'How do you like Laura now?' Audrey asked and she was smiling at her own handiwork.

And Finn only nodded. He drank the water back in a gulp and left the two women in silence.

A strong wind was coming up through the orchard and Laura could feel some part of the sea in it. She stood listening to Dooley and watching a wasp hovering over the windfalls near her feet.

'This tree here has hard red apples,' Dooley was saying, 'sweet enough but not that good for eating. This one over here is the best for that . . . and these apples here, big and green, great for a tart or a crumble. Mrs Campbell does a great one of those.'

'She's going to show me how to make an apple tart before lunch,' Laura said and she picked a green apple and tossed it into the basket.

'So you're going to be cooking for us all,' Dooley said.

'All of you? Does that include the two sheepdogs?'

Dooley laughed at that.

'Well, I'll eat anything,' he announced, 'except for burnt porridge. I won't eat that.'

Laura looked at him and started to laugh too. She didn't know until now that he was part of the package.

'You can have Rice Krispies so,' she said.

He grinned at her and handed her the basket. A long wooden ladder was already propped against the tree trunk.

'I thought you were supposed to be helping me,' she said.

'I have to see a man about a dog,' he replied and he disappeared out through the hedge without looking back.

From the top of the ladder she could see Finn striding across the yard in his straw hat. He stopped for a minute and then headed through a wooden gate that led into the back garden. He stood on the lawn and looked up at the sky with his hands on his hips. Laura could see that he was hot, that sweat was making the band on his hat damp. He went into the house and then reappeared again and headed straight for the orchard. Laura watched all of this, the light cotton of her dress moving around her legs as she stood on the ladder. She climbed up to the top and then pulled herself higher so that she was sitting on a wide branch. When the soft wind came at her back she wanted to lie down in it. Finn stepped through a wooden arch and then reached for an apple and took a big bite. He stood there munching on it with Laura watching, not knowing if she should call out to him or stay quiet. She decided to pick every apple around her and say nothing.

'Laura,' Finn called suddenly.

'I'm here.'

When he looked up at her he gave a laugh.

'You're not stuck up there, I hope.'

'I'm not,' Laura said and she lifted the basket of apples and lowered it down to him.

'And where's Dooley? Ran off and left you, I suppose.'

'He had to see a man about a dog,' he said.'

'Gone to the pub in other words.'

Finn sounded disgusted.

Laura came down the ladder slowly with her back to Finn and

left the hem of her long dress hooked on to a little branch. Each step lifted the skirt higher so that by the time she reached the bottom rung it was up around her knickers.

'Jesus Christ,' she swore quietly and she couldn't reach high enough to pull the hem of her dress loose so she leaned back into it instead and felt it rip, freeing herself and leaving a long ribbon of cotton fabric blowing on the branch.

When she turned towards Finn he was studying the green apples in the basket. He kept looking at them until she started to walk on ahead of him. He was pretending that he saw nothing, not the snowy skin behind her knees or the soft muscle of her thighs that she was too mortified to even think about. She was glad she had packed a second pair of knickers. The scrap of cotton still hung in the tree but Finn's eyes wanted her to believe that he had seen nothing. At that moment even if he felt like laughing he was trying to spare her any embarrassment.

'I'm going to take the car into the village,' he said. 'You can come with me for the spin if you want.'

'Right so,' Laura said quietly and she walked on, wondering how big the tear in the dress was and watching as he swung the basket into his other hand.

The road back into Bishopstown village seemed shorter now and Finn drove his red Mercedes like someone in a hurry. They pulled in and made a wide circle around the pump before parking outside Shaw's shop. Finn leaned back in his seat and pulled a fiver out of his pocket.

'Ask him when the ferry is back and will you get me the *Irish Times*.' He frowned for a minute as if he was thinking. 'And two choc ices,' he added.

When Laura got out of the car he rolled down the window and called after her, 'Paddy Shaw is on the lookout for a wife . . . so

76

watch yourself,' and he was making that smile again as if he was about to laugh but then stopping it.

Shaw told her that the ferry would sail again at seven. He was wearing a white shop coat today and looking delighted with himself.

'The boats have nowhere to dock on the island,' he announced. 'The sea knocked some of the old pier into the water last night.'

And then he was coming out from behind the counter and moving slowly towards her.

'Are you worried you won't get home, pet?' he asked. 'Don't worry at all . . . they're fixing up the pier now and there'll be a ferry at seven o'clock tonight.'

She put the newspaper on the counter and handed him the fiver. It was 23 September 1975 and the headlines said that the IRA ceasefire was over. They had started to bomb the North again.

Finn turned the car around and took the road out past the pump, swinging left down a hill then so that they were facing the White Lake. He turned the engine off and reached for his choc ice.

'I like to sit here sometimes and look out at the lake,' he told her. 'I can't pass it without going down the hill for a look.'

'It's very calm . . . compared to what I'm used to,' Laura said. 'Shaw told me that the pier on the island was damaged by the sea last night.'

'So I heard. Were there any people on it?'

He was tearing the wrapper off his choc ice like a child who couldn't wait to get at it.

'Unfortunately not,' Laura said.

She opened her ice cream and took a little bite. If she was on her own she would have eaten all the chocolate first and then licked off the ice cream part.

Finn looked at her, his face full of surprise, and gave out his big, loud laugh.

'So you're not homesick then,' he said and his shoulders shook inside his shirt from the laugh.

'I thought I was,' Laura said, 'but now I think maybe I'm not.'

'Well, good,' Finn said. 'I thought when I saw you this morning you were making a run for it.'

He looked steadily at her now, turning to face her from his seat. He had already finished the ice cream and held the bare stick between his teeth. He could see the blush coming again but it was smaller now, like a faint glow in her cheeks.

'I was,' Laura said, 'but I came back.'

Finn smiled at her, his eyes dancing.

'I'm glad you did,' he said and he tossed the little stick out the car window.

She was to wait for Dooley at the back of the house. She left her suitcase on the floor of the scullery beside a row of dusty wellingtons and went to sit on the kitchen windowsill outside. The Carpenters were singing on the radio behind her and she sat very still and faced the garden. She did not want to turn around because her face at the glass would give anyone a fright. Audrey had told her to keep the dress but as she waited on the windowsill she began to undo the bun and shake her long hair out.

A peacock appeared and began to call out to her.

'Go back, go back, go back,' it seemed to say. It stepped around the corner again, looking disappointed. Its tail dragged on the ground, wings drooping, its small head cocked. The garden was quiet and lush after the day's heat but the clouds were getting heavy-looking again on the horizon.

The radio grew loud suddenly and Laura could hear the Bee Gees singing. 'Jive Talkin'' – she had danced to it herself one

Friday night. When she turned around she saw that Audrey had begun to dance beside the radio. The kitchen looked yellow in the twilight and through the glass she watched in a coat that still felt damp.

Audrey was skipping around the flagstones like a goat. Her legs were as thin as two pencils and her black curls bounced. She was wearing leopard-print slippers and doing some kind of jig. Every time she crossed the floor she kicked up her legs and lifted another cup and plate. When the table was clear she wiped it in circles, bending her knees in time to the beat.

This is why she needs a rest, Laura thought and she was starting to laugh.

Then Finn appeared in the kitchen and said something to Audrey and she nodded and he left, heading out through the hall to the front of the house.

When the music changed again, Audrey stopped in the middle of the floor and just shook her hair from side to side with her eyes closed. She turned the radio up again and lifting her hands in the air she began to move like a snake. Then she went forward in three marching steps and then back across the kitchen again, twisting her backside in time to the beat.

Someone as daft as myself, Laura thought.

An engine was started somewhere and then she saw the red car pulling a horsebox and bumping up the lane from the farmyard. The passenger door was pushed open and Finn's face appeared.

'Get in,' he said and Laura got her case and climbed into the passenger seat.

'Dooley's at the pub and he's too drunk to stand up.'

Audrey was not mentioned and Laura did not like to ask. She sat in beside Finn and when his foot hit the accelerator she floated. She counted eight white croquet hoops on the lawn and saw a donkey sleeping with its head hanging over a fence.

She looked up at the tall trees that lined the front driveway. She was very quiet. She was still thinking about dancing with him in the kitchen the night before and then driving together into the village for an ice cream. On the way to the island she might pretend he was her husband and why not? It was no harm at all to enjoy a daydream like that. She thought about Audrey in the kitchen with the radio playing. If Laura ever owned a man like Finn, she too would dance.

'Are the storms over?' Audrey had asked over dinner.

'I think so,' Laura had said but it was a bit of a lie. The September storms were unpredictable and often came back for another look.

Anyone from the island who saw the sky now – grey and navy blue and black – knew that the real storm was only warming up. But for now though they were safe in the red car together. She could imagine he was hers and then give him back. The men she usually met belonged in the zoo. They were not like him or any-one in this new place. Martin Cronin was not the worst of them at all but he didn't hold her and waltz in a smooth circle like Finn did and he didn't laugh or talk. The men she knew should be sleeping in sawdust in the reptile house.

Finn changed gear and they moved down the avenue. He adjusted the dial on the radio and began to sing along to it. Laura could make out the red windfalls in the long grass of the orchard. She remembered sitting in the apple tree and him smiling up at her. A scarecrow was slumped in the barley field as if he had been shot.

10

Martin arrived early for the ferry. He had spent the afternoon watching *Jaws* at the new cinema in Bridestown. He had time to kill and at least it took his mind off the embarrassment. He had left the lighthouse after a storm was forecast and lucky for him all the ferries were cancelled. But it was because of a woman and everyone would know it. *Jaws* had frightened the shit out of him. Sitting there at the port, he was sure he would see a leg or an arm floating past. It would be a while before he would feel like going for a swim on Fintra Beach. He bought a bottle of Fanta at the little newsagent's and ate a warm sandwich from a plastic bag. The lettuce had died and taken the bread with it. It smelled like a greenhouse. He tossed the crust into the water and watched the gulls drop down on it. The ferryman and his helper, Francie, stood on the quay and watched the horizon. The water moved and the island stood still behind it.

'You'll go at seven?' Martin said. His voice nervous, hopeful.

'We'll go,' the ferryman said.

If they left on time he could drive to the lighthouse and be ready before the second storm hit.

He opened a new pack of cigarettes and held the foil loosely in his fingers, letting the wind take it. He was feeling sour and hoped a gull would choke on it.

The waves were sloshing under the boardwalk. The sky was getting darker. He could see that it was raining on the island already. The wind rose in a sudden gust making a sail snap and flap but if they left at seven sharp they would beat the thunder and lightning. He had wasted two days and for what? The sheep would be in the paddock stuffing themselves. A bellyful of green grass and in the morning he would find one or two dead and stiff. They would roll over and get stuck like that. They died on their backs because they saw the world differently and couldn't handle it. They were killed by the new perspective.

Laura's face appeared in his mind. The idea of her always excited him. He couldn't help himself. The bitch. He wasn't going straight home anyway. If this little storm blew over he would let the sheep die and go to her house. He thought about the curved wooden porch painted white. The row of windows over the sea, looking east. He would smell the cedar wood in his sleep. Her clothes, her hair and her skin were always full of it. Now that she was gone, he couldn't get enough of her. He wanted to get inside her world now, find a wooden drawer in her house full of her clothes and bury his face in it. He knew where the key was. On the island, it was always easy to get into someone else's house. He would write something on her wall. He would deface it. He would use her bathroom. Overflow the bath. Put her shampoo bottles floating in it. Why not? She wouldn't know a thing about it. She was too busy running away from him. Too busy trying to make a better life for herself. He would give his life to have her back now. That was the worst part. He had bought a pair of navy bell-bottoms to impress her. He had tried. She had run over him. He had made a fool of himself. It was all over the island already. Cronin was still bedding that racy Quinn girl, 'knocking her off'. He had managed to get the last ferry before the storm and had gone to the mainland after her. With a storm coming he had abandoned the lighthouse.

'Ran after her . . . lovesick,' the islanders would say. 'Had he not heard the forecast?'

The ferryman directed him over the ramp. He drove on with a cigarette in his mouth, the smoke rising and making his eyes squint. He parked on the empty deck, feeling the car rock over and back. The waves were getting stronger. One-way ticket now, no going back. So far it was him and the ferryman, and the ferryman's helper, everyone else had decided to stay on dry land, anyone with any sense.

He would have to stay out of McKenna's for weeks now. How the heads would lift to stare at him like cows looking over a ditch. He would drink his Guinness at home, the brown foam running down the side of the free Esso glass, and watch the *Late Late* on his own on Saturday night. He hated her now. She made his life seem pathetic and now that she was gone he had no desire to go back into it.

He would go through her books and tear pages out, slash the oil paintings that covered the walls all the way down the stairs. He had gone down there with her many times and they had done it in a small bedroom full of books. The bed had creaked and he had knocked his head on a painting, sending it sliding down to the floor. She had asked him to stay and he had said yes and then, knowing she was still awake and listening, he got up and left in the middle of the night. He wanted her. He always did – but he didn't want the silver dawn light. He didn't want the breakfast. A woman could get ideas over two boiled eggs.

He lit another cigarette and hung his hand out the window. The ferry horn sounded and the engines started up. A red Mercedes and a horsebox slid into the car park. The horsebox would take some manoeuvring. It would make them late. The driver turned and reversed up the ramp. He did it in one shot.

He looked like a toff, Martin thought. Black hair to his collar and thick sideburns. A good car. A new horsebox. 'A jolly nice tweed cap, by George.' When the car stopped, the driver was sitting next to Martin. He rolled his window down and Martin rolled his up. Then he saw Laura sitting in the passenger seat. He watched as the man stretched himself and then tossed his cap on to the back seat. He took a hip flask from his breast pocket and offered it to her. The sight of her, of them, rocked Martin and made him feel seasick.

He felt himself turn green. He could feel his strength, the things that kept him upright, seep out of his pores, starting in his face. He had pins and needles in his feet. He saw a star or two, flickering. He wondered if he would need to open the window up and vomit. Laura lifted the flask and took a delicate sip. He had never known her to take a drink like that. She flinched at the taste. Smiled a bit. Miss Prim Polly. Sitting up there like Shirley Temple in the front seat and her in a brand-new flowery dress. Where did she get that rig-out? She looked like butter wouldn't melt in her mouth. No one would guess how much she liked being in the sack. Then the toff said something and she looked at him and laughed. What had he said? What had he said to make her laugh like that? The toff paid the fare. The ferry began to move, slowly at first, then it gave a lurch against the waves which were getting high up ahead. It would take an hour to get to the island.

Finn and Laura got out of the car and went to stand at the white rail and look out. There were just the three of them. Maybe we'll have a party, Martin thought. His mood was black and he was still feeling sick. The rain was making spots on his windshield. He didn't want to turn on the wipers. He couldn't stand the noise they made. He would not be going to her house now. If he did he would put a match to it.

*

The sky changed colour. Autumn disappeared and the clouds turned into black polar bears instead. The sun had gone, leaving a yellow stain on the sky behind it. Finn offered her a cigarette and she took one. She hoped he would not notice that she had bitten her nails to the quick. She looked down at her feet, too big, and her hands like boxing gloves. She was about as dainty as Moby Dick.

She sat down on a bench, crossed her legs and began to smoke, holding her elbow in her hand and leaning forward into the cigarette. She had seen Martin's car straight away and knew that he was watching all of this. If Finn said anything even slightly funny she would laugh so hard her head would go rolling down the deck.

The waves were getting higher. Once or twice the spray lifted and Finn stepped back to avoid getting wet. The storm cloud hung over the island and it was getting closer. A black UFO heading east. She knew that he couldn't see it and for that reason he was not afraid. Martin was still sitting in his car but beginning to look left and right. Francie appeared carrying three yellow life jackets.

'Just in case,' he said.

He told Martin to get out of his car and get into the shelter with the others. The shelter had a yellow roof with four grey poles to keep it in place. There was a dinghy attached to the wall and two oars like matchsticks and they tried not to see this. There would be room for four at a push. Suddenly they were on the *Titanic*, minus the chandeliers and the man playing the piano with the water sloshing around his feet. The three passengers sat in a row, strapped in now, on the wooden bench, Finn and Laura sitting close to each other. And then Martin on his own, to one side.

'Isn't this nice?' he announced loudly.

When Laura looked again he was leaning over the side to be sick.

'Every cloud has a silver lining,' she said.

Halfway to the island the ferry and the storm met. It was quiet enough at the start and the ferryman opened the engine up, trying to beat his way through it and get to the island.

'Do you have people?' Finn asked. He was trying to be casual and polite. They were watching the ferryman ride the waves at the stern. The lighthouse looked dead in the distance.

'People?' she asked.

'Family.'

'No. My mother died when I was thirteen and my father was a fisherman.'

Finn looked at her and nodded. 'Was' and 'fisherman' said a lot.

'At first they couldn't find him,' she said, jogging him along.

'I'm sorry to hear it.'

Finn turned the collar of his coat up and pulled it tighter around himself.

'What's it like to be married?' Laura asked suddenly.

She had been on her own for a long time and she was dying to talk. He couldn't help but smile back.

'Ha,' Finn said and he looked at the island. It sloped upwards on the left, grey cliffs, green patches, sheep.

'I haven't been here since I was a boy,' he said.

'And what did you think of it?'

He waited for the right word to surface.

'Desolate,' he said.

'Perfect,' she replied after a pause.

'So why do you want to leave?'

'I meant that . . . the word "desolate" – it's perfect for it.'

They stared into the waves again.

'I came to see the lighthouse then,' he said. 'They say you can see Bishopstown House from the top of it, on a clear day.'

'And did you see it?'

'A mist came in off the sea. I could hardly see my hand in front of my face . . . but we climbed to the top anyway, I enjoyed it. There is something magical about a lighthouse.'

They didn't speak for a while. The waves lifted them up and down in a strange churning rhythm. They were both wet but kept looking at the island as if fixing their eyes on it would keep them safe.

He pushed his hands deep into his oilskin coat and looked at her.

'Marriage is . . .' He stopped and shook his head. 'Well . . . it can be difficult at times.' He raised his eyes, shrugged, smiled a bit.

'Oh,' Laura replied and her ridiculous heart seemed to give a hop-skip.

'But I have a good woman,' he said and his voice was quiet.

Laura thought about Audrey. She could imagine her in a yellow life jacket, watching the storm, worrying about him from a tidy vegetable patch.

'She's a Catholic,' and he said it out over the wind. Laura stared straight ahead.

'I'm a Protestant,' he shouted louder.

She had never met a Protestant before and this one seemed angry about it.

'And do you have people?' Laura asked, trying to change the subject.

Finn took out a handkerchief, gave it a shake and blew into it.

'My mother,' he said and he blinked and gave a long sniff. 'As far as she's concerned . . . there is nothing worse than marrying a Catholic.'

'There are plenty of things worse than that,' Laura said. She looked over at Martin, who was trying to be sick into a Tayto bag.

'Why is the lighthouse not working tonight?' Finn asked suddenly.

'I think the lighthouse keeper is sick.'

She could feel a sudden laugh bubbling up inside her. It was a long time since she had felt that.

When she looked back Finn was smiling at her. He had liked what she said. His eyes were wet but by then everyone and every-thing was wet. Laura did not know anything about the Church. She went to the Catholic one on Sunday because that was where the island people met.

The engine was overheating a bit and the waves were rising and flinging themselves into the boat.

'Keep going,' Laura told the ferryman. 'It won't last.'

'Turn back,' Martin shouted. He was on his feet trying to put a second life jacket on over his head.

'This man is in a panic,' Finn said. He watched him for a moment and then gave a little laugh. 'He's putting it on back to front.'

'He can't swim,' Laura said and now she heard the worry in her own voice.

The boat gave a sudden dip and a wall of water came in, soak-ing them. Around them the waves seemed to reach a rolling boil. Water covered their feet and then splashed to the other side of the deck. Francie came with a black bucket and began to throw it back out. Finn staggered to the car and found another oilskin coat. He put it over her and she sat still as he buttoned her up. He put his arms around her suddenly and held her tight. She knew that he was holding her because he was afraid himself. It was not the first time she had been held like that. He pulled his cap down tightly on his head, buttoned his own coat to his neck and asked, 'Can you swim?'

'Like a fish,' she replied, 'but no one could swim in this.' Under the clouds the sea began to look like treacle.

Martin sat on her other side now, his face green, almost luminous. His black hair was soaking wet. Laura reached over and took his hand and held it tight. She was feeling charitable now, benevolent, and he didn't resist. They were all going to drown. She could have any man she liked.

The ferry rolled sideways and sent them all sliding. First Finn and Laura and then Martin, who landed on her, forcing her left hip into the floor of the boat. The wind rose again and Finn tried to stand up, holding one hand out to help her.

'Sweet Jesus, save us,' Martin said. He had one knee up as if he was genuflecting.

'Sit down,' shouted the ferryman. And they staggered back to the wooden bench, holding on to each other, like triplets.

When they got to the harbour the islanders were all out. They had built a new makeshift pier that ran like a wooden boardwalk out into the water. There were torches and bobbing hurricane lamps. Irene McKenna put a rug over Laura's back. Her sister Patricia was holding a lamp with a low battery and it made a pathetic yellow light. A lamp with a limp, Laura thought. She staggered off the boardwalk and sat down on the wet concrete. Her shoes had fallen off as she climbed down the ladder but she felt safer in bare feet. Hands touched her, patting her back and her head. Father Meehan was there holding a small black Bible and the edge of each page was painted red. Somewhere down low she saw blond hair and then Lucas and he came and put his thin arms around her. Toilet O'Riordan shook the ferryman's hand. Joe Levy handed Finn some tea in a white plastic cup.

'He'll need something stronger than that,' someone said.

Delia O'Rourke was holding the Infant of Prague statue high over her head.

'You can take him in,' another voice said, 'he'll catch his death.'

The islanders laughed. They were cheerful now. This was a celebration. Five people alive when it could have been five people dead. And one of them was Finn Campbell, that big farmer from the mainland. The McKenna sisters were talking about their pub and how Mr Campbell could use their radio and then they could give him a bed for the night. Everyone seemed to have the idea that he was someone important, that he was a big shot from the mainland. Laura could see the sisters' house weighed down with every kind of damn ornament, a shrine in bric-a-brac. A right pair of vultures, enough to drive a man like him stone mad. They were all used to storms and how the sea could turn ugly and if five bodies had been washed up they would have been used to that as well. They began to move away in twos and threes. Finn hunkered down and wanted to know if she was all right.

He put his hand over hers and she could feel the warmth of it. He offered her the hip flask again. This time she made a grab for it and he looked at her, smiling. A car was started then and he became distracted. The front door was opened from the inside and they offered him the passenger seat. To them, he was a prince. They all called him Mr Campbell. They would drive him to the pub and fill him with drink. The others wandered up to the pub on foot. The sky was the colour of charcoal. Only Martin and Laura were left.

'I'm going up to the lighthouse,' he said. For once he made a full sentence, one with a beginning, middle and end. A near-death experience had cleared his head.

The sea had almost pulled them under. She had no desire now to be close to it. She could go to the pub but she would stick out there and feel like a nuisance. She knew exactly the reaction her head coming around the swinging door would provoke.

'Would you look . . . it's the Quinn girl.'

Finn would see then that she was a pariah of sorts. When, she wondered, did she feel it was all right to call him that?

Laura got up from the wet concrete and stood for a minute with the sea wind cold on her face.

She did not know where she was going.

Home, she supposed. The house would be waiting, cold, dark.

The sunset was cleaner now. More stars flickered. There would be no more rain that night.

'I can light the fire . . . you could dry yourself,' Martin said.

For the second time in two days someone was offering to dry her and her awful coat. They really weren't worth it. She considered taking it off and throwing it into the water and then watching as it grew heavy and disappeared, as if she had drowned herself. She needed to be with someone. The idea of Finn surrounded by islanders, laughing, drinking, eating hot food, telling stories, meant she could not be by herself. The idea of walking three miles in the dark along the coast road to her house made everything about her seem pathetic. She realized that she was starving.

Martin stood watching her. His face in a frown, a general look of pain on his face.

'I was thinking of cooking a few sausages,' he said.

11

The telephone line was dead again and Audrey became frightened. She was waiting to hear that Finn and Laura had arrived safely on the island. The wind rose suddenly and it roared high up in the beech trees. She closed the tall shutters in the drawing room and climbed the narrow stairs to the attic. The electricity was gone again and she lit a candle. She hated going up here and yet this was where she felt safe. The big room would be Laura's sitting room. It had an odd shape, high up under the eaves, going into a point at the window, like something in a child's storybook. There was a narrow landing leading to a small bedroom where there was a white bed and a wooden cradle beside it. Laura would have her own bathroom with a washbasin and a tub that stood on short fat legs. At the end of the corridor was a heavy door with an iron latch and then the top of the narrow back stairs that led down to the scullery. She didn't want to go to the wardrobe in the bedroom so she stood on the little corridor, frozen for a moment, with the wind whistling around her and one hand turning the small silver pendant at her neck.

Even now the idea of what had happened in this house could send her backwards into the faded wallpaper. She would turn her face towards it, trying to swallow back tears that were still there and always willing to come out. 'Look at the clothes and look at

the cradle,' Doctor Reilly said. 'Say goodbye, let the grief out.'
But now after three years of letting it out Audrey had begun to
fight against it. She wanted to feel less and be harder. In that way
she would be safe from the pain of it. She wanted to pack her
feelings up in a suitcase and sit on the lid to keep it shut.

The attic smelled like loneliness. The lino was cracked and
against her cheek the wallpaper felt chalky and damp. She took
a deep breath and headed for the stairs again. Coming back down
was like descending Everest. She could feel the heat from the
house rising up to meet her and imagined piles of fresh snow
beginning to melt. On the first landing she could see the wide
hallway downstairs, the swords crossed over the fireplace, the
framed photographs of dogs and ponies, the grandfather clock.
Underneath the attic were softer carpets, a range of different
smells, polished wood, tall gilt-framed mirrors, a mix of colours
from Persian rugs, oil paintings, fresh flowers.

A picture of the ferry on the waves came to her and she tried
to pray about it. Tonight with the wind getting stronger around
the house it was just words going upwards and then disappearing
out through the roof. Once when she was praying she saw stars,
like the ones around the Virgin Mary's head.

'You shouldn't pray on an empty stomach,' Finn said.

It was almost dark and she wanted to go out. She needed to
check that the hens were inside, that the byre door had not swung
open, that the slates were not blowing off the roof. Instead she took
the red velvet back downstairs with her and opened her sewing box
to distract herself. She should telephone Dooley but he would be in
the pub, safely holed up, his hands wrapped around a pint of stout.
At times like this she would like to wring his neck.

Audrey sat at the kitchen table and began cutting the fabric.
The dress would be backless and down to her feet, lined in red
silk. The pattern showed how to make a matching red velvet

headdress. With her black hair, her figure, she would look . . . what did it matter how anyone looked? The thread was taut around her forefinger, the thimble on her thumb like a little helmet.

'Eyes above the nose was all that mattered,' her mother had said. That and working hard, saying your prayers, not getting sick. Her figure was not curved but quite straight, long slim arms, legs like sticks.

Elegant, Finn said. He liked that. He told her that if she was a tree she would be a poplar and they had laughed about it. She had asked Doctor Reilly once about how she could put on weight.

'You can't fatten a greyhound,' he said.

Through the window the sky was black with clouds and night, a single strip of white remaining on the horizon. The trees were rattling, black and bare, branches held out as if asking for help. Inside, the candles on the table flickered and it was hard to see where her needle was going. The emptiness of the house was weighing her down and she suddenly wanted to escape from it. Then she was in the scullery pulling on a pair of galoshes. She crossed the front lawn wearing a scarf tied around her head and one of Finn's long coats. There were branches everywhere and as she walked she began to bend and pick some up. She hated cleaning the house but she liked the garden to be perfect. She squinted up at the roof. So far it looked all right. There were no slates on the lawn but it was hard to see in the dark. Kindling, she thought and she filled her deep coat pockets. She couldn't bear the mess of it. The fence at the ha-ha had collapsed, one long beam lying on the grass, two more flung down into the field. She went for one, the wind making her path difficult, and with a sudden gust the board was lifted up and it knocked her off her feet. She heard the crack of her front teeth and felt pain move through her face. Stunned, she put her hand up and then found blood on it. Surely the ferry would not sail tonight. If it did it would sink.

The thought clanged into her head as clear as daylight. Where was Finn? She tried to think of Laura and could not remember what she looked like.

Then she was crying, the idea of losing him as well as the babies making something inside her break. Her head ached, arrows of pain shooting out from her nose and into her teeth. The red velvet dress. She began to cry again at the thought of it. Her knuckles were grazed and bloody. Why had she not stayed inside to finish it? In another flash she saw her husband's body tossed in salt water. She put her head down and cried into the grass. She cried for her husband and then she cried for the babies she had lost. She cried for the womb, her womb that was careless and unreliable and could not be trusted with something so precious. Audrey sat on the lawn and hugged her knees and felt the wind blow the leaves in a circle around her face. The beech trees creaked over her and she willed the biggest branch to come down and clock her on the head. The last of the children was buried behind the Catholic church and she had never visited the grave once. She had put him in there and that was enough. In her mind she carried him with her, with all the others, like tiny pins inside the hem of her dress.

The wind seemed to be dropping and when she wiped her nose on her sleeve and looked up she could see some stars overhead. Audrey swallowed and took a deep breath.

'This,' she said out loud, 'will not get the dinner cooked.' She straightened out her coat and saw that her pockets were bulging with sticks. First she would make oxtail soup for Finn because it was his favourite. Then she would light a fire and sit down to wait.

When the Guards came she stood at the door and greeted them with the scarf over her mouth.

'Your husband is safe,' they said.

12

Finn lay in the single bed under a pink candlewick bedspread. There were no curtains on the window and a street lamp filled the room with amber light. The pub was closed downstairs but he could still smell stale beer and cigarette smoke. He wondered what it would be like to run this sort of business, allowing all sorts of people into your house – and then stand there laughing and listening to their bullshit. He didn't like strangers in his house and there was nothing he enjoyed more than to walk out early in the morning and watch his cattle get up and stretch themselves. He thought about Audrey and saw her leaning back on white pillows, marking dates off on the calendar as if she was playing bingo. She had wanted nothing more than to be pregnant again. He missed the fresh scent she brought into their bed now but not her constant fretting about what should happen in it. To everyone else she was cheerful, industrious and only he knew that on the inside she was damaged, broken, that losing the babies had changed her. Lately she had been keeping her distance in their bedroom. Finn had felt her grow colder. Now when he lay down on the narrow bed over the pub and began to think about her he felt tired out from all her sadness. He was suddenly weary from helping her to carry that.

Here at the pub, there was a hot-water bottle at his feet and the bed smelled damp. The sheets were beginning to feel wet from his body heat. He had called the Guards on the mainland because the line to Bishopstown House was dead. They were driving out to tell Audrey that he was all right. He was not all right. The ferry's engine needed a new part and it could take days to find it – and until then he was stuck on the island. His clothes were hanging in the small kitchen at the back of the off-licence. He was wearing some other man's pyjamas and when he closed his eyes he could see Laura Quinn's face. The hot-water bottle burnt his foot and he shouted at it.

'Get out to hell,' he said. The sound it made on the lino was 'thud-slosh' and it reminded him of a cow giving birth, the calf dropping down from a height. Across the landing the McKenna sisters thought he was talking in his sleep. He was concerned about Laura, with her blonde hair soaking wet, her damp flushed cheeks. They had left her sitting there with that other oddball on the wet concrete. He felt responsible for her and wanted to know that she was all right. He had no idea where she was but he was sure he could work out where she lived.

Or maybe he just wanted to see her again. He lay very still in the dark and thought about this. She had wrapped her arms around him in a storm and held him. She had braved the wind and the waves when poor Audrey would have been blown away like dust. Laura. So quiet and shy in their kitchen. Who would have guessed what she had inside? She was a good-looking woman really with an easy smile and soft full lips. Her clothes were out of fashion and there was no trace of perfume or lipstick. The sun had given her a mist of freckles on her face and on her chest. He could see her coat, wet and hanging open, her breasts moving freely under her blouse when she walked. She smelled like fresh air and the ocean. Laura wasn't neat and tidy like

97

Audrey and maybe she seemed warmer and more inviting because of that.

He had enjoyed himself in the pub. He had told stories and sung a ballad. They had all laughed at his jokes. He was the tallest man at the bar. He had heard someone say that he was a rich farmer from the mainland.

'He's a fine man ... like John Wayne,' someone said. The women gave him sly looks.

There was a light knocking on his door.

'Are you all right?' a voice asked quietly. It was a woman's voice, crackling with sleep.

Finn froze in the bed.

Patricia, he thought, the one with hair like a crow's nest.

'He's asleep.' Another voice.

'He had a lot to drink. We should check.'

'I'm all right,' Finn called out.

His voice sounded too loud. The idea of the two of them coming at him in the dark had given him a fright. He could hear them shuffling back into their room and the door closing softly behind them again.

He sat up. He could see his reflection in a mirror at the end of his bed. His hair was standing up and the sleeves of the pyjamas were up near his elbows. He wanted to get out of this bed. It felt like a swamp. He wanted to see Laura and to make sure she was all right. It was the middle of the night, but this room and this house were unbearable. The sea looked black from the window, except for a single beam of moonlight, and calm enough. He had the sudden idea of swimming, of running in the dark, the wet sand under his feet, buck naked and diving into the waves. Audrey would not do it – but she would watch him and laugh. And Laura, she would begin running first, beating him to it. She would swim like a mermaid.

He found his clothes in the back kitchen, lit up in pink from the coals in the grate. He stripped off the pyjamas and turned to find his undershorts. The light went on suddenly as he bent over, showing two white backside cheeks. Irene and Patricia were standing there in a mixture of floral dressing gowns, hairnets, slippers, false teeth.

'Jaysus Christ,' Irene said and the two of them got stuck in the door trying to get back out.

Finn took their car without asking. He didn't care what they thought of him now. He had to find Laura and see that she was safe, that was all. He had abandoned her because of a whiff of porter and he was ashamed of himself. He knew that she lived near the ocean in a house made of wood. He would take the coast road and drive in a big circle. He turned on the radio, pushed a lever down to give himself more heat and found his cigarettes. If the ferry had started to sink he would have jumped and taken Laura with him. When the first waves dashed high, covering them, his only thought was that she needed to be safe. Strange, he thought, given that they had only just met. The McKennas had hung a picture of Padre Pio from the rear-view mirror. On this twisty road, he danced around a bit. Finn leaned on the accelerator and turned off his headlamps. He could see everything he needed to see in the moonlight. He turned off the radio again and his cigarette fizzed a little and made a red dot behind the glass. He was trying to make himself disappear. At the pub they said the ferry could not sail yet. The engine had seized, it would take a full day or more to fix it. A picture of his wife appeared in his mind and he lifted it to one side and placed it in the passenger seat.

13

Audrey washed her face and drank warm milk at the kitchen table. The wind had finally stopped and the clock in the kitchen said midnight. But Finn was safe and so was the girl. She could remember her very clearly now. The round open face with pale freckles all over it. A harmless sort. Very pretty in her own way though. She had strong legs, a wide back, heavy loose breasts. If Audrey was a poplar, then Laura was an oak.

She had begun to cry when she looked into the mirror and saw her face. One front tooth was chipped. Her nose, not broken but badly scratched. Her left eye had a pool of green and yellow growing around it. With a slight frown she heated some milk for herself and wondered suddenly where Finn would spend the night. Had the Guards said something about the pub on the island? Yes, it was a B&B of sorts. He would be full of drink by the end of it. She had seen him wobbling in the door more than once. He was alive though and she was grateful for that. She would concentrate on her sewing and the dress could be finished by the time they came back. But when she looked down, the red velvet and the pieces of light pattern paper seemed ridiculous. Finn was alive and poor Laura Quinn must have got a terrible fright. Audrey wanted to make something for her instead of for herself.

Upstairs the small attic window was bare and unwelcoming. Even the green shutters couldn't hide that. She glanced at it and began to imagine red velvet curtains. In the morning she would light a coal fire in the grate and get Dooley to carry some cushions up. A fire and warm red curtains. It would be a kind of welcome – for a girl who would never expect it. The electricity came back and she went upstairs and pressed her tape measure along the window frame. There was more than enough velvet so she could go a length and a half to make pleats. An hour on the sewing machine and she would have them finished, and then fully lined and pressed. She would ask Dooley to hang them in the morning. Then she would make a beef stew for their lunch. She tried to imagine Laura climbing the stairs and in her mind she saw a stray cat carrying a suitcase.

Audrey wondered if she would ever be pregnant again. It was unlikely. Recently she had not wanted Finn to make love to her at all. He would lean towards her in their bed and she would turn over. She got up and went to the long mirror in Laura's bedroom to look at herself. What if there was a baby growing inside her right now and she knew nothing at all about it? But the doctor had said it was unlikely now and, besides, she had always known straight away herself, her hormones jangling at her like cow bells. She could remember walking towards Finn in the lower meadow, wading through the grass, the news ready to jump from her lips. He was fencing with Dooley in the furthest corner, swinging the sledgehammer over the posts while Dooley stretched the wire out. The wind had come in a sudden gust then, lifting dry earth and flattening the grass around her. She had stopped and put her hands over her eyes and whenshe looked at the men again Dooley was on his knees and blessing himself. He said it was 'a fairy wind' and 'a sign of fierce bad luck'.

The mirror was fitted into the door of the wardrobe and

Audrey couldn't help but put her hand to it. She waited a moment longer, feeling the storm fade and the house grow quiet. She needed to get some sleep but instead she knelt at the deep drawer under the mirror and began to take the parcels out. They were wrapped in white tissue paper, each one tied in a bow and labelled. She took out the white socks first and laid them in a row. Then the vests. Next there were shoes – blue and white – and the christening robe that she had crocheted herself. Mostly, she just sat looking down at them. Finn said it was time to let go. He didn't know that there was a curl of dark hair inside her pendant and that she still kept a miniature sock in her apron pocket. More than anything she had wanted a baby boy. Deep down she thought everyone did.

14

On the day after the storm Laura and Finn took the path to the beach. They followed steps made of railway sleepers, lined with gorse, the sand rough with ancient seaweed. The sun had come up early that morning, the sky clear blue and cloudless. The islanders called this kind of day 'a pet'. Heat often followed a bad storm as if to make up for it. She had found him asleep in the car. His head on the passenger side, legs curled, one arm wrapped around the gearstick. Her own car was a black Volkswagen Beetle. It had been her mother's. She had climbed out of bed and straight into her swimsuit and she had planned to drive to Bee's Beach to see if she could find Lucas. She could swim in the bigger waves there, be thrown around in them, and forget. Then Finn sat up and yawned. He wound down the window and poked his head out.

'Good morning,' he said.

Laura stood with her towel over her arm and waited. She needed to ask, 'What do you want?' but there was no polite way of doing it.

'I wanted to see if you were all right,' he said and she blushed.

'I'm grand, thanks.'

He told her that he wanted to go swimming and asked if she could show him the best place. He had slept in the car, outside

103

her house, just to ask her that. Laura would call this day a freak. There was a beach right beside them. She pointed to a small gate at the side of her garden and steps that disappeared down a gentle slope. The beach began at the end of it. On windy days the sand blew up through her house. It formed a long thin line in her bath. Her sheets were usually full of it. His eyes drifted away from the gate and back to the car parked in the grass.

'You have a Beetle,' he said. It was sitting in the morning sun looking smug. The black shell, shining and hot. She would open the two back windows later and feel her knees burn on the seat.

She could also take him to Bee's, she said.

'That's a good beach too but not as safe. It won't be crowded yet.'

Part of her wanted to drive him in her car now. To make the engine rev under her foot. To put a warm bowl of chips and sausages under the bonnet for a picnic. She wanted to open the windows and bomb around the coast road. They would drive fast together and be away from everyone else. If she saw Martin herding his sheep she would give him the two fingers or wave, she couldn't decide which.

When Finn sat up in his car and looked at her she was never so glad to see anyone in her life.

'But Fintra is here. We're right beside it,' she said.

Now he walked on the sand behind her with one of her blue towels around his waist. He was wearing a pair of black swimming trunks and his legs were long and white. Like her he would burn easily. They were like two moths, safer in the dark, protected at night. She wore an old-fashioned red bathing suit that held her breasts in two high points. She had tied her hair in a single plait again down her back. The black umbrella made a shell over her. He carried the picnic basket. She had called it breakfast in the end. The idea of a picnic was something that generally frightened men. Finn was quiet. She knew that he caught the words she sent back over her shoulder. That he felt the same sand, like warm sugar, under his feet. That he would hear the same waves as they got closer. Down here the sea wind had the slightest nip in it. On the cool wet sand the air smelled of fish and salt and seaweed. When Laura turned he had stopped, his hands on his hips, the basket at his feet, looking around, grinning.

'Wonderful,' he shouted into the wind and she smiled at that.

They left their towels together and looked out at the ocean and without speaking they began to run towards it. In a second they were racing, her arms pumping, legs thrashing, their bare feet slapping. The wind became stronger and they battled against it. The sun was getting hotter, the day would be a long one, the last of the summer, a real scorcher. Finn lifted his legs higher in the water and then slowed down when it became deep. When he turned to look she was swimming underwater. He followed. They sprang back up quick enough, water spilling from their mouths, ice-cream headaches. Laura laughed, wiped water off her face and tasted salt. She was well used to that. Without speaking, she moved backwards into a dead man's float.

On the beach he asked her about her mother and father.

'He was from Achill but lived here for most of his life, so did my mother.'

'And you were born here. You've been here all your life?'

Laura paused and looked out over the beach.

'My life is not over yet.'

He laughed at that, bit into a sandwich and lay back on one elbow.

'And where did you go to school?' he asked. 'Here on the island?'

'I just went to the National School. I was always in trouble. The nuns at Bridestown wouldn't take me in the convent school after that.'

105

Here Finn looked up at her, his eyes twinkling.

'You're better off without the nuns,' he said.

'Before I was born my parents had a go at living in America . . . a place called Provincetown. It didn't work out. My mother was happy there but my father hated it . . . He was itching to get back here from the start.'

'I've heard that everyone comes back to the island.'

'Then one night he went out fishing . . . and he never came back. They found his boat aground near Bee's Beach.'

'On the other side of the island?'

She nodded.

'That was before they built the lighthouse. He got lost and hit the rocks . . . They couldn't find him then, just the empty boat.'

Finn looked out at the sea, imagining this.

'The man who bought the boat left it to rot in the harbour. Every day it seemed to sink lower and lose another layer of paint.'

Finn turned to face Laura. She was not tearful but frowning down into the green apple she held in her hand.

'That must have been very hard,' he said.

'Not so bad,' she said, looking away, 'but the harbour's not my favourite place.'

'And your mother?'

'Her name was Eliza. She could read tea leaves. People said she had a gift.'

Then Laura was silent. She looked away and then reached for the umbrella and sat in its shade.

'They blamed her for it.'

'Who did?'

'The islanders . . . The same people you were drinking with last night.'

Her tone had changed a little. There was a slight edge to her voice.

'You're angry with me?'

'No,' she said quickly, suddenly ashamed of herself.

'They think it's bad luck for a house to face the sea and my mother wanted ours to look out at the ocean. So when my father drowned they said it was her fault.'

'It sounds like a lot of bullshit to me,' he said and out of nowhere Laura gave a laugh.

'So . . . what happened?'

Her voice was very quiet.

'She had an accident. A fall . . . not long after my father.'

'I'm very sorry,' he said.

She looked out towards the ocean, her eyes squinting as if she was searching for something in the waves.

'And who took care of you?' Finn asked.

'I did,' Laura replied.

Her left hand was almost buried in the sand and Finn suddenly wished he could hold it. He followed the gentle line of her arm and wanted to go digging for it.

'She wanted to go back to Provincetown. She said it was lovely there. That the sea was a clear blue and that the sky had a pink tinge to it. She talked a lot about the wooden house they lived in and how she found porcelain cups washed up on the beach. She was at her happiest there, I think.'

A white crab sidled past, a barnacle on its back. They watched its slow steady progress as it followed the sound of the waves.

'A hitchhiker,' Finn said and she smiled.

'The islanders call those . . . crabs' wives.'

Here he threw back his head and belly-laughed.

'Have you ever seen a starfish?'

'Hundreds,' she said. 'They're my neighbours. Around here I make friends with sea urchins, clams, jellyfish.'

'What about a seahorse?'

'No.' She shook her head. 'They're so small. Magical creatures. I would love to find one of those.'

'What about that chap on the ferry . . . the lighthouse keeper. Do you know him well?'

'Too well,' she said.

'He seems all right, a handsome fellow.'

'He's handsome for sure . . . but a woman needs a bit more than that.'

He grinned at her and scratched his head. The breeze coming in from the sea was cool again.

Finn sat up and watched the lighthouse.

'I would love to climb it,' he said softly.

Laura said nothing. She began to put their plates and cups back into the basket.

'You're getting burnt,' he said.

There were two red stripes on her thighs already and her back was getting hot.

He sat hugging his knees. She could see faint patches of dry sand on his arms. His spine formed a perfect smooth line down his back.

'Have you ever been up there?'

She wanted to say yes but she couldn't. She wanted to climb to the top as much as he did.

'It's such a clear day,' he said, 'we could see Bishopstown House from it . . . I wonder how we could get inside.'

He sat there transfixed by the red and white tower in the distance. He was still sitting on the sand but now he sounded boyish and excited.

If he had asked Laura to catch the moon for him, she would have tried.

'I'll take you,' she said.

15

In the end it was Finn who took Laura to the lighthouse. She found the key under a stone on the windowsill and they unlocked the door and stepped into a circular room that was painted apple green. It smelled damp and had the same empty feeling as a station waiting room. There was a black door that led into Martin's house. She had seen the other side of that often enough. Here in the apple-green room, though, was mystery and magic, a special place he had kept for himself. The stone steps to the left wound upwards until they came to a door that would let them out at the top of the lighthouse. Under these stairs there was a wide stone hearth and a chair where he sat. There was a jug of old milk sitting on the mantelpiece, several unwashed mugs and some newspapers, which he had left down at his feet. When she had expected to smell the salt from the ocean, Laura smelled only old turf and sour milk.

Finn's feet stamped up the stone steps first and she followed with her head down, out of breath. He climbed on without speaking, his footsteps echoing around the whitewashed walls and hers answering. At the top he pushed the heavy steel door open and they both saw the blue sky, the white of the sun and gasped together, falling out into the air, laughing. Laura ran to the wall first. She had never been so high up in her life. She had never been above the island or above anyone who lived on it. Up here the sun was hotter and the sky was closer. It had never been so blue before and she was dazzled by it. She looked up and it seemed to swoop down on her. In a flash it seemed to tumble and she wanted to run away from it.

'The sky is falling,' she said and she stumbled back from the wall.

Finn placed a hand on her shoulder to steady her.

'The sky is not falling,' he said, his eyes smiling down at her. 'The sky is staying right where it is.'

The wind flapped around them, making them blink. The sea was full of small sailboats in different colours. A few of the trawlers sat on the horizon waiting for nightfall. From here the island was beautiful. Until now she had not been able to see it. She turned to look at Finn who was smiling out at it.

'My God.' He sighed the words out.

'Can you see your house?' she asked and she began to walk around the circular wall.

'Over there in the trees,' but he didn't turn around to look.

Laura looked out across the sea to the mainland and could see no trees at all. Just the red flags at the harbour, grey rocks, a car moving like a toy around the cliff, the big white retirement home called Jericho.

'I see your house,' he announced. 'There are red socks on the line,' and she ran back and followed his point. She had hung out her washing that morning. She laughed and turned to look up at him again.

Laura's cheeks were flushed and he noticed the freckles scattered on her shoulders. He wanted to look into her eyes and he was unsettled by this. He turned away again, looked up at the sky, frowned into the sun. On the ground the people seemed so much smaller than the two of them. There was a haze over the ocean, children on the beach, a blush of sunburn already on their shoulders. He wanted to touch her, to touch this new glow on her. He knew that he should think of Audrey, that he should dig now for a good picture of her and plant it firmly in front of his face. But he couldn't even look in the direction of Bishopstown House. His chest felt tight and it hurt. He could feel some sort of obstruction pressing behind his ribcage. He hated the idea that he had such a good woman at home and he had also found this. He glanced over at Laura. He wanted to take her in his arms and hold her. It was just a thought so there was no harm in it but the very idea made him bite down on his bottom lip. He looked at her again and now she looked back, holding his gaze in her pale blue eyes, showing him honesty, courage. She reached over suddenly, hesitated, and then finally placed her cool hand on his. He was ready to push it away. He would be gentle and yet when it happened he didn't flinch. He was glad. He was thrilled by it. Relieved. They stood there holding hands, the salt wind blowing at them.

'Will we jump?' he asked suddenly, a little laugh beginning to warm his face. His eyes were bluer than hers. A brighter, more intense blue when he laughed.

'I will if you will,' she said.

Her house was warm from the sun and they sank back into it, their swimsuits still damp, sand clinging to their feet.

'Tea?' she asked.

'Yes.'

And then, 'Anything stronger?' and he gave a little laugh.

Laura walked across the room, breaking through a beam of evening sun on her way to the kitchen. She filled the kettle and stood for a moment in the window. The first yellow leaves were falling from the sycamore. There was a bottle of whiskey somewhere. Her mother had kept one for the fruitcakes.

There was a sudden noise behind her and she heard Finn say, 'Plane crash.'

The yellow plane had fallen and they both stood looking at it as if a dead bird had landed in her house. She did not know what this meant. The wooden plane was not broken. It had landed by itself, when the pilot felt like it. She held herself back now, returned to the kitchen and lit the stove to make the water boil up. More than anything she wanted to be close to him. What was wrong with that? Any minute now he would say he had to leave and her heart would die a bit. She imagined sewing him into the couch so that he would not be able to get up. She imagined locking the doors and throwing the key out the window into the flowerbed. She imagined being so close to him that she could climb his ribcage like a ladder. Soon he would say it, 'I must be going,' and she would say, 'Of course,' and she would begin the polite business of letting him back out. She would thank him for his help. They would make arrangements about when he should come back again for her furniture. She would stand on the wooden porch and wave at him, smiling a little, and when his red car had disappeared, she would go inside and sit down on the floor and know that there was another kind of life entirely because she had just been given a glimpse.

Instead he stood up and put the yellow plane on the table, stretched and said, 'I think I'll shave.'

Laura showed him to the stairs in her upside-down house. The small cool bathroom was at the bottom of it. The stairs curled downwards, her mother's paintings lining the walls. Some were just words – 'Help,' one of them called. A small red canoe leaned on the wall next to the bedroom. Finn touched it with his hand as Laura pushed the white bathroom door open and stepped back. He hesitated and finally looked. And Laura looked and she could hear a light whispering sigh that came from deep in his chest. She imagined it was the sound snow made falling off a roof. It was also the sound of a man giving up. He moved towards her, one sudden step and kissed her, holding her face gently and then pulling her into his arms and just holding her where they both let out deep sighs of relief, of joy, of hope.

The sun went behind a cloud and the house darkened. Standing there he smelled like warm ocean and warm sand inside her house. Everything about him was true and good. Everything about her seemed natural, beautiful, new-born, untouched. She did not know that it was possible for a man to make a woman feel like that. She was dazzled by the idea of it. The notion of a love like this gave her a dizzy head. The red swimsuit was still wet on her and her hair was stiff with salt. Goosebumps came up on her arms and her back. Finn held her and stroked her hair. Laura waited patiently. She was just happy to hold him, to hug another warm person and to be hugged back.

When he released her a cloud moved and the house was warm again and bright. What now? her eyes asked. She looked down at herself and began to roll the red swimsuit off. She was not in a hurry to get into bed with him. By holding her as he did he had already made her up. She could have been happy with just that. But she was beginning to shiver. The swimsuit fell in a curl on the wooden floor, the white gusset, full of sand, turned out. More sand fell from somewhere. She didn't know where she had been keeping it. He smiled and pulled at the white string on his trunks. One flick of his wrist and they landed on the side of her bathtub. At times like this, she realized, all men were ridiculous. He took her hand and they walked the narrow downstairs landing together. Her bedroom had no door, just a beaded curtain that rattled like jewellery when they went inside. It was a small room without a wardrobe, just a rail in an alcove where she had hung her only skirt – the blue one she had worn for the interview at his house – and underneath, a pair of black wellingtons, socks scattered beside them. There was a pine chest of drawers at the end of the bed and two tall glass doors, French windows, her mother called them, which opened out into a wooden porch, with its herb and bonsai pots. Her possessions were embarrassing. Her clothes, her underwear from the day before, white pants, a bra, stockings on the line. They looked like they belonged to a lonely woman, she thought. That was the last thought she had.

On warm days she liked to lie down on the beach and wait for the first wave to wash over her. It would touch her toes first and then her calves and then her thighs and in this way Laura allowed Finn to cover her. Sometimes one big wave would surprise her, coming from nowhere, rising up silently and then landing on her with a slap, sometimes turning her upside down with its strength. Mostly, they crept into her quietly, moving upwards, coming in further and being more daring, until she could feel the water seep up her body and make a lukewarm pool around her scalp, with her hair floating in it.

His skin was cold like hers and they pulled blankets over them, got underneath, in their tepee like Indians. At some point he chuckled and she laughed out loud. She remembered her mother reading her tea leaves and she wondered if she could have seen this and what sort of cup could hold these pictures and colours. On another night her mother had shown her how to bake a cake and how to wire a plug. Until now Laura did not know that making love could be like this. Martin ran into the bed like he was late for something. He made love to her like he was in danger of missing a bus. But Finn was different. He was gentle and calming. For her, he was 'live' and 'neutral' and 'earth'.

16

On the same day in Bishopstown Audrey spread the quilt on the kitchen table. Thimbles were placed on index fingers and five women sat down to work. Kitty Corcoran reached for the scissors and then hesitated, looked down at an old velvet dress and touched the hem of it. They had been making this quilt for five months now and it would be finished by Christmas. They had promised to give it to Father Durkan for the big raffle and the money would go towards the new roof for the Bridestown church.

'Go on,' Audrey said and Kitty began to cut through the soft velvet. The other women smiled and listened as someone else's memory was carved up.

Behind them a tray of scones was rising in the oven; on the cooker, a large silver teapot, getting hot. Soon the poplars would stand bare, like black needles. The evening sky was blue with a streak of purple running through it.

'We're nearly back to the dark evenings again,' someone said.

A daughter's red skirt lay in the middle of the table, beside it a husband's shirt, the colour of a buttercup. Audrey added an apron with a tea stain down the front. Shirts and trousers were piled near the doorway, buttons missing, elbows snagged, trousers that had split as one leg was thrown over a fence.

'I made my first Christmas pudding in that,' Emily said, lifting the apron up.

'How did it turn out?'

'Desperate. I put too much brandy in it. When I put a match to it . . . it nearly blew up.'

Here the women laughed. Needles were threaded now and Audrey made the first neat stitch.

'The red rose pieces go around the edge,' she said. 'We'll try blanket stitch first.'

The four women craned their necks to see her work. She turned the flap over to show how it was invisible on the other side.

'God bless your eyesight,' Mary said.

'He proposed to me in that,' Kitty announced and she nodded towards the yellow shirt.

No one spoke for a minute.

'Is he colour blind by any chance?' Emily asked.

Laughter began again softly. In minutes the room would be full of it.

'She was so dazzled she said yes,' Audrey replied.

More laughter.

'Have you any music for us, Audrey?'

At their last meeting they had pushed the table back and danced the Walls of Limerick.

Audrey turned the radio up.

On the table were clothes that carried grass stains, scorch marks, ink and blood. One woman was employed with a scissors to cut these out. The quilt would soon be finished. It was like a life full of sunshine, all romance and no disappointment. In a month or two it would be ready. They had used most of their good memories up.

'Sure, what do you need a housekeeper for?' Mary asked.

'So I can do the garden,' Audrey said. 'I can't stand being stuck inside an empty house.'

'You have a wonderful pair of hands . . .'

'Is there anything you can't do?'

'I can't drive,' Audrey said and she gave a little laugh.

She had spent the day cleaning out the attic so that it would be ready for Laura. They had interviewed four women for the housekeeping job but they were all sergeant-major types and Finn said they talked too much.

'I don't want some battleaxe bossing me around in my own house,' he told Audrey. They liked Laura because she was quiet and easygoing, the type of girl you would hardly notice in the house. She couldn't boil water but teaching her to cook would give Audrey something new to think about.

She put an old Persian rug on the floor of the attic sitting room and Dooley helped her install the little electric cooker. A leather armchair came up from the study, old now but soft. There was a scrubbed pine table from the basement for the little kitchen and a small dresser that had been out in a shed, lined now with blue and white striped plates and cups. She did not know what Laura would bring from the island but she guessed that she wouldn't have much. Dooley did as he was told, his thin arms doing the lifting, his cap turned backwards on his head. Audrey pointed out more pieces of furniture and ignored the sweat coming through his shirt. For every hour that Finn was gone she added something else. The red velvet curtains had matching tie-backs now and blocked out the draught. She put a jug of fresh milk in the fridge and some butter on a blue plate. A freshly baked loaf was waiting in a tin box. There were white cotton sheets on the bed and four wool blankets. When she closed her eyes she saw Laura shrinking down and imagined tucking her in at night.

Finn had promised that he would stop drinking after they were

117

married and he had mostly kept his word. That was nearly twelve years ago now. When she walked up the aisle she could smell booze off him at the altar rails. After they moved to Bishopstown House, he ploughed the fields to grow grass and barley and she stretched her veil over the raspberry bushes to keep out the birds.

The children who would save her from her feeling of emptiness didn't come. First she counted weeks, then months. Minutes mattered, even seconds, any form of time but years. Years were for old people. Years were for mountains and planets and coral reefs. Finn and Audrey could not grow old like other couples. Theirs would be a marriage of days.

On Easter Sundays Finn took her to the fairy fort. The rain stayed away and the horses galloped in a circle around them. The air was fresh, the grass still full of winter, matted yellow and wet. They walked out together, bound tightly, needing each other, stepping high over the tall grass and matching the other's pace. He did not take her hand. There was no need for that. He lit a fire and she spread a picnic out over the rocks. They boiled eggs and ate them staring down from the fort. The clouds moved and the April sun came out in long yellow shafts.

'We're like two people in a holy picture,' she said.

The first baby was lost in a summer meadow. She jumped down from a fence and caused it to fall out. 'It wasn't your fault,' everyone said but at night in the dark with her husband sleeping, it was Audrey's own jump that shook that baby out. She got up and went outside and weeded the garden in moonlight. In her mind she called that baby 'Sean' but never said his name out loud. When the sun was lighting the horizon, she found a scrap of red fabric and cut out a small letter 'S' and sewed it into the hem of the patchwork quilt.

The second baby was lost early on a January morning when

Audrey walked through the silver frost. Her heart was happy and light inside her and the birds were making cold little chirps. The grass was frozen white and she saw a robin. The women came and made some quilt with her. They said it was God's will but Audrey blamed herself. She could not forget the white and silver of the grass and the robin's red breast. This baby she called 'Adele' and when she embroidered the letter 'A' into the corner of the quilt no one liked to ask her what it meant.

In the darkness Finn would find her and she was glad of it then. When the bedside light disappeared they seemed to fall downwards into each other's space. All day she would want this. Her husband's face near hers, his stubble on her cheeks. During daylight hours, they were serious and businesslike. They worked the onion drills together, they examined the windfalls in the orchard, they painted the outside loft.

The last baby was born at eight months. Stillborn – or born still as Audrey preferred to think. This one she had held in her arms. She had felt his warmth and his weight. She had pressed his damp hair into her breast. The smell of him made her dizzy. It was Finn who uncurled her arms, lifting each of her fingers away and making them straight. Audrey's heart felt hollow then. The wall was no longer robust and thick. It did the job of keeping her alive well enough but it was worn thin from the feelings that were coming out. She asked Doctor Reilly for something that would help her to sleep. He gave her morphine and when she woke up her heart felt like an empty sack.

They dressed that baby together and buried him behind the church. A strange and savage act, she couldn't bear to think of it and she could not bear to name him. No one came except the priest. There was a warm shame attached to losing the babies as if the parents had been careless. The neighbours would come later, carrying whiskey, casseroles, flowers. But there in the churchyard with the rain pelting their backs, no one but a father and a mother had the right to look.

They had a long talk with Doctor Reilly then. Not at the dinner table but at the surgery across his wide mahogany desk. And there was no drinking or dancing, just his solemn face looking into theirs as he told them that Audrey's body needed a good long rest and even then there wasn't a great deal of hope. And Audrey had agreed because since losing the last baby she wasn't interested in housework. She only liked to be out in the garden or down the yard with her hens. She couldn't stand to be inside, polishing silver or dusting the banisters, listening to all that silence.

Here Finn glanced over at her and gave a little laugh.

'Good luck with that,' he said to the doctor. 'This woman of mine is always on the move.'

'A bit of gardening, plenty of fresh air, quilt making . . . that's all fine,' he said, 'but I want you to relax and forget about . . .'

There he stopped.

'We'll see how you are in about six months,' he said.

'And if I rest?' Audrey asked.

'I don't know, is the honest answer,' Doctor Reilly said. 'But at the moment you just need to rest more and mind yourself.'

At night in the kitchen Finn held his hand out to Audrey and she took it. They stood for a moment, leaning on each other, and then beside whatever fire was left they began to dance. His feet in leather slippers and his hands rough from farm work. He held her close and she could smell tobacco from his lapels, soap from his shirt. There was a red Pelican pin that said he had given blood. He held her close and she would cry down into his shoulder a bit. In his arms, Audrey found a hiding place. Her husband knew her pain and tried to take small shavings off it every night. He took those shavings and filled his own pockets up.

120

The fire flickered and the second record dropped. Sometimes they danced to Bill Haley & His Comets. When he jived with her it was as if he was steering the car around the hairpin bends of Kerry. Her hair came undone and soon they were both laughing and Audrey would give a little shout. They said nothing at all to each other. They just danced and danced and then fell back on the couch laughing and breathless. With the curtains opened the two of them could be seen for miles across the flat fields covered in frost.

Finn stoked the Aga and made tea that they took up to bed with a plate of biscuits. They read books out loud to each other and listened to the radio. Anything at all except the silence. The silence meant that they were together and still lonely and that there would never be a child in their house. So most nights they read out loud or danced, otherwise the sadness would get inside again, in a slow steady drop.

17

Laura knew that Finn was gone. She knew that if she turned over, she would see the empty bed, his side cold now and the pillow crushed. The new day brought light rain and a mist that clung to her windows. Clouds hung low and the foghorn sounded. She had known many days like this, days when the island lost its lustre overnight and became a wet ball of moss and lavender. Finn would have crept out without making a sound. She had often heard Martin leave and had said nothing. She had listened to the bed creak softly as he sat up. She had felt his frightened eyes on her as he checked that she was asleep. And she had gone along with it because who would want to hold on to a man like that? Go on, you eejit, she had thought, and then I might actually be able to sleep.

She had heard shoes pulled across the floor gingerly, a tiny grit under the sole, enough to wake a field mouse up. One night he was in such a hurry he left his drawers in the bed. Another night, one black sock. So she knew too how bare feet sounded on her floor. How the wooden boards made guilty feet stick. Once he let a shoe fall from under his arm and cursed at it. 'Jaysus, fuck,' he whispered – and then actually believed that she could have slept through it. Perhaps she did, she thought, perhaps she dreamt all of it, otherwise when the next day came it would have been hard to live, hard even to get up.

Laura lay on in her bed without moving. She had not heard anything at all during the night and she was afraid to look. The bedroom curtains moved with a light breeze and she felt cold air wash over her face. Her first thought was that it would not be possible to see the lighthouse from the coast road on a day like this. The red and white top would have disappeared into the mist. Martin would be up there now, sweeping his steps. And if she and Finn went up they would see nothing except each other, and then she wished for this. She saw the two of them up there, laughing in the blue sky, and found it hard to believe that it had ever happened.

She began to move her foot backwards, letting her heel take the first knock-back. It was the only part of her that was able for it. She would know it was over if her foot made it to the other side of the bed. Suddenly there was a sound, a long sigh, and then a deep inhale of breath. This was something she had never actually witnessed, she realized, the sound of a man waking up. She sat up in a panic. A warm hairy arm came around her then, pulling her closer, a hand placed gently on her kneecap, pushing also, so that her buttocks fitted neatly into his hips. Laura heard herself swallow noisily. She had trouble stopping herself letting out a whoop. Her eyes were wide open now. She was more awake than she had ever been in her life. She was so awake she wanted to jump up, jump out of the bed with a stretch and a shout.

Finn's breath became slower and she listened in wonderment as he fell back asleep. She closed her eyes again and smiled. The bedside clock said a quarter past eight and the seaweed would not be collected. Outside, the rain was getting heavier and the sky had darkened. She did not know what day it was. In the normal world this would be a Saturday, she thought.

123

When Finn woke he could smell bacon frying. It came from somewhere over his head and he remembered then that he was in a house that was the wrong way up. He remembered a yellow aeroplane and the white trussed ceiling of the sitting room and two rocking chairs parked at a stove. He could hear the sound of a spoon scraping the pan and imagined two eggs being basted, the fresh yolks sitting up, plump. Another smell intervened, a foreign one.

I'm not a coffee man, he thought.

He stretched, jumped out of bed and pulled on his trousers. He had slept like the dead and felt fresh. The storm at sea had been forgotten. He would need to take the McKennas' car back. His own car was still at the harbour, an empty green horsebox attached. He thought about the black Beetle parked near the hedge. His mind worked its way through these things and then like a dream that had been forgotten, it came back to him. When he sat on the bed, her bed, tying his laces, it hit him like a mallet.

'Laura,' he said.

In the bathroom he looked at his face in the mirror, the first layer of fear surfacing as he used her pink soap. She had put a clean towel out for him. He put the seat down on her toilet and sat on it. This wasn't a simple thing. He needed to get it straight. True, she was not like anyone else he had ever met. Now she was upstairs frying rashers for him and making coffee because she didn't know that he never drank it. He did not think about Audrey at all now. He didn't need to. She was all around him, in him, in the threads she had used to darn his elbows and socks. She was the life he was going back to. Audrey had a permanent trail of breadcrumbs out. His return to her was so obvious it didn't warrant a thought. Finn stood at the foot of the stairs, frowning. She was up there, waiting, fresh-faced and wondering. He had enjoyed her and could not feel bad about it. He was not the sort of man to have regrets or to leave in the dark. The dark was for sleeping in. He wasn't a coward. But he did need to leave now and he had to do it without destroying her. He climbed the stairs to the sitting room slowly, feeling himself go down instead of up.

Laura was standing at the small table next to the kitchen, an apron hanging around her neck. She was wearing a loose blue jumper and a pair of white slacks. Her hair wasn't combed. She had tucked it behind her ears, a sheet of white blonde falling on her back.

'Good morning,' Finn said.

'Hello,' she replied.

She was holding the frying pan, ready to put his breakfast out. There was something motherly about the way she straightened the knife and fork at his plate. Then she dipped her head down to hide a blush. She served eggs and bacon, black pudding, fried bread, a favourite of his. Finn realized that he was hungry enough to eat the plate. They sat opposite each other in silence and began to eat.

'A dark day,' he offered.

'It is,' she said.

'I'd murder a cup of tea,' Finn said, and Laura went to get a bigger pot.

There were knives and forks clanging, a spoon adding sugar to the tea, the paper napkin had Christmas holly on it. They leaned on these props, used the cutlery like stilts. The clock in the kitchen said a quarter past two. The rain was falling slower now, in long steady drops. The sea would be as calm as the White Lake today. He would leave on the ferry at four o'clock.

Finn caught her eye then. He put down his knife and fork and smiled at her. He reached across the table and took her hand and held it.

'Don't be upset, Laura.'

She watched as he drank some more tea and spread marmalade on his toast. Every mouthful she took felt like it could choke her. She ate the yolk out of her egg and left it at that.

'Now . . .' Finn announced.

He joined his knife and fork and placed his hands flat on the table.

'The job.' He had lowered his voice a bit. 'The housekeeping position . . .' He stopped and looked right into her, his mouth set, his forehead making ladder rungs. He shrugged, looked awkward as if he was waiting for her to speak.

'It might not be a good idea now,' he said quietly.

He was firing her before she even started.

'No,' she replied.

It had begun as a gentle conversation across a breakfast table and it was clear to her now who was in the driving seat. She waited to hear 'but' or 'and' or 'however' to see if this road they were on had any kind of bend.

Finn tilted his chin and his eyes moved to the open window.

'So . . .' he said and he faced her again.

Laura's heart shifted gear and filled her chest.

'Will you sell that car to me?' he asked.

His voice was low. His eyes soft, full of sorrow. From lovers to second-hand car dealers in a heartbeat. The sound she imagined was a full tray of crockery sliding into the kitchen bin from a height. Once, when she didn't feel like washing up, she had thrown the dishes out. She was not cut out for the housekeeping job anyway. Earlier that morning while the man who had left his watch on her nightstand still slept, she realized that she could not take it. She had swallowed that pill herself but only because she had moved on and was hoping for something great. What she had now was the day before, the night, not even the following morning together, he had already spoiled that. The goodbyes began very early when the man belonged to someone else. Through the window she saw the Beetle, looking dumb and innocent, a strange love token between them now. She remembered sitting in it as a child in summer and melting crayons on the seat.

On the other side of her house, the one that faced the road, a car pulled in and the engine was turned off. Footsteps moved over the gravel and Laura held her breath.

'Hellooooo,' a voice called. Laura shut her eyes.

'Is it a rooster?' Finn asked.

'Irene and Patricia,' she said in a low voice. 'They probably want their car back.'

Finn looked at her, his eyes warming up and in a moment they were both beginning to laugh. They couldn't help it. He grew quiet then and sat very still. He did not move from where he was sitting and he was not the kind of man to duck behind her couch. Laura got up and walked to the door.

'Hellooooo, anyone at home?'

In her mind she saw herself with a shotgun, blowing their heads off.

The McKenna sisters were standing on the wooden porch examining the chives, gone to seed, in a pot, her old bicycle leaning against the shed, heavy with rust. They were like two hens staring into grit, hoping to find a barley seed in the dust.

'Good morning, Laura,' Irene said. When she smiled her teeth were like a gate. 'We were looking for Mr Campbell.' They had borrowed a green van from the grocery shop. Their own grey Ford looked like an elephant standing in the grass.

'He left your car here,' Laura said and she nodded towards it. 'He wanted to thank you but he was in a rush.' She swallowed. A trickle of sweat was moving between her breasts. She did not care about herself. The whole island would be talking about her and Martin anyway, it was him she was trying to protect.

Patricia and Irene stood and waited, the same tight smiles fixed on their faces.

'We need it for the Cash and Carry,' Irene said, 'otherwise he could tour the island with it.'

'Was he in a rush?' Patricia asked suddenly.

She was standing a little behind the older sister. When she asked her question, her head popped out.

'He was worried about his wife.'

'Ah,' Patricia nodded.

'Was he,' Irene said in a flat voice.

They waited for a moment and looked at Laura. She felt like a criminal being nailed to a cross. Then they walked back down the steps again carrying their handbags like weapons.

Finn revved the engine and reversed the Beetle out. He held the steering wheel tightly, put it in gear and turned the car to face the road. She had not asked him for anything at all and if he was honest there was nothing about Laura that he didn't want. But he had Audrey. Audrey was there first. He needed to drive away from here but he found that it wasn't as simple as that. He waited for a moment and then pushed the clutch in again and turned the engine off. Laura was standing on the porch with one hand lifted in a delicate salute. In the other she held the cheque for the car neatly folded. He needed to say something. Anything. He couldn't just drive off. He tried to turn the key again but his fingers didn't have the strength. He opened the door quickly and walked back up the steps.

He did not know what to say so he said what he thought might be the truth.

'I want to see you again, Laura.'

And she said nothing. She already knew that what he said would be turned over and over in her mind, probably for the rest of her life. He didn't kiss her goodbye. He lifted one hand and placed it on her cheek and Laura tilted her face and leaned into it. At that point Finn meant everything to her. And when she looked up at him, her eyes clear blue and without tears, he would have promised her anything. He also knew that the drive to the ferry in the Beetle, the journey on the ferry itself, the drive back to Bishopstown House and the sight of Audrey – would cool him down and dilute things a bit.

Laura took off her glasses and ran down to the beach. She walked out towards the sea and carried the previous night with her. The memory was still fresh and for now there were all sorts of possibilities. It would fade, she knew that, but in the meantime she could imagine and hope and those moments would be like stars exploding, dazzling her.

On the beach she opened the cheque out and her heart fell down a few hundred feet. It fell so fast that she had to catch her breath. It fell so far that she felt her own bones rattle around it. She licked her lips and tried to taste him. She sat on the beach until it was dark, hugging her knees, feeling foolish. The light came on in the lighthouse. The foghorn sounded. If Martin was up there he would be able to see her sitting on the beach. Men wanted only one part of her. She looked at the cheque again and wondered if she had made a mistake but she hadn't. She knew now that he wasn't coming back. She had wanted him to have the car as a souvenir of her and the island, a gift that would connect them – but *he* had just wanted to buy the Beetle for his wife and he had paid her far too much . . . to take the sting out of it

*

129

Finn drove to Bishopstown House late in the evening.

'The afternoon crossing was delayed again,' he said and Audrey could not help but smile at him. He looked apologetic and windswept and handsome. When he saw her bruised face he took her in his arms. He held her close to him and she was lost in the tweed of his jacket where she could smell tobacco and Pears soap. She pulled him closer. There was no smell of drink at all from him. He had come bouncing up the drive in a black Volkswagen Beetle, jumping out then, laughing at his own gift with Dooley behind him in the red Mercedes and the empty horsebox.

'I am so happy to see you,' he whispered and he kissed her lips.

'Where's Laura?' she asked suddenly and she looked around his shoulder to the car.

'She changed her mind,' he said simply and he gave a quick shrug. His voice was loud, determined. Then he sighed and pulled a face.

'She has a fellow on the island, I think,' he added and he looked down for a moment at his boots.

'Oh,' Audrey said and she could not explain why she felt so disappointed. The girl had nothing and she had wanted to take care of her. That was all. Now she wondered what had happened to scare her off.

'Come on,' Finn said and he pulled her across the gravel and put her sitting in the driver's seat. Here Audrey began to touch the inside of the car and she was like a child in it, quiet and wondrous. She ran her left hand over the smooth knob of the gearstick and tapped the horn, laughing at the odd honk that came out. She turned on the ignition and pushed the accelerator with her foot.

'Where did you get it?' she asked.

'Do you like it?' he replied. 'Put it in gear.' The car lurched forward and Audrey gave a sudden scream and a laugh.

'Jesus Christ,' Finn said. Audrey pushed her foot in further and headed straight for a load of sand in the back yard.

'Clutch . . . brake!' he shouted but she put her foot on the accelerator instead.

Together, they drove up the steep angle of the sand and straight down the other side. It happened in an instant and then the engine cut out. They looked at each other and began to laugh and laugh. She did not know how long they sat there laughing but when they finally climbed out the sky was full of stars and the windows were fogged up. That night they shared a bottle of wine and made love in the sitting room. Audrey forgot to ask again about the car or why Laura had changed her mind. The world felt warm again and she only cared that he was back in it.

18

After the storm Laura had given in and followed Martin to his house. She watched as Finn was driven away to the pub and then the harbour was deserted. Friends were scarce and she was hungry and tired. Martin finally broke through with an offer of pork sausages and fried bread. When they reached his house they stood for a moment in the moonlight.

'Wait here,' he said.

She stood meekly in his doorway and felt ashamed of herself. Now that she had agreed to go with him he was already back in the driving seat. He unlocked the heavy door to the lighthouse and began to climb the steps. She listened as his footsteps grew faint and imagined a heaven for mountain goats. More than anything she wanted to follow him but she was not invited. Being up higher than the island would help her to breathe, to concentrate, to believe in herself. It would be something, she thought, if they could share that. Instead she watched his back with tired eyes and saw where the key was kept.

Laura waited for a minute and then pushed his front door open with her foot. The hallway was as she remembered it, dank and cold and the colour of a raspberry from the Sacred Heart lamp. Three coats hung on a coat stand with a pair of green waders underneath. His mother watched her from a black and white photograph. She was wearing a hat that looked like a piss-pot on her head. The idea of that made Laura laugh quietly. Then in the silence of the hallway she stopped short and asked herself, what had started that? Where had these new laughs come from now? Finn, of course. He had had the same effect on his wife. In a warm flash she remembered their kitchen, the heat of the Aga, the smell of a freshly baked cake, the beautiful Audrey and how when she spoke to him there was always a hint of laughter in her voice.

The eyes in the holy picture were half closed and heavy. The rest of the island was celebrating because the ferry had reached the island safely and even Jesus looked half cut. The house was cleaner than she remembered and in the distance she heard the cuckoo clock. It was getting late and the seagulls had gone to sleep.

She sat on the first step of the stairs until he came back. First she heard the radio he was carrying and knew now that the weather forecast would follow them for the rest of the night. He turned on the lamp on a low table and looked down at her. His eyes seemed dark and fearful. It was the first time she had seen him look afraid. He frowned and then held out a hand to help her get up. A good start. A gentleman inside trying to claw his way out.

'I think,' he said, 'I'll have a bath.'

Laura wondered if she was asleep and dreaming.

'The fire is set,' he said. 'You just have to put a match to it.'

He disappeared down the long corridor into his new green bathroom that was reserved for special occasions. He opened the door that would separate them now with frosted glass.

'The sausages are in the fridge.'

First, she imagined drowning him, both hands leaning on him, in over the bath. Then she imagined the cast-iron frying pan embedded in his head. When he turned on the light in the bathroom, it looked like he was in a greenhouse watering plants.

She walked into the kitchen and stood there trying to decide what to do next. Then the light suddenly went off. Martin appeared again and flicked the switch. He stood beside her and frowned at it.

'It's on a timer now,' he said. 'It's more economical like that.'

'It's even more economical,' Laura said, 'if you just sit in the dark.'

Martin stood under the bright light and looked at her. He was trying to decide if what she said was funny or not.

'Are you having the bath?' she asked.

'There's no hot water,' he replied.

'That's very economical too,' Laura said.

She watched as he became busy in the kitchen. He lit the range and a smell of frying sausages rose up. Then the light went off again and she got up and found the big black switch. He buttered a fresh batch loaf and put big slices over the heat. He made tea in a heavy brown pot. The light went out again and this time he put it back on himself. They sat side by side on the low couch and ate with plates on their laps. In another minute they were sitting in pitch black.

'Do you want to watch the television?' he asked.

'All right.'

The Sweeney was on and they sat in front of it without speaking. They stopped getting up to turn on the light and stayed in the strange flickering shadow from the set. He did not make any move to touch her. He sat very still on his side of the couch. Later, when the flag appeared and the national anthem was playing, Martin cleared his throat.

'The reason I like to see you in the afternoons is because I have to be near the lighthouse at night.'

Laura remained silent.

'The day I went after you to the mainland was the first day I ever left the lighthouse – and you know why I did that.'

She looked at her feet.

'You can come here later in the day . . . if you like.'

He reached over and took her hand. His was rough and she was surprised by the pleasant warmth of it.

'I suppose we could get married,' he said and she felt like a cockle that was closing up. It was not a proposal but a statement. A couple of days earlier and she would have accepted. On Monday she would have been happy with that. Now she wanted him to say he was sorry for everything. She wanted him to soften and warm up a bit. At this point in time he was like a wet crab beside her on the couch. And yet what were her choices? What life would she have by herself? Finn was what she wanted but she stood no chance of ever getting a man like that. Martin did not ask to touch her and she did not ask to be touched. He had learned something on the way here and she was glad of that.

'I'll have to think about it,' she said.

Her voice was perfectly level. There was no kindness and no cruelty in it. Martin gave a little bow and leaned back on the couch, satisfied. If the light was on she guessed she would see relief written all over his face. Relief in small ink letters on his forehead. Relief repeated over and over like lines on a board by an errant student. Relief in giant letters – a big 'R' covering one side of his face. And yet she remained somehow fond of him. 'Fond', the awful milk-and-water sentiment that he had given to her in the past. Was 'fond' enough to make a marriage last?

When he fell asleep she pulled a blanket over them. She was still fond of him then and could ignore the whistling snot in his nose as he began breathing heavily in and out.

It was getting bright when she left, the sun coming up white on the horizon. It was six o'clock in the morning. She lifted the latch on the back door and was greeted by the sound of the sea, before stepping out.

19

There were no more clear days after Finn left. The sun disappeared and the sky turned yellow like old buttermilk. The rest of September passed slowly and Laura felt like she was sleepwalking. She went to the village and bought bread and a turkey gizzard. At the school gate she became entangled with children rushing out. She forgot her change and had to go back to the butcher's. A dog followed her down the street sniffing at the plastic bag.

The sky seemed lower now and the mist came down again. Sudden flurries of autumn leaves came at her like snowflakes. The islanders could see only the white edge of the ocean and the wet grey cliffs and occasionally the top of the lighthouse. The sheep climbed higher. They moved into the clouds like wool angels and some never came back. She continued to gather seaweed. She avoided Martin and he kept his distance.

Closer to winter the island seemed to shrink and the islanders closed their curtains and stopped looking out at it. Their whitewashed houses made a neat row of yellow lights along the dark coast road up from the village. There were fewer houses after Fintra and where the rocks were steep up around the lighthouse. Inside, the women painted gull's eggs and arranged shark fins and old crab shells on their windowsills. They made baskets from rushes and every bathroom had a shell for a soap dish. Men and women gathered in the pub and the church and the post office and talked about what might have happened between Finn Campbell and Martin Cronin and Laura Quinn.

Laura stayed inside and people rarely saw her. For them she lived between mouthfuls of sour stout. She existed in the moment when a stamp was bought and licked. She was packed with groceries into brown paper bags. Delivery boys had their own spin to add to it. She missed Lucas, his fair hair and his gentle silence.

She retreated and felt herself suffocate. The walls moved towards her, like the house was trying to squeeze her out. The pain she felt was tremendous and there seemed to be a mountain of it. It was not heartbreak at all, just a huge disappointment. A longer word and a bigger idea. A giant kick in the arse and on this occasion the boot went as far up as her heart. The women on the island said she deserved to be on her own. That Martin was too good for her and that she was a woman who couldn't settle herself. One minute she was leaving the island and the next minute she couldn't get enough of it. Once when she walked into Molloy's shop, Irene McKenna stood and faced her.

'So are you still courting Martin Cronin or what are you at?'

Irene just stood there with her basket over her arm and asked her out straight. The shop that was already quiet enough became silent.

'That's one for *Mastermind*,' Laura said.

Irene McKenna should have been in the Gestapo, that was what Martin said. She couldn't stand not knowing everyone's business. She had to ask Laura or she would have burst with the frustration.

And Laura bought all the wrong groceries then because she was distracted. A newspaper. Brillo pads. Four duck eggs.

138

Rain came late in September and Laura could not sleep. One night with Finn and she became heavy and dull in herself. Her legs dragged, her arms ached. She thought it might be her body mourning the loss, fighting with her as it gave up the idea of being loved and touched. She took to making the cakes that he said he liked. Victoria sandwiches, that was the one he talked about. She remembered sitting with them in the warmth of their kitchen as she counted the six eggs out. She yearned for them – Finn and Audrey – not even him but them, just the comfort of their life, as her flour was sieved. She added homemade raspberry jam, fresh cream slathered on thick. They came out of her oven hot. She sat at the small table and ate them by herself. She baked early in the morning before the sun came up. She would eat two for her lunch, another for supper, another to help her to sleep. In between eating she was waiting, even though it made no sense. Her waistline thickened. She thought about Audrey and let her skirts out. She found a pair of her father's trousers and rolled the legs up. She wore his Aran jumper and looked like a sheep in it. She pulled it on and got lost inside it. One night to stop herself from thinking about Finn Campbell she took a scissors to her hair and cut it short.

'Now I really look like a less-bean,' she said.

The weather got warm again in October and in the afternoons she would sit under an umbrella at the top of the beach steps. From there she could see the spot where they had sat. She could see her red swimsuit, his wet hair pushed back off his forehead. She could feel the sun warm on her shoulders. Once she put her hand up as if to push back the fog, as if wiping a window clean, to see inside his life. She cried then. It came eventually. And she was sick. She stopped eating the cake and everything else she took came back up. She cried more. Her tears filled the house up. They covered her floor and her couch and her bed at night.

She wanted someone, anyone, to be kind to her. She bought a second-hand TV and spent December and January watching it. And all the time she imagined Audrey unbuttoning her coat, coaxing her into the warmth.

Spring came again and someone left flowers on her porch. A small twisted bunch of purple heather with brown string tied in a knot. She stood and looked down at it, afraid to pick it up. It was not from Martin. He had called over once. He had pulled up his car and sat in the rain without getting out. She was sitting inside the window waiting, so there was a sort of stand-off. Eventually he blew his horn at her.

Always the gentleman, she thought.

She came out. He wound the window down.

'I heard you got fat,' he said. 'I wanted to see for myself.'

And he drove off, his exhaust fumes adding to the mist, him disappearing into it.

'The Hound of the Baskervilles,' Laura said.

Lucas Boyle left more flowers, placing them like letters on her woven mat. Once she found him there and he raised his hand, flat in the air.

Hello, his small hand said.

Hello, her bigger hand said back.

He had grown taller. His hair was still almost white. Laura grew warm at the sight of him. She opened the door for him but he shook his head. He turned and galloped like a goat down the steep beach steps. He was in bare feet. She worried that he would cut himself.

More heather came in small bunches. Laura had enough for a hedge. She hung it from the beams in the ceiling, placed some in a vase at her mother's picture, put more beside her bed. When she slept she dreamt she was on the moors all night.

On another morning she waited for him and saw him push

himself through her fence. He came inside with her and they sat on the couch and ate cornflakes.

A week later when it was almost June again, she woke, wet.

She could not get up. She felt some kind of pain. Then she felt she could die because of it. She had wondered when it would start. This was the last of her memory of Finn trying to get out.

There were footsteps on the porch. Small feet. The mountain goat was back. She began by calling softly. She sobbed. Then she bellowed his name out,

'Loooooooooooooo—CAS,' and again 'Loooooooooooooooooooooo—CAS.'

He came to the French windows in her bedroom and stood looking in. Cat and goldfish. He placed both hands against the glass. Laura felt herself grow hot and then cold, her throat gurgled when she swallowed. Her body was drenched in sweat.

Lucas touched the door handle and then turned it, stepping inside like he was walking on glass. He looked around her room, eyes wide.

'I need help,' she said.

Me. Lucas touched the centre of his chest.

'I have . . . pain,' Laura tried to explain.

He nodded. He looked around again. He stopped then and stared at the painting over her bed. She was dying and his attention span was short.

'Lucas . . .' she pleaded.

He stepped up to the bed, looked down and put one small light hand on her stomach.

Laura felt the room turn and spin. Stars appeared over her head.

Lucas placed one thin arm on top on the other, smiled down at one elbow and rocked.

A *baby*, his arms said.

For once Laura was glad he couldn't speak.

Lucas found the midwife waiting. She was stirring her soup at the kitchen table, lifting the carrots on a spoon, like a woman with no appetite. When she saw him she got up and raised a broom handle to the ceiling and knocked three times.

'It's time,' she shouted up.

There was no note of panic in her voice, no urgency even. It was as if they had been waiting for a bus. Her daughter rattled down the stairs, carrying a big bag, wearing her coat. Her red hair was curled like her mother's. She was a novice, being trained by her mother, like the chimney sweep who sent his own children up.

On warmer nights Laura had taken to walking and crying. They had seen her on the road late at night. Her nightdress barely covering her. Her wellingtons with the toes cut to let her swollen feet out. Her belly had ballooned. When she glanced down there was nothing else to look at. She felt like she had stolen the moon and was trying to run away with it. She knew what was happening and only wanted to stop it. But the baby kicked her out of the bed. It wouldn't even let her sleep. When she sat in the bath, it lurked like a crocodile under the face cloth. When the water grew cold it kicked and made her get out. When she ate curry she belched and farted and the baby kicked and kicked. It could do whatever it wanted and she was powerless and now it was getting ready to break out.

'God is good,' the midwife said. 'She didn't try to do it by herself.'

She put the soup bowl into Lucas's hands and told him to sit. He was worried about the big bag and imagined they would put the baby in it. As soon as they were gone he sprinted over the gorse. When they arrived in their car he was already waiting at the house.

The midwife had never spoken to Laura before. Even now she didn't say much. She took one look at Laura, put a hand on her forehead, called her 'pet'. Laura groaned. She panted. She tried to stop more sounds from escaping by keeping her lips tight.

'Let it out,' the midwife said.

She drank tea with her daughter. She ate a biscuit, crunched on it, shook crumbs off her fingers. She stood up.

'I'll take a wee look,' she said.

Lucas stayed high up in the kitchen boiling water, pot after pot. He carried them down the stairs, leaving them in a long trail outside the bedroom door, as if the roof had a leak. On the way back he put his fingers into his ears and climbed back up. The midwife took her knitting out.

For Laura the world had gone from grey to red overnight. She refused to look lower than her bosom. Further down had nothing to do with her. She could only see the moon she had run away with, and down further the man in the moon was trying to get out. She made sounds inside her head. She went over the words of 'Yellow Submarine'. She reminded herself that it was almost summer. She hummed. The midwife nodded. Her needles clicked.

'I don't get involved until the pushing starts,' she said. Apart from that she was still and silent.

In her mind, Laura was pushing them out on their heads. Their charity was overpowering. Their kindness made the morning sickness come back. And yet as evening came and she faced another night, not a mother yet, the baby battling, knocking, elbowing, shouldering, she was glad of them. A baby, she realized, had a way of mowing through a lot of shit. It had a way of clearing the air between people, of patching things up.

The midwife said, 'I'll take another wee look.'

When the daughter stood up Laura became frightened.

'I can see a fine head of dark hair,' she said.

Laura wanted to scream, run away and yet the idea of a 'fine head of dark hair' – a new small head that belonged to someone else – made her heart lift and soar like a kite. She was surprised, addled, she had not expected the happiness that came with this. Now she too wanted it out. She heaved. She pushed. She clenched her teeth. She cried. She closed her eyes and heard, 'Look, look, look.'

The mother and daughter sang it out together. They held him high, two hands catching him under the armpits, long legs dangling, fists clenched, chin trembling, eyes opening, seeing her – with her chest still heaving, her eyes watering, her sweat-drenched skin – but seeing her, for what she was – the centre of his universe.

The baby came and made her crazy. She took one look at him and a new idea, one she had never had before, came bounding, galloping, racing into her head.

'I am loved,' she said.

20

June 1976

Madness. That's what Laura called it. Some queer place put together by hormones and a lack of sleep. Days ran into each other and most of them felt like one long night. The moon appeared and there was real green cheese on it. The baby got bigger and Laura got smaller. He drank so much milk that it felt as if her insides would come out. Not her innards, not her guts, but her thoughts, the secret words that only she was intimate with. Then another layer of crazy came because of general disbelief. He couldn't be hers. He was a bloody nightmare and he was also magnificent. She was not capable of building a thing like this.

She named the boy Matthew.

'Why?' someone asked from the end of her bed.

The islanders came to see the baby and said the daftest things. Since Matthew arrived they were all talking in their sleep.

'There's the little man for you now,' said Patricia McKenna.

'No time at all and he'll be sitting up eating an egg,' announced Toilet O'Riordan.

'Boo-boo-goo-goo-cuckoo-cuckoo,' said the dwarf.

When the baby gave a milk-filled burp, they all chorused, 'Good man yourself.'

The baby looked away. He was trying to get some sleep. He couldn't care less what they said. He thought they were all talking shite.

'He's doing his business now,' the midwife's daughter announced.

They all looked at Laura and she looked back at them. She had no idea what they were talking about. The midwife changed the nappy and congratulated Matthew on the contents. In one of her earliest maternal moments, Laura spotted the small cushions of his bottom and wanted to cover him up. Only a mother had the right to admire that. In secret she would want to kiss it. They were all craning their necks when the nappy came off. When he grew up he would kill her for allowing it.

Laura turned her head away from them and thought about Finn. She remembered waking in those warm arms, in the same spot, under the same window, under a grey sky, and now this. There was joy, a real diamond of it, but it was small now compared to the fear she felt. The people who had shut her out, who had closed doors on her, came now, lining up outside, like cows at the parlour waiting to be milked. The baby arrived and opened them all up to her. He was like a glue that bound them. Because of him, they smiled and brought gifts. Patricia McKenna baked a lasagne. Her sister brought a new wooden crib. Toilet O'Riordan carried in four wool blankets. Milk – there was oceans of it. When Matthew cried, it ran in rivers down her front. He opened his eyes and she saw someone who was wiser than herself. He suckled like he had done it before. He looked around the room as if he had built the place.

'He's a real professional,' the midwife said.

She was still there with her daughter. Like two clucking hens, they had taken up residence. The daughter seemed human enough but she rarely spoke. Laura did not know how to put them out – and besides she needed them and that was the worst part. For now they changed the nappies and washed them and lifted Matthew up to suck.

Laura lay like a cow that had fallen into a ditch. Lucas came with his mother and pointed the baby out. When Laura saw him she began to cry. She told them that the name was 'Matthew Lucas' and everyone's eyes settled on her to see what name she would put next.

'Quinn.'

But she said it to herself.

She shaped the name with her lips, said nothing at all, she didn't even whisper it out. Her tongue could not get up from under the embarrassment. No one cared really. That was the gas part, Laura thought later. The baby was the putty that filled all the ugly cracks. One look from him and everyone got stupid. He moved his eyes to the left and turned them all into dimwits.

Everyone came – except Martin.

'He's up in the lighthouse,' Mary Brennan said, 'keeping watch.'

Laura had no thoughts for him at all now. Her eyes were directed on to her baby's face. They all thought that Martin was the father. They expected him to come into McKenna's later and wet the baby's head. Now there would be a wedding as well, they said. From where Laura was sitting propped up with white pillows, the room and the island were spinning like a carousel.

'When will I feel right again?' Laura asked the midwife's daughter, who looked into the middle distance.

'You were never right,' the midwife said. It was meant to be a joke but no one laughed because there was more than an ounce of truth in it.

'You'll never be the same again,' the red-haired daughter said. When her mother wasn't looking she reached for Laura's hand and held it.

'It's like learning to live a new life.'

'I want my old life,' Laura said and here she began to cry a bit. Her own life had been awful but now she was suddenly fond of it.

'It is still your life – just a new version of it.'

Such wisdom, Laura thought, from someone who was saving herself for the altar rails, from someone who wouldn't even take a lift from a man, never mind climb into the back seat. She was sorry when she let her hand go again though.

'I'll come again,' the daughter said and she whispered the next part. 'Without my mother.'

'What's your name?'

'Rose.'

'I'm Laura. This is my son Matthew.'

They looked at each other and smiled.

'I can give you some Panadol – for tonight.'

'I'd like that.'

The midwife came back and took the baby away from Laura as if she owned it. Then Laura found the strength to thank her and tell her that she was ready to be on her own at night. Then she remembered that she wasn't on her own any more and that she wouldn't be on her own again, probably not for the rest of her life, and even when he grew up and left her and the island, he would always think of her because she was his mother. No one else could be, no one else.

21
July

Martin watched this world from the lighthouse. He carried a camp bed up and slept there on the calmest of summer nights. He looked to the east and could see a thread of smoke coming from Laura's house. When the sun rose he watched to see the baby's face in it. He wanted to see the child but she wouldn't ask him over and he wouldn't go without an invite. Once he saw her pushing the baby on the beach in a wheelbarrow and he nearly took a fit. He didn't know what to do with himself. He went to the mainland and bought a big pram and a teddy bear and wheeled it back. He had to take it on the ferry and those that didn't turn away looked inside and started to laugh. He had embarrassed himself, and yet the idea of the baby going down to the village in a wheelbarrow was a bigger embarrassment. The whole island knew it was his. One of the McKenna sisters said that the boy had his widow's peak. Until now he didn't know he had one himself. The baby came and shone a spotlight on all of them. He came and swapped day with night.

He walked in the dark with the pram, wheeling it along, listening to the jig and squeak of its springs and wishing he could hear sounds of another sort. Now and then he would look down and imagine a small round head looking back up at him, lips making a tiny trumpet and then a raspberry sound, and the idea of it made him laugh. He had never cared that much for Laura until lately. Now he was looking into an empty space and imagining their baby in it. An empty pram wheeled along the coast road at night, he could not imagine anything as sad as this.

When he got to the house the lights were on and the curtains pulled back. He could see her on the couch, lying back in a dead sleep, her mouth slightly open and a small dark head, also asleep, on her breast. The two of them had just crash-landed there, a mother-and-child train wreck. They couldn't even make it to the bed. There were nappies on the table and talc, a soft rabbit with a white cottontail on his behind. The floor had a cup and saucer on it, a round bite taken out of a biscuit, a half-eaten bowl of tomato soup. Martin considered knocking softly but the baby was sleeping and he knew that she wouldn't want it to wake. He parked the pram on the wooden porch, put the brake on and walked back to the lighthouse. He felt a bit better then, a bit lighter in himself. Whatever was going on behind those windows, he was a small part of it.

The next day he went to the church and did the Stations of the Cross. He used them to pass the time, like playing patience or stacking dominoes. He didn't care about Jesus. He was blinded now by his own life. It had been very dull once. When he came to the one with Mary Magdalene, he thought about Laura and blessed himself. He dabbed his fingers into the holy water font and found comfort in the smell of melting wax and incense. At least he was welcome here. In the afternoon hours, it was empty and he felt safe. He couldn't go to the pub or the shop now. They were all talking about him and Laura and now there was their little child born out of wedlock. They wanted to know when they were getting married and he couldn't stand listening to it. He

150

came in here and pretended to pray and hoped he would bump into the priest. He had an idea of striking up a casual conversation with him, like two farmers leaning on a fence, except that he would be refilling the holy water font and Father Meehan would be gathering novenas left at the St Antony and St Jude statues.

Instead the parish priest walked up to him. 'I believe you are to be congratulated,' he said.

Father Meehan looked over his glasses at Martin with one eyebrow raised, a single strand of grey falling into his face. Martin gave a soft 'Ha ha' and wiggled his arse a bit, like a dog trying to wag himself.

'I've been meaning to talk to you, Father,' he said.

'Oh yes?' Father Meehan stood firm with his Bible under his arm, waiting.

'It's about the wedding,' he said.

'The wedding?'

'I'd like to set a date.'

The priest paused, took off his glasses and chewed on the arm for a minute.

'I've always thought the church looks its best in the afternoon light . . . Would you agree with that, Martin?' he asked.

'Oh yes, indeed, it's beautiful in the afternoon light.'

Neither man spoke for a minute. When Martin looked down, he saw how the priest's black shoes pointed at his wellingtons. He wondered if he was wearing platforms.

'A wedding,' the priest said. 'Well, I'd have to see herself about that.'

Martin didn't speak.

'I mean I would need both of you here,' Father Meehan said. He was speaking now as if Martin was deaf.

'Herself is keeping to herself,' Martin said. He smiled a big soft smile for Father Meehan. They were getting more like those two farmers at the fence now, he thought.

'Is she indeed?'

'Oh, she is . . . keeping indoors, hardly seeing anyone at all.'

'That's funny, I heard half of the island was up at her house.'

'Oh, not at all, Father, with the baby and everything . . .' Martin stopped.

The church was beginning to feel hot.

'I'll need to see the two of you at the parochial house before I set any date.' The priest's voice was firmer now. He sniffed and lifted his chin up.

Martin was silent.

'I called in myself last week,' the priest said lightly. 'Lovely little child.'

Martin could feel himself beginning to grow faint.

'Not a bit like you,' Father Meehan said and he walked off.

Martin sat down in a seat to say the rosary. A moment later and he had his head between his knees. The priest turned and had another look at him from the sacristy door.

'Coming in here,' he murmured, 'like a cock with two tails.'

22

August

There was no bath for the baby so Laura used the kitchen sink. She would sit him up on the draining board in the middle of the cups and plates. There were Brillo pads and washcloths and used saucepans and the baby didn't mind a bit. The baby didn't mind about anything. So long as Laura fed him and washed him and held him and then left him alone so he could sleep, the baby couldn't care less.

His big eyes followed her around the room.

Where do you think you're going? they asked.

As soon as she sat on the toilet he would start up. It was as if her warm skin on the cold plastic seat could set an alarm off. He would roar so loud that she was sure he would be heard on the other side of the island. She was afraid that Martin would come running, or worse, that bloody midwife. She got used to piddling with the child sitting on her lap.

'Is nothing sacred?' she asked him.

No, his eyes said back.

She had no idea that someone so small could produce so much shit.

She laid him on her knees and changed the nappy. She could

do it with one hand now, the pin between her teeth, a real expert.

'Matthew,' she said in a gentle voice, 'I never knew anyone to shit his drawers so much.' So far they had very little in common but he seemed to smile a bit at that.

Matthew came and the light was different. The quality of the air in her house seemed to change overnight. It was warmer and cleaner with him in it. Laura used some of the money left by her mother and now the kitchen shelves were stacked with white nappies and cloths. Small vests and bibs hung on a rail near the stove. Another rail held mittens and socks that looked like they were made for a mouse. The old furniture looked like it had been reupholstered. Someone saw her with the wheelbarrow and a new Silver Cross pram was left on her porch that night. It was a real Rolls-Royce of a thing, with big bouncy springs and a hood. Laura peered inside and wondered if they could both get into it. He slept in the bed with her at night. She was the protector and yet she had never felt so safe in her life. He slept and she watched over him. The tiredness was like being dragged by the hair out of the bog. Martin did not visit her. Rose came instead and suggested that he might be waiting for an invite. To invite him would be to announce that he had fathered the child. Laura would not do that. That invite would stay locked inside her head.

Matthew suckled and slept. He cried and suckled and slept. He cried and suckled and shat his drawers and slept. She cried and he cried. He wailed and she wailed too, their voices going up like a choir to the roof. No one knew what they were doing, what they were on about. They were together in their own mad place. Laura had to keep the baby alive and that was her only clear thought. When she got up at three in the morning, staggering with sleep, she reminded herself of that. She had to keep the baby alive and, in doing so, stay alive herself. Outside of that, no other thoughts could exist. He suckled with his eyes closed, making little sighing noises. Her weight dropped. He was sucking all the fat out of her and putting it on to himself. Laura felt like she was climbing Everest with a giant baby on her back. At times he caught her unawares and looked up into her eyes and she felt herself completely melt.

The men didn't matter at all now. Martin, she decided, was an eejit but he had bought the big pram so he had some kindness left. He called late one night after midnight when the baby was asleep and asked her to come with him to see Father Meehan. He stood on the front porch holding on to his cap and looking frightened.

'Now?' Laura asked.

She was beginning to think he belonged in the mental.

'Tomorrow,' he said. 'After mass,' and there wasn't much tenderness in his voice.

They both knew that the baby couldn't be raised on an island like this out of wedlock. Laura knew that Mattie needed a father as well as a mother and she saw that Martin Cronin would do as well as anyone else. He didn't propose and so she didn't have to accept. He just asked her to go and see the priest with him and it was easier for her then to answer yes.

She was too tired and too busy to worry about Finn now. He had promised her nothing. She had no energy left for the wondering and the hoping and yet she did not completely forget. She just shut that part of herself away until she had more time for it. She despatched that Laura to the beach to think about Finn, to watch the lights flicker on the mainland and to wait.

It was late afternoon when she heard a faint knocking on the front door. She put Mattie into her bed to sleep and the sound continued, polite but determined. It wasn't Martin Cronin anyway. It was a Wednesday and he would have taken the boat out.

She had often helped him gut mackerel and fry them on the cast-iron pan on Wednesday nights. She remembered the blood and the newspaper print and how she had buried the parcel of guts and how his cat had dragged it back out. Mattie was sleeping with both arms up as if he was triumphant. Laura climbed the stairs and saw a woman standing on the porch. Her colours were faded through the glass of the door but she could see a light fine-knit cardigan the same colour as a lemon. The woman wore it on her shoulders with her arms free and it would never have occurred to Laura to wear a cardigan like that. The only lemons she knew were hard with dots of blue mould on them, lined up with old butter wrappings, inside the door of her fridge.

Audrey had her back turned and she was leaning sideways, dead-heading one of Laura's geraniums. Her chin was up, breathing in the sea air, and one foot was pointed to the steps. The Beetle was parked on the grass at the front of the house, looking like it belonged there. Until now Laura did not know how much she had missed it. The giant bug, her own overgrown cockroach. She had been a fool to sell it. She had been a fool full stop, she thought. She turned the door handle and Audrey swung around. Her black curls didn't move much and her arms were slim and suntanned. To Laura she seemed to have a very long neck.

'Hello, Laura,' she said. Her voice was a sliding scale of shyness, nervousness, good humour, suspicion, relief.

'Hello.'

Audrey had come to find out something from her. That was the suspicious part. Laura heard it like a dog hearing a silent dog whistle. It was as quiet as a falling leaf.

'Will you come in?' she said.

By now Laura knew that women who got married had long necks and toenails painted the colour of seashells. For women

156

like her, too big and with glasses, her job was to sit in the congregation and try to smile back.

'There's someone for everyone,' her mother had said.

Now, seeing Audrey, who seemed to shine a little at her, the black penny dropped and dropped.

'No, Mother, there is not.'

Audrey stepped inside smiling and as she looked around her eyes grew wider. She put her handbag on the floor and rested both hands on the back of the rocking chair. The stove was black, unlit, the red chimney pipe curling up to the white rafters and out.

'What a lovely house,' she said.

She was walking around now, her long white skirt floating around her. She was not wearing stockings and her ankles were smooth and pink like a child's. Laura stood still and watched her, her own bare feet flat on the wooden boards, her legs as white as her nightdress. For once she was wearing knickers but knew that her breasts could be seen through the cotton and in a minute Mattie would wake.

When Audrey reached the table she saw Laura's wedding dress spread out there, the long strip of tulle that Laura had bought reluctantly because someone said she would have to cover her head in the church.

The two women faced each other.

'Well, I'm not surprised you didn't want to come to Bishopstown . . . Why would you want to leave a lovely house like this?'

The white dress lay perfectly still on the table and neither woman mentioned it.

'Would you like tea?'

'I'll have a quick cup.'

Laura wanted to ask, 'Why are you here?' but she was afraid to

157

say anything to her. She moved to the kitchen and felt her own breast milk run in a trickle down to her stomach. The kettle went on to the range with a clank. Still Mattie didn't wake. She would let him sleep and sleep. She turned the radio on to block out the silence.

'Now,' a whispering voice said, 'we'll play a few reels from Joseph Potts.'

A fiddle gave a squeak and Laura filled the teapot up. She knew that the other woman was looking at her back. The brown freckles that would show through the cotton of her nightdress. The broad shoulders, good to push a car with, the legs that were good for walking and standing but not so good to look at.

Audrey sat at the table and Laura sat opposite her, still in her nightdress.

'Will you have a biscuit?'

She reached up to a shelf and produced a tin of Kimberleys. They each took one and she felt ridiculous. The open window caused the curtain to give a sudden flick. It was cold and Laura got up to close it.

'The summer is over,' Audrey said and her voice was full of sadness. 'I hate the short days, the long nights,' and she shook her head.

Laura did not know what to say to this.

'I'm getting married,' she replied.

'Well ... there's news!' Audrey put her head back and laughed, delighted.

What is she so happy about? Laura wondered.

'Is that your frock?' and she was up from the chair and moving towards it.

'Well, it's just beautiful,' she said, 'and you'll be beautiful in it.'

The lie she told was like a turkey in the room, one that was overstuffed.

'And what's your fellow like?'

There was no sound from the small fellow downstairs yet.

'A bit of a dry shite,' she said under her breath.

Audrey took a sip of her tea. She had a way of holding the cup to her lips as if she was drinking from the holy chalice. This must be 'refinement', Laura thought.

Audrey opened her handbag and took out a cigarette case.

'Would you like one?'

'Yes . . . thanks.'

They lit up and smoked for a moment in silence.

'You're not gone on him . . . is that it?' Audrey asked.

'I like him well enough.'

The idea of marrying Martin Cronin came to Laura then and she felt a cold sweat rising up.

'The dress is rotten, isn't it?'

Audrey tilted her head sideways and smiled over at it.

'It needs to be taken up an inch or two, give it a good wash and press it – and you'll be gorgeous.'

In that second Laura believed her.

'And the bride has to dance. It's a tradition on the island.'

'What will you dance?'

'The hokey-cokey,' Laura answered.

Their eyes met and they laughed.

'I could show you the hustle . . . or maybe an easy reel.'

Laura thought about this, Audrey with her pencil legs and ballerina feet, and Laura looking down at her own two sods of turf.

'No, thanks.'

The music changed to disco on the radio and suddenly Audrey was on her feet and pulling Laura with her.

'Now,' she said, 'watch,' and as Laura stood there feeling limp Audrey began walking in time to the music.

'That's all there is to it. Now come on ... follow me,' and Laura began to move slowly behind her, feeling that she had all the grace of a polar bear on ice. The two women tramped across the floor together and the music changed again and here Audrey gave a little yip that made Laura take fright. Audrey jumped into the air and her skirt lifted and away she went, around the stove, around the chair, behind the couch and out across the floor again. She caught Laura's hand and they ran together, both laughing now, and for the first time ever she began to feel light. They ran through the open door and around the house, jumping over the long grass. The sea moved below them and for a moment Laura wondered if they would run through the dunes and down into the water but Audrey pulled her back up the steps to the porch again. Inside, the music stopped suddenly and they leaned on each other, laughing and out of breath.

'I told you,' Audrey said, 'a child could do it,' and Laura was smiling at her, her eyes shining and wondering why she felt so happy in herself.

They were silent then and from downstairs a single steady cry was issued.

'What's that?' Audrey looked frightened. 'What is it?' she asked again. 'A cat?'

'That's Mattie,' Laura said.

The baby was carried up the stairs, his cheeks blazing, bright-eyed and fuzzy-headed with sleep. He sat in Laura's arms, both hands on her shoulders, his face pressed to hers, his tiny mouth quiet, soft lips parted.

'Oh Jesus,' Audrey whispered and she put her hand to her face to laugh quietly. 'Oh Laura, Laura ... he's beautiful.'

They stood together near the stove and because of Mattie everything shifted into another place.

'How old is he?'

'Nearly three months.'

'Could I hold him?' Audrey asked. She sounded shy now and her eyes were wet.

'I need to feed him,' Laura said. She was saying no at last and for once there was no need to apologize.

'Oh, of course,' and Audrey started to arrange cushions on the couch and when Laura began to nurse she took their cups into the kitchen and rinsed them under the tap. She was lit up by the sight of him and, as usual with Mattie on her knee, Laura felt like she was safe.

Audrey sat beside them and took the baby's hand. He was finished feeding and studied her carefully with great interest. She lifted him on to her knee and he placed one fat little hand on her face. Audrey laughed at this and Laura watched and smiled.

'We were having a rest when you called,' Laura began. 'You'll have to excuse the state of the place.'

Mattie smiled at Audrey and she whispered into his ear, 'You're a beautiful boy, aren't you?'

He lifted his hand to the row of pearls she wore around her neck. He held them and pulled them towards his mouth.

'Why don't you have a rest?' Audrey said suddenly. 'I'd love to take him for a little walk.'

The pram was parked in the garden behind the house with the blankets folded back but Laura did not know what to say to this. So far she was the only one who ever took Mattie out.

'I would just love to push him in the pram for a bit.'

When Laura looked over she could see that Audrey's eyes were pleading with her to say yes.

'All right,' she said. 'Maybe take him down that road to the left, you can get a good view of the sea . . . but keep the hood up . . . and here,' she grabbed a white knitted hat and put it on his head.

161

He smiled up at her and she smiled back. Audrey was quiet now and obedient. She listened carefully when Laura showed her how to manage the pram and where the brake was. Laura pushed it over the grass and then stood and let Audrey put her hands on it. She watched as Audrey began to push and Mattie leaned back and lifted his feet.

Audrey walked down the road with her head held high and her chin up. She tried to breathe evenly, matching the rhythm of her feet, in through her nose and out through her mouth. On the bend she stopped, a sudden blast of air catching in her throat. It was late afternoon now and getting cooler. She tried to swallow but her mouth was too dry to allow it. The sound that came out was more like a gasp, the same noise as a creaking gate. She wondered if Laura could see her ramrod spine and rigid shoulders from the window. The baby watched all of this with mild interest. Audrey wanted to be happy for her but self-pity was already pushing out in front. Then came the sour taste of jealousy – and she was ashamed of it. She swallowed and tried to concentrate on moving the big pram into the grass – but the jealousy came back again and it was sickening, a fat pillow leaning on her good nature and crushing the life out of it.

She had taken the car for a spin and then ended up at Laura's house. She had often wondered about her life on the island and the world she had chosen over what Audrey herself had offered. Deep down, she wanted to know a bit more about the storm and the night Finn stayed on the island. She was not worried, just curious, and she had planned to mention it and then sit quietly in the sun-filled room and watch as Laura tried to fill the silence up. Audrey needed to sit in her house and look around and see if Finn had been there, if he too had sat on that sofa, if she could possibly imagine it. Why would she think that? She wasn't sure

162

herself. She had arrived at the wooden house like a Sunday driver, without any real purpose, other than to 'have a look'. Then there was the wedding dress and Mattie – which she had not expected at all – and everything else became irrelevant – Mattie, trying to sit up in his pram now and becoming impatient.

The clouds drifted and a late sun came to soak the wet air up. The baby looked left and right. He lay back and smiled up at the seagulls. The wind had a chill in it and down below the sea was stirring itself in grey and white. She tried to hum a tune softly and smiled down at Mattie who obligingly smiled back. She had never seen anything so beautiful in her life. And now she was baffled – how a plain girl like Laura could make something like that – and she, Audrey, could not. And this baby was an accident, a mistake. And now a gunshot wedding and wouldn't everyone know it? A part of her wanted to say 'up the pole' but she swallowed that back.

She came to a picnic area and parked the pram high up near a wet wooden seat. She put the brake on and together they sat and watched. The sea tumbled around her.

How long, she wondered, before I have to go back?

The baby sat very still and examined his fingers, his face incredulous as he held his own thumb up and stared at it. More than anything she wanted to lift the baby out and hold him. Laura hadn't said anything about that. She could say that he was crying and that she had to pick him up. Audrey gently loosened the straps and lifted him out. His legs gave a little kick when he was airborne and he was happy to sit in her arms and look over her shoulder. She sat there, holding him close, feeling thrilled, and almost dazed. She dipped her nose in at the back of his neck and she could smell his warm baby scent. She saw the soft crease between his shoulder blades, the gentle half-circle of tiny boy shoulders. She glanced at her watch and knew that she needed to get back. She had been gone for over half an hour. It wasn't fair to have Laura worry even if Audrey was feeling sorry for herself. Putting the baby down again would be difficult. The wind got up and blew her hair back from her face and Mattie put his hand up and caught a strand of it. She hugged him close, rocked him over and back. Her mind was swimming and then she reluctantly lifted him back into the pram and fastened the straps. She leaned in and kissed one soft cheek. Mattie looked out at the sea as if he hadn't noticed.

She found Laura standing on the grass verge outside her house. She was dressed now but her face looked stern, a thin crease of worry in a straight line down her forehead. She seemed to relax when she saw them though, her shoulders falling, her hands reaching for Mattie, touching his face and his hands to see if he was cold.

'Was I too long?' asked Audrey.

''No . . . it's all right.'

'I'm sorry . . . you were worried.'

Laura carried Mattie up the steps and she didn't invite Audrey inside. It was as if she had been forgotten there in the grass. She waited for a moment and then climbed the steps after them and stood in the doorway.

Laura and Mattie turned and looked together.

'I just wanted to say . . . if you ever need anything at all, don't hesitate to call us.'

'Thanks,' Laura said and her voice was flat with no tone at all in it. The 'us' part felt like a slap.

'I hope you have a wonderful day.'

'What?'

'For your wedding.'

'Oh.'

'I wish you long life and happiness,' and before the door closed Laura felt Audrey's lips brush her cheek.

Laura watched from the kitchen window as Audrey reversed the car out. She gave a quick flicking wave over her head and drove off. For Laura, the only person who had tried to teach her something had disappeared from her life.

23

Martin walked into McKenna's and called for a pint. The men at the bar nodded and he smiled at them with his tongue out between his teeth. He pushed his cap back on his head and put one leg over a stool and waited. He was wearing the new black bell-bottoms. There were three women smoking and playing Twenty-five in the snug. They sat with their fat knees apart, shoes flat on the ground, stockings in wrinkles down near their feet. Someone was slapping rings on to the ring board around the corner in the lounge. The dwarf winked at him and wandered behind the counter and brought out a bag of peanuts.

'You can put those back,' Irene McKenna shouted.

She was at the far end of the bar slicing ham and cheese for sandwiches.

In two days' time Martin would be married. He would have a woman to keep him warm at night and a ball and chain at his feet.

The men at the bar watched him, grinning, one or two nodding as if there was a joke floating around. Smoke hung in a cloud over the bar, the electric kettle overflowed and Patricia McKenna came in cursing from the lounge. She made three hot whiskeys and carried them to the cardplayers in the snug.

'Those are on me,' Martin said and his tongue moved inside his cheek.

'You're a happy man, Martin Cronin,' one of the men called and a ripple of laughter followed.

'And whatever these men are having.'

Patricia began pulling pints and made a clucking sound like a hen on eggs.

'I'll have a brandy with mine,' someone called.

'And a ball of malt.'

'And two fingers of whiskey.'

The bar hummed with laughter as the measuring glasses clinked under the bottles of spirits.

Martin tried to smile and peeled a few notes from his wallet.

The men moved back from the bar and made room for him to pull his stool in.

'You're the happy man,' one of them said again.

'Happy out,' he replied.

'A fine woman.'

'A fine woman indeed.'

'And a ready-made son . . .'

And here there was silence and one of the men looked down at his feet.

Patricia stirred three more hot whiskeys and began to slice the lemons.

'A lovely little child he is,' she said.

'He is.'

'Do you think he looks like you or her, Martin?'

'Well, it's hard to say . . .'

The men smiled long slow smiles into their pints and then stared at the bottles behind the bar in silence.

No one spoke for a minute so Martin continued.

'Some say I'm there around the eyes.'

'Oh, around the eyes . . . yes, yes, I could see that.'

'When I look at him . . . I think he has my mouth.'

'Oh, he has his mother's mouth, I think.'

Here there was a muffled laugh from the snug followed by silence.

'Women in pubs . . .' one of the men began and he shook his head.

'Now back to Mattie . . . he has his mother's mouth, I think.'

'I think he has her eyes as well,' Irene said.

'Well, that doesn't leave anything at all for poor Martin.'

And here the men laughed again.

'He had his widow's peak,' one of the men said and he looked down and laughed into his sleeve.

Martin took a drink and wondered why he was not enjoying this as much as he should.

'Is he a good sleeper?'

'I believe he is.'

'You'll find out soon enough.'

More laughing. Martin swallowed. The dwarf offered him a peanut and then stared at him with wild eyes until he bought him a drink.

The men began to talk about other things, the weather, the tides, the day's catch, the quality of the pint.

'And what's wrong with the pint?' Patricia wanted to know.

'It's a great pint.'

'Best I ever had.'

'A very good pint.'

'It's a bit sour,' Martin said.

'And you should know,' Patricia replied.

'What did I do?' Martin shrugged his shoulders and looked around the room for help.

'And there's more than one man with a widow's peak,' Irene added.

The men grew quiet then. They sat and supped their pints in silence. Three musicians came in and the fiddle-playing started up. The men switched to whiskey and they gathered around Martin to sing ballads. He sat quietly at the bar and tried not to look at them. He watched as Patricia and Irene moved up and down with drinks. He drank in silence. There was a white shirt in his wardrobe and it was starched so much that it could stand up by itself in the church. The bed was a new one, a double with a green buttoned headboard made of velvet. He had bought a second-hand Hoover for Laura and two good flowery housecoats. He had felt like celebrating something but the talk at the bar had given him a headache. He didn't know what they were laughing about. It felt like swimming in high tide with an undertow at his feet. He had bought them all drinks and they had given him nothing but guff. What did Irene McKenna mean? There was more than one man with a widow's peak . . . was that what she said? and the same thought would keep him awake all night.

24

October

On the morning of the wedding the straw boys came and picked Laura up. They pulled up in a Ford Escort and walked through the front gate of her house. They were wearing straw baskets on their heads so she didn't know who they were but because of some daft tradition on the island they were going to steal the bride and then return her for a ransom.

'These fuckers,' she said and she stood inside the window watching them. Her mood was sour like vinegar. Outside, the sky was blue and clear. She had known as soon as she opened her eyes, from the light that came through her curtains, they were going to have a sunny day for this wedding in October. She was suddenly very fond of her bedroom now, in particular the bed and how it creaked when she turned over. She liked the orange lamp and the locker on one side of it. She liked the idea of having the bed to herself and Mattie at night.

'You're a band of fuckers,' she told them, 'coming in here and taking money for wearing baskets on your heads.'

The straw boys helped her into the back seat and put a blindfold over her eyes.

'Rot in hell,' she told them.

One of them pulled the blindfold down then so that it covered her mouth instead. She had to laugh a bit with them over that. They took her around the island, past the lighthouse and behind McKenna's pub where they stood around smoking in the broken glass and bottle tops.

'Not the first time you were back here,' one of them joked.

'You can drive me around for ever if you like,' she said.

'We need to get the ransom from the groom first.'

'The groom is as tight as a duck's arse,' the other one said.

'Where is he anyway?'

'Someone said he was up at O'Boyle's helping a cow to calve.'

'Ha, ha, ha.'

Laura stood and listened to them. Martin had made the house nice for her. She had already heard about that. The idea of him making preparations made her feel sick. The expectations he had. The idea of him and her together, husband and wife, was as romantic as cement. She had no choice in the matter. She had known it from the moment Mattie put his head out for a look. If he was to have any chance in life it was inside wedlock. In her mind she saw a padlock around her neck.

'Cronin is as tight as a drum,' the straw boy continued.

She wished his cigarette would set his head on fire. She wasn't even married yet and she was already ashamed of her husband. Finn. He galloped past as he usually did. She was getting used to catching him in her fist and throwing him out before he reached her heart.

The other straw boy pushed her against the wall gently and kissed her on the lips.

'Ha, ha, ha,' one said. He was the smallest. There was no doubt that it was the dwarf. He would want a kiss as well, she supposed. This was another part of the custom she knew nothing about. It reminded her that there was a life somewhere outside of this. She

171

kissed them one by one and couldn't see who they were but she felt rough straw on her face.

There would be dancing later and she would have no part in that. As soon as the church was booked the rest of the island was humming. The excitement was nearly too much for them. They would do the Paul Jones like a circle of elephants. And Mattie would be at home with the midwife. She was only doing it for him. The least he could do was show up for the photographs. She had bought him a bow tie and a small dark suit but the priest would have none of it.

She had woken early, feeling like a plank, like an ironing board, not able to get up. She was sure Martin Cronin had come in and nailed her to the bed during the night. Her head was full of dread and sleep. Rose had come in and held Mattie and then the straw boys arrived and Laura looked at her.

'So you're in on this,' she said.

'It's not every day you get yourself a husband.'

Laura stood with a wellie on one foot.

'Where's your sense of humour gone?' Rose asked.

'The tide took it out.'

The dress was still on the back of the bathroom door. She was steaming it to get rid of the creases. It was white cotton, broderie anglaise. It had fallen off the hanger and she had found it in a ball at the bottom of the wardrobe.

'What are you going to do with your hair?' Rose asked.

'I might put a clip in it.'

The straw boys put her into the car again. She was to lie on the back seat and they were going up to Martin Cronin's for a look. When they got there he was already in his wedding suit. He was standing out on the lawn talking to Toilet O'Riordan. Martin was freshly shaved and wearing a cream khaki suit.

'Would you look at *Daktari*?' one of the straw boys said.

She lay on the back seat and could see the windows of the big dark bedroom. She tilted her chin up and looked into the sky and it didn't seem big enough. She would marry him and be smaller inside herself. She would marry him and try to avoid him for the rest of her life. She would marry him and set fire to that cream khaki suit. She had never thought that she would need Martin Cronin to make her respectable. It had taken her months to say yes. He had waited in silence and then one night at her gate she nodded to him and he took that as a thumbs-up.

'We have plenty in common,' he told her and this was meant to melt her heart.

'Yes,' she answered, 'we're both as odd as two left feet.'

Inside, Mattie was learning to roll over. He could tip a box of breakfast cereal on to the floor. He reached for the table leg and the kitchen drawers and saw no reason why he could not have them. She had no idea why but the boy was born with hope.

The straw boys took her home and Rose was waiting with the iron in her hand.

'Your dress is ready,' she said.

'Go on to the church,' Laura told her.

'I'll take Mattie to my mother's.'

'No, I'll take him on my way.'

Rose stood for a minute in her bridesmaid's dress. Her cheeks were flushed and her lips were pink.

'You look like a rose,' Laura said and then, 'I'll see you at the church.'

The door slammed shut and outside the sun was lower in the sky. It had the unusual quiet of a day that was full of heat.

Another pet day, Laura thought, another freak.

There were some tourists left on the beach. A white car had gone too far into the soft sand and the owners stood staring at it as if it was a spaceship. Laura watched for a minute and then pointed out the railway sleepers to them. If they could get the back wheels on to one they would be all right. They looked at her and looked at the sleepers. Even though it was all very clear it was as if she was speaking in a foreign language. The man began to ask her questions then and Laura, feeling that she had helped enough, walked off.

'Sorry,' she said, 'but I have to get married.'

Her little boy was in her arms.

He said 'Dee' and 'Va va va'. Once or twice he said, 'Ma-ma,' and looked surprised.

Mattie knew her now and understood that she was more than the hired help. They were friends. They were more than friends. That penny was beginning to drop. They were more than mother and son. What was the word for 'forever connected'? Laura wondered. She was already late for the church but she sat on the sand and tickled his bare feet. She knew how to make him laugh. His laugh was like medicine for a broken heart. She took him in her arms now out to the shallow waves. The water was lapping gently, with the tide going out, and he looked down and watched this with great interest. His face registered astonishment, delight. She had never met anyone who was so pleased with life.

Laura and Mattie faced the sunset together. She could feel the cool sea breeze on her forehead and through the thin white cotton of her dress. The rest of the island was waiting at the church. Someone had made a garland of white flowers for the photographs. She had seen it over the door earlier and had wanted to vomit. Afterwards there would be tea and sandwiches in McKenna's. And after that . . . the Paul Jones, the Siege of Ennis, the Walls of Limerick – and the dwarf would get into the circle and dance. And after that . . . Laura looked down at the sand.

She had put her bouquet into the pram as well as her

wellingtons, his favourite toys, a small bowl of mashed potato, nappies. She pushed the pram up the steep gravel path and looked down over the island. The wind was behind her now and it made the canvas hood on the pram flap.

'So help me Jesus,' she said and with that she took off.

She ran down the steep hill into the village, past the post office and around the church. No one heard the sound of the wheels when she ran past. They were inside wondering what the bride would be like and looking forward to the free sandwiches.

Only Rose saw. She was standing on her own at the door of the church, feeling less like a rose now and more like a tulip. She saw a streak of white, the big blue pram being bounced off the footpath, the baby sitting up in it, laughing his head off.

'That's the mad bitch,' she whispered.

She had been looking forward to the wedding for months. Then she leaned on the holy water font and began to laugh.

The ferry was late leaving. There were too many tourists shuffling on and too many sunburnt legs. Laura made it to the pier and gave a shout, not a real word at all but some version of 'help'. Where was she going anyway? The pram would travel up a tree-lined lane to a low yellow house. That's where she was going. There was nowhere else. She had nothing to give him except Mattie but Mattie was everything she had.

The ferry began to move off.

'Come on,' someone shouted but the boat was drifting silently, two feet from the pier, three, five, six.

'Come on,' someone shouted again and Laura considered jumping the gap. She looked at the pram and wondered if it would float.

If she had a small oar she and Mattie could paddle it. If she had an aeroplane, she and Mattie could fly it. If she had a life, she and Mattie could live it. The ferry was packed like a beehive

175

and one of the bees looked back at her and waved. She lifted one hand in the air, not sure if she was waving or trying to call them back.

Mattie sat very still and watched her face. Everything he needed came from that place. She turned the pram around and walked back to the church.

25

Martin and Laura took turns washing in the green bathroom. He had left a blue towel out for them and a sliver of Lux soap. The water was lukewarm and she filled the bath and lay down in it. She wore her glasses and looked up at the ceiling. She lay back and imagined that she was in the ocean. The water lapped around her and a cold drop landed on her foot. She noticed that the toilet had a furry green cover on it. He had dressed it up for her. He had bought the toilet a hat.

Martin tapped on the glass in the door.

'Are you going to be all night?' he asked.

She pretended he had said, 'Are you going to be all right?' and answered, 'No,' in a voice that echoed.

Through the frosted glass he seemed vague and lifeless, a man with a loose shape and not much of a face. She could make out maroon-coloured pyjamas. Later that night and perhaps for years after, she would have to see him like this. She put her toothbrush into the glass with his and then lifted it out again and put it lying down on the small glass shelf. Now and then she would stop and listen for the sound of Mattie. He was sleeping at the midwife's house and she was missing him. There were things that she had done wrong and things she had done right. There was a morning when she had considered dropping him out the window into the flowerbed. He had been crying his head off. At five in the morning she had imagined it rolling down the hill to the village. Then he made a grab for her hair and whipped her glasses off instead. While she was singing to him, he snatched at her bottom lip and did everything he could to tear it off.

'Boys will be boys,' people said and they always gave a little laugh.

My boy is a lunatic, Laura thought and she stood in the green bathroom and missed him. Her boy had fat cheeks and giant brown eyes. Her boy had eyelashes that were real chimney sweepers. Her boy was a little beauty who could not bear to be dressed. Once she had rolled on the bed, wrestling with him and his eyes said he wasn't having any of it. He would not have fallen far if she had dropped him out the window and in that moment she had really wanted him to be outside in the flowerbed, with her standing, empty-armed, in the house, by herself.

But it didn't happen. She was the mother now and that meant making loaves and fishes of herself. She didn't drop him out the window, she held him tighter, gritted her teeth and prayed to her father and her mother – and then watched in wonder as his eyelids became heavy and he fell asleep. They had both slept then, arms entwined, her hand holding his small foot, and they were still friends when in the late morning they woke.

She sang 'Carrickfergus' and 'Away in a Manger' to him making up words and he laughed.

'You're away in a manger yourself,' his eyes said.

'Away with the fairies,' she said back.

There were things that she did right. The dressing and the feeding and the bathing made him glow like he had been polished. And on hot days in summer they played in the sand or lay under the giant elm tree, looking up at the leaves together. He lay back, mesmerized. She lay back, mesmerized. She was glad she had not dropped him into the flowerbed.

Martin had bought him a new white cot and it looked like a good one. There was also a red aeroplane made of paper hanging from the lightshade and there was a blue and yellow kite. It was her first night without him. It was decided that the little man shouldn't trespass on the wedding night. It was the big man who decided that and on that day, Laura just kept answering yes. She knew Mattie would have had a screaming fit anyway. He had never slept without her any night. Now to be put into the small beige room across the landing from her. He would scream like a banshee and rattle the walls of it.

But Martin had bought him a kite and the idea of him doing that made her agree to it.

They sat up in bed beside each other for a minute, their hands resting on the pink eiderdown. He had made up a new room for them, with a bedside lamp and a double bed. Laura sat waiting, dreading the darkness, dreading the click of the electric switch. The lamp was made from a wine bottle covered in seashells. She could name every one of them. She would have liked to spend the night doing that or gathering shells and softening putty and making more and more lamps.

As soon as it was dark Martin climbed her in the same way he would climb a gate. She tried to remember what it had been like before, why she had come to him so easily, what it was that she had liked. But then she had no one at all. No one but herself. In the last year she had climbed up that ladder a bit. He was not one for foreplay. He was the sort of man who took his dinner on a cold plate.

'Well, what's the view like from there?' she wanted to ask but a part of her had died earlier at the altar, the joking part, and all that was left was the one that said yes.

Martin pushed himself into her with a grunt and made a noise

179

that sounded like 'Ha'. He had not forgiven her for wheeling the blasted pram up the aisle with the baby shouting at the top of his voice. The baby with his 'Va va vas' right through mass.

'Va va vooom,' someone said and the islanders started to laugh.

Father Meehan didn't look happy at all, not even when he had given him the tenner in the envelope. That was the part when the priest usually came to life and seemed to lighten up a bit. And they gave him a good chunk of the wedding cake.

Now in bed Laura cried and the tears ran down her temples and in no time at all her hair was soaking wet. Martin was already at her to grow it back.

'Your dress is lovely,' he had told her as they left the church but later he said there was something a bit odd about a woman with hair so short, like she'd had ringworm or lice or had been let out of an institution, he said.

That was on the way back from the wedding party and he was driving them to his house.

'Keep talking . . . you're making my knees weak,' Laura had said.

He didn't carry her over the threshold. They were both a bit too weary for that and Martin was worried about his back. Instead he turned the handle and pushed the door open.

'In you go' was all he said.

Afterwards Martin sat up on one elbow and reached for his cigarettes.

'Smoke?'

'Yes.'

Always yes.

Across the island she knew that Mattie was crying. In the same way the seagulls circled before a storm she could sense it. She knew that he was circling another child's cot looking for her and trying to console himself. He was slapping other people's hands

away from him and he wouldn't eat or drink. There were warm
tears sitting on his cheeks.

Martin slid a cigarette out of a new pack and she heard the
match strike. The room lit up and in this brief flare they both
looked frightened. It was almost dawn and they were married.

26

November

She boiled the eggs and the cuckoo clock called the hour. Over breakfast she would decide everything. Not that a mistake had been made in marrying him – she already knew that – but the size of the mistake. It might be the size of the island or even the fresh blue sky over it or it might be the size of a pullet's egg. Mattie was settled in his high chair beside her. He held a toast soldier in his hand, squeezing it like a tube of toothpaste. Martin waggled his fingers in front of him like a magician performing a trick and Mattie gave a slow reluctant smile at that. The range got going and the room warmed up. Snow was forecast for the end of the week. She watched as her husband sawed the top off his egg with a knife. She preferred to use a spoon and knock hers on the head.

'Snow later in the week.'

'The air is full of it.'

'Tea?'

'Just a hot drop. Thanks.'

Mattie began to tap a spoon on a plate and they both smiled at that. He watched to see how much more he could do before someone became irritated. He kept it going and he killed the silence. A slight frown wandered over Martin's face.

'You're a great wee fella,' he said and then, 'When will he start to walk?'

'He hasn't started to crawl yet.'

'What age is he now?'

'Nearly five months.'

Martin nodded.

'That's good bread.'

'I bought it at the shop.'

He looked a bit disappointed when he heard that. He drank some tea and looked out the window.

'I need to take the boat out . . . while I still can . . . The fish will be in the shallow waters.'

In her mind Laura saw the boat turned over on the shore and her there, hammering holes into it. He was already getting on her nerves and this was how she comforted herself. She pushed the thought out.

'Be careful,' she said.

Martin watched her for a minute and then when she stood to clear the dishes, he grabbed her and pulled her down on to his lap. He kissed her cheeks, her neck, her mouth and Laura gave a gasp and struggled to get back up. Mattie was starting the tap-tapping on the plate again. He was looking out the window and not a bit interested in what they did.

'Martin . . .' Laura whispered and she managed to give a little laugh.

'Now, now, Mrs Cronin,' he whispered back.

He pushed her off his lap gently and got up and walked out into the hallway. She heard the sound of heavy boots being lifted and laced and then disappearing down the long hall and through the door that led into the lighthouse. Laura sat down again and looked at the empty eggshells on their plates. The mistake was bigger than she thought.

The snow came and brightened the house. In the morning she found Mattie staring up at the Jack Frost flowers.

'Come here, will you,' she said. He was pulling out the curtains but she spoke gently to him, always gently, her lips touching the dark curls at the back of his neck.

The islanders stood in their doorways and looked bewildered. Everyone was friendlier and they walked through the snow and ice holding on to each other for support. After three days of it they had to stay inside and Martin came down from the lighthouse.

'There are no ships,' he said. 'No trawlers, not even a rowboat.'

They stood and looked at each other for a moment and the child watched this. The child with his rock pools of eyes, all seeing, all knowing, making judgements.

In the bed, there was another island between herself and Martin already. The old-style eiderdown folding into hills of pink and green flowers. He wore a jumper over his pyjamas and Laura had two hot-water bottles at her feet. They both slept facing a window. On a clear day she could see the wet moors and the heather. When Martin opened his eyes he saw the sea and the yellow coast. She knew that he was selfish, that he would even try and steal a good view from his wife. She watched as he got up and could not believe that she had married his white ankles and his yellow heels and his big maroon pyjamas.

Until now the lighthouse had saved her but in three feet of snow and with chunks of ice bobbing on the water, Martin had no business there. Instead he came down in the middle of the morning and stood looking at her. The gate creaked and Patricia McKenna walked slowly down their path holding on to the wall to save herself.

Laura watched her creeping along from the window and

Martin went to the door. She was wearing flat leather shoes and the path was like a skating rink.

'I hope she gets the flat of her arse,' Laura said under her breath.

Patricia moved along, almost at the door and Laura could feel the blast of cold air as her husband opened it.

'Well,' he managed to say but just looking up quickly was enough to unbalance her. Her two feet shot up and the rest of her followed. She was airborne briefly and then back down with a crash and a rattle. A handbag skated into the flowerbed and Martin went sliding after it and his feet went from under him then.

Laura stood and watched them trying to get back up.

'God is good,' she said.

Patricia managed to get to her knees, her nylons sticking to the ice, and then when she put one foot out as if she was genuflect-ing, both shoes went from under her again.

Laura looked down at Mattie.

'There's a woman out there doing the splits,' she said.

'Laura,' Martin shouted and she began lifting the breakfast dishes and pretended not to hear him. She hummed a tune and laughed down her nose, holding her breath and nearly choking herself.

'Laura . . . are you deaf?'

She imagined killing him. A good whack of the cast-iron fry-ing pan on the back of his head.

Patricia was sitting on the ground, afraid to move, and Laura hoped that her arse would be frozen to it. She put on a pair of Martin's boots and went out and shook salt around them. If she was a giant, and sometimes she felt like one, she would eat them with chips. She was gaining weight again and her hair was grow-ing back.

'That's contentment,' the midwife said when she met her at the shop and Laura had laughed like a lunatic.

'She's not all in it,' the shopkeeper said.

She wanted to tell them that her husband was a miser and until she married him she didn't know the half of it. The man she married was an awful mean shite. He peeled the notes out of his wallet before she went to the shop and then counted the change when she came back. And she was afraid to buy herself an ice lolly and if she did she kept her mouth shut in case he saw that her tongue was pink.

'That's contentment all right,' she said.

In the afternoon Laura carried Mattie upstairs and got into the bed with him. Later Martin came up and, without undressing, got in as well. The baby lay between them, kicking both legs in the air and then banging them back down again.

'That's one way of keeping warm,' Martin said and she couldn't help laughing.

They both warmed their hands on him. Their whispers made a cold fog in the bedroom. Once when reaching for Mattie's hand, Laura took Martin's by mistake and he held on to it.

'You have warm hands,' he said. His felt cold and like they were made of wax and then they were kissing. Martin got up on one elbow and sniffed. His nose was cold and red at the tip.

'I think I'll make a pot of tea and bring it up,' he said. 'After that . . . would you think of cleaning up the house?'

'I'll think about it,' she said.

The snow forced them to stay close to each other and they were quiet. It was as if their jaws had frozen and they were too cold to speak. Martin stoked the range and the three of them slept together in front of it. In the mornings they ate porridge from the saucepan like they were having a picnic. They took turns spooning Mattie and he was entertained by this. In the pale morning light, keeping each other warm, Laura felt more hopeful. She had not quite given up the idea of killing him with the frying pan but she had to admit that her husband was not the worst person she had ever met. And this, she supposed, was a better start than most couples had.

27

The snow thawed and Martin went back to the lighthouse. The weeks passed slowly and Laura wore the flowery house-coats that he had bought for her, alternating between the green leaves and the red flowers. When the sun shone on her she felt like a garden. She took out the mop and the duster and looked at them. Then she sat down at the table again and stared into the rhubarb patch.

'Look, Mattie, a bird . . . look, Mattie, a sheep . . . look, Mattie, a dog.'

An army of small boys was marching through her life. She smiled into his honest face, knowing that he was free from guile, free from guilt, free from expectations or any real thoughts and it seemed more important than cleaning to make the sounds of birds and sheep and dogs. She could not remember what he looked like when he was born now. She could not remember what he looked like last week.

In the afternoon they sat on the horsehair sofa and read the old newspapers. She watched as he tore out small strips of paper and stared as they stuck briefly to his fingertips. Later he would move away and leave a pile of shreds behind him like a giant paper haystack.

'What in Jaysus' name happened to the paper?' Martin asked.

'Mice,' Laura said.

'You're supposed to keep house.'

He was standing behind her with the eyes of a man who was haunted. He was like a man who was being driven out of his house by dirt. Deep down she knew that she was torturing him. That there was a name for what she was doing. In another country, there would be a law against it. She was letting his house go to hell and beginning to enjoy it. He wasn't paying her and he was tight with his money anyway and she would retaliate now by letting the dirt pile up.

No one came to visit. Martin was given Ryvita crackers and old cheese on a side plate for his lunch. He began to look lean, the sallow skin around his eyes starting to hang just a bit.

She looked around the kitchen and wondered if she should throw the old Christmas cards out and make way for the new ones. But then maybe he wouldn't like that. She could see dust sitting on the television but what was the point in chasing something off when it would be back again next week – and the week after that. She imagined climbing the dishes in the kitchen sink so that she could clean the grease off the lightshade. She thought about all of these things and got tired just imagining the work. In the end she took Mattie in her arms and walked around the house without her glasses. Once she walked into the cat's bowl and discovered a mouse drowned in milk.

'And you were going to get a job doing this?' Martin said.

He drove the three miles to McKenna's for a pint and a ham and cheese sandwich. As soon as he left, Laura took Mattie out. She would walk the road in big strides, her hair flying behind her like a flag. It was still that strange colour, blonde with streaks of almost pure white. If it wasn't for the pram, people would have thought she was a ghost. But the pram made everyone friendlier and they stopped her to see how little Mattie was. On the way home from the pub, Martin would pass them and he would signal and then pull wide and not stop. At first she would raise her hand in salute and he would lift his hand as he went past. Then they stopped doing that. Laura knew that it was hopeless but she didn't know how long it would be before he threw the two of them out. The first time she had slept with Martin Cronin she had killed herself; now, as his wife, it felt like she was dying twice.

He went to war with her over the cleaning. He took the money away and did the shopping himself. He told her to stay at home and he went out and bought some mince and a turnip. He bought the same things every week. She asked for a new toothbrush and never got it.

At home she made him burnt omelettes and the smell fell like a depression on the house.

'You're a slattern,' he said and he took to cooking for himself.

She began to glow from her walks around the island. Her face was rosy from the wind and Martin became a thinner, quieter version of himself. At night he stepped through the black door and locked it behind him and she knew that he was sitting in the round green hallway with another coal fire burning in the grate. They were reaching a point where they could hardly stand each other. She knew that he boiled his own kettle now and made tea for himself and she realized that there was little hope for a husband and wife who had separate fires to warm themselves.

'You're to stay at home,' he said. His voice was low and quiet and he sounded depressed.

'I can't keep the child inside,' Laura said and she swallowed her tears back.

'There'll be no more walks around the island until you get the house straightened out.'

'He needs fresh air.'

'I know he does . . . and I need a wife.'

28

Before it was fully light Laura walked the two miles to Bee's Beach. The November wind was coming in over the dunes and lifting light sand with it. She left the pram and her shoes near the railway sleepers and walked on in bare feet. Her own house looked down at her from the other side of the cliff and it was surrounded now by long grass and weeds. The 'For Sale' sign was nailed to the front gate but so far no one wanted it. When one tourist asked to see inside, she put the price up.

She found Martin's boat turned over on the sand with some lobster baskets and ropes underneath. It was painted pale blue and called *The Island Jessie*. Now as she stood over it with the baby under one arm and a hammer and a nail in her pocket, she wondered why he hadn't named it *The Island Eejit*. She put Mattie down and he flipped himself over on his stomach and began to play with a clump of seaweed.

Laura walked around the boat and examined it inside and out. Then she knelt down on the sand as if she was saying the rosary and without looking up once, knocked one small hole into the prow. It would not be enough to sink the boat or to drown him but it would be enough to give him a good fright and maybe then he would stop annoying her. She was sick of his badgering and an hour baling water out would be like a meditation for him. He would come home after that and be glad of some hot tea and stop giving out to his wife. Then she put another little hole in the bottom of the boat for good measure and this one was under the seat to cover up her handiwork.

Drops of rain began to fall on the sand and she called out to Mattie. He was still lying on his stomach looking at the shells and the seagulls were hopping around him, not sure if he was a threat or not. She trotted along the sand and scooped him up and put the hammer and nail into the pram, under the mattress. She stood at the top of the path and looked back. It was easy enough to get rid of a husband, she thought, if things ever became too much.

When she got home he was standing at the garden gate, waiting. His shirt was unbuttoned and she could see that he was wearing a miraculous medal around his neck. Three sheep had trespassed into the gooseberry bushes and when they saw Laura they lifted their heads and stopped chewing for a minute.

'I told you to stay at home,' he said.

Laura looked back at him and said nothing. If he said something nice to her for once they might have a chance. There was still a soft spot in there somewhere but he had never tried to find it.

'Are you deaf?'

She stayed quiet.

'You're soft in the head,' he said.

'I needed to get out.'

'Where did you need to go in the dark . . . are you mad?'

'I'm not mad.'

'Will I have to have you certified?' he asked.

'I cleaned the house,' Laura said, feeling like a child.

'I always knew you weren't right . . . I was warned but I didn't listen. I didn't have sense.'

192

Laura's heart sank and she felt her body grow limp. She listened to these words and felt her clothes hang on her as if they were wet.

'There are plenty of people who would testify to it,' he went on.

She stood very still and said nothing. Her time with Mattie began to flash past her in a series of small bright postcards. She felt like she would suffocate. The thing that he was hinting at took away her breath.

'Now, don't make me do something I don't want to do . . . or I'll take the child and send you off to the madhouse.'

Here Mattie smiled and pointed at the sheep.

'Baaaaaaa,' he said.

'That's my wee man,' Martin said and he put one hand on the baby's head.

'You're so sure about that,' Laura whispered.

The clouds were thick overhead. On a day like this they would never lift and the island would stay in a grey fog. She felt her own hair prickle and rise on her neck. Martin's nostrils flared and she could hear him breathing as he thought about what she had said. She wanted to bite her tongue off but it was too late for that. She watched as he turned and walked inside. The sheep ducked their heads down to the grass again and began to eat.

29

Martin rowed out into the waves talking to Mattie. He had propped him up in a lobster basket and then tied the basket to the seat. It was a rite of passage, the fisherman and his son rowing out into the moonlight, and it was never too early for a boy to start. Besides, Laura had annoyed him with that dig about him maybe not being the father. Of course he was the father. She went down to the bathroom and he took Mattie out. The waves came in a steady waltzing rhythm now and the boat rose and fell with it. He rowed with his back to the horizon and now and then glanced back at the island. Behind him the moon seemed to fade a little and the sky was a shade of dark ink. He turned his head to see what kind of wave was coming and then lifted one oar and steered with it.

He usually fished in shallow waters but now he decided to row further out and around Goat's Head. To his right was the light-house and underneath it his own house and his life. By now Laura would be out looking for them. She would be running around the house crying and shouting, her face the colour of ashes. It gave him no satisfaction to give her a fright but he was with his son and he didn't need her permission. He had forgotten to take Mattie's coat but the blanket was wrapped around the basket and he was wearing one of Martin's woollen hats.

Man and boy, father and son, he thought and then he said it out loud to Mattie, who smiled and then looked a bit worried.

The sky grew darker and Martin lit the hurricane lamp. After Goat's Head he would throw down a line and see if anything would bite. He thought about his mother then as he often did when he was rowing. Mattie was beginning to cry. The wind rose suddenly and blew into his face and his eyes were streaming and red. The sea was getting rougher now and the waves coming up high around the sides of the boat. When Martin got closer to the black line of Goat's Head, he looked up at the sky and he saw Laura standing in the middle of it. She was on the cliff edge like someone who was going to jump. Then he looked down and saw two inches of water in the bottom of the boat. Mattie was beginning to cry harder now.

'Shhh . . . Shhh,' Martin said.

He stopped rowing for a moment and when the boat rose up high and dipped on the waves, the water moved up from the end and covered his feet.

'Shhhhh,' he said to Mattie again.

Martin's arms were limp now, with the oars held loosely and he watched as more water came in whenever the boat dipped. He lifted a bench out near the prow and found a fresh hole in the wood. He needed to get the water out but he had nothing with him except the plastic cup from his flask. And the waves were higher and sending more water in over the sides. There had been no mention of this in the forecast but the sea was often un-predictable around Goat's Head. Martin tore bits out of an old sail and tried to block the hole up. Deep down he knew it was hopeless. He found another hole in the floor down near Mattie and he tried to stuff it with some rope. The rag at the other end was already soaking wet and beginning to come loose. The boat was getting lower in the water. He was racing with the sea and he couldn't keep up. He looked at Mattie, who had gone quiet. He began to say a Hail Mary under his breath.

Laura stood on the cliff like the Statue of Liberty, one arm raised in salute. She was too far away to shout anything to them and too far away to help. A white van crawled up the gravel path and disappeared around a bend. There was no life jacket in the boat. Martin began to work silently. He had one orange buoy and he would tie it to Mattie and the lobster basket. It was enough to keep the child up. He himself could drown, no question, he already knew that. The foreign sound of water trickling on to wood and then the sloshing noise of it was all a fisherman needed. The sea was pulling the boat further out. He stayed calm and quiet for Mattie's sake and wondered how long it would take.

The boat was too far out to row back and he could feel the cold of the water moving slowly over his ankles. It would go down in minutes at this rate and he would try holding on to it with whatever pride he had left. Mattie could float in with the tide and have some chance if Laura worked quickly now and ran for help. They would find his own body in the morning curled around the Black Rocks.

Martin thought about his mother. He asked her for help. He imagined her high in the heavens throwing down a net. Laura was still on the cliff, standing perfectly still like she was carved out of it. The boat sank lower and he lifted Mattie in his arms and kissed his cheek. The water was up to his knees and in a few minutes the boat would sink. When it went under he would need to lift the boy and push him as far away from it as he could. Then he would hang on beside him. He would say things to comfort him. He would sing that song from school he knew and sing it through chattering teeth. He would do anything to stop the boy from slipping under. He would turn the lobster basket and the buoy towards the island so that Mattie would not have to see him sink.

The boat tipped to one side suddenly and Martin lifted Mattie in the basket and flung him high, towards the stars and the flickering grey moonlight. The air smelled of frost. His ears were already numb on the sides of his head. Martin leaned and let himself slide into the water. He went under and then bobbed up close to the basket. The baby wasn't crying at all, that was the worst part. His face was white and he had gone quiet. Martin called out to him and then disappeared again, under the water.

The sea glowed silver around him when he came up again. The seagulls sounded anxious. In his mind his life had been wonderful. He had a child and a house and a wife who was all right. The waves around him turned yellow and there was the buzz of a small engine behind them. Laura appeared in a motorboat with Toilet O'Riordan and a big search lamp. The boat belonged to Tommy Nolan. To Martin it sounded like a giant honeybee and she was riding on its back.

They fell on the sand and made a tight circle. Laura wrapped Mattie in a warm blanket and put him to her breast. Martin looked at Laura and then reached for her and pulled her close. He held her together with Mattie, tight into his chest.

'You saved us,' he said. He was shaking with cold and his eyes were black with fright.

'But I did it,' she said into his hair. 'I put the holes in your boat . . . I had no idea you would row out around Goat's Head.'

'I know but I wanted Mattie to see the lighthouse from the water.'

'I nearly drowned the two of you.' Laura knew she would have nightmares about that.

'Yes . . . but then you saved us.'

Martin knew that Laura would leave him. He was not meant to have a wife. He was not built for the drama of marriage and neither was she. After less than two months with him she would pack the blue case and go and once again he would feel a mixture of regret and relief. He would go back to his old routines, a soft egg for breakfast and a rasher skin for the cat. A pint after lunch. The news. The paper and to the lighthouse at night. His routines were like the lines of string that surrounded his cabbage patch. Necessary, but light. In time, he would lose his hair and buy a set of false teeth. Now and then one of the islanders would make a bad joke about marriage and he would be forced to grin at it. The women would try to entice him to one of the dances at the back of the pub and he would go to be sociable, sitting at a low table, lit up by the new flashing disco lights. The music would start and he would watch them all out on the floor jigging about – and he would go home on his own and get a good night's sleep. He wouldn't dance. Not without Laura. Now and then he would remember things about her. He would make a pot of tea and remember how she liked it, weak, the colour of an old dish-cloth, and the house would feel empty and he would miss her a little. The boy was probably not his at all. He knew that now and yet it was the boy who would break his heart. He could hear her moving around downstairs in the kitchen with Mattie now, talking to him, the words going over and back. The boy warmed the house. His voice, sweet and innocent, coming up through the rafters.

30

The frost had turned Bishopstown House silver and Laura watched as a rooster crowed in the yard. He stretched his neck out, opened his waxy beak and let out a good long screech. His small head looked like a walnut. He was in every way ridiculous. He gave his wings a satisfied flap and walked off.

All men are the same, she thought.

It was the middle of November and someone had hung two peach-coloured sheets on the line, beside them a man's white vest and underpants. She had spent most of the night at the ferry port on the mainland with Mattie buttoned inside her coat. They had found a wooden bench in the waiting room there and tried to sleep. She had missed the last bus to Bishopstown and she couldn't go back to the island. She hadn't expected a frost. Mattie had slept and nursed and his breath had made a wet circle on her vest. He was nearly six months old and for him nothing was any different. Attached to her, only the day had changed. In the early morning an old man in the waiting room offered her a green apple from a string bag and watched as she ate it.

'Thanks,' she said and she avoided meeting his eyes.

He was from the other side of the island. He was one of the men who had helped to pull her dead father out three days after his boat went down. He remembered her too but neither of them wanted to mention it.

'You're up early' was all he said.

There was a faint smell of toast off him. Now they had the green apple to connect them instead of that wet night on the beach. He told her that he knew someone driving out past Bishopstown House and he could drop her at the back gate.

An early sun appeared and sent orange and red beams up over the cowshed. The sheets were frozen on the line and so were the underpants. Laura stood with the pram watching them. The back door was open and there was a light on in the kitchen. Her thoughts were still tangled inside her head. When she tried to decide what to do she saw lichen and seaweed. Martin had started to treat her like a human being recently but it was too late for all that.

A black Shetland pony was eating hay near a wooden fence. In her mind she was putting Mattie on his back and giving him a ride. The pony nodded his head and shook the hay about. He had legs like stumps and he was standing up to his belly in it.

She began to wheel the pram to the back of the house. She had worked out what she would say but the words already felt like chewing gum in her mouth. The windows were lit up and she saw Audrey at the kitchen table.

Audrey, in a red angora jumper, kneading bread.

Laura stood and watched for a moment. The river had been frozen in parts and everything around her was quiet. This house seemed to dodge the elements. There was no wind here and the small birds hopped about without opening their beaks. The silence was killing her and her feet on the gravel sounded monstrous. A robin landed on the pram and looked up at her. The cold had made him brazen. A few nights below zero and he had lost his marbles.

She went over her lines again. Small stars appeared to her right and she lifted her hand and swatted at them. She moved to the window and stood looking in at the woman baking bread. She was lifting the dough out of the bowl and laying it down in a tin. She produced a short knife and made three little nicks. The oven door was opened quickly with a cloth and she shot the loaf tin in.

Then Audrey turned around and their eyes met – and Laura could hear her own heart beating inside her chest and she was frightened by it.

'Ba ba ba ba ba,' Mattie said.

The big Aga was still there, throwing out a red heat. The same copper pans lined the walls and seemed to watch her. The mop and the bucket were waiting like old friends and so was the apron with the straps that crossed at the front, like a straitjacket. Audrey reached for her with hands that were covered in flour. She pulled her into her arms and held her for a minute and Laura stood still, feeling that if she hugged her back she might break her in half. She felt like a walrus, like a mist landing on them, asking for charity and being barefaced about it. She would ask about the job and try to take the sting out of it. It wasn't even eight o'clock in the morning yet. Most people wouldn't be up. But Audrey welcomed her and she would have two white handprints on her back to prove it.

Another door opened behind them and Finn appeared in a long wool coat and a hat. He was carrying a bucket of water and his hands looked angry and red. Laura turned and faced him properly, the frosted air crackling around them.

'Sit down here,' Audrey said and she was pulling a chair out from the long table.

'This girl is frozen,' she said to Finn, 'and the baby,' and she was reaching for the handle on the pram and beginning to push it towards the heat.

Finn stood and watched for a minute. His eyes were hidden under the brim of his hat. It looked like Donegal tweed and he had some fishing hooks and feathers stuck into the side of it. His mouth was slightly open as if he was making an 'Oh' sound. He passed the bucket to his other hand.

'The tank in the yard is frozen,' he said, 'the cattle have no drink.'

Audrey was shaking oatmeal into a saucepan.

'Have you a kettle?' he asked.

She passed him one from the heat without really turning and he closed the door again, leaving a trail of steam behind him.

Audrey spooned some thin porridge into Mattie and he opened his mouth up like a fish.

'I was wondering if you still needed a housekeeper,' Laura asked.

Audrey was sitting with her back to her. The copper pans were brighter than Laura remembered. At the top of the table was an egg-stained plate.

'What about your husband?' Audrey asked and she managed to make this awkward question sound all right.

'I should never have married him.'

Laura lifted Mattie on to her knee and began to unbutton his coat. A tractor rumbled in the yard and she could hear Finn shouting.

'I just thought that . . . maybe you might still need help.'

'We always need help in a house like this,' Audrey said.

Tea was poured into big blue cups. Audrey sliced brown bread and scrambled eggs to go with it. She sat and watched Laura eat. Mattie pointed at the windows and laughed up at the lights.

'I'll talk to Finn,' she said and Laura nodded, still looking at her plate.

And that will be the end of it, she thought.

The attic rooms were painted cream and white. There were red velvet curtains on the little window and they seemed too grand for it. An iron bed stood where the ceiling slanted and, next to it, a small wooden cot. There were freshly ironed sheets and a patchwork quilt. The fire in the grate burnt red and crackled. Laura was to have her own radio, Audrey said. Her own coal bucket. Her own teapot. Her own fridge. Her own bath and sink. She could have one afternoon off every week and one Sunday in every month. There was a bookshelf with three cookbooks lined up on it. And in a small cupboard in the hallway, more blankets, cups, plates, some cotton dresses and some white aprons, stiff with starch.

The little bathroom was cold and she was reminded of the island. There were coloured mosaic tiles on the floor and big old-fashioned taps that dripped. Mould had made a map of America on the ceiling where the steam rose up.

The women stood for a moment in the white room and when Audrey spoke her voice echoed around it.

'Have a hot bath,' she said casually. 'It will do you good.'

Laura wondered if she smelled bad. She had washed earlier that day but seeing the house and then Audrey had made two wet circles appear at her armpits. When Audrey tried to take her coat she had refused to unbutton it. Seeing him standing there in the kitchen then and saying nothing at all to her had made a long trickle of sweat run down between her breasts.

'So it's all right that I stay here . . . with the baby and everything?' she asked. 'I mean,' and here she stopped and swallowed, 'your husband might not like it . . . the baby crying at night.'

'Leave Finn to me,' Audrey said and she smiled at her as if they had a secret.

'Have you talked to him?' Laura asked.

She looked down at her feet. She was being impertinent. She knew she was overstepping the mark.

'Not yet but I will.' Audrey's voice was brisk now, with just a hint of annoyance in it. 'You get an early night, you need some rest,' and she leaned in quickly and kissed Laura's cheek. 'Everything will be all right, Laura,' she said.

After dark Audrey brought up beef stew with boiled potatoes on a tray, and for Mattie a bowl of rice pudding and a bottle of milk. He smiled up at her and she gave a little gasp and smiled back.

One smile from him, Laura thought, and I can go anywhere I want.

When Audrey left she ran the bath and sat on the side of it, feeling sick. Audrey had left some clothes on the chair for her. An Aran cardigan and a tweed skirt, her cast-offs, let out a few inches to go round her hips. There were woollen tights, slippers, a new white silk slip. Laura washed her knickers out in the bathroom and hung them from the mantelpiece. She used the two brass candlesticks for pegs. They reminded her of one of the tourist tents on the island. Steam came off them and caused the mirror to mist. The cot was a bit small for Mattie. He was curled up in it now, fast asleep, like a big cat.

Deep down she had prayed for the smallest sign from Finn. A tiny signal passing between them that she could have read like a flashing light. She had wanted to see his eyes light up for a second with recognition, a brief nod of his head, a smile given with a twitch of his lips. She did not expect him to welcome her but just some small acknowledgement that they had met. All she got for her trouble was an angry man in a tweed hat. He had stood there without any warmth for her, and Mattie had said 'Bam!' and pointed. She had sat at their kitchen table rolling scrambled eggs around in her mouth, feeling weak and humiliated.

The taps squeaked when she turned them off and there was a mousetrap in the corner of her room.

When, Laura wondered, will I have a house without mice in it?

The water and the steam warmed the little bathroom up. The water was very hot and there was plenty of it. She climbed in and sank down until it covered her head and she stayed there for as long as she could, her ears filled up and any sound blocked out. She blew bubbles, thought about the sea and the two dolphins she saw once, and she bobbed back up. She shook her head and began to breathe. The map of America was stretched out over her head in a mixture of green and grey mould. In a few days they would run away again. She would get the boat to America as her mother did. It was her last hope. She lay back and put her feet out over the end. She had painted her toenails red once and when Martin saw them he started to laugh.

'I've never seen anything so ridiculous,' he said.

She missed him a bit now but she wasn't sure what exactly she missed. She reached back and found an old bar of green Palmolive soap. It was dried up and felt like cement. She held it under the hot water to make it soft. The last housekeeper would have used it. In a sitting room downstairs and on the other side of the house, Finn and his wife were talking. She would have liked to be a fly on the wall for that. She wondered if there was anything at all about her that he sometimes thought about and missed.

31

Finn knocked twice on the attic door and stepped inside. He had left his wife sleeping and then stood at the bottom of the narrow staircase, looking up. The hallway below him was dark and quiet. A single chime came up from the grandfather clock. He had watched *Upstairs, Downstairs* with Audrey in the sitting room. She had one eye on the new television set and the other on her needlework. She seemed happier in herself. The idea of another woman in their house and especially the baby seemed to make her quieter and more content. He could offer no reasons yet for putting the girl out. Audrey was happy and that was enough. He had plenty of money in the safe. He would go to Laura in secret and persuade her to leave the house.

He left their quiet bedroom with the bay windows that looked out over the fields and the mountains. He prayed Laura was still awake. Then he prayed that she was already asleep. He crossed the landing and opened another door to the attic stairs. There was a strip of orange light under the door so he knew that Laura was up. The stairs creaked and he leaned heavily on the old banister. He hadn't climbed these stairs for years, not since he was a boy and this was where his toys were kept.

When he had seen Laura standing there in the kitchen his heart had nearly stopped. He had not been right since the storm and the island anyway, when nature, the elements at their wildest, had tossed them into each other's path. Dooley had been drunk again and Finn had had to drive her to the ferry. He hadn't planned it – and yet he was happy as they went down that dark avenue together, happy when the wind shook the old boat, happier still when he woke up cold and stiff in his car and there she stood, prettier than he had remembered, golden, somehow, in the morning sunlight.

But afterwards on the farm he had felt weighed down by her and guilt and drawn then to the worst kind of work. He got up before sunrise and worked long after dark, turning the land into his own personal Lough Derg.

Audrey would see the funny side of that, he thought, him being a Protestant. That's if there was anything at all for them to laugh about.

They picked stones in the lower meadow, a job that was back-breaking and mindless. Finn and Dooley sliding in the muck, their hands red raw from the cold, their fingernails thick with dirt. Dooley objected most to cleaning out the duck house but Finn was determined. He had no choice but to shovel and Finn wheeled the full barrows of droppings to the slurry pit.

'A duck is a dirty bastard,' Dooley said.

And in between these acts of penance, Finn made love to Audrey. He took her to see a show in Dublin and they stayed in a nice hotel for a few nights. A gold necklace in a velvet box appeared with earrings that matched. And there was the new pressure cooker which she loved and set out on the kitchen window to rattle and hiss. He tried to rub out what had happened on the island. He wanted to cover it over now and forget. He regretted telling Laura that he wanted to see her again but didn't all men say those things when trying to escape? But he didn't lie to people as a rule, as a rule he was arrow-straight. He liked

207

honesty, he liked the truth. A spade was a spade and everyone should know where they stood. But in that moment outside her house he had meant it and he was moved again by the flicker of joy that had crossed her sad face. And later at home in Bishopstown the girl and her sadness seeped into him, moving around his mind at times like a ghost. She didn't have much and whatever about the night they shared, she didn't need the lie that followed. If he allowed himself to think about her he would begin to soften and he didn't want to do that, he couldn't. The idea of losing Audrey or causing her more pain made him frightened. So he thought only of his wife and when he couldn't do that he exhausted himself with work.

Now Laura was under the eaves of his house and his wife was sleeping one floor below. He had stood there in his own kitchen trying to remember the cattle that had gathered at the gate, crazy with thirst, steam coming up from their backs, and looked and looked at her until he realized that his breath had stopped. How long had he stood there? What had his face said? He was glad he was wearing a hat. He was glad for the kettle that was handed to him quickly, piping hot. He had left and walked out into the white morning sunlight, dazzled and light-headed. He had left the women in the kitchen together with a baby that was falling asleep. In the yard, he had shouted at Dooley and kicked out at one of the cats.

Now he found her sitting on the side of the bed, wearing one of his wife's old nightdresses, her white calves bare, and a pair of big blue knickers steaming at the fireplace. He stood for a moment and looked down at her, the underwear between them like a surrender flag.

'Hello,' she said.

Her voice was low and he could see that she was frightened.

The fire was dying and there was no coal left in the bucket.

'Are you warm enough up here?' he asked.

'Yes.'

Laura folded her arms and looked down at her feet.

He sat into the armchair and crossed his legs. One hand went to the pocket of his dressing gown. For as long as she could remember Laura had sent men fumbling for their cigarettes. He didn't offer her one but struck the match on the fireplace and tilted his head back and began to smoke it. He was better-looking than she remembered. His hair was still very black, longer now and there was more of a curl in it. His forehead was broad and weathered. She put different pieces together to try to rebuild the man from the beach. She watched as he smoked his cigarette and felt like she was about to get a death sentence.

'This used to be the nursery,' he said.

He looked around the room and lifted a loose flake of tobacco from his bottom lip. Laura pulled the Aran cardigan around her.

'Look at this,' he said suddenly and he got up and lifted one of the red curtains back.

His name was scrawled in red crayon. 'Finn' in big childish letters that went up and down. He gave a little laugh but when he turned his face to Laura there was no trace of happiness in it. Finn stood in his pyjamas and a Foxford dressing gown. He was wearing thick woollen socks and no slippers. He stood there at the window smoking and looking down at her and neither of them was able to speak. Eventually he sat down in the armchair again and tossed what was left of the cigarette into the coals and watched it smoke. He leaned towards the fire with his elbows on his knees and raked his hair back with his fingers. He was still looking down into the red coals when he began to speak.

'Why did you come here, Laura?'

'I had nowhere else.' Her voice sounded insolent.

'Nowhere else? For a housekeeping job?'

He swung his head up so he could see her.

'Your wife made me feel welcome . . .'

'Audrey makes everyone feel welcome.'

There was a hint of annoyance in his voice and she was not sure which of them he was annoyed with.

Laura looked at the boy asleep in the cot.

'I heard you got married,' Finn said.

'Yes.'

'And what happened?'

He sounded fed up, bored.

'After I got married . . . I realized that I didn't want to be married at all.'

'Oh,' he replied and then, 'ha . . . well, you wouldn't be the first to realize that!'

There was no humour in his voice when he said the words.

Mattie turned over in his cot. He moved himself around and then slept on his front with his bottom up.

Outside, a fox made its hoarse screeching bark.

'They sound like banshees,' Laura said.

'They're after the hens,' he replied.

She was feeling the cold now but didn't want to go and sit with him at the fireplace. Once she had imagined having some kind of life with him. Now she was just hoping for a conversation that was friendly. She was hoping that he wouldn't throw her out of his house.

'I'm sorry,' she said in a very low voice.

Finn turned and looked at her again. He gave a sigh and leaned back in the chair.

'I don't want to cause trouble for you,' she said.

Laura stood up and rubbed her hands at the fire.

'If I could stay for a day or two . . . then I'll go somewhere else.'

Finn took a deep breath. The relief on his face made her heart twist.

'Will you go back to the island?' His mood had suddenly brightened.

She shook her head.

'I was thinking of going to America, giving me and Mattie a new start.'

Finn nodded.

'How old is the baby?' His voice was quiet.

'Nearly six months.'

'Born in June?'

'Yes.'

'I can help you with money,' he said, 'if you need it.'

She went down on her knees and leaned towards the embers to warm herself.

'I don't want your money,' she said quietly, 'I just wanted you to see your child.'

His big bones seemed to shrink down when she said this and her own nightdress made a tent around her feet. A father, a mother and their child. Together in a madhouse. Close to her ear was the silk cord of his dressing gown, the wool was thick and she could imagine crawling inside it for warmth.

Finn got back into bed beside Audrey. He lay very still with one hand on her hip. The moon cast a grey shadow over them and she stirred in her sleep. He lifted her nightdress up from her thigh and kissed the warm skin underneath. His wife smelled like lemons. She smelled like summer-time. When he saw Laura earlier in his kitchen with the boy who looked like him he saw his life end. Audrey turned over and watched him, her eyes still sleepy and her eyebrows arched in mild surprise. Things were better between them now. When they went to bed at night she had stopped keeping her distance. She rolled over now and kissed him on the mouth. He kissed her back, holding her face and then stroking her hair back from her forehead.

'What's the matter, Finn?' she asked. He didn't answer her question because he couldn't. Instead he turned on to his back and gave a long whispering sigh.

'The girl can stay,' he said.

32

Spring came late on the mainland. The mountains stayed white and the snowdrops on the lawn looked miserable. In the mornings, Laura carried Mattie down the back stairs, shivering. From a window in the return she could see that a light was on in one of the sheds. The sheep were lambing. She had seen some of them waddling in. Puffballs. Clouds with black stockings on. Finn's coat and hat were gone from the scullery. He was already up and working with Dooley in the yard. Two midwives in wellingtons and rubber aprons.

In the kitchen she stirred the porridge and squeezed the oranges into a jug. She liked to be here in the warmth with Mattie, spooning him a soft egg and telling him about the day ahead. When she heard Audrey going into the dining room, she went in after her, ready with her question.

'Good morning, poached, scrambled or fried?'

Audrey had adjusted some more skirts for her and there were new black shoes and tights. The white aprons held her together and saved her from looking like a witch. She thought about the housecoats that Martin had bought her and only missed the flowers. She was beginning to feel happier at Bishopstown. She began to enjoy keeping it clean and putting everything in its proper place. Her mother had taught her this and with

Audrey's help it was coming back to her. It was a long time since she had shared a home with someone and this house was warm and there was always plenty of food in the pantry. On Sundays Audrey took her to the church and she felt like a big doll again, propped up beside her. The farmers there had red hands and the women still had the track of their pillows on their heads. Everyone had their mouths open, breathing or yawning or just staring into space. When the collection plate came she turned it upside down and they all went on their knees looking for the coppers.

The dining room was warm enough even though the fire was just starting. Audrey was wearing a yellow polo-neck and standing with her back to the radiator. She smiled at Laura and asked, 'How is little Mattie this morning?'

'He's grand, having an egg in the kitchen.'

'Finn has been up most of the night with the lambing,' Audrey said and she glanced out the window.

She looked down at the table then, set with two places, the silver and Wedgwood laid out carefully by Laura the night before.

'I think I'll eat with you and Mattie in the kitchen,' she said.

A pot was bubbling quietly on the Aga.

'What are you making?' Audrey asked. She had pulled up a chair next to Mattie and was pretending to eat his toast.

'It's a beef and Guinness stew . . . I need to cook it for a few hours.'

At first Audrey had cooked everything and Laura had watched carefully beside her, asking questions and writing everything down. Audrey was gentle and patient with her, like an older sister showing her how to do her homework. When she made her first full meal, Audrey took Mattie for a long walk down to the river and back.

Laura only saw Finn through the windows, in a red tractor that bumped out over the fields or leaning on a stick watching his Charolais cattle graze. She would see him walk a horse around the paddock in the evening and in the mornings he read his newspaper and said, 'Fried, please,' without looking up. She grew used to seeing him disappear in his sheepskin coat, and when the weather became warmer, his panama hat. Doors closed behind him, lights were turned off and she would find the room empty except for his cigarette smoke.

Audrey put the kettle on and took some bacon out of the fridge.

'I think we should bring the men some breakfast. We can make them some tea and hot sandwiches,' she said.

'And maybe some of that tea brack I made,' Laura added. 'I'll bundle Mattie up.'

The yard was dark and empty and they followed the sounds of buckets clanking until they reached the big shed. The men were inside, sweating, the air filled with the sounds of new life and the warmth it brought with it. Finn and Dooley were kneeling beside a ewe and around them the new lambs were trying to stand on wobbling legs and suckle.

'We brought you some breakfast,' Audrey said.

Finn didn't reply but stayed where he was with one hand resting on the sheep's back.

'This one is in trouble . . . it's a small ewe with a very big second lamb.'

Laura put the basket on a bale of straw and stepped closer.

'Can you not pull it out?' she asked.

Finn looked up at her and frowned a little, surprised to see her there in the early-morning light.

'She's a small ewe . . . and I'd need a very small hand.'

A moment passed and Laura looked down at her wellingtons. They were an old pair of his and she could feel that one sock was already wet, the damp creeping around her heel.

Laura smiled and opened her hands out towards him.

'Laura . . .' Audrey said and she shook her head and moved towards the wooden door. Her wellingtons were white with pointed toes and Laura had never seen anything like them. They were too clean and more like dancing shoes.

Dooley chuckled quietly and sat back into the straw. The ewe gave a groan down low in her throat.

'You could lose her,' Laura said and she was still holding her hands out to Finn.

He reached for one then and turned it over in his.

'I think Audrey's are smaller,' he said and there was the slightest flicker of mischief in his eyes.

'Oh sweet Jesus,' Audrey whispered. She stood for a moment rooted to the ground and then gave a sigh and handed Mattie over to Laura.

Laura stepped back and watched as Audrey began to roll her yellow sleeve up. Her hands were as small as a girl's and her arm slender and wiry. There were no freckles, just a smooth stretch of olive skin. She pushed the wool sleeve up high towards her shoulder and they stood and watched as she began to push her hand in.

'You're looking for a foot,' Finn said quietly. 'Keep going . . . that's it . . . that's it.'

'I can't feel anything at all,' Audrey said.

From where Laura stood she could see that Audrey was gritting her teeth.

When she pulled her hand out she had a fistful of black pellets.

'Ah Jaysus,' Dooley said.

Laura looked down into Finn's face and turned away in case she might laugh.

'Do you want me to try?' she asked.

'I can try again,' Audrey said and she was more determined now.

No one spoke for a moment.

'You put your hand up its backside,' Laura said.

The sheep looked around, bewildered.

Laura had watched the men on the island often enough and found the foot easily and pulled. Then Finn leaned in, his hand over hers and pulled too.

The new lamb flopped on to the ground. Dooley whistled a tune and began to shake the new straw out.

On Monday Laura washed Finn and Audrey's clothes. They ate the breakfast that she cooked and she went upstairs and stripped their bed. She had been there for nearly three months and she knew now that Audrey wore silk nightdresses and that he wore blue cotton pyjamas. She had seen the twisted butt of his cigarette in a white ashtray on the nightstand. Once she pressed her face into his pillow before pulling off the case. Audrey liked the mattress to be aired and for this Laura had to tip it sideways. On Saturdays they left an envelope of crisp notes for her on the kitchen table. They were generous but she didn't need to buy anything. She sent some of the money to Lucas Boyle's mother and asked her to buy books and shoes for him. And his mother wrote back and thanked her and told her that Lucas had started to talk and Laura was happy to hear it.

At night she watched her own son sleep in the attic and sat by the fire sewing. Audrey had taught her how to thread a needle and make a row of very neat stitches. If Laura made a mistake she was very patient with her and when she baked a good cake or cooked a roast Audrey was quick with her praise. Now Laura could reline Finn's tweed jacket and she filled in the holes in his jumpers and knitted new heels for his socks. She enjoyed this work and it was better than gathering seaweed. She liked to think that Finn was carrying small parts of her in his clothes.

A tiny camel coat with leather buttons and pockets appeared and Mattie looked beautiful in it. Then there was a new red jumper, a pair of very small jodhpurs and black riding boots.

'He's not able to walk yet,' Laura said.

'That's the best time to start,' Audrey replied.

From a window as she pushed the Hoover around the landing, she saw Mattie on the Shetland pony and Audrey leading them around the park.

33

On an evening late in February Laura found Finn milking. He was sitting on a low blue stool with his head resting on the cow's stomach. The cow was a Jersey with shiny black hooves, refined, good-looking. Laura stood and listened as the milk began to stream into the bucket and the cow flicked her tail at him like a wet dishcloth. It was a quiet hour in the day, when the birds sang a bit here and there and it was too early to start dinner. The cow flicked her tail again and caught his jaw with it.

'Easy, easy,' he said loudly.

His face was streaked with cow shit. He shook out a white handkerchief and in her mind she was soaking it in salt and ironing it.

Laura picked up a bunch of straw and held the tail steady for him. She stood there, attached, feeling like a bridesmaid, and this was how their second conversation took place.

'Well,' he began, his voice heading towards the cow's hooves but he sounded friendly enough.

'Well,' she said back in a different voice.

'You're out for your walk.'

'It's a nice evening for it . . . I think we've seen the last of the frost.'

'Where's Mattie?' he asked.

'With Audrey . . . in the garden.'

'She's grown very fond of him.'

The cow twisted her head around and looked at them as if she was listening. A cat stepped into the barn, wrapping herself around the corner, her paws soft.

'She's in for her supper,' Finn said.

There was a dirty blue saucer on the ground with traces of old milk and hay stuck to it. The milk slowed and the cow lifted her foot to disturb a fly that had settled. Finn got up and drew his stool back. He straightened his cap on his head. Laura released the tail and waited. The barn smelled of hay and manure and it was just she and him, with a dainty cow standing between them. A late afternoon sun was making a pink square on the floor. Laura went and stood in it. It made her feel happy again, less cold, more welcome.

'How long do you plan to stay here?' he asked suddenly.

He walked towards the creamery can and began to pour the milk into it. It came out smelling warm and it was the colour of custard.

'I'm not sure . . . for as long as you want.'

Finn stopped with the bucket half empty and turned around to look at her again. He stood there with the milk still moving and stared down into her face. It was the first time he had really looked at her. It was the first time she noticed the frown line that had formed between his dark eyebrows. His mouth, his teeth, the stubble on his chin hadn't changed. His eyes were the same blue but there were grey stones of worry in them.

'For as long as I want . . . ?'

He put the bucket down and took a step towards her.

'Laura,' he said quietly, 'I don't want any of this. You here with Mattie . . . you gave me no choice. I can hardly turn the two of you out of my house.'

'What else could I do?' She looked back at him, her hands low and clasped in front of her apron.

'Listen.' He stepped closer. The light in his eyes had changed again and what she saw now were flickers of panic.

'You need to leave here, this can't go on . . . Audrey—' He stopped and Laura reached for his hand and tried to hold it.

'You told me you wanted to see me again.'

'Never mind what I said . . . do you not understand? What happened between us was . . . nothing. Audrey is my wife.'

Laura let go of his hand and he caught hers then. He held her with his thumbs around her wrists as if to stop her from running away from him.

'Is Mattie nothing?' she asked.

'Go back to the island,' he said quietly. 'I can come and visit the boy there . . . if that's what you want.'

The cow watched them and lifted a foot, growing impatient. Finn untied her chain and when he opened a wooden door that led into the field, she reversed herself out of her pen and broke into a trot. Through the doorway, Laura watched as she bucked her back legs suddenly, her udders jiggling as if she was a young one.

Finn bolted the door and came back to their square of sunshine.

'I can't go back,' Laura said.

He sighed and looked up at the rafters. He sat down on a bale of hay, his shoulders hanging. He took a deep breath and found his cigarettes.

'Do you want one?' he asked.

'All right.'

'Sit down here for a minute.'

Laura sat on the bale beside him. The stubble nipped at her through her light skirt. He handed her a cigarette from the box and she took it, her hand trembling. He looked into her eyes and gave a sigh and she felt her head go swimming.

'There is another way,' he said and he turned and looked at her again.

'A way . . . where everyone benefits . . . you and especially Mattie.'

Laura sat still and looked at the tip of her cigarette. Her nails were short and there were hacks on her fingers from the housework.

'Let's think about this for a minute,' Finn said.

A lawnmower started up in the distance.

'You could leave Mattie . . . here . . . with us.'

It was the last thing she had expected.

'Leave Mattie here? Why would I do that?'

'Think about it, Laura.'

He got up and started to pace around, his hands in his pockets. The walls around them were whitewashed. There were laying boxes built into them, empty now except for old hay and dust. He waited for her to say something. She sat very still, frowning up at him. She had never seen such a worried man in her life. The cat appeared again and lowered her head into the saucer and began to drink milk like she was ravenous.

Finn came back and hunkered down beside Laura.

'What kind of life can you give him?' he whispered.

She didn't answer.

'We could give him everything a boy could ever want . . . a good school . . . he could travel . . . he would have this house . . . the gardens and the farm . . . wouldn't you want that for your son?'

Laura took a deep breath. She was feeling like she might suffocate. She looked between her knees to the bale and wondered if she could burrow into it. When she tried to get up she was unsteady on her feet. Finn reached for her elbow and held it for a second.

She pulled her arm away again.

'I'm not leaving Mattie. I would never leave Mattie.'

'Laura . . .' Finn's voice had some note of fear in it. 'He is my child too. I do have a say in it.'

'But I'm his mother.'

'Yes, but he's not even one year old. He won't remember any of this.'

'And what would Audrey think about it?'

'We've already discussed it. It was Audrey who brought it up in fact. There's nothing she wants more than to care for Mattie. She already loves him as if he was her own child.'

'But he's mine,' Laura whispered. 'I've minded him since he was born. For eight months . . .'

Lately Finn and Audrey would stop talking when she came into the room. Now she knew what they were discussing. How to take Mattie away from her. How to separate the mother and the son.

There were tears lodged in her throat that needed to get out.

'You've been planning this all along,' she said.

Finn walked away from her and began to put his jacket on.

'What is it you want from me?' he asked and his broad shoulders had shrunk again. He held his hands out as if he was perplexed, as if her being there had cast a fog over everything.

She knew what she wanted but he was in no mood to hear it.

'Do you want money? Is that it? I can give you any amount you want.'

'I don't want money,' she said.

'What can you give him?' he asked again.

'I'm his mother,' Laura said and her voice was very quiet.

He looked at her as if he hated her.

223

'Listen,' he said. 'Last week that social worker, Mary Costello, came here. She had been to the island looking for you. She asked a few questions and from what I heard no one there had a good word to say about you.

'What can you give him?' he asked her again.

'I'm his mother. I love him.'

Laura looked up at him and wondered how he could not understand this.

'You are his mother,' Finn said quietly, 'and when he gets a bit older . . . you'll embarrass him,' and he walked out into the yard, a bucket of milk swinging against his leg, milk slopping around his feet.

34

The seagulls were flying high so she knew that a storm was coming. The forecast was for rain and the river was already running high. A white cat appeared on the bank like a ghost and sat there staring at her. Laura thought about her mother and wondered if she was watching her. She always came into her head when she was in a crisis. She went back into the house and looked for Audrey and found her in the big bathroom with Mattie. She had only been in this room to clean it so she stood for a minute on the short landing and knocked.

'Come on in,' Audrey called and Laura stepped inside and closed the door behind her.

She had never really noticed the room before but now, after talking to Finn, it seemed different. There was a pair of pink slippers next to a weighing scale, a pink robe hanging on the back of the door. The bath was bigger than hers and it was surrounded by white candles. She could not understand why anyone would need candles in the bathroom unless there was a power cut. On a low table near the window there were several glass bottles of perfume. The toothbrushes – blue and red – were kept in a glass near the sink. She saw Finn's razor, his shaving cream and brush, standing up in a little mug that said 'Pears Soap'. Four small photographs in a strip were stuck into the mirror. They were black and white, the kind you got for a passport, taken in one of those little booths. Finn and Audrey, looking squashed and laughing, their faces close. Laura knew now that their world was small and tight and that there was no space for her in it. She would get a passport for Mattie and start a new life somewhere else.

She watched as Mattie had his hair rinsed and smiled up at them, blinking when the water streamed down his cheeks. Audrey made a lather of soap and used her hands to wash his neck, his back, his stomach. She smiled up at Laura. She was on her knees at the bathtub, her white sleeves rolled up, her hair loose and damp from Mattie's splashing. From where Laura sat she could see how his skin was glistening and wet and how Audrey's arms looked lean and tanned next to it. She watched the pink tips of his toes coming up through the water and the small perfect arches of his shoulders. She did not need to look for the long smooth line of his spine, she had traced it with her fingers, a thousand times. Audrey trickled water into the tub with the sponge and he watched this and laughed.

'He loves the water,' Audrey said.

She turned a little and leaving one arm around Mattie she leaned her cheek on the side of the bath and watched Laura's face.

'Is something wrong?' she asked and as usual her voice was full of kindness.

'No . . . not exactly.'

Audrey sighed softly and went back to running the water down Mattie's back. He kicked his legs and gave a little shriek.

'You're not happy,' she said and her words headed down into the water.

Laura sat and looked through the window towards the orchard. Summer was coming. She could feel the first warm signs of it.

There was something about the way Audrey spoke to her that made her feel sorry for herself.

'Is there anything we can do for you?' Audrey asked and Laura could feel tears building up in her throat. Audrey lifted Mattie out of the bath with his legs kicking. She laid him on a white towel and began wrapping him up.

'You're not going to leave us, I hope.'

She looked up and waited for Laura to answer. Mattie watched his mother from the floor, his hair still wet, his eyes happy and bright.

'I couldn't imagine the house now without Mattie in it. I couldn't bear it, I think.'

Laura sighed and looked down at her fingertips. The skin on her thumbs was dry and cracked. She had ignored Audrey's advice about wearing rubber gloves.

'And we would miss you too, of course.'

Audrey's shoulders seemed to sink a little and her body became smaller. She patted Mattie's hair dry and shook her head slowly.

'Is it the work?'

'No, no . . . it's not that.'

'Or do you need more time off?'

'I don't know what to do with the time off I have.'

'Do you need more money because . . . ?'

'No, no, thanks . . . the wages are grand.'

Audrey sat on the floor and held Mattie on her lap. Laura uncrossed her legs and stretched them out. They sat there quietly together for a moment and neither woman spoke.

'Is it Finn?' Audrey asked.

This time she didn't look up.

Laura took a deep breath and waited.

'He can be hot-headed,' Audrey went on, 'and he's not used to a stranger in our house.'

So that's what I am, Laura thought.

'He is a good man . . . very generous, honest.'

Laura listened to all of this and tried to believe it.

'I'm a bit homesick,' she said finally.

'Well, I can understand that. Maybe you should take a few days off and visit the island.'

'How did you meet?' Laura asked and she kept her voice low and quiet. 'You and . . . Mr Campbell.'

Audrey seemed surprised by her question and gave a little laugh. She sat back on her heels and looked out the window.

'I was staying with a friend of mine in Drumquin, her brother asked me to a dance and Finn was there too, he was his friend.'

She got up then and began to let the bath water out.

'And what happened?'

'He gave us a lift home, asked for my address . . . and we began to write.'

'Who wrote first?'

Laura couldn't help herself now and to this Audrey looked out the window again and frowned. It was as if the answers she needed were in the hedges and the grass.

'He did . . . he was very charming.'

'But there must have been something else.'

'Of course . . . there's always something else,' and that was all she said for a moment.

'The first time we went out he took me to the airport restaurant for dinner.'

'To the airport . . . in Dublin?' Laura asked, and here both women began to laugh.

'He drove me the whole way to Dublin and back. Can you imagine?'

They looked at each other and laughed again at the idea of it.

'But after that – there was no one else . . . for either of us.'

'No one else?' Laura asked.

'No one else,' and here Audrey looked, for the first time, into her eyes.

She lifted Mattie into her arms and kissed the top of his head.

'He was full of surprises then. We had Chicken Kiev and watched the aeroplanes landing and taking off – the airport was the "in" place to go for dinner. Sounds daft now, doesn't it?'

Laura leaned over and lifted Mattie on to her knee. He patted her shoulders and laughed.

'Mama,' he said, 'Mama,' and the two women smiled. Laura was close to tears and could not explain it.

Audrey spoke very quietly then. 'Sometimes I walk around the house with Mattie in my arms and I pretend that he's mine. I know it sounds silly but I can't help it. The first time I held him he filled a gap in my heart.'

Upstairs Laura put Mattie into his cot and showed him how to join his hands. Then she touched his forehead with his fingertips so that he was blessing himself. She kissed him and waited for a moment with her face against his, listening to his soft breath, inhaling his scent and feeling him slip away from her, to sleep.

35

March

Laura climbed on to the roof and stood between two yellow chimneys. She gripped Mattie in her arms, looked up to the night sky and bellowed. She had discovered a trapdoor in the attic and it led to the stars and fresh air again. By standing out here she had her own freedom on the top of the house. In the very far distance she could see the lighthouse and knew that Martin was working. She was supposed to be downstairs herself getting ready for the party but instead she was standing on the roof roaring her head off. She had not been right since talking to Finn in the milking parlour and now she had seen the two of them kissing. It was not a quick peck but a kiss with real warmth in it and something inside her broke into small pieces. Finn and Audrey were together – a husband and a wife – and regardless of what had happened between her and Finn, she could not separate them. Deep down she had hoped that he would want her, that what had happened on the island could happen again in this house – but the kiss she saw was real and it caused her to snap.

Her voice came out in another long squeal and in it were the oven gloves and the starched aprons and the awful tights that clung to her legs like Robin-run-the-hedge. Audrey had asked her to dress like that for the dinner party and Laura cried out again and this time it held the starched linen napkins and the blasted crab bisque that was too salty and had to be put down the sink. When she cried out once more it was for herself and Finn and she was trying hard now to spit her own broken heart out. But Mattie put his soft hands against her breast then and said, 'Mama' – the best word he could find, his voice coming out clearly, gently and whatever was broken inside her didn't hurt so much. He looked into her eyes and seemed to say, What the hell are you shouting about? Finn couldn't matter now – not when she had her boy to mind. The roof would become their island. On the clearest mornings they would count the different reds in the sunrise.

Downstairs the rooms were full of fresh flowers and there were four ducks roasting in the oven. Crystal wine glasses stood on the long table and the Wedgwood was laid out on a lace tablecloth. The wine was to change for every course. Tiny coffee cups appeared like something from a doll's house. The first headlamps moved slowly down the road and a record came on for the dancing. She had never felt less like dancing in her life. From the outside the house glittered up at her like Christmas.

On her way down she passed their bedroom and Audrey was smiling up at Finn from her dressing table. He had one hand on her bare shoulder, leaning down. She was wearing a red chiffon evening gown and looked beautiful in it. Then Audrey saw her and called her in.

'Look, Laura,' she said and she sounded breathless.

Finn sat on the end of their bed and put his black polished shoes on. He was wearing a white dress shirt with dark braces and looking around for his cufflinks.

'Look,' she said again and this time she placed one hand

to the string of pearls, white and glistening, around her neck.

'Pearls,' Laura said and she nodded.

'Natural pearls,' Audrey said and she was smiling and flushed. 'A present from my husband.'

When she stood up, there was a long train at the back of her dress. Laura had never seen anything like it.

'You look like a queen,' she said.

Finn didn't look up. He finished tying his laces and pulled at his cuffs.

'Natural pearls,' Audrey said again. 'One for every year we've been married,' and she smiled at the necklace in the mirror.

'The oyster makes them to protect itself,' Laura said suddenly but Audrey wasn't listening.

She was opening a jewellery box on the dressing table and taking out a pair of gold cufflinks. As Laura stood there waiting, Finn turned his wrists up.

'Now don't forget, Laura,' Audrey said, 'it's champagne first for the toast.'

'What are you toasting anyway?' she asked and her voice came out sulky and quiet.

'Our anniversary,' she said. 'We're twelve years married.'

'Congratulations.'

The skin on Laura's forehead felt as if it was stretched tight.

Audrey adjusted her husband's bow tie and gave his cheek a little pinch.

'Very handsome,' she said and Laura stood there seeing herself in their mirror, in the white starched apron.

Looking like a right gobshite, she thought.

Downstairs she waited in the hallway near the lamp and went over her lines with the stuffed fox.

'Good evening, may I take your coats please?'

'This way to the drawing room, sir.'

'Would you like a glass of champagne, ma'am?'

'For our first course we are having crab bisque.'

'Would you care for some roast potatoes?'

'Coffee, sir? And some petits fours?'

Audrey said it was a success when no one really noticed that the housekeeper was there. But Laura didn't care now what anyone thought and for once she thought it would be nice to be noticed.

Later she was to eat a bit in the kitchen and wait until they were finished and then start the washing-up.

'Like a dog with a bowl in the corner,' Laura said to herself and she was annoyed with Audrey for suggesting this.

'Good night, sir. Good night, ma'am.'

She was to stand inside the front door with their coats. She was already exhausted by the thought of it. She might just kick them up the backside on their way out.

When the car turned around on the gravel it made the hallway bright and Laura stood for a minute as if caught in a spotlight. The doorbell jangled and she saw a blonde woman wearing a lot of make-up and her hair done up like bread rolls on her head. Laura went to the drinks trolley and poured herself a whiskey and drank it.

She opened the door and stood there for a moment looking at them. She was supposed to say something but she couldn't remember what it was. She closed the door again. Through the glass the man lifted his eyebrows and began to laugh a bit as if he was embarrassed.

'Good evening,' Laura said finally, 'may I have your coats?'

She knew then that she was supposed to invite them in first but she had forgotten that part. They stepped into the hall smiling and then Audrey and Finn appeared and there was a lot of kissing and crying out and Laura was left with the expensive coats and scarves. Where was she supposed to put these? She rolled them up and left them on the yellow couch under the window. The drawing-room door closed and she went to the trolley and took another drink.

'Down the hatch,' she said and she raised her glass to the stuffed fox.

'Good evening, ladies and gentlemen, may I take your coats?'

'Good evening, give us those coats.'

'Good evening, throw your coats on the couch. They're all in there . . . as drunk as sticks.'

Laura brought in the champagne and poured a glass for herself and stood there with the guests.

'To life,' she said, raising her glass.

Finn turned the music up and Audrey looked at her and shook her head. Laura went into the kitchen to carve the ducks.

When the door opened again she was carrying the carving knife and the woman with the blonde hair in rolls gave a little gasp.

'It's time to go into the dining room,' she said but no one moved.

Her hair had come loose and there was a long streak of duck fat down her apron. Finn looked at her with half-closed eyes. Then he looked at Audrey and grinned.

'I said – will you go into the dining room now and sit down.'

The guests put their drinks on the table and hurried out.

'And what are we having?' Audrey gave her a prompt.

'Crab's . . .' She stopped.

'Pardon?'

Laura looked hard at the soup bowls.

'Piss,' she said finally.

'Bisque,' Audrey said and she cleared her throat.

Laura left the room and began to laugh down into her apron.

Audrey followed her to the kitchen. She stood and watched her fill the coffeepot and didn't speak.

'After the coffee . . . I think you better go to bed.'

Laura carried on as if she hadn't heard a word.

'Would you care for some roast potatoes?' She seemed to remember one rolling off a plate. Then there was the spinach that landed on a woman's foot. She had stood there and watched as they ate everything she had cooked. They didn't speak to her and no one even said thanks or that it tasted good.

'You greedy bastards,' Laura said.

Audrey lifted her glass quickly to 'my wonderful husband'.

Finn stood up and proposed a toast to 'my lovely wife'. The others clapped and cheered and tried to drown the housekeeper out.

It was late when Audrey and Finn went to bed. They had stayed on in the kitchen and finished the washing-up. The cutlery was dried and polished and the tablecloth left to soak.

'It was a disaster,' Audrey said on the stairs.

'Everything she cooked was very good . . .'

'Her legs were plaiting under her with the drink.'

'She had had a few, no doubt.'

'We should let her go,' Audrey said quietly, 'but that will mean losing Mattie . . . and I don't want to do that.'

It was a while before Finn spoke and when he did he sounded very tired. The stairs creaked and when Laura peeped out she could see them sitting together on the top step.

'How badly do you want him, Audrey?'

'More than anything in the world.'

'Then maybe we should talk to Mary Costello or Father Meehan and see what they think.'

'And what will we tell them . . . that she got drunk?'

'Among other things. Didn't Dooley say he saw her out on the bloody roof? Is she right in the head, do you think?'

Audrey didn't answer.

They got up and walked arm in arm to their bedroom.

'Poor Laura,' she said then, 'she's just not able to cope. Bringing up a baby on her own is too much.'

'Then maybe we can step in and give her some help . . . give her a break.' Here there was some kindness in his voice that Laura recognized from when they first met.

'I would give anything to be able to care for that little boy,' Audrey said.

Laura stood very still on the back stairs and listened and then she found the blue suitcase and began to pack. Finn and Audrey's bedroom door was closed now and their voices were muffled. They talked on and on, quietly and in secret. Mattie slept soundly and she sat on the side of the bed watching him, until the sun came up.

In the early hours she opened the trapdoor again and climbed out. She would cook their last breakfast in the kitchen and take the ferry back. When she looked down, Finn was standing on the front lawn in his pyjamas looking up at her. He was trying to say something but when he opened his mouth no sound came out. Dooley appeared carrying a ladder and then they both stared up at her as if she was the Virgin Mary appearing to them on the roof. In her mind she considered blessing them. 'The baby, the baby,' someone shouted then and it sounded like Audrey. Audrey in her pink dressing gown and slippers clip-clopping out of the house. She realized then that Finn thought she was going to jump, that what had happened between them could send her flying to a ground made solid with another late frost. White crystals covered the box hedge. The shrubs in the garden had been blackened by it. 'No man is worth breaking bones for,' Laura wanted to tell him but what was the point? Instead she would go back to her wooden house and read tea leaves. When she looked towards the island now though, she couldn't see it. A thick fog had come down and the lighthouse and the people had disappeared into it.

36

Laura watched the morning sun brighten the attic and looked out the window towards the island. It was not possible to see the sea from here but if she closed her eyes she could imagine hearing it. She could not stay in a house any more where the furniture was polished and the beds were made and the husband and wife loved each other. Laura knew that she did not belong in a world as perfect as this. She held Mattie in her arms and kissed his cheeks.

'I'm taking you home,' she said.

She sat in the window seat and could see the chimneys of Drumquin in the distance. The lawn was deserted again and she could hear Finn and Audrey coming up the stairs and closing their bedroom door. The river stretched like a ribbon in front of her and she would follow it. Most of her wages were saved and she still had the money her mother left her. She could go to America or she could start again on the island and open her own seaweed baths. She thought about the grey rocks and the seagulls on the island, the broken-down barbed-wire fences with black plastic caught there in tatters. There were signs on the road that said 'For sale, sheepdog pups' and 'Topsoil wanted'. The people who lived there had nothing, except a plot that a parent or an old aunt had left. Some of the houses had no roads leading to them at all. The coast road shrivelled up after the lighthouse and then turned to a gravel path and then to grass covered in sheep tracks. The people had nothing except each other and the sea and the rocks to look at.

She waited until half past seven and then went downstairs and got the breakfast ready. She took particular care with their porridge and mixed some Jersey cream into it. She wasn't wearing the black linen dress or the apron any more. She had her case packed and closed on the bed. Mattie was already wearing his coat and eating his breakfast in his chair. She put a fresh white tablecloth on the dining-room table and stood there in her old blue blouse and skirt. She had found the cardigan with the holes in the elbows and the shoes with the broken heels that her mother had worn before her. She did not know what they would say to her but whatever was coming she wanted to be in her own clothes to face it. She would say sorry to Audrey first. Audrey who had taught her how to cook and clean and had never once made her feel like a servant. She would stand there and say sorry to her from the bottom of her heart. She would not even look at Finn. She would cook him the soft fried egg with the crispy bacon that he liked. She would stand silently at his shoulder and slide the plate on to the tablemat and then silently step back. On her last day in his house, she would be nothing but the perfect servant.

She sat at the kitchen table and ate her own breakfast and then she heard them coming quietly down the stairs. She had expected to see them in their dressing gowns again but instead Audrey was wearing a grey suit and Finn was in his good tweed jacket.

'Good morning,' they said and Laura waited until she heard the chairs scrape the floor of the dining room and then she went inside.

'I'm sorry,' she said simply, '. . . for everything.'

239

She stood there and felt some white morning sunlight on her face. She had washed her hair and it lay in a pale sheet on her back.

'Now, Laura,' Audrey's voice came first and Laura thought she could hear a tremor in it. 'Don't worry at all about it.'

She was sitting across from Finn and there were dark circles around her eyes. Her face was pale and she looked as if she had been crying all night.

'None of us got much sleep . . . so let's not even talk about it,' she said.

Laura glanced at Finn and waited for him to say something. The newspaper remained folded and he sat very still and looked down at the tablecloth.

'Let's just forget about it,' he said and he lifted his spoon and began to scoop up the porridge.

'Laura, you look tired. Why don't you go upstairs and have a rest?' Audrey said.

'I'm planning on going back to the island . . . I think it's better for me and Mattie. I was thinking of going now, this morning, after you've had your breakfast.'

Audrey glanced at Finn and he looked up at Laura at last.

'There's no need for that,' he said. 'Take the rest of the morning off and we'll talk after lunch.'

'Where's Mattie?' Audrey asked.

'He's in the kitchen . . . having his toast soldiers.'

'You can leave him here with me while you sleep.'

When Laura woke she sat up straight in her bed. The grey light of morning was gone and the house was very quiet. She had slept for hours and the ferry would leave at two o'clock. She picked up her suitcase and went downstairs to find Mattie.

Instead she found Audrey waiting at the bottom of the stairs.

'Hello, Laura,' she said and she swallowed and then lifted her chin up. She was still wearing that grey suit and holding her hands together down near her skirt. There was a gold brooch on her lapel and her hair was pulled back into a low ponytail. Laura could see the first grey hairs at her temples.

'Have you been to mass?' Laura asked. 'You should have woken me.'

'No. I didn't go to mass today.'

Around them in the cool dark hall the air seemed different. The furniture hadn't changed at all but when Laura opened her mouth it was as if the air had a different taste. The grandfather clock was still inside the door. The small brass gong was standing under the window. The little drinks trolley with all its glasses washed and shining stood in the shadows under the stairs. Laura's eyes were still heavy with sleep and she needed a drink of water. She glanced in the direction of the kitchen and Audrey put one hand on her arm as if to stop her.

'Will you come into the drawing room, please?'

'Why?'

'We need to talk to you.'

'Where's Mattie?'

'Matthew is fine. Please come inside.'

Laura saw then that the door was already open and the soft cream and green flowered rug was waiting. She crossed the hall with Audrey and could not understand why she was suddenly shaking.

'I'm sorry about the dinner party.'

They stopped at the doorway and it was Audrey who hesitated.

'I had a long talk with Finn last night. He told me everything,' she said. 'I know what happened on the island.'

Laura stood very still and looked down at her. For an odd moment she wanted to put her arms around her and comfort her

241

but she felt too awkward. From where she stood she could see Audrey's gold wedding band and her engagement ring that had three round diamonds.

'I had an inking,' Audrey said quietly as if she was talking to herself. 'An idea that maybe . . . but who wants thoughts like that?'

Laura turned towards the door and took another step but Audrey stopped her again.

'There are some other people here . . . who want to talk to you.'

'Who?'

'Father Meehan, Mary Costello.'

'What are they here for? Is that the one we call Holy Mary?'

'She's a social worker, Laura, and the sergeant is here as well.' She glanced down at the floor and then looked up at Laura.

'Where's Mattie?' Laura asked again.

'Don't worry, he's fine,' and then Laura felt her warm hand at the small of her back, guiding her in.

The people who wanted to talk to her were sitting at the fire. There was tea on a low table and she could see that they were eating her fresh scones with damson jam. The sergeant was smiling and he had left his Guard's cap on the piano stool behind him. He was saying something about the local rugby team.

'They have no scrum . . . no scrum at all,' he said, his voice rising as she came in.

Mary Costello was sitting at the end of the yellow couch holding a cup and saucer and she gave Laura a smile as she lifted her cup. Then there was Finn, sitting in his usual chair, his long legs crossed and a cigarette in his hand. The fire was blazing and the flames came up from under fresh ash logs that sparked and crackled.

'Sit down here, Laura,' Finn said and she saw then that a

special green leather chair had been parked in the middle of the rug and she was to sit in it and face this firing squad.

The door opened and Father Meehan came in, rubbing his hands.

'Well, there you are now,' he said to Laura.

Audrey offered him another cup of tea and he said, 'Just a hot drop then.'

There were no scones left at all and someone had dropped jam into the butter dish.

Laura sat very still and listened as silence came. The casual words seemed to fall away and cups were replaced quietly on their saucers.

Father Meehan spoke first.

'This is difficult for all of us here, Laura,' he said.

She could feel the fire at her back and she wondered if the chair could melt from the heat. The room was so quiet without Mattie. She wished she could feel the weight of him on her lap. The clock on the mantelpiece chimed once. She had never missed him so much in her life.

'We're all concerned about you, Laura,' Mary Costello said quietly and she leaned towards her as if she was trying to push these words into the green chair.

Father Meehan went on and now he was speaking to her with his head tilted to one side.

'We are all different in this world,' he said, 'but when a child's safety and welfare are at stake . . . there are times when something needs to be said.'

The sergeant cleared his throat and looked down into his cup.

'We're worried about the child,' Father Meehan said and he wet his lips and looked up into Laura's eyes.

'Mattie?' Laura asked. 'Why?'

'We're concerned that he might not be safe.'

'Of course he's safe . . . Why wouldn't he be safe?'

'We're concerned that he might not be safe . . . with you,' Mary Costello whispered.

'With you.' Father Meehan added the same words quietly and nodded as if it was the saddest thing he had ever said.

Laura could feel herself sinking. It was as if she was looking at a map and she had just realized where she was on it.

'Where is he?' she asked. Her voice was steady and she tried to breathe.

'Now don't make things harder for yourself,' the sergeant said.

Laura looked over at Audrey. She was sitting on the arm of Finn's chair holding on to his hand. Finn sat very still and when he finally looked at Laura, his eyes were like two grey stones in his head. He said nothing and his face reminded her of one of the deserted cottages on the island, with the broken windows, so you could see the fields through it.

'We've spoken to a number of people about you and some even came forward of their own accord,' Mary Costello said.

'Who have you talked to?' Laura asked. She could feel herself and the green chair melt into the carpet.

'Some people from the island . . . People from the village . . . and now Mr and Mrs Campbell, who are well respected in the community . . . John Dooley, and some of the people who were here last night.'

'And what are they saying about me?'

No one said anything for a minute and Laura looked at each face in turn.

Finally it was Finn who broke the silence.

'That you might not be able to manage . . . raising a child.'

'Manage . . . but . . .'

'We've had our concerns for a while now. You left your

244

husband and we heard that you might be fond of a drop,' Mary Costello said and she gave a little nod of her head.

'I hardly drink at all,' Laura whispered.

'Apparently last night there were . . . a few problems. The guests here . . . well, they were very worried about their own safety at one point.'

'You came into the room . . . brandishing a knife,' the sergeant added.

'And what were you doing this morning, taking the baby out on the roof?' Mary Costello asked.

'Mattie is safe with me,' she said. 'Mrs Campbell will tell you that.'

Laura looked over at Audrey and when Audrey looked back she gave the slightest shake of her head. Then she looked down sadly at her hands which were folded on her lap.

'Sometimes decisions need to be made for the good of a child,' Father Meehan said. 'I mean to say . . . sometimes other people need to step in and . . . put the child somewhere safe.'

She could hear her own heart beating. It had travelled upwards from her chest and it was beating hard near her throat.

'It wouldn't be permanent,' Audrey said quickly.

'Well, that's not certain either,' the sergeant added and he grimaced then at his own words.

'Where is Mattie?' Laura asked again in a low voice.

The sergeant leaned forward and joined his hands so that his fingertips were pointing at Laura.

'If in time we felt you were managing better, then we would all reconsider and the plan would be that . . .'

'That we would give him back,' Audrey said and now her voice was suddenly bright.

'He's not yours to take,' Laura replied and as she watched, Finn clenched and unclenched his fist.

'Please . . . Where is he?'

Audrey spoke up again.

'If anything was to happen to him I would never forgive myself,' she said.

'You will never forgive yourself anyway.' Laura spoke quietly and she could feel a tear begin to make its way down her cheek. The way they presented her with all of this made her begin to wonder if they were right.

'There's nothing wrong with me,' she said and she was crying now.

'It is very hard for a woman on her own to manage,' Father Meehan said.

They sat there in a circle around her and listened as she wept.

'Please tell me where he is,' Laura said and no one answered and in her mind she was running through the rooms, opening doors, brushing against walls, calling, calling, calling until she could hear his voice, 'Mama, Mama, Mama,' echoing around the house.

'Where is he?' she asked again and now she sounded worn out. She got up from her chair and ran for the door. The sergeant caught her arm as she went and he spoke gently to her.

'Now, don't make it worse for yourself. You're not a bad girl, we all know that.'

Audrey got up and Laura could see that she was crying as well.

'Laura,' she said and she took her hand. 'He's somewhere safe now and if you like . . . we could care for him here. That means he won't have to go into any kind of . . . place.'

'Do you mean an orphanage?' Laura asked. Her head was spinning and the ground was moving towards her.

'He's not an orphan. He has a mother,' she said before anyone answered.

*

246

She sat upstairs in the attic and looked into the empty cot. There was no point in running and screaming through the house like a mad woman because he was no longer in it. Everything was too quiet and empty without him, especially herself. She looked at the small cotton sheet and closed her eyes to imagine him. His long dark lashes resting on his pink cheeks. If he was there she would touch his nose with her fingertip. His voice would be calling out to her, the babble that could be heard like music through the house. She had lost him and there was nothing she could do about it. They had taken him away when she was asleep. The best they could offer her was a home for him in this house. At least she would know where he was, they said. If she climbed to the top of the lighthouse she might see him running on the grass at the front. On a clear day it might be arranged that he and she would fly a kite, one on the island and one on the mainland. She would come back some night and take him back but she didn't say that. They thought she had a slate loose and no one wanted to actually say it. Now she thought she was going around the twist herself. They could give him everything and she had nothing at all for him except herself. From what those people said that didn't count for much.

She was to visit a special doctor from the mainland. A woman who understood what went on inside people's heads. There was medication, they said. She wasn't to drink. If she had any suicidal thoughts she was to contact Father Meehan even if it was in the middle of the night. She might need to go into a special hospital if things didn't improve. A place where they had all kinds of treatments. They would assess her after a month, then after three months, then after six. At the end of a year they would make a decision about where her son should live.

In the meantime she would see him once a month. They would take him to the island or she could go to their house.

A year without Mattie, Laura thought. There was all sorts of talk and plans and she wanted no part of it. What was 'once a month' when she had been with him for every day and night of his life? She might as well be standing at his grave.

The taxi came and she stood beside it with the priest and the sergeant. They would take her back to her house on the island and set a date for her first visit.

'Come on now, Laura,' they said.

'You can both drop dead,' she answered and she looked at Audrey instead.

If they had decided she was a nutter then she might as well go along with it. Finn was not there to say goodbye and she was glad of that. Only Audrey stood at the big double doors with her arms folded, her hands catching her elbows, as if she was cold. Her eyes were still red and her lips seemed thinner as if her smile had been lost. They kept on talking to her as they stood there on the gravel, promising her this and that, and she held on to her suit-case and heard none of it. Instead she tried to remember her last day with Mattie and how many times she had kissed him. She could only remember him sitting behind her when she was plucking the ducks and he was trying to catch the floating feathers.

Laura turned around to face Audrey again. She still had a question for her and she needed an answer. She walked back to the door again and looking straight into her face. 'How can you do this?' she asked. 'How? Tell me now so I can understand it.'

'Oh, Laura . . .' Audrey said quietly and she seemed to hug herself tightly for some kind of comfort. She looked away then and squinted into the sky and that was the only answer she seemed capable of.

'If there's any God at all,' Laura said, 'you'll go straight to hell for this.'

248

The sound of her own voice seemed too loud and the trees around her were wild with starlings.

She cried all the way to the boat and when the priest tried to comfort her she turned to the window and stared out. She put her hands flat on the glass and pushed. She felt as if she had been split in half. She concentrated on breathing and standing up and then walking and that would be enough for a start. When she found herself alone again in her house she thought she could hear him crying. She looked around her but could not see him. It was like hearing the sea inside a shell, a strange whispering sound that she knew would haunt her.

37

She went back to the island and found that a tree had fallen on her house. The roof was crushed, the gable split in half. There were branches meeting her inside the front door. It was still locked, the key under a shell on the windowsill where she had left it. Daylight was coming in through the branches and there were green leaves brushing against her face. The crash had been recent. There was a freshness to it and the branches were leaking new sap. In one part there was a nest with a single blue egg in it. A circle of feathers and twigs that glittered because the bird had found some Christmas tinsel.

Clever little bird, she thought.

Laura sat on the floor and cried with the branches. She cried for herself and for the tree and for the bird who had lost its egg. She cried for any living thing that had been a mother and had lost its chick. She thought about the sheep and had more respect for them. She had seen them on the side of the steep paths, nuzzling the little body, frozen in snow, its eyes taken out by seagulls and rooks.

The house was brighter than before. When she looked up she could see the sky through the roof. In summer she would lie on the couch and bake herself. Most of the time though she knew it would be wet. The tree had come in and broken her house and now it gave some sort of shelter in its place. She had no desire to cut off the branches. She put her hands on the bark and felt its rough skin instead. She imagined she was patting an elephant's big foot. Part of the south gable was gone but mostly the tree had done for the roof. She wanted to keep the tree and sleep under it. She could not bring herself to go downstairs. The last time she had been down there she had had Mattie in her arms. Something inside her shifted suddenly and for a moment she wasn't able to breathe right. Whatever it was hurt her so much that it blocked her windpipe. With him she was allowed into the world, without him she was disconnected. Mattie had anchored her. He had pulled her down and stopped her from floating off into space.

She sat on the blue sofa under a canopy of leaves and no one came to visit her. There was no glass left in the windows and the wind was blowing straight into her face. The sea seemed closer than before and if she closed her eyes she could imagine it swirling around her feet. The front door was swinging on its hinges and in the first week of March there were sudden grey flecks of sleet. She wore the same clothes every day. The blue cardigan and the blue skirt. She had let them take her child away. What sort of mother would do that? One who was short of feelings. One who couldn't feel the cold. She watched as a man walked a white dog on her road.

'Look, Mattie, a dog, see that, Mattie, see that dog?'

She thought about the white cat on the river bank. She closed her eyes. She woke on a Wednesday feeling stiff and smelling mildew from her clothes. When she turned around she saw Martin Cronin standing on her porch.

He was wearing the cream fisherman's jumper and there was a hole in the front. His jacket was green and waterproof, the check cap the same one she remembered. She sat very still and looked at him. He stood without moving. There was a chainsaw in one of his hands. Laura didn't get up.

'I hear you have a tree down,' he said.

She looked at him again but didn't speak. He took his cap off and scratched the top of his head. He looked around the room slowly and without any awkwardness, as if it was his own house. His eyes took in the kitchen with the used plates and cups in stacks. He took in the tree with the leaves that were withering now as if autumn had come into the house. The wind whistled around him and he sat down on a wooden rocker and began to rock gently with the chainsaw on his lap. Laura sat very still and watched him, her eyes round behind her glasses. She did not want to see anyone but he didn't bother her too much.

'How is your boiler?' he asked suddenly and Laura looked down at her feet. 'We'll have to check that it's working. You'll need a hot tank.'

She only heard 'we' and then tuned out after that.

In the end he put the chainsaw on the floor between them and offered her his hand. She saw that it was calloused, that he had a small c-shaped cut on one finger from a fishhook. Everyone on the island had a cut like that. It was unusual for Martin though and it meant that he hadn't had his mind on the job. She looked at the hand as if it was not human but a strange object made from wood. When she put her own into it, it was out of curiosity and she was surprised by its rough warmth. He pulled her to her feet and guided her into the kitchen where he steered her on to a low stool. She sat there and held its round sides as if she was in danger of falling off. Martin went back into the sitting room and glancing back at her once, he pulled the cord on the chain saw and stood for a moment with it bubbling and revving in his hands. The diesel fumes rose and he looked at the tree for a second, choosing his target, and then looking back at Laura again he leaned in and began to cut the tree up. The noise filled the house and the smell of fuel was a comfort. She could hide behind all of it and watch him do his work. She had liked the tree and she would miss stepping around it. She would miss the inconvenience. She knew that he would cut it into logs that would end up in her stove at night.

Martin looked up through the roof and said he would need to borrow a longer ladder.

'I can put some plastic over it today and then get some of the men to help me. We'll have to measure up for planks before we can fix it.'

Laura had always known that there was some kindness in him but this was the first time he had come to her and released it. And it was because of Mattie. He had changed him and brought the good part out. She could tell by Martin's eyes that he knew what had happened and now because he too loved the boy he was trying to help her through it.

Martin swept up the sawdust and put the logs in a stack at the side of her house. A car passed him on the road and he waved. Some part of her knew that he had been seen helping Laura Quinn and that he was not ashamed. He found cardboard and taped it over the broken windows and he wrote down some measurements for glass. Through all of this, Laura watched and could not speak. Her own loss and her shame was causing her to choke. He filled the kettle and made tea for them and then he nodded once at her and with one hand on her arm, he guided her back to the sitting room again. It grew darker and they didn't put on the light. Laura sat on the couch and looked over at Martin. She could hear him swallow and breathe in and out through his nose. She watched the space that he was in and it felt like she was seeing a priest behind the screen in the confessional box.

'I lost him,' she said.

'I know.'

'How did you hear about it?'

'They came asking questions.'

'What did you tell them, Martin?' and even as she said the words she already knew that he wasn't to blame.

'Nothing,' he answered. 'I was on my way into town. I had a few lambs for the mart. I had no time to talk.'

'But they knew . . .'

'They said they wanted to know something about my wife. I said I had no wife.'

Laura had nothing to say in response. He had denied her and that didn't matter a bit. She would have done the same thing herself.

'Maddy Hughes had something to say though. And the Farleys up the road. And that old bitch Patricia McKenna stuck her oar in. Even Boy Lucas's mother, although she wasn't the worst . . . but when they put it all together . . .' and here Martin waited and picked the words, 'When they put it all together . . . I believe it didn't sound too good.'

Laura and Martin sat in the dark and then she began to cry. She put her head back and cried soft tears up towards the roof. She had cried a lot since Mattie had been taken. Now even her crying was different. It was soft and weak like an animal that had been caught in a trap.

'Would you have said anything good at all, Martin?' she asked and she took her glasses off and wiped snot and tears on to her sleeve. Sitting there beside him she could smell his oilskin coat and old sweat off herself.

Martin stayed quiet for a minute.

'I would have said that you didn't deserve to lose the boy,' he said. 'That is what I would have said.'

Laura put her head down on his lap and wept and he put one hand on the back of her neck and rested it there.

'I'm lost, Martin.'

He waited for a long time before answering.

'As am I,' he replied.

The furniture grew. The gas cooker towered over her. The windows became monuments. She sat opposite her mother's rocker and talked as if she was still sitting there. Once she lay on the wooden floor and traced the dark rivers that ran through it. The windows were replaced and the grass was cut. It was still the most beautiful house on the island but without his little say-so what was the point? On the nights when she felt stronger she tried to face it and on nights like that she would go and sit on the beach and let the waves come closer and closer until she got drenched. She would lie on the sand then, flat out and soaked. For some reason it was slightly easier to bear when she was thoroughly wet. And then suddenly she was stronger and well enough to stand up and begin the walk back. But the sun coming up like a raspberry made her forget again and suddenly she was pointing it out to him and saying, 'Look, look,' and with that she went down on to the sand again and lay with her face in it, hiding and buried.

On another night she imagined that it was not possible – that losing him was something she had dreamt. She would go out and look for him. She would shake every tree and beat back the grass. She would hold him again. She had to believe that. Some nights she pretended he was there, otherwise she would die from the pain of it. She wondered if there was a voodoo doll with white hair in someone's house on the island. Her heart was riddled with pinpricks.

38

17 March

Martin came again on St Patrick's Day. He knocked on the glass in her door and stood looking at the empty window box.

When she answered he said, 'Do you want to go to the parade?'

She was wearing one of her old white nightdresses and the wind made it wrap around her legs. The forecast was for snow again. The winter had stretched into spring and there seemed to be no end to it. She had been on the couch cutting her toenails and thinking about seeing the head doctor the following week.

'The parade?' she said. For a minute she thought he wanted her to be in it.

'The Balally Pipers are playing. They're meeting up at the National School and then marching down the coast road. The fat Farley girl is going to lead them.'

The shamrock was limp in his lapel but he sounded interested. He had the hungry look of someone who had been up too early and had washed himself in cold water before mass. She could imagine the pipers, blue with cold, crying into their whistles. The whole island would be out. Martin's green bathroom came to her in a flash. She had a hard time believing that she had been in it. That she had stood in his house, that they had shared the same bed and sink.

She went downstairs and took a bath and considered drowning herself. It was becoming a daily ritual for her, lying there and imagining going under the water, the idea itself bringing a kind of relief. Instead she got out and found a pair of clean corduroys and the Aran jumper with the round neck. It still smelled like her father when she was inside it. He was close to her again in a whiff of coarse yarn and pipe smoke. She put a red scarf around her head and tied it the way Audrey had shown her. Her hair was still wet when she clipped it up.

She sat into Martin's car and he glanced at her and winked. She looked straight ahead and wondered if they were the 'village eejits' that people often talked about. It had occurred to her to wink back. They passed the pipers who were sitting in the boot of someone's car, their round white knees sticking out.

'A cold day for kilts,' Martin said.

He parked the car at the high end of the village and they sat under a sign that said 'McGrath's!' and 'Breakfast served all day – and lunch!'

The pipes gave a squeal and the parade began to move slowly past the old Sunrise guesthouse. A wooden fruit crate hung on the door that said 'Parcels Here' in bad handwriting. It had been closed up for years. A tangle of wooden chairs was piled up inside the front window. Father Meehan marched behind the pipers along with four altar boys, their surplices flapping, their faces frozen and white. Molloy's hardware shop had a sign advertising itself on someone's trailer. Two youngsters carried a banner that said 'McKenna's Select Bar'. A tractor appeared carrying St Patrick on a front loader and the crowd cheered and clapped. He waved and then blessed Laura and Martin.

They got out of the car and began to follow the crowd down the laneway to the village beach. People stepped out of her way and were quiet around her. One of the tourists asked if he could take her photograph. She knew what he saw of course, the sea and her wind-burnt cheeks, the red headscarf and behind her a white cottage with green shutters on the windows. There was even an old black bicycle leaning on the gable. He would get her to stand there and then go back to America and show his friends what Whale Island was like. He would say, 'This is one of the islanders,' and they would see that she was ridiculous.

Laura went to the cottage and stood where he asked. She stood in the middle of the narrow gravel lane between the cottage and the long green line of windblown rushes that ran down to the beach. The sea was wild and grey behind her. Mrs Murtagh came out and shook the dust from the mat on her doorstep. She was wearing a long black dress with her hair in a bun. She went back inside like one of the weather people as soon as the camera came out.

Laura took her glasses off and stood there and waited. The tourist adjusted his lens and began to click.

'That's perfect,' he said.

The crowd waited quietly behind him. Martin leaned on a wall and spoke to Barney Maguire. They lit cigarettes, sheltering the match in cupped hands. The islanders continued to gather behind the man with the camera, and without her glasses Laura could see heads without faces and she preferred them that way.

She began to move and the tourist said, 'No, wait, just one more . . . near these rushes.'

She glanced back and saw that the whole island was watching her. No one said a word and she stood there for a moment, waiting. She thought one of them would say something but instead she got blurred people and silence. She turned her back and began to walk across the patchy grass, following a line of broken sheep wire that led her down to the beach. Only Martin followed her. She knew that it took courage now to do that but she didn't want it. She wanted to be on her own now and she didn't appreciate whatever it was that he was trying to offer her.

The wind threw dry white sand at them. It had the same sting as salt and they walked on through it. They came to a railway sleeper and sat down together. A tourist couple came towards them wearing coloured hats and holding hands. They asked Martin if he would take their picture.

'It's our anniversary,' the woman said.

'How long?' Laura asked, suddenly interested.

'Forty-five years,' and the man and woman looked at each other and laughed as if the whole thing was a joke.

'I can't believe it,' the woman said and it sounded like she really meant that.

Martin lined them up on the sand and they put their arms around each other. The waves hit black rocks and sent the spray high, soaking all of them. The couple grabbed each other and laughed. The camera clicked. Laura looked into the sea and missed Mattie. She was in some sort of pain and getting used to it. She knew now that it moved around her body, at times taking root in her chest, and today, because Martin was trying to distract her, it had settled in her mouth like a toothache.

'You need a plan,' Martin said.

He had given the camera back and then came and sat near her again. The parade was moving further up the coast road in fits and starts. The pipers would only play for a few minutes and then they got into cars to warm themselves.

Laura wanted to ignore him but it was hard not to move closer to him in the cold.

259

'Come on up to McGrath's for some coffee and a slice of cake,' he said.

The idea of eating made her feel sick.

'What sort of plan?' she asked.

Martin got up from the sleeper and took a few steps down the beach. She could hear shingle cracking under his boots. He stood with his back to her, his hands on his hips. The wind blew his hair straight back from his face and she realized in an unusually clear moment that his profile was perfect. 'His side-face', as the islanders would call it. There in the blue wind she looked at him and saw a work of art. Laura heard her own thoughts then and she wondered if she was completely mad now or if she was just off her rocker a bit. Sitting there in a huddle, admiring Martin Cronin in the wind, she realized that the real madness only came now – and it must have been caused from losing her child and the white loneliness that had followed.

He turned and caught her eye and smiled. They looked well enough together and they both knew it. On the outside they were no different from the other couple on the beach. Inside, it was a different story. When he looked at her again, she looked away. There were only so many times you could plough the same field and expect something green to come out of it.

Laura got up before he could offer his hand and walked ahead of him towards McGrath's. She had put her glasses back on and as she passed through the broken stone walls the people who had hung around talking grew quiet again. She looked into their faces and they looked straight back at her now as if they were also in pain. She realized in that moment that the whole island missed him, that they were mourning him as if something of theirs had been lost.

In McGrath's, Bridget Nolan stood behind the counter and told Laura about the cakes.

'We have lemon drizzle cake – and this one is chocolate strawberry – we have a tea brack, ginger cake, apple and rhubarb crumble . . . and, of course, apple tart.'

Martin stood at the glass counter and seemed dazzled.

'I'll have a slice of apple tart,' he said and Bridget laughed.

'Playing it safe, Martin,' she said.

The apron was tight across her round stomach and Laura wondered if she was eating many of these cakes herself. She told Martin to get her some tea and she sat down at a corner table. Bridget came with the tea on a tray and a slice of lemon drizzle cake.

'It'll do you good,' she said.

Martin sat down and poured the milk and then the tea into the cups.

'What sort of plan were you talking about?' Laura asked.

He sipped his tea and grimaced as if he had been scalded.

'To get the child back,' he said.

39

The doctor who was to examine her head arrived in a hackney car. She was carrying a purple handbag and had shoes to match. She had a fancy purple shawl that kept falling off her shoulders.

'I'm Doctor Marron,' she said and she produced a box of tissues and put them on the table between them.

'What are they for?' Laura asked and Doctor Marron gave a big smile and shrugged.

She was the sort of woman who smiled when there was nothing to smile about.

'So, Laura,' she began, 'you've been having some problems.'

She sat back in her chair and watched Laura's face.

'People often find the first assessment difficult. If you feel like crying that's all right.'

'Thanks,' Laura said and she looked out the window.

She had no intention of crying. By now she was used to covering her heart and would not open it up to a total stranger.

'If you could just tell me a few things about yourself, I can make an assessment.'

'Like what?'

'Like . . . what are you thinking about at the moment?'

'I'm thinking about my son.'

'That you miss him?'

'I don't think about missing him.'

'Then what were you thinking about?'

'Just him. How he was. How I remember him.'

'Can you tell me about your mother . . . ?'

'She read tea leaves. She was very good at it. She had long curly hair. She died.'

'How did she die?'

'I can't remember.'

'And what was your father like . . . ?'

'He had glasses. He wore an Aran jumper and smoked a pipe. He died too.'

'Were there any siblings?'

'No.'

'Is there a history of mental illness in your family?'

'You would have to ask my parents about that.'

'Were your schooldays happy?'

'No.'

'Have you had any significant relationships?'

And here Martin floated into her mind as if he had wings. She did not know what to say about him. She would not have used the word 'significant'.

The doctor tilted her head to one side as if she was amused.

'You really need to cooperate with us,' she said finally.

'Why? Why do I need to cooperate with you?'

'We're trying to help you.'

'Can you help me to get him back?'

'Perhaps. In time.'

Laura felt that the woman was useless. She had expected her to have a special machine with wires and lights for looking inside her head. She would have liked to show her the jumble of thoughts that whirled around like a sandstorm, the plans, the hopes, the dreams, the disappointments that she had had. Her head was like a chocolate box, turned upside down a few times so that every different flavour had lost its place. The doctor in purple sat back and smiled gently at her as if she was the strangest creature on earth.

Laura didn't speak now and the woman opposite didn't speak either. Instead she rearranged herself on the chair, pulled the shawl back up on her shoulders and prepared for a wait. She didn't know how comfortable Laura was with silence.

The clock on the wall ticked. From time to time the doctor wrote something into a small ring-bound notebook.

Probably her shopping list, Laura thought.

Three cars passed on the road and the sky lost its brightness. Before long a grey shadow had crept in. The women didn't eat or drink. Laura had nothing that she cared to offer her. They had made tea at the start and now the milk had a fly floating on it. Laura watched its wings and imagined drowning in sour milk. The doctor wrote something else into her book. She asked if she could use her bathroom and Laura pointed it out.

When she came back upstairs she said, 'You have a lovely house . . . very unusual.'

'Like the person living in it,' Laura replied.

The woman gave a little laugh and stretched herself. She stood in the middle of the floor and arched her back and stuck her elbows out.

'Eeeeeee – aaaaaaaaaaaaaaah,' she said softly and Laura watched.

'I have a one-year-old daughter myself.'

'What's her name?'

'Mary Ann.'

And for a moment the two children were holding a beam for them to stand on.

The doctor crossed the room in her big shoes and clopped like a pony. She had a big behind too and Laura wondered if she would need a lasso to get her out of her house.

'There is some medication that might help.'

'For what?'

'To calm everything down. They're not magic beans . . . they just put you on an even keel.'

Laura had never been on an even keel and wondered what that would be like.

'I'm going to recommend that you try these. It's a low dose of Valium. See how you get on and I'll see you again in a month.'

Laura looked at the small white box as if it would blow up.

'In the first week or so the pills might make you feel worse.'

'Great,' Laura said.

She got up and followed the doctor to the door.

'You should also try to get to bed early. Get fresh air every day. And a lot of my patients find that yoga helps.'

Laura smiled for the first time that morning. She had heard about the yoga hippies on the mainland. She could just see herself now standing on the side of a hill, bending and stretching with the sheep.

She sent word with the fat Farley girl.

'Tell Martin Cronin to come up to the house.'

The girl stood frozen to the spot and curled her top lip. There was a gap between her front teeth.

'You want me to walk the whole boreen road just to tell him that.'

'Yes or you can have a kick up the backside,' Laura said.

'You're mad,' the girl shouted and she took off in a slow trot.

She reminded Laura of a baby elephant, only not as pleasant. She had seen her lead the parade down the coast road with the green beret cocked on the side of her head, grinning insanely, delighted with herself. She knew that the girl would go to Martin because she was afraid not to. Half the island thought she was mad. The other half thought she was a witch.

A fog came down and Martin spent the night in the lighthouse. He drank tea and closed his eyes and thought about Matthew. The light turned around slowly and made a grinding sound. It lit up his face and then turned it black again. He saw Laura behind his eyelids and had black and red thoughts.

The Farley girl had appeared at his hedge when he was out clipping it. The weather was getting warmer. He had taken his jacket off and hung it on the handle of the rake. In the morning the air smelled green and wet. He worked on in his shirtsleeves and felt his back getting damp. His arms were thin and sinewy, covered in black hairs. A thick blue vein ran like a rope from his elbow to his wrist. He had made a bonfire out near the orchard and put the couch and chairs on it. He had cleared out the kitchen presses, finding cans of fly spray, bottles of turpentine, old goose fat, brushes solid with paint. He had lifted the lino up and found more lino underneath it. He bought a new red carpet and walked on it in his bare feet.

Martin painted the skirting boards and opened the windows. He found some of her clothes hanging in the wardrobe and lifted them out and laid them on the bed. He straightened the white dress up so that it was like a person lying beside him. He lay down flat and tried to imagine her in it. She had driven him stone mad. He couldn't wait to get her out of his house. And yet, as soon as she had gone a new silence settled. It made his ears ring and gave him a pain in his head. Before her he had enjoyed his own company. He had been dull but content. Now she had ruined that. He didn't want to lose her completely and yet he knew he

266

could not take her back. He imagined walking out on the long pier with her, a grey slab of concrete surrounded by black rocks. He wondered if they could find some middle space to exist together. A husband and wife who got on well enough and used up most of their time walking over and back to each other's houses.

The Farley girl annoyed him. Just the sight of her tomato face, the straight girlish hair blowing around her head. She was puffed and defiant when she reached his gate.

'How is your mother keeping?' he asked.

He leaned out and clipped an errant sprig.

'She's grand,' she said. She had come up the road marching and swinging her arms like the sergeant.

'The Quinn woman wants to see you.'

'The Quinn woman?'

'The daft one who lives on our road.'

Martin put the clippers down and heard the blades scratch the concrete path. The first buds were out on the lilac bush. His mother had told him that it was bad luck to bring lilac into the house. His underwear was swinging on the line. A pair of white Y-fronts, a vest, a pair of black socks. If this picture was in a catalogue, he thought, the caption would be 'Bachelor' or 'Loneliness'. Just as his mother, with her tweed coat and her big round shoulders, would have been 'Salt of the earth'.

'She has a name,' he said.

The girl stood and looked at him and he could see her eyes narrow and move sideways as she tried to understand what he meant. She knew she had offended him in some way and now with the fog coming in she wasn't feeling as brave.

'Mrs Cronin,' she ventured.

'Ha' was all Martin said and he gave a quick shake of his head. He hooked his jacket off the rake with one finger. The new terrier appeared and began to bark at the girl. They both watched as the dog's hackles travelled in a fan up his thick neck. He began to dance around her feet and snap.

'Will he bite?' the girl cried out.

'He might,' Martin said. He felt for his car keys in his pocket.

'Her name is Laura,' the girl said and there were tears welling up.

More annoyance, Martin thought.

'That's right,' he said. 'Now go back and tell her I'll be there in the morning.'

'Are you not going to give me the lift back?'

'The walk will do you good.'

The girl's bottom lip gave a wobble.

'Off you go now.'

'But . . .'

Martin put his hand into his pocket and took out some baling twine and tied it around the dog's neck.

'Here,' he said, 'he'll keep you safe.'

The girl took the string reluctantly.

'What if the fairies lift me?' she asked.

'They wouldn't be able,' Martin said and he walked back to his house. He turned at the door and watched the two of them on the road. The donkey started braying over the wall, giving them a good send-off. He wondered what Laura wanted. He had some idea. He would ask her in the morning if he was the child's father. He had never got a definite no or yes. The terrier was bought for company but he didn't miss him at all now and the dog seemed happy enough with the girl, his short tail up like a cigarette butt.

40

In the morning Martin drove through the fog to find Laura. The white headstones in the children's cemetery looked lonely on the hillside. They were gathered together in the middle of nowhere, Eliza Quinn there with them, the headstones like a swarm of bees made from cement. No one ever went to visit them and they weren't allowed into the main cemetery because they had never been baptized. Matthew would end up there too if he died. The idea made him wind down his window to breathe.

The fog lifted as the car climbed Goat's Head.

'God is lifting his tablecloth,' Martin said. It was Laura who had told him that once.

Blue sky appeared and the seawater smelled clean and clear. He could see her down on the beach gathering seaweed, the giant cage on wheels making two long lines through the sand. The tide was going out and it had left silver rivers behind it. The sand was smooth where she stood and then fell into gentle folds with the waves. Further out it became soggy and he had seen a horse sink to its neck there once and drown. The same thing had happened to the whale that Lucas Boyle found.

He parked his car at her house and then took the wooden steps down to the beach. As he passed her gate he reached for a second pitchfork. She stopped what she was doing and looked up, her hands dropping a wet shell into her apron pocket.

'Morning,' she said.

'Not a bad day,' he replied.

The seaweed was lush and wet, oozing its amber jelly. That was the kind that made the best bath. The tourists came to the island for that and for the scenery. They paid good money to lie back in brown water and make their skin soft. It had become a ritual for most of them and they came back again and again for this. Once Martin had walked past the window and seen two fat German women taking a bath together. One had her head sticking out of the steam box and the other was lying there in the bath with her arms and legs spilling out.

'Not a pretty sight,' he told the men at the pub later.

They gathered the seaweed together. Now and then one of them broke a shell under foot and once their pitchforks tangled. Otherwise the only sounds came from the seagulls and a single curlew in the marsh. Their eyes met and they were like two scorpions fighting. Laura gave a little smile and he saw then that she looked different. Her hair was pulled back from her face and she wasn't wearing her glasses. He stood and looked out at the sea and wondered if it was possible for a person to change. Her skin was still pale and translucent, a faint blush in her cheeks from the early-morning wind. The freckles were still scattered everywhere like confetti but her eyes had a new light in them.

When the cage was full she said, 'Come up to the house for breakfast.'

The house was warm and it smelled of coffee and freshly baked scones. The table was set with a blue cloth covered in small pink flowers. There were pale blue cups and saucers, slices of fresh brown bread, a jug of cream and plum jam. He took off his jacket and he watched as she went to the oven and took out the tray of scones. She pressed one gently with her finger and nodded. The house was clean and he could see that the green gingham curtains were freshly washed and ironed. The floor had been polished and the books were lined up neatly on the shelves. She was wearing a pair of jeans and a thick brown belt, a polo neck and a colourful scarf.

'Spring cleaning?' he asked.

Laura came and sat at the table. She had made tea for him and poured coffee with cream for herself. The news was playing on the radio and they both listened out of habit to the weather forecast.

'I'm getting the house ready for Mattie,' she said. 'I was thinking of changing his room around as well. I got some new wallpaper. It's sky blue and covered in little red aeroplanes.'

'When is his first visit?'

'It was supposed to be today but they cancelled it because of the fog. It's meant to be every four weeks but they had to push this one back because the ferry got cancelled . . . I haven't seen him since I was at Bishopstown House myself.'

'That's just the start of it,' Martin said. 'Next thing you'll be seeing him once every six months.'

'I was thinking about what you said . . . about getting him back.'

Martin looked down into his cup.

'Do you think I could?'

'I think you should try,' he said.

The morning sun appeared on the table between them and he placed one hand there and he could feel that it was warm.

'I think, as his mother, you have the right. None of these people – the priest, that Mary Costello woman or the damn Campbells – should separate a child from its mother . . . or his . . .'

Martin stopped and he didn't speak for a while and when he did he was awkward, as if the words were heavy and he had some trouble getting them out.

'Are you sure that Matthew isn't mine?'

Laura put her glasses on as if they would help her to think.

'I'm not sure about anything,' she said.

'You'd make a great politician.' There was a slight sourness in his voice.

'That's the truth,' she replied.

'Fair enough then,' he said. 'Well, I'll help you anyway. I don't like to see those rich people doing whatever they want.'

'And what about Father Meehan? You'll see him at mass and have to face him yourself.'

'I haven't been to mass for weeks . . . When I heard what they did to you and Mattie I wasn't able to go back.'

'So you've stopped doing the collection plate.' Laura's face was beginning to smile at the thought of this.

'They can get the fat Farley girl to do it . . . and she can ring the bell too if she likes.'

He reached for his inside pocket and took out a small notebook and pencil. When he opened it flat on the table she could see that he had been recording the weight of his lambs in it. 23lb, 26lb, 28lb, 21lb. The big one must have been a pet lamb, she thought.

'How well do you know their house?' he asked.

'Like the back of my hand.' Laura got up and pulled the curtain over to block out the sunlight.

'Do they lock all the doors at night?'

'He does,' she said. 'It's like a ritual he has.'

'What sort of man is he?' Martin's voice was suddenly quiet.

'He's all right. She's nice enough . . . or at least I thought she was. She's a good cook.'

Martin nodded.

'Are you sure you want to go back?' he asked.

Laura began to gather their plates. She tried to imagine going to the house in the dark and she became frightened. She tried to imagine never holding Mattie again and the idea of that was worse. She cleared the table in silence and then sat down on the couch.

'The window in the kitchen, the one that opens on to the smaller garden . . . the lock is broken. In warm weather they slide it up and lift the table out.'

'What do they do that for?'

'They like to eat outside,' she said and then, 'They're rich,' as if this explained everything.

'What they did to you,' he said quietly, 'it wasn't right . . . Just because they have a big house and some money doesn't mean they can do whatever they want.'

He came and sat on the couch beside her. He didn't seem as brave now and when he spoke his voice shook. The idea of sneaking into a big house like a criminal was beginning to frighten him a bit.

'If you could get in . . . would you know where the boy sleeps?'

'I think so.'

He opened a pack of cigarettes and pulled two out.

'Here,' he said.

'What else can I do?' she asked suddenly. 'I can't just give up and I can't have them coming and checking up on me here for the rest of my life.'

When she looked out the window she saw that a robin was balancing on the clothes line in between the pegs. He slipped and bounced back up. He slipped again and bounced. He reminded her of herself.

273

Martin got up and threw his cigarette into the kitchen sink. He put his jacket on and straightened his cap.

'I'll collect you tomorrow evening.'

Laura looked up, surprised. She had been waiting for him to chicken out.

'I'm coming with you,' he said.

41

Martin called to her house close to teatime. He was wearing a black cap and a black polo neck. He stood on the porch dressed like a cat burglar and Laura knew that in another life all of this would make her laugh. She took a blanket and some milk for the baby. She had also bought a new soft rabbit and a story-book.

'What's in the bag?' he asked. He looked at her suspiciously as if she might be carrying explosives.

The ferry left on time and it was a calm crossing. They shared a ham sandwich and Martin had a packet of fig rolls and tea in a flask. He opened the packet and slid it towards her. The boat was bouncing softly and they could see the mainland.

He drove the car off the ferry and through the village in silence. They turned their heads together then to glance down at the White Lake. They saw the grass verge where they had argued. They reached the yellow house in twilight. The sight of it shocked them and they parked near the front gate and stared at it.

'What time is it?'

Martin looked at his watch.

'Half past six.'

'He won't even be in bed yet. Drive around to the back.'

Laura opened her door and Martin followed. He waited until she had one foot out on the gravel and then he did the same.

She turned and looked back at him.

'I have to do this by myself,' she said and he nodded, pulling his leg inside. She could see that a weight had been lifted off his shoulders. He was a bigger coward than she was. And still he was there with her when she had no one else. She also wished that he had offered to come up to the house with her anyway. She was worried about walking up the long gravel lane in the fading light.

She climbed over the gate that she knew was bright red and had a tight rusted bolt. A handful of bats swooped over her. She needed to walk the long straight stretch of laneway and then, when she went around the first bend, she would see the lights of the house. She could hear the river in the distance. It sounded low, more like a trickle. March had been a very dry month.

She could see one light through the trees and knew that it was from the lamp on the hall table. The big drawing-room windows were in darkness and there were no lights on upstairs. She crossed the lawn, her footsteps becoming silent, and held her breath as she stood in the dark at the front of the house. She had never seen it like this before, a low black rectangle except for one orange-coloured light. The black and cream tiles of the wide hall were lit up. She could see how they shone through the glass in the porch. The kitchen door was closed and she saw the edge of the banister to the left and on the other side the study and dining-room doors. Finn's overcoat hung near the front door and next to it Audrey's favourite umbrella. She had not imagined coming to the house to find that there was no one in it. She tried to breathe slowly and then folded her arms, catching her own elbows. She didn't know where they could be and she knew that Mattie was with them. For the first time in his life, she did not know where he was. The idea alone made tears rise up from her throat and when she inhaled she made a tight gasping noise.

She walked to the door and turned the handle, knowing that she had no chance of getting inside. She had an idea of running through the house, in and out of rooms and down the long upstairs landings, trying to find him. The door opened easily and it surprised her. She stood and looked into the hall. The air smelled of polish and there were roses in a vase. She watched as some pink petals fell and landed on the floor. She knew that they had not been away for very long. The roses were still fresh and there was a smell of baking in the air.

Laura crossed the hall and opened the kitchen door and here she felt the familiar warmth on her face. She could see red embers in the Aga and some shirts hanging on the pulley dryer overhead. She turned on the light and stood there for a moment. Strangely, she missed sitting at the long kitchen table. She missed her talks with Audrey as they sat together shelling peas or making jam. She missed how they both shared Mattie and told each other little stories about him. He would sit on the floor near them, gabbling, playing quietly with Audrey's pots and pans.

She turned then and walked to the first kitchen window. She leaned towards the glass and then gave a scream as she saw someone else looking in.

She screamed again and staggered back into the kitchen chairs. Two hands reached for the frame and lifted the bottom up and Martin put his head in.

'It's only me,' he said.

'What in Jaysus' name are you doing?'

'Shhh. Shhh,' he said and he put his fingers to his lips. 'They're coming home.'

Laura watched as he pulled himself up over the sill and slid like an eel on to the floor.

'I saw the red car on the road. They're coming in the front

entrance. I saw the two of them . . . and your little man sitting on her knee in the front.'

Laura gave a sudden smile at the thought of seeing him. Martin turned off the light in the kitchen and they stood together watching the car travel past the front of the house, its headlamps lighting up the trees.

'What will we do?' Laura asked. She was holding on to his arm now and looking for an answer in his face.

'What will we do?' she asked again.

A key turned in the back door.

'Hide,' he said and before she could say anything he was running quietly up the wide front stairs. Laura had no choice but to follow him. From the stairs she could hear voices behind her and Audrey was talking about the village fête.

'We should have entered Matthew,' she said. 'He was the bonniest baby in the field.'

Finn laughed and he lifted his cap off and put it down on the baby's head. Laura could not see Mattie's face but she saw two small hands lifting the cap off again. He was wearing clothes she had never seen before. A navy-blue jumper and a pair of cream corduroy trousers. He had a pair of brown leather boots that laced up the front and she wondered if he had walked in them yet. She crept up the stairs after Martin and he turned left and walked into their bedroom with the big bay windows.

They stood in the dark and looked at each other. Martin opened another door and she could see that the nursery had been moved into Audrey's dressing room. A small lamp with the moon and stars on it was lit up near a cot. The cot itself was made of dark shiny mahogany and it reminded her of a sleigh. There were rows and rows of picture books on shelves and more toys than she had ever seen. A jack-in-the-box. A toy garage. A lorry filled with wooden zoo animals. A red racing car that he could sit in. A wheelbarrow. A space hopper. She stepped inside and sat near the cot on a white rocking chair.

'This,' she said, 'is where Matthew lives,' and she stretched her hand out in a circle around her. She could hear Martin sigh. He was carrying the plastic bag with the blanket and the milk inside it. He sat on a soft red chair near her and they waited in silence together.

Music started up and Laura gave a jump.

'We have to go downstairs,' she said.

'And then what?' Martin's eyes were wild with fear.

'They're going to come up here to put Mattie to bed . . . and they'll find the two of us sitting in his room . . . like two stooges.'

Martin sat very still and imagined this.

'Right so. Will you do the talking or will I?'

Laura didn't answer. She got up and began to walk like a blind person towards the stairs. The music got louder and when they looked down over the banister she could see that Audrey was dancing with Mattie in her arms. Laura and Martin hunkered down together and looked through the rails. The hall was lit from the kitchen door now and it seemed as if Finn and Audrey and Matthew were in a triangle of gold light. Music was coming from the drawing room and Laura knew that one of them had put the record player on. She had heard this song before and she had already seen them dance to it. She held the wooden rails tightly and watched as Audrey took the little boy in her arms and began to shuffle across the hall.

'"You are my sunshine, my only sunshine,"' the man on the record sang.

Finn laughed and clapped his hands and Laura could see that his face had changed since she had last seen him. It was as if being a father had softened him, as if having a child had worn him down at last. Audrey danced back across the hall again and

279

dipped Mattie towards him at the end. She was counting out loud and getting out of breath and every time she crossed the room, Mattie gave a delighted shriek.

Martin put his arm around Laura's waist and she was at that moment happy to have it there. They watched as Finn got up and put his arms around Audrey and Mattie and how in that moment they all danced together.

'"You make me happy when skies are grey,"' the man on the record sang and Laura held the rails tighter and kept looking down, down.

The house was warm and safe around her. Even now she did not feel like an intruder. The grandfather clock gave a solid tick and chimed the half-hour. She could see more fresh flowers in a vase in the return of the stairs. She could smell lilac in the air. In a week or two there would be new leaves on the hydrangeas. Audrey would collect warm eggs and feed one to her son. There was a photograph of Matthew on the hall table. There was another one on the wall with Finn carrying him on his shoulders.

A lot can happen in a few weeks, she thought. A few weeks is a long time for a little man.

Laura got up slowly and looked around.

'This way,' she said and they began to tiptoe down the long landing to the right. The floorboards creaked under the rugs and she knew where to step left to avoid the one that was broken. She placed both hands flat on the wall and then pushed and a secret door opened with a creak. They stepped through it and it led to a plain little corridor with bare boards and whitewashed walls. There was a narrow staircase on one side and she stopped for a moment and looked up towards the attic. There was no light and the moon had turned their faces silver. When Laura looked at Martin now it was like looking into the lake and seeing another, more frightened version of herself.

'Go down here,' she said. 'You'll find a door at the bottom. The bolt is stiff but it takes you out into the garden. I'll meet you back at the car.'

Martin stood without moving.

'Go on,' she whispered and she turned her back on him and waited. She listened as his footsteps disappeared down the stairs and stood there for a moment and remembered. She thought about wearing the aprons and climbing up and down these stairs. When she looked back now it was as if she had been part of a family for the first time in her life. The hurt felt heavy on her chest and she began to climb the narrow staircase. Her room was exactly the same except that Audrey had taken the white sheets off the bed and the patchwork quilt was turned back to show the pale blue ticking on the mattress. The fireplace was dark and cold but she could see the door to the bathroom and the row of cookbooks on the wooden shelf. She sat on the bed and faced the window and she knew that if she reached to her left, towards the end of the bed, she would feel the empty wooden cot.

She stood at the window for a minute. Martin would be heading down the back lane now. She could imagine him running, his footsteps rattling over loose stones, his breath coming fast, the relief at seeing his car and then the waiting.

She went down the narrow attic stairs and back on to the big warm landing. She stopped at their bedroom and put the grey rabbit and the storybook into Mattie's cot. The music had stopped now and she sank down to her knees and watched again through the wooden banister rails.

Audrey sank into a chair in the hall and Laura watched as Mattie turned his face up to hers and put both hands on her cheeks.

'I better get his bottle ready,' she said and she stood up and handed him with a smile to Finn.

281

Laura got up and leaned back against the wall. She rested her head on one of the portraits. She thought about leaving by the back stairs but there was a thought in her head and she could not make it go away again.

'I have to see him,' she whispered, 'I have to see his face.'

She could see the three of them through the kitchen door and she began to walk quietly down the stairs. Finn was sitting on a chair at the end of the table and he had Mattie on his knee, facing him. Audrey was near the Aga heating milk and the glass bottle was sitting in hot water. Laura stepped closer and waited near the hall table. She could see their black telephone and letters addressed to Finn and Audrey Campbell.

'Hello,' she said but no one heard her.

Audrey poured the milk into the bottle and Mattie began to laugh when she shook it in the air.

'Mattie,' Laura whispered and still no one turned around.

Then Audrey crossed the room to close the window.

'I must have forgotten to shut this,' she said.

Laura began to cross the hall and she felt as if she was floating. As she moved she saw that Audrey was turning from the cooker and then lifting a cardigan off a chair and heading towards the back door. The door opened with a creak. Mattie sat on the table, patting Finn's shoulders and swinging his legs.

The back door gave a rattle and she could hear Audrey's footsteps disappearing down the yard.

Laura stood in the doorway, behind Finn and still he could not hear her and then Mattie looked up. She looked straight at him and he looked back at her. She looked into his eyes and saw again that they were beautiful and that he had not really changed at all. His eyes were the same but it was as if he could not really see her.

'Mattie. It's Mama,' she whispered and her mouth stayed open with the shock of it.

She waited and counted the heartbeats that she felt inside herself.

One – two – three—

How long does it take for a boy to remember?

Four – five – six—

How long does it take to forget?

Laura watched as Mattie began to smile back at her, his dark eyes suddenly lighting up.

'Mama,' he said.

Martin was waiting in the car. In a few minutes he saw her come running, her hair loose and flying behind her. She got into the front seat and without saying anything, he started the engine up. They drove away, sending the gravel flying, and headed for the long straight road to the village. When they came to the lake he realized that she was crying and he pulled over and parked near the edge. They looked out over the calm water and he handed her a fresh white hanky. He lit a cigarette for her and then offered her brandy from a hip flask.

He put his arm around her and could feel that she was shaking.

'I was never going to take him,' she said. 'I just wanted to see that he was all right.'

Martin nodded and she could hear him rubbing the stubble on his cheek.

'I wanted to see if he had grown much . . . if his hair was still in curls at the back.'

Martin sighed in the dark.

'He looked happy. Didn't he look happy? Could you see that?'

'He looked happy for sure,' Martin said.

Laura got out of the car and walked down to the water and he followed.

'All I want is for him to be happy. I want him to have a good life, a better one than I had . . . In a while he won't know any different. He's nearly forgotten me already. It's as if I didn't exist.'

'I don't think that's true,' Martin said and his voice was very quiet.

'Oh, it is. He's doing really well and from now on they can send him to a proper school and he can learn to talk French, and he'll travel and have nice friends . . . Don't you see, he'll never want for anything?'

'He'll want for his mother.'

'He'll forget all about me.'

'But what about you? How will you feel about that?'

'As long as Matthew is happy . . . I'll be all right.'

'But how will you feel?'

Laura didn't speak.

'Laura?'

'I'll die every time I think of it.'

They stood together and listened to the soft waves at the edge of the water. It was dark now and lights were appearing in houses on the other side of the lake.

'You think I'm a coward,' she said.

'I think you're brave.'

'You think I'm a bad mother.'

'I think you're one of the best I ever met.'

'And they love him . . . Could you see that they love him?'

Martin nodded and bit down on his bottom lip.

'Not the way you did,' he said.

Martin finished his tea and handed the cup to Laura. It was May and they were sitting in her kitchen in the late-evening light.

'Summer is coming,' she said. Outside, the Jack Russell was eating long blades of grass.

284

'That's a sign of rain,' Martin said.

She put her glasses on and looked into his cup and gave a sigh and handed it to him again.

'The tea is too cloudy,' she said.

He poured a second cup and after he drank it he handed the empty one to her again. Some leaves were caught together in a clump and all of the others were scattered around the cup.

Laura shook her head and took her glasses off again.

'What is it?' he asked.

'I'll give you the good news first.'

Martin didn't speak.

'You'll have good health for most of your life. You'll die a beautiful death and you won't be on your own when you pass.'

Martin frowned at her and straightened his shoulders.

'And what's the bad news?'

Laura looked into his eyes and a part of her wanted to laugh.

'They're only tea leaves, Martin.'

'Your mother was never wrong.'

'I'm not my mother.'

'Go on,' he said.

'You might lose your marbles,' she said.

'What?'

'You'll go round the twist a bit . . . I mean towards the end.'

'Jaysus,' Martin whispered and he rubbed his forehead with his hand.

The dog was scratching at the door and Laura got up to let him in. He came scuttling across the floor and began to jump up and down at Martin's lap.

'Around the twist . . .' he repeated and he shook his head.

'Not for a long time yet,' Laura said. 'And I might be wrong . . .'

He sat and stared out the window.

'More tea?' Laura asked and she held the spout over his cup.

'No, thanks.'

She drank her own tea in silence and then glanced into the cup and gave a little laugh.

'What do yours say?' he asked.

'Well, they don't tell me I'll be in the mental.'

She waited for him to say that she was already mental but he didn't.

She looked into her cup again and smiled.

'They keep telling me that I'm going to drown,' she said.

42

June

Summer came quickly. In one day, blue sky and green leaves appeared. There was a sudden burst of heat early in May and the islanders threw their doors and windows open to it. They turned their backs to the ocean and took their kitchen chairs outside. They liked to watch the cars that passed their houses, to see who was out and about on the road.

On her last day on the island Laura got up early and took a long soak in the bathtub. She lay back in the water and looked around the room as if she was taking an inventory of her life. A bar of white soap, a stale facecloth, a dried-up spider, the chain on the plug beginning to rust. Sand in corners. Sand in cracks. Sand that gathered in soft drifts when she emptied the bath. She washed her hair and put on a new summer frock. She made her breakfast and sat at the table with a book. She had taken to reading the poetry of William Butler Yeats. Her dress was white and covered in small red flowers; here and there, in between pearl buttons, green ivy leaves curled. The blue suitcase was packed and waiting near the doorway. The morning sun was on her, drying her hair and making it shine. She didn't bother wearing her glasses any more. Her skin had a fresh crop of freckles on it. She had a stripe of sunburn on her nose.

A car slowed down on the road and she wondered who was coming. She stopped chewing and listened, expecting to hear Martin's step on her porch. He called in most days, sat with her, sometimes not talking, just sitting and drinking tea before heading for home. He bought her a new television for company and he would stop by in time for the news. Sometimes he was welcome and he was also a nuisance. She glanced to her right and through the window. She could see the leaves flicking on the sycamore and behind that the sea. The tide was turning and she could feel it turn around and come back towards her. The waves churned further out, white horses gathering, ready to bring sea urchins, crabs, whelks and more seaweed in.

Before daylight she marked the wall with a pencil behind her bed. She left a mark for every day she was without him. When his first birthday came in June she couldn't face the day at all. She told herself that she would stop thinking about Matthew when the pencil ran out of lead. For now she closed her eyes and imagined what he was doing, where he was, what he looked like. Her memory of her last day with him was fading but she could still see him catching a white feather in his hand. This was the clearest picture she had of him. He looked at the feather and smiled up at her. That was the one she framed and hung in her heart.

Another whale had been found and it had survived. Laura saw it first and she found Lucas and took him down to the beach so he could claim it as his. In the mornings they sat together at her kitchen table and she began to teach him to read. They started with letters and sounds and soon she was sticking labels to everything in her house. In less than thirty words he could read the names of all her belongings.

The islanders had started calling on her again. Because of

losing her son, she had gone from being a witch to being the fairy queen. They talked about her in the post office and decided she was gifted, that she could heal them and tell them what their futures held. So the women came and talked about their troubles and the men held out hands that were covered in warts. The O'Boyles came with ringworm. Lucas wrote her a message on a cereal box, asking for a better voice. They all went away believing in something. They paid her with topsoil, eggs and pots of jam. She sat there every morning waiting for the cars to arrive, reading Yeats and with her hair on her shoulders, damp and warm.

The footsteps came closer and when she looked up she saw Finn Campbell.

He was in short sleeves with long brown arms and the white straw hat in his hand. He stood there looking in at her and Laura did not get up to greet him. She sat looking back and he stood, his head bowed, with this odd sunhat making a round shadow on the ground. He pushed the door open and stepped into the room.

'Hello, Laura,' he said.

She lifted her chin in reply but couldn't find words to speak to him. He sat down on the wooden rocking chair and began to spin the hat between his hands. Laura took a sip of tea and saw that her own hand was shaking. The cup found the saucer with a clatter and she looked up at him. Even now there was no point denying it. She still had some love for him and the sight of him had sent her gliding upwards, only to be put back down on her chair again.

'It's a powerful day,' he said.

She could see that he was uncomfortable but she was happy enough about that.

'It is,' she said.

She buttered a piece of toast and turned to look down at her book again.

'You came to our house,' he said.

'Yes.'

She didn't look up.

Finn nodded. He looked as if he was in some sort of pain.

'You left something behind.'

Laura imagined the flask and the blanket. The little rabbit in the cot giving the game away.

'I wanted to see him.'

'You could have told us. We would have liked you to visit.'

'I didn't want to upset him. I just wanted to see for myself . . . that he was all right.'

Finn leaned back in the chair as if he was suddenly tired.

'So . . . are you leaving him with us?'

'It's what you want, isn't it?'

'You know it is . . .' but he sounded quiet and sad about it. 'He's doing very well. I think he's happy with us, Laura.'

'I could see that.'

'But we want you to see him . . . to spend time with him . . . yourself,' Finn said.

Laura got up and walked into the kitchen. She stood at the sink with the tap running, watching how the water bounced back up at her from a white plate.

In her mind she was lifting the pitchfork. Later she would sit outside with Martin and tell him about it.

'And what did you do then?' he would ask, his eyes round.

'I stuck it into his arse.'

She walked back into the sitting room and stood facing him. The water had made the front of her dress wet.

'Your frock is wet,' he remarked and she could see he was trying to make things lighter.

'I'm finished with aprons,' she replied.

She lifted a second cup and poured some stale tea for him.

The sun was on the table and she could feel it warm on the back of her hands. She had picked one of her mother's old-fashioned china cups, in plain white, so she could see the leaves.

'Drink this . . . I'm going to read your tea leaves.'

Finn frowned up at her and then drank the tea back and handed her the cup. He took a deep breath and sat back in the chair and rocked a bit.

'That's right,' she said, 'you sit back there and relax.'

He looked worried and she could see how he held the hat tighter in his hands.

'Well, you'll have a happy enough life from now on, but . . .' here she reached for her glasses and put them on, 'I see a difficult death.'

Finn said, 'Well, thank you for that.'

'You're very welcome,' she replied.

'Laura . . . He will always know where he came from. He will be told about you as soon as he's old enough to understand.'

She took the cups and put them into the sink and left him there in the warm silence. A bird was singing outside the kitchen window and she opened it up and let the song float in to them.

'I have work to do,' she said quietly.

She stood under the arch that led to the kitchen with her hands on her hips.

'Why did you come here?'

Finn's expression had changed and he seemed duller. He was like a man who was suddenly depressed.

He looked straight ahead through the row of windows. The sea was closer now, the tide would be high. By nightfall it would be right up to her house.

'His birth certificate.'

'Ha,' she said.

Laura wondered when he would kick her in the stomach,

291

when one of his rocks would hit her on the head. She reached into the drawer of her desk and lifted the sheet of paper out. It had been folded in half and for a moment she considered opening it and taking a look. It was the only part of Matthew that she had left. After this there was no turning back.

'I want you to promise me that you won't change his name.'

'His name is Matthew . . . and it always will be.'

'Matthew Lucas,' Laura replied.

She stood up and put the birth certificate on the table.

'I'll leave it here for you.'

Finn had put the hat back on his head and he scowled up at her from his chair. He seemed to have sun in his eyes even though it was down near his feet.

'Did I matter at all to you?' she asked suddenly.

He took his hat off again and put his head to one side and looked at her. Everything in his face seemed to soften and move slightly, his shoulders dropping, his fingers not moving, his hands relaxed.

'I didn't know how things would turn out, Laura.'

He looked into her eyes and then, giving a long sigh, he reached out and took her hand. Laura could hear the clock tick from the kitchen. His skin felt leathery from farm work and her hand felt small inside it. A ship's horn sounded in the distance. The first of the new cruise liners was coming in. It was to go around the island and dock for a few hours at Bee's Harbour.

'Did I matter at all?' she asked again.

'Everyone matters,' he said.

Laura closed her eyes and gently pulled her hand away from him.

She crossed the room and lifted the blue suitcase and he watched as she walked past the windows and took the steps down to the sand.

Finn let out a sigh of sadness, of relief, and got up and left with the door banging behind him. He had dreaded this journey to the island and yet what could he do except face it? Mattie was happy with them and she too had seen it, but not for the first time his thoughts wandered over to her and what it was she felt. He tried in that moment to imagine it and remembered himself and Audrey standing in the cemetery with the priest, the rain beating on their backs. Until then he had not known that such a loneliness could exist. Yes, he knew how she felt.

Finn watched as Laura walked away from him and on the beach she turned around once to look. And now he delayed, waiting for something, some final gesture, a small wave, forgiveness? But she stood very still and the wind lifted her hair and covered up her face.

43

Martin saw her from the lighthouse. She was wearing a white dress and there was no apron or pitchfork. He watched as she pulled the cage with her, standing for a moment with one hand shading her eyes and then pushing her way through the first salt-water river. He squinted when she stopped to take her sandals off. Then she walked on without them. The white cruise ship appeared on the horizon and he could hear a curlew calling. It was a lonesome sound, eerie, like a warning, telling the island that people from the other world were near. Laura unbuttoned her dress down the front and when she reached the last button, a sudden gust of wind lifted it high into the air. She wasn't wearing the red swimsuit as he expected. Instead her bra was unhooked and her knickers fell away and stayed on the wet sand behind her.

He watched and blinked into the sunlight. No one in their right mind would swim in that kind of current, not even Laura who was born and reared on the island. By now the tide had turned and the cage was at the edge of the water. Martin went inside and found his binoculars. He could see her clearly then, climbing into the cage, naked and curling up like a baby on the floor. He gave a sudden cry, whispered, 'Sweet Jesus,' and began to run down the steps calling out to her. She was going to go the same way as her mother, except she would use Fintra instead of

White's Cliff. He tripped and fell hard near the bottom, landing on his arm, and he heard his own bones breaking. There was some fresh blood on the wall beside him and the bone had broken up near his shoulder. The pain came suddenly and covered him, making him dizzy, forcing him to sit on a step and bend over. He thought about Laura, cold and without clothes, the water getting higher around her. He crawled down the corridor to his house and the Jack Russell appeared and began to lick the blood from his ear. He found the phone but there was no answer from the Guard in the village.

'You lazy bastard,' he roared into the receiver.

He lifted his car keys and now the dog was dancing around him. The terrier was delighted and sniffed at the drops of blood that were landing on the floor.

The water would be closer now, the waves lapping around her.

He got into the car and tried the ignition but there was no sound out of it.

Martin put his head against the steering wheel and tried to breathe slowly. He turned the key in the ignition again.

'Please,' he said but nothing happened.

'Please,' he said again but it sounded like the engine was already flooded.

'You're a heap of shite,' he told the car quietly.

He could imagine the water curling around the wheels of the cage and beginning to come in small waves over her. Soon she would be sitting in it. Soon it would be like cold arms wrapping around her. He turned the key again. The water would climb to her waist and creep up towards her shoulders. The car battery was flat and he sat for a moment with one hand in his hair. He put his head back and cursed quietly.

'Jaysus, fuck and bollox.' He said it like a prayer.

The trees around him were spinning. The dog began to bark

in the garden and the sheep stopped grazing. He was trapped and so was she. She would drown in minutes. Then the sea would begin to pull away again and leave the empty cage on the shore. He had tried to help her before. He thought that he had come to know her. The tide would be coming in fast now. It would fill the cage and gently lift her out and turn her over. Martin closed his eyes and with his good arm, wound down the window for air.

February 2009
Jericho

44

Laura was tired of the sea. She had looked at it for so long that all the changes, the tides, the churning of the waves, the calm days, the storms, the many different coins of light bouncing off its surface, merged now into one big grey-green thing. There were only two days when it was really blue. One was the day she fell in love with Finn Campbell, the other was the day she tried to drown herself. Every other day it was distant, remote, occasionally beautiful. The sea was like one of those Swedish women she had heard about, lovely in its own way but cold. No wonder she was bored.

Then the ambulance came over on the ferry and they lifted her out of bed crying. Her bed was rank. It smelled like piss and feathers and sleep. A cosy nest, the most comfortable there had ever been. Lately she had been like an old badger making circles in it before lying down to sleep. Now the islanders would set fire to it. They would go through her things and take her mother's teapots and oil paintings. The young man with the white hair had called the ambulance and let them in. He stood watching as they took her away and then he locked the door and gave her the only key. She had known him all his life. He was an albino and he was crying a bit when he hugged her and said, 'Goodbye.'

She couldn't remember his name at that moment so she just

said, 'Bye.' There was a big label and a string on the key. 'My house', the label said. She knew now that she was losing it. The albino's wife had put a few things into an old blue suitcase. That one should have been labelled too. 'My life', she thought. Later she would find a photograph of a baby and an Aran cardigan in it. There was no nightdress or underwear. Laura had no need for such things. She lay waiting in the ambulance for the ferry to sail and imagined that she was in a white limousine.

'Are we moving yet?' she asked.

'Are we moving yet?' she asked again.

She was still wearing her wellingtons on the stretcher. The nurses didn't know it yet but they would have to cut them off and boil her feet. She had not seen her toes in weeks. When she imagined her feet she saw old potatoes covered in clay and going to seed. The ambulance men were nice to her. They carted her off and didn't baulk at the smell in her house. One of them found an old raincoat and he put that with the suitcase. This was the sum total of her life. A small blue suitcase and a raincoat she didn't recognize.

She wanted the ferry to be late but it came on time. It backed into the harbour and took them all away with it. Through the window she saw the seagulls laughing down at her.

'What are those things?' she asked. She enjoyed pretending that she was soft in the head.

'Seagulls,' someone said. They sang the word out as if it was from a nursery rhyme.

She knew that she would be hearing a lot of that. The ambulance bumped off the ferry on to the mainland and the driver joked up front. She could see the Jericho nursing home through the windows. She had watched it often enough from her own beach. A big white castle with ugly towers decorated with crows. On the lawn she saw a few of the other old crocks. The women had hair like dandelion seed. Three men were lining up at the end of a long grass strip and attempting to play bowls.

'They could knock someone's brains out,' the driver said.

Here the spin of the world was slowing down and she slowed down with it.

'So this is how it happens,' she said to herself. 'Slower, slower, slower and then not at all.' She didn't believe in fading away. She would find a nice young doctor who would move things along for her. Fading was for the movies. She wanted to go out quick.

'You can play bowls too,' one of the nurses said cheerfully.

'Bowls my arse,' Laura replied.

She turned her face away. Her hair was still long, the colour of primroses now. Her eyes, bluish, like the sea, with a mixture of skies hidden in them. She had stopped crying as soon as she left her house. She knew they were coming to take her. She knew that it was only a matter of time before Lucas and his wife decided to step in. There was only one thing she wanted to say to all of them and they weren't really interested. They would drop her into a wheelchair and then drive off for someone else.

She fell asleep before she said the thing she wanted to say. She was still sleeping when the doors opened and the stretcher came sliding out. The wind rose and it blew her hair around like feathers. She slept in the foyer and again in the big silver lift. She woke up near a busy nurses' station and the man who filled out the forms smiled at her as if she was from the circus.

'Your date of birth?' he asked.

'I'm seventy-two or three,' she answered.

He reached for his calculator.

She would have liked to say it to him too. To him she wanted to shout it out.

A nurse helped her off the stretcher. She stood her up and tried to put on her raincoat. Laura woke up properly then and caught sight of herself in two glass doors. She still couldn't remember that coat. It hung on her limp, and she looked like a cloud in it. She made small steps and her wellies squeaked. She took another step, squeak. Two more short steps, squeak, squeak. Deep, deep down in the bottom of her there was someone who wanted to laugh. The other part, which leaned heavy on that one, stopped it coming out. She would die here and they were treating her like an eejit. That wasn't something to laugh about.

She sat very still, sorry now that she was stinking the place out. In the white room they would undress her and give her one of those gowns that opened down the back. Then the world would see the cheeks of her backside poking out like two old windfalls. She didn't care a bit about that. It was the sound of the water in the distance that frightened her. A little woman with a violin came in but Laura did not know what to say to her. She was holding the bow over her shoulder like a fishing rod. They brought her into her own room and Laura began to cry again.

'You'll upset the others,' one of the nurses said.

It was a battle now and she had to get a few punches in before they really got into it. The scissors appeared and she felt herself being lifted into the air. She stiffened her legs and sent herself higher so that her head knocked against the bed frame.

'Now that's what happens,' the nurse said, pleased with herself.

Laura had something she wanted to say to her. There was another nurse who looked at her over her glasses as if she was a real museum piece. Then there was one with henna-dyed hair that made her look like an old rat and another one with a big backside.

'Should I play?' the violinist asked.

Laura stared at them all blankly. She was stripped bare now and under a smooth white sheet. They were beginning to work on her boots.

'What would you like to hear?' the little woman asked. She looked straight into Laura's eyes and Laura looked back. She thought the ambulance was taking her to the old folks' home but maybe it was to the asylum she was sent.

Someone was running the bath and it sounded like a waterfall in the distance.

The nurses began to bathe her. They knew she was from the island. There was a wild look in her eyes like she had birds trapped inside her head. When they lifted her from the bath, naked and dripping, she was like a shipwreck. Rock pools had formed in the deep hollows inside her hips. She tried to say something to one of them but they couldn't understand what she said. She tried to sit up. She opened her mouth and tried to explain that it was important. Then she lay back on her pillows again and gave up. One of the nurses sat at the bed and the violin case closed with a snap. She seemed to sleep peacefully then with one leg turned out. If she had been upright she would have been balancing on one foot. In sleep she was radiant.

Then she opened her eyes suddenly and stared.

'Would you like me to play something for you now . . . to help you to sleep?'

'All right then.'

'What would you like?'

'"Yellow submarine",' she said.

The nurse made a clicking sound with her mouth.

The thing Laura had wanted to say was 'I was young once.'

45

April

In a room that looked out over the ocean, a grey-haired woman unpacked a bag for her husband. She put a pair of blue pyjamas under his pillow, his razor and shaving brush beside the bathroom sink. She folded his walking stick and put it into the wardrobe and it crossed her mind that he might never need it. This thought rested on her briefly like a cloud and it was an effort to lift it. Their son had bought the walking stick and the magnifying glass. At what point, she wondered, do parents want gifts like these? It was springtime now but the daffodils did nothing to cheer her. Lately when he poured the tea his right hand shook. He would stand watching the fields or the television or listening to the radio and sometimes forget to close his mouth up. He had developed a peculiar habit of piddling in the flowerbeds.

A nurse came in with a blood pressure monitor.

'The doctor would like to run some more tests,' she said.

'What sort of tests?'

'Another chest X-ray . . . some more bloods.'

Finn stood at the window and listened with one ear. In his mind his heart was being asked to jump hurdles and skip rope. But still he faced the ocean. He could see the evening sun disappearing into it. He could see the island turn grey and the old lighthouse, red and white on the highest point. As long as he stood there, everything was normal. As long as he didn't turn around he would not have to face it.

'I'll leave you to get settled,' the nurse said and she pushed the blood pressure monitor out again and closed the door.

He stayed at the window and Audrey sat down behind him on the side of the bed. His tweed jacket fitted his broad shoulders neatly and his hat was still pulled down on his head. By now she knew every crease of him, the thin folds that gathered at the back of his neck, his hair, in dead grey curls, flattened. They had shared a bed for more than forty years. In the mornings he reached out for her hand and she would wake to find him holding it. As a younger man he would not have done that but now he was nearly eighty years old and he was afraid. Old age made him love her more and she was not offended by this. She knew every mark on him, inside and out. She would recognize his shadow on the ground. She knew where his walking stick stood, where his clean underpants were and where the blue pyjamas were kept.

She did not know that this time was coming, that after years of taking care of him she would be visiting him in the Jericho nursing home. That it would be up to someone else to hold the soup spoon to his mouth, to dress him, to place his slippers on the floor beside his feet and say, 'The left one first.'

'Your husband is a very sick man,' the doctor said. 'Too sick to be at home.'

The tea trolley came, crashing and banging, and the woman pushing it announced her arrival.

'Now, will you be having your tea?' she asked.

In all the time Audrey had planned their trip to Jericho, she had not imagined this either, that a woman with permed hair under a floral cap, noisy and over-familiar, would try to feed her

305

husband. He turned then and taking off his cap, he sat on the side of the bed and pulled the tray up.

There was a grey fillet of plaice with a slice of wet lemon sticking to it, two slices of bread with butter in two small gold packets, jam in a tiny plastic box, a Mr Kipling cake, tea from a doll's teapot. She poured his tea and watched as her husband cleared his plate.

He spoke to her for the first time then.

'Not too bad,' he said.

His blue eyes were clear and bright when he looked at her and in response she had to look down at her lap. It will be harder, she thought, if he tries to make the best of it. Tomorrow she would bring hyacinths for his windowsill and she told him this.

'What?' he asked.

'Hyacinths,' she shouted.

'Oh.'

They sat together on the side of the bed and the woman with the floral cap came back.

'Did you enjoy that?' she asked loudly and she wheeled her noisy cart off.

Audrey wanted to take his big hand in hers but she was afraid that if she got soft it might upset him.

'You better head for home before it gets dark,' he said.

She did not know what the house would sound like without him in it.

They sat for another few minutes. He reached for his inside pocket and produced a big pair of glasses held together with Sellotape.

'I suppose I'll do the crossword.'

She pulled an armchair across the floor and watched as he got settled. She hovered, about to kiss his cheek. She swooped in then and gave it a peck, her movements awkward, childlike. She

306

looked at him with his newspaper folded and the biro tapping on the page as he began to think.

She had a picture of him in her mind then, ploughing a field pursued by a flock of seagulls. With so many memories to unearth, her mind had chosen this. Then she saw him carrying their son high on his shoulders. She imagined the drive home without him and her breath went cold inside her chest.

'Well, goodnight then,' she said and she stood waiting for something.

'Goodnight so,' he replied.

46

Audrey went home to the empty house and felt safer when she locked the door behind her. Out of habit she stopped for a moment and listened for his footsteps and then his cough on the stairs. She had been warned about his chair in particular. How she would notice it suddenly and then wonder as she stood there, a duster in one hand and polish in the other, how her husband had suddenly disappeared.

'Move his chair,' Mary Coffey said. 'Put it into another room so it's one less thing to bear.'

'And then what?' Audrey asked. 'Take the rug that was under the chair or the bookshelf behind the chair or the reading lamp that hung over the chair?

'Then what, Mary?' she asked again. Finn's chair, Finn's room, Finn's house. Her husband's loose threads were caught everywhere.

Her friend held her hand for a moment.

'No, Mary,' Audrey said. 'It's better that I get used to living without him. Anything else will be like running from my shadow and I could be doing that for the rest of my life.'

So she went inside bravely and stood in the hall. The grand-father clock ticked solidly. A fly bumped against the glass door.

So much and so little has changed, Audrey thought.

She opened the door to the drawing room and waited for his chair to fly at her through the air. It was, as she expected, in its usual place, on the other side of the wide marble fireplace and under the lamp with the green bobbled shade. His other glasses, she remembered now, were on the top shelf of the bookcase. She crossed the room, glancing for a moment at the freshly swept grate, still warm from the fire the previous night. They had had their own favourite chairs. She had dozed here every night and he had watched her. They had had their own sides of the bed which in all their years of marriage had never changed.

A car moved on the driveway, the sound of the gravel under its wheels causing her to look out. The postman was late today and she could hear a hen cackling in the distance.

I need to find that nest, she thought, or else a clutch of chicks is going to appear. She held the arms of her own chair tightly and tried to think about the red comb on her favourite hen. She could imagine the chicks floating lightly then and the hen's umbrella wings as soon as danger appeared.

Through the bay windows she could see the Ox mountains, more beautiful than ever and also higher than before. They were impossible to climb anyway, but without him, each one was like Mount Everest now.

'How wide the world,' she said, 'without you in it, Finn.'

The clock on the mantelpiece chimed again.

She climbed the stairs and stood for a moment at the top looking down into the hallway and listening to the silence of the house. In her mind she became a strangely divided person, a patchwork, a kaleidoscope, a multicoloured tapestry of herself. She felt herself lift off – as if the logical part of her mind gave way and stepped aside for the emotional, less sensible part. She wanted to walk back down these stairs, each step solid and certain under her foot, and turn the handle of the kitchen door.

He had become fussy lately. He wanted a poached egg one minute and then sardines on toast the next. He had taken to anchovies briefly and he liked them draped over two scrambled eggs. Regardless of whether he was hungry or not though, Audrey knew that he didn't like the tea to be late. It was six o'clock and she knew that if she looked into the pantry, she would find tins of sardines and anchovies, which she herself detested, in the saddest little stacks.

She crossed the short landing and climbing another flight of stairs she opened the door to their bedroom at the top.

It's just a room, she told herself, and I need to change my clothes and hang this suit up.

She put her handbag on the bed and went to his wardrobe instead and began to move her hands over his clothes. He still had all the suits he had ever owned. 'The one he married me in', and 'he danced a few foxtrots in that'. If she lifted a sleeve and placed it to her nose she knew that she would not smell her husband. She would only smell suits that should have been thrown out. 'Your husband is a very sick man,' the doctor had said. Then they had given her tea and made her sit down, as if that would help. Now she lifted an empty jacket sleeve and held it as if she was shaking his hand and it occurred to her, suddenly and tragically, that Finn was sleeping in a narrow white bed now and that he would not be coming home.

She sat on the bed and took off her shoes. She lined them up beside the wall and then took off her suit and hung it up. The bed was as she had left it. The sheets not changed since their last restless night. She went to his side, lifted back the covers and got in wearing her slip. The cotton was cold against her legs but here she could feel him, here he surrounded her as he always had. Here under a tent of covers, they had talked for all their years, at night. She turned over on to her side, pulled her knees high up to her chest, caught the sheet and pressed it to her face. Audrey lay, eyes open with no tears and no sleep coming, one part of her still numb and without any sense of what was actually happening, and the other white-faced and terrified.

47

Matthew knew where Jericho was. He knew that it was the last white castle on the mainland and after that there was the sea. He had stood close to it once with his father, looking out at the island. Inis Míol Mór – Whale Island. On a school tour they had done a nature trail there. The bus took the boys along the winding coast road and then up to the lighthouse. They had to shelter from a sudden rainstorm and the lighthouse keeper taught them how to play checkers and patience. They found crabs with broken legs and a dead seagull and a pair of swimming trunks on the beach. Most of the houses were deserted, piles of stones left and one or two walls. He carried minnows home in a jam jar and emptied them into a cattle tank. They died then or were swallowed up by the Friesian herd.

'I see the sea,' his father would shout and he would drive the car right down the ramp on to the sand. He wasn't afraid of any-thing. He could swim in any kind of current or tide. He had saved a man from drowning once.

Matthew paid for the taxi and glanced up at the windows. Behind him a man was clipping a hedge. There were three old people smoking in a gazebo and a woman with white hair floated by wearing an oxygen mask. Two men shuffled past with Zimmer frames. He knew about Jericho, everyone did. He found it hard to believe that his father would end up there. He went to the reception desk to ask where he was and said his name out loud while such a name could still exist. He stood at the desk while the nurse ran a pen down a sheet of paper.

'He was on the ward,' she murmured. 'And then . . . oh yes, he's in Room Five now.'

Matthew wondered what happened to a name after someone died. He wondered if the words would disintegrate, or if the letters rearranged themselves to name someone else.

An old woman was walking slowly down the corridor holding on to the wall. The palms of her hands were pressed into it. Someone else in a wheelchair was demanding a taxi to the church.

'Did you take your tablets?' the nurse asked.

'You're talking about tablets; I'm talking about a taxi.'

The nurse at the reception desk leaned out and pointed with her pen.

'Take the lift to the third floor and turn left at the double doors upstairs.'

Around him everything was moving. Nurses walked quickly, old people shuffled past in dressing gowns. He did not want to see his father here. He did not want to see him in a place where everyone was in pyjamas. A woman ran down the corridor crying, 'Help, help, help,' and one of the nurses rolled her eyes and said, 'There she goes again.'

Matthew stood in his jeans and jumper, his hair in loose curls and he remembered that he needed a haircut. The nurse behind the desk watched him for a minute.

'You're tall . . . like your father,' she said.

He nodded and smiled.

'Room Five,' she said again. 'Some of the doors are left open . . . keep looking straight ahead.'

He had no idea why she would say this but she had kind eyes. He knew he was tall like his father and he also knew that he was adopted. 'My name is Matthew. I'm adopted,' were two pieces of information that went hand in hand. He had never not known about it or about the woman from the island who had known his father briefly and then drowned. Finn and Audrey had taken him to see her house once but it was a long time ago and he couldn't remember it now. It had never really mattered to him but standing on his own in this long green corridor he suddenly missed her without knowing why.

On the way to the lift he glanced left and right and then mentally closed the doors inside his head. He looked at his feet and listened to his boots squeaking. He got into the lift and tried not to think about the people with yellow faces and white hair. He was thirty-two and he had never felt so young in his life. He knew he would open a door soon and find his own father, another old man, sitting there. He would see him in his pyjamas at two in the afternoon like everyone else. He would be sitting up in bed or on an uncomfortable wooden chair and he would look into his blue eyes and together they would acknowledge what was happening – that Finn was frail and fading, the same as everyone else.

He found the white corridor and stood at the doors watching. There was a new quiet here and the nurses were dressed in pale pink. A violin was playing somewhere. Bach's Allegro Assai, he recognized it. Doors opened and were closed again discreetly. The nurses' station was full of flowers and thank-you cards. There were nice pictures on the walls and everyone spoke in whispers. Matthew took a deep breath and without thinking any more about it, he found Room Five and stepped inside.

His father was lying back on the white bed. The TV was silent. There was no newspaper in his hand. There was no pen to do the crossword. His pyjama top had opened down the front and Matthew could see an old suntan V on his chest. The rest of his skin was blue white. His arms were thinner than before, his legs, still long, stretched out. His feet were swollen and in white tennis socks. His father had never worn sports socks in his life.

'Ah,' he said when he saw his son and he nodded.

There were no tears in his eyes, just a quiet calm sort of light. Matthew dropped his bag and went to kiss him. He put his arms around his shoulders briefly and felt how small he was.

My father is dying, he said to himself.

He went to the end of the bed and put his hands deep into his jeans pockets and finally met his eyes. He nodded back at him and tried to smile but he felt like crying instead.

'How are you, Dad?' he asked.

The words came back to him and sounded ridiculous. Surely there was some other question to be asked. Surely there was a whole new set of emergency vocabulary that could be pulled out at a time like this. He was being polite. He didn't know anything else.

Finn pulled a face and gave a big shrug. Then he smiled.

Matthew pulled up a chair next to him.

'How are things at the university?'

'Great, nothing different. My first-year English class is very good.'

'Keats? Shelley? Wordsworth?'

Matthew smiled and then laughed.

'I'm doing Shakespeare with them at the moment. *The Merchant of Venice.*'

Finn folded his arms and looked off into the distance.

'But love is blind and lovers cannot see / The pretty follies that themselves commit . . .'

In that moment his voice was different. He was, as he used to

315

be, loud and sure of himself. His eyes found a spot somewhere and he concentrated and remembered every word.

'I loved it,' he said simply, 'and I can remember it as if it was yesterday, walking on those cobblestones . . . happy days.'

Matthew nodded.

'Happy days,' Finn said again.

'Where's Mum?'

'She went to get some lunch.'

The usual stuff went on around them, Matthew thought. And at the same time people were dying, one by one. No one had any control over anything and still everyone was so quiet and calm. The violin played on. His mother was eating a sandwich in the canteen. His father's pyjamas were unbuttoned. The bathroom door was open. A trolley rattled past the door. And his father lay on the bed and recited Shakespeare. Everyone was oblivious to the end, or else they were so shit scared, 'all the usual stuff' was there to block the idea of dying out.

The air between them seemed dense and Matthew was suddenly tongue-tied. There was so much and so little to talk about. He traced the bedspread pattern with his index finger and when he looked up, his father was staring out the window, lost in some distant thought. He lay back on his pillows and watched the sky as if he was trying to remember something. He took a deep breath and closed his eyes. Matthew listened to him breathing and could think of nothing at all to say to him. He racked his brains but he was stuck. He looked out the window too and reached for his father's hand.

48

Lucas Boyle came wearing dark glasses to visit Laura. He brought her flowers that he had picked from her garden. Bearded irises, the first lilies, long wisps of sea grass.

'Are you sure these came from my garden?' she asked.

'I tidied the place up a bit.'

He pushed the dark glasses up on his nose.

'You look like a rock star,' she said.

Laura took a deep breath and relaxed back on her pillows. She hated trying to talk to someone from her bed. Lying there gave her a double chin and the words went down and lodged between her breasts. Most of the people who came to visit her in Jericho were only coming for a look. They pulled up chairs to both sides of the bed and leaned in like they were going to play cards over her legs. They looked around the room to record everything and then stared at her so they could go back and tell it to the island.

'Ah, God, she looks desperate.'

'I felt so sorry for her lying there.'

'She has no one at all, you know.'

She was trapped under the white sheets and couldn't get away from them. No decent conversation could ever be had when one person was lying in bed.

Lucas didn't say much. He just sat there quietly and looked at her with his head to one side. His wife was hovering in the corridor.

'So they're looking after you well?' he asked.

'They're talking about sending me home next week.'

'You do look better.'

'I suppose I should, after two months in this place . . . but my lungs are finished. Kaput,' and she looked out the window. 'Don't smoke,' she said.

A nurse came in and took her blood pressure. She handed her two pills in a small plastic cup. When she was gone Lucas sat down on the wooden chair again.

'How do you like my new teeth?' Laura asked and she pulled her lips apart to show him. She had practised this smile in her hand mirror. She had been sitting there in bed smiling at herself.

'They look nice.'

'I feel like I have a piano in my mouth.'

'They'll have to settle down a bit.'

'And I have new glasses.'

She pointed to her handbag and made a great ceremony of unhooking the clasp and finding the case and opening them out. She put them on and sat there blinking at him.

'Very nice,' he said and he smiled at her.

'They make me look brainy, I think.'

When Laura laughed it sounded like a cream cracker being crushed.

She looked around the room for something else to talk about.

'And they're giving me an oxygen tank. I'll have to wear my own little mask . . . and I'll pull it around behind me like a dog.'

'Well, you had a dog once.'

Laura shook her head.

'No . . . that was Martin's.'

Lucas nodded.

'He thought you were dead, you know . . . that you drowned yourself.'

'Did he now?'

'The whole island did. It looked like it . . . then he fell down the steps of the lighthouse trying to save your life.'

'My hero,' Laura said.

Lucas looked away for a minute.

'Most things end up back on that beach. I didn't think that you'd drowned . . . There was no body,' and he looked down at his hands folded on the bed, embarrassed.

'No body at all,' Laura added.

She gave a shrug.

'I tried to drown myself but the sea wouldn't take me . . . The cage went down but I was thrown back up on the shore. I couldn't even do that much right.'

Here they looked at each other and began to laugh.

'And I nearly froze the arse off myself,' she said.

Behind her glasses, her eyes twinkled.

Neither one spoke for a moment and Laura stared at the tall trees outside her window.

'I didn't know what to do so I let the sea decide for me . . . it spat me out . . . so I knew I would have to go on and live out my life.'

'Where did you go?'

'To America . . . in a grey raincoat and not much else.'

Lucas nodded.

'I got a job on a big cruise ship . . . It was the first one to stop at the island and I knew it was my chance to escape.'

'You walked down to the harbour and asked for a job?'

'The tourists were flooding the island and everyone was distracted. I was just another person carrying a suitcase. There were no islanders down near the pier at all. They were too busy making money from the Americans and McKenna's was packed to the rafters. Irene and Patricia, God rest them, must have been rushed off their feet.'

'And where was the cruise ship going?'

'To New York. I asked one of the porters if there might be any work. I had a passport in my hand and I knew how to work in a kitchen. I think he took a bit of a shine to me. He brought me on board to meet the cook.'

'And then they found your clothes on the beach . . .'

'It was a perfect day to slip off . . . The village was so full of people I thought it would sink. I told the cook I'd scrub pots and wash floors for him, anything at all for my passage, and he took me on on the spot.'

'And what did you do in New York?'

'A lot of different things . . . I cleaned houses and big offices at first and then I worked for years in a B&B in Brooklyn. At night I read tea leaves in the Village and I made great money doing it. The Americans pay a lot to know what's up ahead.'

'Did you ever meet anyone famous?'

'I saw Bob Dylan once . . . he was an awful-looking sketch.'

Here Lucas laughed.

'You should have got an autograph for me.'

'Eventually I'd saved enough money to buy the B&B – the owner was a friend of mine by then and she gave it to me for a good price. I looked after a lot of young Irish people coming over and trying to start a new life.'

'It must have been some change from the island.'

'It was but my mother had organized a passport for me before she died. I didn't even know I had one until I found it in a drawer. I sent it off with the forms to get a new one – and it was as if she was helping me to escape. New York seemed like the best place to start.'

'And what was it like living there? I've heard it's an exciting place.'

'It's like being in an asylum every day of your life. But if you have a few pounds in your pocket it's all right . . .'

Here Laura's voice trailed off.

'And did you ever marry?'

'Only the once . . . I still called myself Mrs Cronin in New York.'

'You never divorced him?'

'What was the point? I didn't want to get married again and neither did he, I think.'

'No . . . Cronin didn't show any interest in other women on the island after you left.'

'That's true love for you,' Laura said and her voice was dry when she said it.

'But you came back to the island.'

'Only to die,' she said simply. 'But this time I could afford an Aer Lingus flight.'

Her eyes drifted off and she was lost in thought again for a minute.

'I wish I could stay longer,' Lucas said quietly, 'but we left the baby with my mother.'

Laura nodded. She wanted to grab his hands to stop him from leaving but some lonely shard of pride prevented it.

'The next time bring the baby . . . I'd like to hold him.'

A monitor began to chirp behind her and Lucas watched it.

'Don't worry about that . . . that's just my oxygen tank. It's reminding me to breathe. It thinks I might forget . . . can you imagine that?'

Lucas smiled down at her and waited. The monitor chirped again.

'It also thinks I'm deaf.'

She lifted the clear mask and snapped it over her nose and took a long sniff.

She looked up at him from behind her glasses and the mask.

'How do you like me now?' she asked. 'Do I look like I'm going into space?'

Lucas stood for a moment at her bed. The oxygen tank was making a pumping sound followed by a rhythmic hiss. She knew that leaving was awkward for the people who came to visit. There was nothing as bad as going back to real life, just walking off, and leaving someone else lying there in the bed. She closed her eyes and began to breathe deeply. She would do them all a favour and pretend to fall asleep.

49

Before Jericho, Finn's time with Audrey was not complicated. It was filled with things like All-Bran and weekly excursions to the supermarket and broken sleep. And in between those things they concentrated on staying warm, taking each other's blood pressure, keeping a yearling or two, hens – and more recently a handful of coloured pills. He knew that she would pack the last bag for him. Other women, the more romantic kind, would collapse at the idea of finding those clothes. But when the time came she would drive home and go straight upstairs to the icy bedroom and begin to pack. He didn't care what she put into the bag, he trusted her with all of that. She would unzip a small black holdall and put a well-ironed blue shirt inside. She would roll his old college tie neatly and take down the best sports jacket he had and the most comfortable shoes. And none of this would surprise him a bit. His wife had been packing suitcases for him all of his life. Sometimes they were the size of a television and other times they were the size of a cereal box. The shirts were always perfectly ironed and arrived at the new destination without a single crease.

What is a wife? he wondered. Someone who cares enough about a man to organize the loose rolling rocks of his life. And when the time came, without anyone noticing, she would translate all of it into softer, kinder words for their grown-up son. When no one was watching she would speak to a nurse and quietly point out the small black bag.

'His clothes are here,' she would say. The shirt he was to be buried in, ironed and waiting inside. When she heard about his illness she was in no way soft or romantic, in fact she was downright unfriendly to him at times. She was like an old fisherman mending a net. She tied loops and fixed holes and held everyone together in it.

Finn closed his eyes and waited for sleep. He lay in the strange orange glow of the night light and listened to the beeps and rattles and wide-awake voices of the hospital at night.

He sat up slowly and saw 2am on the clock.

'Well, well,' he said to no one but himself.

He moved his legs over the side of the bed and could feel the tiles cold under his feet. He used the back of the chair for support and in two steps he made it to the window. He was finding it harder to breathe lately but if he could open the window he would hear the sea and breathe with it. He found the latch and when the blast of cold wind came in, it sent his hair up in wisps and made the door of the room slam shut. He stood there and saw that it was raining. There was a dark puddle on the windowsill and the gardens were wet and silent.

The door opened and a nurse told him to shut the window and get back into bed.

'It's raining,' he replied.

'I can see that.'

'When will I be going home?'

'Everyone asks the same question.'

She was straightening the sheets on his bed.

'Everyone wants to know when they can get back out and I can't tell you that . . . but soon, I hope.'

'No one ever comes back.' He had said this to Audrey once. They were arguing about the church again and she said something awful about hellfire and he replied, 'No one ever comes back!' He shouted it at her actually. He spat the words out. He was already sick then and he was afraid.

The nurse stepped in again and adjusted his heart monitor. She scribbled a note on to the clipboard and put it on the end of his bed. She moved silently towards him and gently lifted his wrist to take his pulse. He could hear her breathing. He could smell her perfume and feel her warmth close to his cheek. What was it like to have warm skin, to have a life stretch out in front of you? He had had those feelings once. Now he couldn't remember it. She poured some water into a paper cup and left it for him on his locker. He kept his eyes closed. He had learned that it was easier to pretend to be asleep, easier than trying to make chat with a nurse half his age, in the middle of the night. She left silently, like a vapour, he thought. The door closed softly and he fell into a light sleep.

When he woke up again there was an old man standing beside his bed.

'What do you want?' he asked.

'You're in my room,' the man said.

'This is not your room. Now get out.'

The man walked to the window and looked out at the lighthouse.

'I'm afraid to close my eyes these nights,' he said.

He came back and stood at the bed again.

Finn gave a sigh and glanced over at the door. There was a switch somewhere to call the nurse but he could never find it. He began to pull himself up in the bed and his elbows shook with the strain of it. Lately he had been amazed by his own weight. His feet landed on the cold hard floor and he poked his toes into leather slippers. He walked around the bed, using it for support, and then launched himself at the bathroom door.

A second light flashed on and he stood at the toilet. The sound he made was a trickle and then silence. He moved his feet, farted, made another trickle and then stopped. He pulled at the cord on his pyjamas and turned, moving slowly back to the bed, forgetting to flush the toilet. He caught sight of his reflection in the mirror then. A yellow face with the skin tight over it, his hair in wisps, his neck white and scraggy. He stood there and began to cry into the sink.

The man came and watched from the doorway.

'What are you crying for?' he asked.

Finn shook his head and went back to sit on the bed.

'I don't feel too good,' he said.

'Neither do I.'

They sat on the side of the bed together.

'I remember what it was like to talk to a girl and now they don't even think I'm human,' the man said.

Finn lifted a juice carton and gave it a shake. There was a way to open it but for now it was a mystery. Audrey would know how to do it. She would know what flap to lift. He poured some more water and held the cup unsteadily to his lips.

'The hardest part of being old is that you have no business talking to a young woman, no business at all, in fact trying to talk to one could get you arrested,' the man continued.

'I walk past them and they don't even see me,' Finn said and he looked off into the middle distance for a moment to imagine this.

'I think I'm still young . . . I am young . . . inside my head.'

The man left and Finn got back into bed and thought about

Audrey. All joking aside, romance or no romance, if it came down to it, he would still slay a dragon for his wife. She would pack his last bag for him. She would pick out his last suit of clothes. What thoughts would come and frighten her when she stood alone in that cold bedroom that faced north?

50

In the mornings Audrey shaved him and Finn knew that this routine was keeping her from falling down. The electric razor buzzed as she drove it around his chin. She covered his cheeks with it and he pulled a face. Then she combed his hair and dabbed some sort of moisturizer anywhere she saw those little white flakes. The pink toothbrush came next. He liked to catch it in his teeth and hold it there. Even now he enjoyed this small struggle with his wife, their last tug o' war, when she pulled and he pulled and neither one wanted to give in. Two Catholic priests came to see him. They came as soon as he was wheeled along those bright corridors to the dying place. They didn't think he would notice the softer carpets under his wheels and the fresh flowers and the thank-you cards but he did.

'I won't get out of here now,' he whispered to Matthew, 'I'm too far gone.'

The priests drew the curtains and said psalms into his ear and because he was not ready for it yet, because he didn't know then what was coming himself, something inside him, deep down in his animal part, gave way and broke. And then Finn's voice was heard in yelps and howls so that Audrey came rushing back.

'One of them asked him what sort of funeral he wanted,' the nurse said.

'Damn and blast them,' Audrey whispered.

She stood very still then with one hand placed on his forehead. She barked orders at the nurses, 'Hand me this', 'Get me that' and as each day passed from there, time seemed to slow down and Audrey was angry with everyone and especially angry with death.

Once when Matthew came in, she was there already and the sun was not even up.

'I woke up,' Finn was saying and he was not looking at Audrey but straight into the wall over her head. 'I woke up and there was no one here. There was no one here and I didn't know where I was.' And Audrey was holding his hand and crying. She was saying, 'I won't leave you. I won't leave you. I won't leave you,' over and over. And Matthew, seeing them as they were, holding on to each other, closed the door quietly and slipped away again. That night she sent him home and slept on a mattress beside Finn's bed.

Audrey and Matthew began to talk. He listened without moving and then picked up the words and posted them into his head. It seemed to be about life and love and love leaving and then dying and dead people and death. It was not about him or Audrey. It was about Finn and Finn dying. It was his vital organs and now there was something else to speed things up.

'A big stroke . . . last night,' she said.

They sat side by side on the grey plastic chairs and he tried to think about his father. In his mind he was a lion. A lion behind the wheel of a Renault 19. He had loved that car. They all did. Once he broke the gearstick and they had to reverse the whole way home. 'This family in a nutshell,' he had roared. Matthew could see that day now. Their heads inside the car window. The bay pony standing on the back lawn. His father swimming out to sea in big black trunks late on a summer evening. It didn't matter that they were in reverse at all. He roared into the phone. He roared at the television. He roared at them. Once Matthew opened the bathroom door and there he was, sitting on the toilet. And he didn't roar at all. He just said 'Ha ha' softly and tapped the ash from his cigarette.

'Let's get a cup of coffee,' his mother said.

There was a red light over Finn's door and this meant that they could not go inside. Matthew liked when the light came on. He imagined his father going on air for a live interview with God. Instead the nurses, three of them and always one big strong man, were just moving him into his chair. And what was the point? He could not remember the last time Finn gave a good roar. His mother was telling him in a roundabout way something he already knew. Deep down Matthew understood that his father was sinking, that it didn't matter if he was lying on the bed or sitting in a chair, one minute he would be there, and the next he would be gone.

Audrey stopped walking and turned to look up at him. They stood for a moment, balancing together on a heartbeat, the noise silenced around them, the gurneys floating up into the air, the nurses flying with wings and Matthew knew that she was telling him something that was out of this world.

'It won't be too much longer now,' she said.

Through an open door he saw an old man in green hospital pyjamas still wearing his check cap in the bed.

He knew his mother was trying to break it to him gently. He looked down at her and marvelled at how small and brave she was. They never got the coffee. They just walked around in a big loop.

51

Laura's suitcase was packed. There were three pairs of nylons, a pair of slippers and a pink nightdress inside. The clothes she was wearing had belonged to someone who had passed. She took the bar of soap from the bathroom and put it into her cardigan pocket. She looked at the white towel and considered taking that too but the suitcase was already locked. The small teapot from her breakfast tray was still warm when she fished out the wet teabag. The pot fitted into her handbag and would be useful for reading tea leaves for someone she didn't like. For people like that, she went for the meanest-looking pot.

She sat at the window and waited. The sun had come up over the forest, making every cypress tree in it glisten. Lucas was on his way from the island to take her home. She thought about going back to her house, with the sloping roof, the garden ugly with dandelions and bishop's weed. She had tried to get away but the island always pulled her back.

'Here I am now,' she said, 'sitting in a dead girl's dress.'

There was a new pendant hanging around her neck. It was called a 'Panic Alert'. If she woke up in the middle of the night and needed something she was supposed to press it. She was a good bit over seventy with a pair of lungs like old bagpipes and eyes that were getting steadily worse. What, she wondered, would constitute a panic? If she wet the bed? If she needed a glass of milk? If she wanted to talk? If she needed to see another person's face? The last one was the one that usually woke her up. She looked down at the big red button and traced her finger over it. She always thought she would end up with a string of old pearls around her neck. Audrey had given her some fake ones once and Laura gave a thin smile at the memory of it.

'You can have them if you like.'

On her way back on the ferry she had pulled them from her neck and dropped them over the side. Who wanted pearls that had been warmed already on another woman's neck?

Laura pressed the red button. It was there under her thumb, big and round and red. She couldn't help it.

A nurse appeared at the door, her face worried, expectant. She frowned when she saw Laura just sitting there, smiling back.

'Hi, Deirdre,' she said.

'Is there anything wrong, Laura?'

'No . . . I'm grand, thanks.'

The nurse turned to leave.

'You're like the little boy who cried wolf,' she said.

'Hmm. Hmm,' Laura said and she smiled and stood up.

She checked again that her suitcase was locked. That her handbag was over her arm, that her glasses were on her nose and that she had her oxygen mask around her neck.

'Come on, you,' she said to the tank on wheels and she began to pull it behind her down the corridor.

The ferry was running late. She might as well go for a walk. It was good to move on her own down the corridor, past the nurses' station, and to wear clothes even if they had belonged to some- one else. She came to a crossroads and more rooms that looked out over the sea. The tank beeped and she snapped the mask on and took a deep breath. The air felt cool and good inside her chest. She took another breath and began to walk. She wondered how long she would last, living on artificial air, like a deep-sea diver with her tank. She made no sound with her feet and when she looked down she saw red velvet slippers in a size too big. When, she wondered, had shoes become redundant? When had it become acceptable to wear slippers in public?

The doors to her right were open and she glanced at the many different scenes being played out, a wife plumping pillows, a man staring up at a television set that was too loud, two nurses getting ready to change someone's sheets, a breakfast tray being lifted out. They all had the same things in common, one person in bed, the wait giving them a grey face, and someone else watching from a chair, looking tired and anxious. The nurses were busy taking care of everyone and yet when it came to the sad idea of passing, they seemed to be oblivious.

And fearless, Laura thought.

She stopped at a small room where a man in a check cap was lying back on his pillows. Two nurses were standing over him and beginning to lower his bed. Laura adjusted her glasses and lifted her chin up. She stared and then squinted at the face in the bed. She stepped forward and her tank gave a hiss. She tilted her head and stretched her neck out to get another look. One of the nurses saw her and with a gentle hand pushed her back and closed the door in her face.

'No one is allowed in here,' she said.

But the room was empty, Laura thought, empty of that man and his life and the space he had kept for himself.

She turned the handle and stepped inside again.

'Laura,' the nurse spoke quietly, 'you can't be in here now.'

The man was still wearing those awful free hospital pyjamas and his cap had been taken off and put beside him on the bed. Laura looked down at his face.

'Is he dead?'

'Laura . . .' The nurse spoke now in a more urgent whisper. 'I have to ask you to leave. Only his family can be here.'

'Why are you whispering?' Laura asked. 'He's as dead as a maggot.'

The man's mouth was still open and his eyes were staring upwards. It was as if he wanted to see out through the roof of Jericho and up through the clouds and then further up to some-where else after that.

'Do you know who he is?' Laura asked.

'No one knows who he is . . .'

'Hmm,' Laura said.

She began to sit and one of the nurses scooped up a light wooden chair and put it under her. She leaned into the bed for a closer look.

'Toilet O'Riordan. I'd know the old head of him anywhere.'

The nurses stopped adjusting the bed and looked at each other.

'Have some respect,' one of them whispered.

'He couldn't shut his mouth when he was alive either,' Laura continued.

She moved her face closer to his and wished he would shut his eyes and stop gaping up at her.

One of the nurses gave a long sigh.

'Rest in peace, Toilet,' Laura said.

On her way back she passed the corner room and saw an old man sleeping with his face turned to the window and his hands folded on his chest. His room was full of fresh-cut flowers. Someone had put a nice hand-made quilt over his legs. A young man sat next to him on the chair with his forehead down on the bed. His hair was dark with flecks of gold through it and it spread out in curls on the white bedspread. Laura did not want to stop and look. She knew what was happening there. Through the crack of the door, she could see the losing and the loss.

52

The wardrobe door creaked and Finn knew that they were sending his clothes home. He knew that as each day passed, they were looking at his belongings and knew now that he would not be needing them. He heard Matthew plead for his hat. 'He never went anywhere without it,' he said. Poor little boy. And Audrey replied through gritted teeth, that was how she covered up her heart now, 'He won't be needing it where he's going.'

So his hat and his overcoat were sent home. His Foxford dressing gown then and that was harsh. It meant he would never be getting up, never leaving this bed again. Finn could see quite clearly that he was dying now but to accept that he would never stand up again and never walk, that was strangely hard. His breathing was irregular and prone to stopping and everyone in the room counted to six or eight or ten. And then it would start up again.

'A big man,' he heard someone say, 'and a big man even now.'

'Death does not shrink everyone,' someone else said.

On Tuesday he said his last words and they were, of course, unremarkable and before them such a mishmash of thoughts and sounds. His life was still not flashing past him. There were no flashes of any sort. Just a simple, very calm, bus-stop wait. And he was aware of every part of himself. The colourful stuffing that made him a boy and after that a man. Memory 63. The short trousers he wore to Sunday school, sitting in the pew behind Dorothy Newton and how she wet the seat and how under it, on the red carpet, the urine looked black. And she was a single woman, had never had a child, her body shouldn't have given her trouble like that.

And he remembered peculiar things and was able to say to Matthew, 'Go down to the shop and get me a small bottle of Seven Up.'

And Matthew, who came into the white room at night to hold his hand and thought he didn't know it, went running to the shop and bought four bottles.

'He doesn't know what he wants,' Audrey said.

So his last words were asking for something and his last living thoughts were around the state he was in and more than anything what he felt was thirst. The blasted thirst. So in the end he didn't say goodbye at all.

He said, 'Mattie, get me an orange.'

And Mattie did and Finn remembered looking at it, drinking in the smell of it, holding it at a distance, like the sun coming into his room at night. And after that he discovered he no longer needed to speak. He could speak but he didn't want to. Matthew would understand that. He had already asked him to scatter his ashes on the island. That was all that mattered and he had managed to say that.

Audrey was still making sure the nurses had all the well-ironed pyjamas. The doctor said he was the best turned-out man in the hospital. That made her glow. He had felt that. They had never been the perfect two. No. Fought a lot. He had been unfaithful once and she had forgiven him for that. She had made the best of it and they were still somehow joined. And not because of Matthew, no, but because of something else that really did mean 'until death do us part'. And here it was. Memory number 1. The first time he saw her. Sitting on a stool in Drumquin drinking a Coca-Cola.

Boy oh boy, he thought. She knocked him sideways.

At the beginning, out of nowhere, tears rose up but most of that stuff was winding down now. At first he was frightened and he didn't want to go at all. Every time he saw someone he loved he just burst out into this awful blubbering and wailing again. The words that came out were in a language even he didn't recognize. The first time was with Matthew, holding his hand in an iron grip as if to stop himself from drowning and his wife asleep in the chair. He loved to see her like that. All her busyness gone. Her face slanted on to her shoulder and if you could hear above the noise of the ward, the tiniest baby snore. He looked at her and knew that he would never again sit in an arm-chair and look across the room and see her. And he started that awful bloody wailing again. He couldn't help it. Matthew stood over him, patting him like a dog and really begging him to stop. Embarrassed for his father and embarrassed for himself. Finn stopped abruptly then, not because he had begged him to but because he had forgotten what it was he was crying about. What he wanted to say, what he was trying to say was 'No one ever thought as much about a woman as I thought about her.'

'He's finding it hard to go,' the nun said.

'Dying to die . . . but can't,' whispered someone else.

Memory number 2. Going into some big department store in Dublin and buying her that dress. The white one with the big red flowers on the skirt part. Her black hair and pale blue eyes. He couldn't take his eyes off her. Those were the words he wanted to say to her so often and couldn't. Those words had sat between them for half their lives. No matter what the latest fight was about he wanted to say them and couldn't. He had tried to say them very recently and still couldn't. Yes but she knew. Or did she? It was too late to say them now and too late to ask. The best he could do now was mumble, slurring all the words out to Matthew. The words felt gluey and he couldn't understand him. They were perfect when they left his brain. But Matthew couldn't make them out and Finn tried again, each word pushed out like a ball of dough from his mouth.

'Tell Audrey I love her,' he said.

53

Matthew carried the small square casket in his arms. A white ribbon had been tied around it so that it could be lowered down, and then taken off again by his mother and tied in a different, more manageable loop. That was how they did things now, each one helping the other, but they were confused. They were still trying to get used to playing these new parts. Because now that he was *gone*, and there was a sad little word, Matthew and Audrey were on their own.

They had argued about the funeral.

'He wanted to be cremated,' Matthew said. 'He asked me to scatter his ashes on the island.'

'Cremated? And then what? We could end up with some other man's ashes in the pot.'

'It's called an urn . . . not a pot.'

'And what about a grave? A proper grave with a headstone.'

'But he's not here now . . . in a grave *or* where his ashes are scattered. You of all people shouldn't believe that.'

'I need to know where his bones are kept,' she said.

Now there were rocks and dry dusty earth and Matthew reached forward to help the undertaker and he began to silently fill in the small three-foot space. Then he stopped suddenly and handed the shovel back and began to walk down the concrete path by himself. He did not want to bury his father. He did not want to be the one to shovel in more dank earth. Instead he climbed the high cemetery wall and stood looking out, trying to get away from it. He could see their house in the distance and he stood there with the wind blowing his hair and his coat back, listening to the choir sing, 'The Lord is my Shepherd'. He told himself that he didn't mind, that he would get over it, that he was not the first son to lay his father to rest.

Gone, the word came back to him again and he wondered if it was possible for anyone else to hear it. The first time was in Jericho when the nurse had unhooked the tubes and wires and let the side-bars of his bed down. He heard it again as they joined Finn's hands and lit a red candle under the crucifix.

It rang out in the crematorium when the awful opaque curtains began to slide across. First one and then another and when everything was creamy white he knew for sure that his father was gone.

'A cruel wrench,' Audrey said.

'Gone' as the priest asked him to lower the casket in.

'Gone' as Matthew threw the first fistful of gravel in.

'Gone' as his mother laid the wreath.

'Gone' as the choir began to sing.

'Gone' as Matthew stood frozen to the spot.

'Gone, gone, gone,' he said to himself and still he could not fully grasp the real meaning of this little word.

'A grave is never easy dug,' the priest said pleasantly.

No matter how many times Matthew turned it over in his mind, he would never recover from seeing his father stretched out on that bed. He would never be able to find the words to describe how it felt when Finn began to grow colder, when each part of him left this earth and how he had put one finger into the crook of his father's elbow for warmth. For feelings like those there was no language yet.

In the end Finn was to be divided. Most of his ashes would be buried for Audrey to visit on the mainland, a smaller part – could it be his heart? Matthew wondered – would be scattered into the ocean from the island.

54

The women came and they began a new quilt together.

'It's time to start getting out,' Mary Coffey said.

'What do you want me to do?' Audrey asked. 'Go on the internet and find a date?' and here everyone laughed. Her voice bubbled up to the kitchen rafters. The kettle began to whistle and the big silver teapot was already hot.

'He's only been gone a few months,' Audrey said quietly.

'No matter, this is all part of the process, and women are better at it.'

'What process is that?'

'The grieving process,' Kitty said. 'I read a book about it after Brendan died, Lord rest him. Staying at home is easy but the next thing you know, a year has passed, and people are not worried about you any more and then you creep out and they won't notice – you'll walk into a room full of strangers and there will be no welcome in it.'

'So what social delights are you suggesting?'

'It doesn't matter what it is, all that matters is that you're out,' and here Mary lifted her hands upwards, palms flat, 'out of this house!'

The women didn't speak for a moment and Emily put on her glasses and examined some thread.

'There's bingo,' she said cheerfully. 'That's on Mondays.'

And Audrey listened and quietly imagined it. Sitting in the dusty hall in a row of plastic chairs, her backside growing numb as she put red marks into a box.

'The Legion of Mary is on Wednesday nights and we say the rosary in the old folks' home on Sunday evenings.'

'You might as well come around here then, I'm an old folk myself,' Audrey said.

'And we leave the statue of the Virgin in houses where we feel people have the need for it.'

'It can bring great comfort to people who are bereaved,' Kitty added.

And in her mind Audrey imagined this also. A small Japanese car making its curling way up the front avenue and then sliding politely into her husband's old parking space. Two humble faces standing on the gravel, the statue like a baby in their arms. The Virgin Mary in a clear plastic dome like something that had been won for throwing hoops at the Christmas bazaar. She shuddered when she thought about it.

'If they come around here,' she said, 'I'll hop the statue off their heads.'

'And what about all that money you have?' Mary asked.

'What about it?'

'Well, don't you think it's time you spent some of it on yourself?'

'I'm keeping it for Matthew.'

'Matthew has enough and isn't he talking about going to London?'

'Why don't we all go on holiday, Audrey?' Kitty asked. 'To Portugal or the Canaries . . .'

'Next thing you'll want me in a red bikini on the beach,' she replied.

*

343

Audrey did not know how to grieve for Finn. She did not know how to do anything now except to put on her red apron and work. She moved around the house mechanically, starching sheets on the lawn and turning the mattress. Her alarm clock was shrill at seven and she swung her legs out of bed and took off in a pony trot. Her head was dizzy, a part of her brain still dreaming as she bumped her shoulders against walls before sitting on the icy toilet seat.

'Why am I getting up?' she asked herself suddenly.

'Why am I up . . . for who, for what?' and then she began to move again, pulling up her underwear as she went, before the thought took root.

Before daylight she began to take his clothes from the wardrobe. She gathered different tweed suits and jackets and trousers together and decided where they would go, which should be burnt and which should be sent to charity shops. She looked at the soles of shoes and filled a bag with six pairs for Oxfam and then she wondered what it would be like to see her husband's shoes on someone else's feet. She sat back on her hunkers for a moment to think about this. So another man might stand beside her in Tesco and she might look down and see her husband's feet. They were his shoes, not his feet, she told herself firmly, but the sun came up grey and purple that morning.

The colours of loneliness, she thought.

She put fresh flowers into a vase on his side of the bed and lay down and tried to go over recent events. She had lost her husband. Yes. She was a widow now. Yes. She was no longer a wife – and yet she did not know how to be anything else. Audrey curled her legs up and pulled his pillow towards her. She would put his clothes and shoes under the stairs and wait. She could not let him go, not yet. In her mind, she and Finn were still joined together, so tightly bound that they moved through each other and out the other side.

One Year Later

55

The house was pale magnolia now and not the sunshine colour Laura had told him about. There were sheep grazing on the front lawn, leaving it bald in spots. The shrubbery was overrun with thistles. A goat was tied to a post in the middle of the grass, circles of dark green around him where he had relieved himself. Lucas knocked on the door and waited. He could see a small attic window covered over with ivy high up in the roof. The yellow house was like a shell now and the woman who lived there would be a smaller shell inside it. He had often seen this on the beach. A winkle inside a land snail, rattling around and around and not able to get back out, both empty together, trapped and useless. She came to the door quickly enough but then stood there looking out through a crack, her eyes full of suspicion, blinking up at him in the early-afternoon sunlight.

'Who are you collecting for?' she asked.

'I'm not collecting for anyone, I'm from the island . . . my name is Lucas.'

The words came out in a hurry, tripping and falling over themselves.

'I thought you were a ghost,' she said and Lucas smiled at that. His hair was still very blond and the white spring sun was making everything shimmer. He was finding it hard to speak to her. He remembered how Laura had taught him the alphabet and how each letter had a sound to go with it.

'Are you Mrs Campbell?'

He swallowed and wondered again what had persuaded him to come here and introduce himself like this. His mother's old bungalow had been like a museum, filled with every piece he had ever found on the beach. A thousand shells or more, washed and polished and arranged on small white shelves. Swimsuits, bikini tops, underpants, flip-flops, bedroom slippers, rubber ducks, a wetsuit, snorkels, an airbed, a Union Jack beach towel, brown Guinness beer bottles, one black wellington boot, a pair of small red ones, a collection of coloured sea glass, the edges dulled by the waves and sea salt, a few handbags, several beach balls.

His wife called it 'his junk'. He had married a niece of Patricia McKenna's, a small butt of a woman who had inherited the pub when her aunt passed.

He had tried to explain that it was not what he had taken off the beach that mattered but what was left after it. A beautiful emptiness with nothing but the wind and sand filling it.

'Rubbish belongs in a bin,' she replied. 'Unless it's of some use it shouldn't be taking up precious space.'

He had lifted his treasures into black bags and taken them to the dump. He held on to a few pink shells for luck and he stood now on the gravel outside Bishopstown House turning them over and over inside his pocket.

'Audrey?' he asked again quietly.

The woman gave the slightest nod and her eyes were narrow behind small silver glasses. Her white hair was unwashed and flattened into her head.

'What do you want?' she replied.

She opened the door a little wider and Lucas watched as a

soft grey cat appeared and began to wrap itself around her legs.

He moved a little closer.

'I'm a friend of Laura Quinn.'

He could see how the words fell on her, how each one left a dent. She folded her arms slowly, pushing her hands up into her sleeves for warmth. The wind was rising and four jackdaws marched along the roof. One hopped down on to the gravel, his eyes like wet ink.

'If it's OK . . . I'd like to talk to you for a minute.'

Audrey looked out over his head to the grazing sheep.

'You better come inside.'

The big door was opened back with a creak and in the darkened hallway he could see a wide oak staircase and two swords crossed over a fireplace. A pot was burning in the kitchen. He could smell scorched potatoes and hear it hiss. He glanced at her and she gave a sudden sniff herself and then hurried across the tiles to the wide door of the kitchen. She was wearing small bootee slippers like all the old people did but somehow her clothes seemed older than she was. Inside her light cotton slacks her legs had shrunk with only the bones left. Hydrangeas had turned turf brown in a vase near the telephone. In the kitchen he heard her swear quietly and lift a small grey saucepan.

'Just some old stew I put on for myself.' Burnt to shit, she said under her breath.

She was standing at a small electric cooker and next to it a big Aga that had not been lit. A Dimplex heater on wheels turned itself on with a little click. The clock on the wall ticked loudly. To Lucas in the silence of a cold afternoon, it was like a shout. They sat down opposite each other at the table and Audrey folded her arms again. She was wearing two woollen cardigans, one over the other. Behind her a green bowl was filled with eggs, piled high.

'Well, what is it you want?' she asked again.

'My name is Lucas Boyle . . . I'm a friend of Laura Quinn.'

Lucas took his glasses off and rubbed his eyes.

'Poor Laura,' Audrey said suddenly, her voice quiet, her eyes drifting towards the window as she thought about it.

'I know she worked here for a while.'

'She did,' and a slight smile crossed the woman's face. 'I taught her to cook.'

Lucas returned her smile and could see that it was a mixture of happiness and sadness.

'Will you have tea?' she asked and before he answered she was scalding a pot and beginning to cut into a burnt fruitcake.

'This one got a bit overdone,' she said.

They were sitting opposite each other again.

'How did you know Laura?' she asked.

'I knew her when I was a boy . . . on the island.'

'And you're still on the island?'

'Yes . . . and always will be, I think. I couldn't imagine living anywhere else.'

'And are you married?'

'Yes . . . and we have a six-month-old baby, a little girl.'

'Well, you'll have someone to mind you then.'

Audrey's face seemed to close over for a moment.

'There is nothing worse than loneliness,' she said.

Her eyes were fixed on her plate and Lucas could feel that she wanted to draw whatever warmth there was out of him. It took a lot to tell a stranger that you were lonely, he thought, but it didn't matter to her. All she wanted was to talk to anyone except herself. He could see that for her being alone was a cancer, that loneliness had sucked away all life and hope.

'She had an unfortunate end,' Audrey said and she stirred the teapot and began to fill his cup. 'Laura,' she added as

350

if there could be some confusion around who she meant.

Lucas thought about the shells he had collected. His wife said that holding on to things was pointless, that everything and everyone had to have a purpose. He had grown taller than anyone ever expected. At six foot four he wondered now how much precious space he filled every day and if he was of any use. He had been warned that his wife was a go-getter, an industrious little woman, a Protestant. The islanders said she would turn him inside out.

'Laura is alive,' he said.

The teapot came back down to the wooden table and again Audrey looked down at her plate. She pressed three fingers to her lips and it was as if she was looking for a place to hide herself, under the used butter knife maybe or behind a slice of fruitcake.

'She's not well,' Lucas continued. 'Her breathing is very bad. Some days she's able for a short walk on the beach and she's very clear-headed. Other days . . . she just sleeps.'

'Where is she?' Audrey asked.

'On the island.'

Lucas drank some of his tea and let his shoulders sink down a bit. The worst part was over. In his mind he had a sudden picture of himself and Laura running on the beach, something to do with a whale, how her hand held his, how safe he felt.

'She told me a lot about you. About this house. About you and Mr Campbell.'

'She wasn't a bad girl at all,' Audrey said. 'But it's such a long time ago now.'

'She doesn't know I'm here,' Lucas said.

'But why are you here?' she asked and she looked up at him.

He paused. Any moment now and their eyes would have to meet. He would see a grey sea in hers and she would feel slightly dizzy at the sight of his dancing pupils.

'She's dying,' he said.

56

Matthew reversed the old Beetle out of the garage and parked it near a cloud of pink clematis. This morning would come, he knew that, the morning when he would get up and take his father's ashes to the island. He had found the clothes under the stairs. His father's old jumpers, tweed suits, shoes that were tearing through plastic bags trying to get out. He didn't want them to go but his mother was peeling away layers of his father now, she was trying to push the last parts of him out.

The night before he had found her sitting in the kitchen. He had watched from the doorway as she sat at the long table in a row of empty chairs. This was the life she had now, she told him, and she would have to make the best of it. But the house seemed to be falling down around her and there was no light in her eyes when she spoke. Matthew knew that without Finn she could hear the clocks ticking and her own lungs taking a breath and she was asking herself that awful question, 'Now what?'

He had dropped his bag on the floor and walked to her with his arms open and lifted her up in a hug. She cried a bit into the corduroy of his jacket and then pulled away again, shaking her head.

'Have you eaten? What will you have? I have beef stew. Sausage rolls? There's some beer in the fridge.'

He told her that he was going to the island in the morning and she nodded, opening her mouth to say something about the tides or the weather and then growing quiet again. She went to the oven and took out a red saucepan.

'Would you like me to come with you?'

'Of course.'

'We'll take the old Beetle,' she said. 'I had a new battery put into it last week.'

They drove out the lake road leaving a trail of blue smoke behind them. The shops in the village were still closed with bales of newspapers stacked outside. A lone white dog trotted up the middle of the street, sniffed at the ground and then disappeared around a corner. Matthew turned the car left for Jericho and headed out to the coast. He opened up the windows and they sat in the car park near the beach and Audrey poured coffee from a flask. The small box was on the back seat and when he lifted it up and closed his hands around it, it was like a bird he was going to let out. To his right he could see the windows of Jericho. The tide was coming in, soft white foam moving towards them in ripples. He was glad that she had agreed to come with him.

'I see the sea,' Audrey said.

The ferry crossed the water in a heavy shower. The sea was calm and the rain fell straight down, making dots and circles. The island was in front of them and they were heading towards it. When Matthew looked up he could see the clouds moving and the sun trying to come out again. He kept one hand in his jeans pocket, holding on to the wooden box, keeping it safe and warm.

'Nearly there,' Audrey said.

The island seemed to rise in front of him and he could hear the heavy chains hit the wood on the stern and then the ramp going down again. There was a cloud of blue smoke when the

drivers started their engines and the Beetle made a growling
sound.

Audrey pointed to a signpost and told him to take the lower
coast road. There was a village pub with an old chipped sign that
said 'McKenna's Select Bar' and they went inside for lunch.
Three men in caps leaned into the wooden counter and the air
smelled of stale beer and cigarette smoke. The woman behind
the counter turned around and stared at them. Then she
pretended to be casual as she asked them what they would
like.

'Two ham sandwiches and a beer, please . . .'

'Draught all right?'

'Bottled, if you have it.'

'We only have draught Heineken or I can give you a bottle of
stout.'

She glanced at the men and grinned.

'Would you like a bottle of stout?'

'No, thanks. A glass of Heineken is fine . . . and a pot of tea for
my mother.'

They sat down at a low round table and listened and Matthew
watched in wonder as this other life was taking place. The sea
was moving in the distance. There were more spots of rain on the
windows. The people here had nothing at all to talk about.
Lonely bachelors who came into the pub to use words that they
might otherwise forget.

The woman wiped the table and brought out a plate of ham
sandwiches.

'Touring the island?'

'You could say that,' Matthew said.

'Well, we have a big event at the old lighthouse later on
tonight.'

'What's that?'

'We're going to light it again. It's in honour of the old lighthouse keeper who died a while back.'

'Ah,' Matthew said and he smiled. 'I'd like to see that, I like lighthouses.'

'Let the light shine on,' one of the old men said and the others nodded.

'Poor Martin. He didn't have much luck.'

'A decent poor divil.'

'He wasn't the worst.'

'No, he was not.'

'As dry as a stick.'

Everyone nodded.

Outside, Matthew started the car again and glanced at the passenger seat. His mother had hardly spoken since they arrived on the island.

'Where would I find a really nice beach? I mean . . . the best beach on the island,' he asked.

'That would be Fintra,' she said, glancing out the window, 'the nicest beach on any kind of day.'

She pointed towards a narrow lane leading off the main road.

'Up that way and take the first left. We'll pass the old light-house, I think. Keep going for about two miles . . . and you'll find a white timber house.'

Matthew parked and looked out over the ocean. The sky was clear again and the water was as calm as a lake. He glanced up at the white house and could see that it had a new roof and it had been freshly painted. There was a white swing on the porch and red flowers on the windowsills in boxes. The gate had a sign hanging by a thin chain and it said 'Private Beach'. They sat in silence for a minute and the late-evening sun came out.

Audrey wound the window down and took a deep breath. She

355

knew that if she stayed she would see the sun setting in pink and red from this house.

'Matthew,' she said quietly. 'This is the nicest beach on the island and beside it is the best-kept house.'

He moved to open his door but then stopped and looked at her.

'Are you coming with me?'

Audrey shook her head. She waited for a moment without speaking.

'I'm thinking of leaving Bishopstown,' she said. 'The house is yours now and you can sell it if you want . . . but I need to make a new start. I was thinking of moving back to Kerry to live with my brother.' She took a deep breath and swallowed.

'Would that be all right with you, Matthew?'

'Of course . . . if it makes you happy.'

The sky was getting darker now and one or two early stars came out.

'And I had a visitor last week,' she said quietly. 'A young man called Lucas Boyle. He lives on the island . . . and he was a close friend of your mother's.'

Matthew closed his door again and turned in his seat to face her.

'She's alive, Mattie . . . and this is her house.'

She continued to speak to him in a low tone, her voice steady and her words clear and precise – and Matthew sat in silence and listened. When she finished the sky was dark and the old light-house had lit up.

'My mother is still alive.' Matthew whispered it to himself.

Audrey paused for a moment.

'Your real mother,' she said.

He opened his mouth to say something but she stopped him.

'Your real mother,' she said again and her voice was clear now and firm.

They sat together and watched as the lights came on beside them in the white house.

Matthew took a deep breath and swallowed. He sat very still and stared into the twilight.

'Should you come in with me?' he asked finally and when he looked over at Audrey there were tears coming down her cheeks.

She shook her head quickly and opened her bag for a handkerchief. He wiped the inside of the windscreen and turned on the ignition for warmth.

'Go on now,' she said quietly. 'It'll be all right.'

The white gate gave a creak and he climbed the steps to the porch. He stood at the door for a moment and then knocked gently on the wood.

He heard footsteps move towards him, a sound he recognized as bare feet on wooden floorboards.

'Who's there?' a woman's voice called.

Through the glass in the door he could see a yellow aeroplane high up in the rafters.

'It's Matthew,' he said.

57

Audrey found the old record player and a stack of LPs bought in Dublin. The Chieftains, the Clancy Brothers and Johann Strauss. She pulled one out of its sleeve and looked at the label. 'Toss the Feathers', it said. The needle still worked and she was filled with anticipation when she heard the little crackle it made on the vinyl at first.

The music rose up then and filled the house and Audrey's hand, feeling like it belonged to someone else, leaned in and turned the volume up, and as she did, 'God forgive me,' she said under her breath, 'a widow is not supposed to dance,' and yet she did not mean any of it.

Her foot began to tap and then she closed her eyes and swayed and as she did she lifted her dress and swished the skirt over and back. The small parlour was dark and there was no space here for feeling ridiculous or ashamed or anything other than how the music moved through her body and made her heart pump fresh blood. She had learned to dance in kitchens in Kerry and it was second nature to her. She had loved the raw fever of it, the reckless, breakneck pace, the yips and yahoos that went with it. Where she grew up this was how people met, across kitchen flags, in bare legs and flat shoes, with the fire low and the windows open to save them from the heat. Frosty air would come in and hit them as they crossed the room, in the middle of their chests. Eyes met, shoulders bumped, every man and woman in the room made completely alive by it. She had danced with Finn like this, unselfconsciously, his eyes sparkling at her and as she remembered she lifted her feet higher and began to move around the house. She did not know how long she danced, but in the days and weeks that followed, late in the afternoons, with her house becoming untidy around her and the garden hedges growing wild, Audrey went back to the parlour again to forget about her loneliness and to dance.

58

On the edge of the earth, Laura saw beautiful things. The pictures that came to her were random and out of sequence and each one was a surprise, a backward glance at her life. On the outside her skin returned to its former pink and looked fresh again. There was a glow, a dew that hung over her, and it belonged to someone else. Lucas stood in the early-morning light and watched her sleeping. He pulled the covers up around her and put his hand gently over hers.

'Her hands are cold,' he said.

Laura's fingers moved. She had been sleeping for two days. Behind closed eyes she saw a broken blue couch left out on the grass. She saw her own mother, dead for years, knitting a sock. White sand passed over her in soft waves as it made dunes behind Fintra Beach. Her mind had become a silent slide show and she watched it all with mild interest, detached and calm, between awake and sleep. Death was no big deal – not when you were the one who was dying. And all the time those memories in colour glided back and forth. Sometimes she felt like talking and there were still days when she could sit up. But today she didn't care enough and besides the pictures were interesting. Her wedding dress moved in front of her. Herself and Mattie were running barefoot on the beach. The black Beetle was parked in the long grass. Finn came and went and he didn't matter now. Martin was laughing down from the steps of the lighthouse, the sound echoing around the whitewashed walls.

Matthew moved into her house and the islanders came and kept a vigil. She knew that it was spring from the scent of the hawthorn blossoms and on a clear day they carried her bed upstairs. Then someone else suggested taking the bed down to the beach.

'Will you put me down, you band of half-wits,' she said.

The sea was the one thing she would not get excited about. At one point when they were climbing the stairs with the bed she had begun to slide down to the bottom of it. She knew then that she was much smaller now, lighter, an old feather of a thing that could disappear into thin air. It was Matthew who stopped her from falling. His hands lifted her up, her thin legs dangling. She could have fallen out and rolled like a ragdoll down the stairs – and no one said anything and then Laura and Matthew looked at each other and began to laugh, a big belly laugh full of noise and warmth. She was laughing so much that it was hard to breathe then and the men around her became concerned. They tucked her in under the covers again and lifted the bed up into the air.

Audrey came and washed her hair and she lay perfectly still and allowed this. She could feel the teeth of the comb on her scalp and then her head being lifted up from the pillow, balanced on one hand and her hair stretched down into a shiny white braid. Later Laura would wonder if she had imagined it. She lifted one hand and tried to touch her hair but instead she found real pearls around her neck – she knew by the weight of them. She whispered to Lucas to take them off again and to give them to his wife. Her breathing was easier without them. Close to her throat they had felt cold and foreign.

Soon Laura was floating high up over the world in a place by herself. And there was a new feeling that she was starting to move higher – that she was on the edge of the earth and still not ready to step off. She wasn't afraid of dying at all – she just wasn't ready yet. And she could feel some kind of heat underneath her, the furnace that would launch her into outer space. And today, and yesterday, she had had the feeling that someone was standing behind her. That someone was waiting and wanted to hurry her along. 'Who was that?' It was a minor enough irritation. She thought she could smell her father's pipe smoke, her mother's perfume. And all she wanted to do was to turn around and look whoever this was in the face.

The islanders came to say the rosary and they annoyed her. They whispered out prayers for her soul and asked for a happy release. They did not know that she was listening to all of it, that on the inside her mind was active, jumping softly, bouncing with magical pictures, and instead saw only the worn-out woman on the bed. Her breath loud, at times gasping and painful for them to hear, was of no consequence to her now. Her toes turning black, she couldn't care less.

But they were drinking her tea and closing in on her. She opened her eyes suddenly and said, 'Will you all get out to hell!' Outside there was a swamp of wet moss and heather and she hoped they would get stuck in it. Mattie had fallen asleep on the bed beside her. Truthfully, she didn't know for sure who his father was. But what was truth when he had a better life than hers? They had all heard her final words. They just didn't know it yet.

'I did my best for the whole bloody lot of you,' she said.

They were more profound inside her head.

As for the islanders she wondered why they were all crying. Was it because they would have no one to talk about after she was gone? She cleared her throat and told Lucas and his wife to go and she could hear them sniffling. Could they not see that she was happy, that Laura was at her most beautiful now? There was only one person in the room that she really cared about and he was sleeping beside her. There was love in the world when his hand was in hers.

Acknowledgements

The idea for this book came to me in 2006 as I watched the Atlantic roll back from the rocks of Mulranny Beach in County Mayo. I had no idea then that my life was about to change and that I would soon be setting up my desk in a different house, at a different window, with a new baby in tow. I have always believed that some books want to be written regardless of what is going on around them, but this one would not have happened at all without the love and unfailing support of my (often sleep-deprived) husband, Steve. So, thank you, Steve – at last I get to say it.

There were many other good forces at work, too. My readers, Juliet Prendergast, Deirdre Harrington and Emer O'Beirne, gave the kind of encouragement that propels a book forward. I remain indebted to my agent Faith O'Grady for her gentle cajoling, professionalism and good humour, even when the work was slow coming her way. Cat Cobain's enthusiasm as well as her intelligent and sensitive editing have been a tremendous help to me. I'm really happy to have her on my side.

My mother, Eleanor Jameson, comes from Tubercurry in County Sligo and, so, without realizing it, helped me to find a natural setting for my story in the west. I have borrowed many a turn of phrase from her, and thanks are not enough when I consider the inspiration and life force that she is. Shortly after beginning the book, my father passed away, and I thought often of him when writing. A straight-talking man, I could always rely on him to give a direct and honest opinion on any book. I can only hope that he would have enjoyed the result. Finally, a special thanks to Arthur, for sleeping when he did, for being an inspiration and a joy. Of course, I could not have described motherhood without him.

© Leah Verwey

Alison Jameson is an Irish writer who studied English at University College Dublin and went on to work in advertising for many years. She now writes full-time and has published two previous novels, *This Man and Me* (which was nominated for the prestigious IMPAC Award) and *Under My Skin*.